Coven at Callington

The Cauldron Effect, Volume 1

Shereen Vedam

Published by Shereen Vedam, 2020.

COVEN AT CALLINGTON
First edition. March 31, 2020.
Copyright © 2020 Shereen Vedam.
ISBN: 978-1989036419
Written by Shereen Vedam.

This book is dedicated to

Jane Austen and Georgette Heyer,

for introducing me to the Regency era,

and to J.R.R. Tolkien,

for sharing his love of fantasy with all of us.

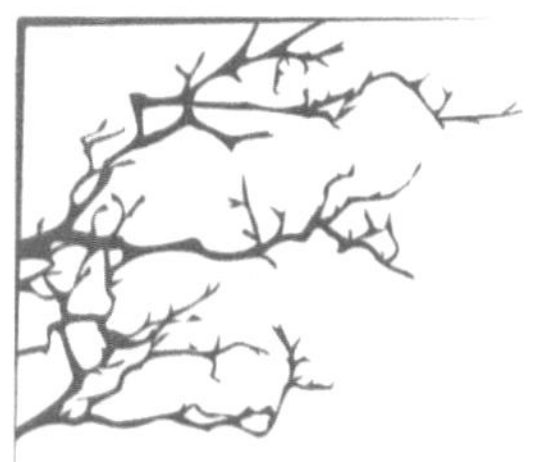

Author's Note

In all 3 of the Cauldron Effect books, you'll find openings to each chapter in *italics*...this is to distinguish these special scenes from the rest of the chapter.

These chapter openings will give the reader an added quirky perspective of the ongoing story from a different point of view than the main character. These scenes could be from the perspective of an inanimate object, an animal, a bird, or even a celestial being.

If you find these openings unsettling, skip them. You'll be able to follow the story without these "extra" scenes, though reading them will give you a more entertaining journey into this fantastical world.

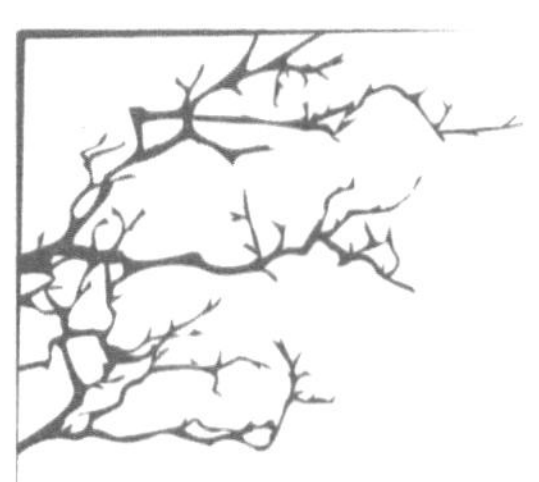

Prologue

Switzerland, Summer Solstice, June 1454

"This be truly odd, Andreas." Johannes, a polecat, stood up to sniff the closest tall stone his friend had brought him to inspect. There was a gaggle of them, all lined up, straight as a man-made fence, across the recently empty landscape.

His nose suggested these stones may have been roasted at some point, like in a forest fire. One sniff and his throat felt dry and itchy. The sharp scent was unfamiliar. Keeping well back, he used his whiskers to sense its makeup. This stone was vibrating! As if it were alive and purring. Were all of them doing that?

"They weren't here last night." Andreas, a fellow polecat, scratched at the white fur that made up his neck bib. "Yet, this dawn, they're blocking my path to the lake."

Johannes clacked in scorn. While immensely tall, each stone was only ten steps wide, leaving a wide gap before the next stone. There was plenty of room to scoot through, though he didn't want to be the first to try.

"Where do you suppose they came from?" Andreas asked.

"Who knows?" Johannes inched closer to inspect the line of stones that seemed to stretch forever in either direction. "They smell ashy. Have you touched one yet?"

"No! You do it. Bet you won't."

Johannes sighed. That's why Andreas had asked him to come. He knew Johannes couldn't resist a challenge. The moment anyone said, bet you can't do this or that, Johannes felt compelled to try. The urge to lick the darn stone trembled on his tongue. He leaned forward.

The air before him erupted like a hot spring, scorching his extended tongue and flinging him backward.

He landed painfully on his left side and Andreas landed with a thump beside him. His friend's bushy tail filled Johannes's sore mouth. He spat out the tail and scrambled to get his feet under him.

"Ayee!" Andreas squealed and raced for the cover of trees.

Panic battering in his chest, Johannes glanced back at the stones. His breath caught at the sight of tall humans dressed in bright coverings standing perfectly still in front of each stone. They looked as surprised to be there as Johannes was to see them.

Johannes turned and raced after his friend. He had to break this habit of blindly responding to challenges.

"DYTEL!" HIS MOTHER'S voice sounded an alarm.

Eight-year-old Dytel snapped his eyes open expecting to find they were trapped in a dark void or still in their world, waiting for a new chance at life. Instead, before him was a different place. He glanced up at his mother in wonder. "My spell worked!"

They were encompassed by greenery. Ancient trees, vibrant bushes, and grasses sprinkled with wild flowers carpeted the ground. Trembling with excitement, he reached out to a nearby tree and traced the bark of its giant trunk. It was real and stretched high up as if to touch the blue sky. Even the air seemed different, not thick and murky. He breathed deeply, expanding his lungs, relishing the fresh clean scent. There were animals, too! He'd only ever seen such creatures in statues and drawings. Here, they were alive!

What's your name? he asked the one that was long and furry, with a pointed face that quivered. The little animal screamed in his mind and raced away. Dytel laughed. It could hear him and speak back, in a fashion.

"Dytel, stay with me!" His mother's arms wrapped around him, pulling him close, tight. She was afraid of this place. Why?

"Mother, we're here. Really here."

All of his life, he'd heard stories of a place like this. A world that looked the way their Wyhcan world once had, in the days before their sun began to die.

Dytel, ever dreaming of visiting such a legendary land, had come up with an extraordinary idea. One that made coming here plausible. He had convinced his father the spell could succeed. Then his father had talked the Grand Coven Council into believing his boy's idea was workable.

With their world on the brink of destruction, desperate measures were needed. Having tried and failed to save themselves, listening to a far-fetched idea from a warlock child became not only feasible but also paramount.

His father organized the casting using the strongest warlocks and witches left alive in their world. Despite all his pleading, Dytel was not one of those picked to cast the daring spell.

Still, it was *his* idea that had made this event possible. The spell had called for magic-ingrained megaliths to be whipped toward the new world, a world of legend and old witch's tales. Once the stones landed and took root, the Wyhcans would use the magic embedded in the stones to transport themselves between worlds.

"Where's father?" Dytel leaned around his mother to gaze eagerly down the line of warlocks and witches stepping away from their transport stones. Strange. Some of the stones had no people before them.

"Where's father?" he asked again, a sliver of doubt gliding down his back. "Why isn't he here? Mother, where are all the spell casters?"

Chapter 1

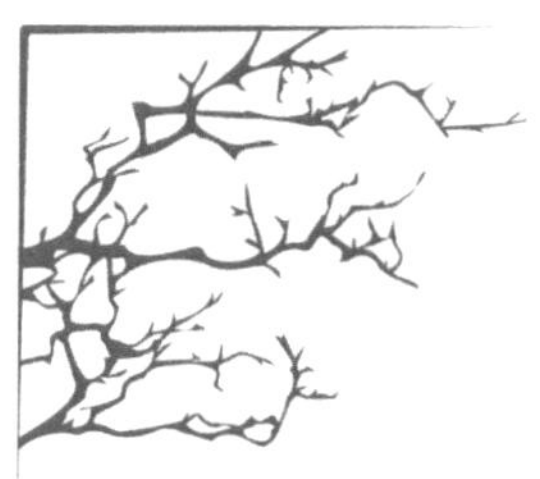

*L*ondon, England, September 1815

Ernest, a lamp-post on St. James's Street, flickered his flame to signal George, on Ryder Street. "Have you heard the latest, George? There's talk of a mad plan to light all of London with air."

"Gas, Ernest, not air. It's said to produce white jets of flames. Pall Mall's lit so and the theatre districts are in the works. Shouldn't be long before they reach us."

Ernest fluttered his golden light in disgust. "Will never happen, George."

"Progress, Ernest. Can't stop it."

"I tell you, it'll never hap...now, what's this? There's movement below."

"Night watch?" George asked as a cool autumn wind swirled around him, fluttering fallen leaves.

"Not unless he's taken to skulking in the dark. Where did they all come from?"

"They?"

"Hounds. Big, black ones. Five, to my count. Tails down, hackles raised, ears back." His light quivered. "George, I sense trouble."

"Then this is your moment, Ernest. We were created to warn people of dangers that lurk in the dark. So, flare, my friend. Flare as if you are about to be extinguished!"

THOMAS DRAKE SAINT-Clair, Earl of Braden, normally viewed all strangers with suspicion. Tonight, he'd succumbed to the temptation to trounce an unknown opponent, even if only with cards. Little wonder. At one and twenty, he had finished his formal training and been christened a Guard of the Green Cross. The guards were part of a secret limb of the Anglican Church ruled by the Archbishop of Canterbury, their sole purpose to vanquish dark creatures of the underworld set to lure, kill or defile humans.

After only a year of active duty, however, Braden's assignments had recently dried up. For weeks now, no alarm bells clanged within the body of the Church. No urgent messages came from the archbishop that in some forgotten corner of the British Isles trouble blazed. The war with France was over, but had a truce been called by Hell?

Ahead of his carriage, an unusually bright street lamp highlighted an orderly row of narrow brick houses. Movement caught his eye and his instinct for trouble flared. He rapped on the carriage roof to signal a stop. Before the vehicle halted, he flung open the door and jumped out.

"Something wrong, milord?" his footman, Garth, called out from beside the driver.

"Shine the carriage lantern over there." Then he saw it. A crouching dog. Braden's pulse slowed. A dull life, indeed, if all he chased were shadows of pets. He waved to Garth. "Never mind. It's merely a dog."

The dog's eyes shifted, glowing an eerie yellow, and Braden's blood surged. Hellhound!

"My sword!" he called to Garth.

With a metallic hiss, Garth withdrew the weapon and tossed it to him.

Agamore was Braden's broadsword. It settled with a familiar weight in his grip. The unearthly hound sprang for him and Braden smartly sidestepped, deflecting the hound with a powerful sweep of the back of his sword. The blow flung the hound against a nearby brick wall.

"More of 'em." The carriage driver's voice was pitched in panic. The horses shied in response.

Deep-throated growls from the alley affirmed his driver's keen sight. Three, no, four more hellhounds slunk out of the dark mouth of an alley.

Fortunately, no pedestrians or vehicle traffic yet. The quiet was unlikely to last with White's attracting customers around the corner. The noise of the frightened horses alone could awaken those sleeping in nearby rooming houses.

"Get the carriage away," he called to Garth as he advanced with swift jabs and slashes, herding the snarling creatures back toward the narrow alley. He'd dispatched three before they realized just how skillful he was with his weapon.

A backward check showed Garth shoving a fallen beast into the alley entrance. Then a hot flare at Braden's back warned him that Garth had erected one of his magical barriers so innocents would pass by oblivious.

Good man.

Just the reason he allowed his intractable footman to remain in his employ, despite Garth's unhealthy fondness for using magic at the least provocation. Magic was deemed a product of the Devil by the archbishop, just as the miraculous feats guards performed were considered gifts from God.

Since his acquaintance with Garth, however, Braden had been struggling with his Church's definition of magic. For in no sense could he ever see Garth as evil. The man had too good a heart.

With the carriage moved off down the road, the alley turned dark but then a nearby sputtering street lamp flared. The light fell clearly across the two remaining hounds within the brick-lined battlefield. The larger shaggy beast appeared similar to a hellhound, but he had claws in place of nails and crimson eyes.

Vague memory of an ancient folk tale sparked recognition of the beast's fluid shape. A barguest? Those shape-shifting goblins were reputed to be cunning and deadly.

The creature jumped across from wall to wall. Braden swung the broadsword in a high arc, aiming for the beast's underside. The barguest leapt to safety and then swiftly attacked, pinning Braden.

Deadly claws skimmed past his arm, scraping the brick. Braden shifted and lunged before the barguest could recover. The wily fae sailed out of reach.

Braden released a pent-up stream of invective about the creature's lineage.

On their fourth skirmish, he almost had it. The barguest twisted midair, so only the flat of Braden's sword connected with its leg. Though howling with satisfying agony, the barguest dodged out of reach. The beast was crafty.

Its strategy of attacking, retreating to avoid Agamore's bite and attacking again, physically drained Braden.

His muscles ached from swinging the sword, so he broke away. He panted and the air that poured into his lungs reeked of spilt blood and entrails. Salty sweat dripping down his face stung his lips.

Barguest and hound switched places, perhaps to conserve strength. Braden lunged with a fierce thrust, and made contact with the hound. Blade sliced flesh and the fae hound bellowed in pain. It jerked back, slammed into the opposite wall and then scrambled to escape.

"Kill it, guv'nor," Garth shouted in encouragement.

Braden grunted. "What do you think I've been trying to do?" He dove at the fleeing hound, but it bounded away and his sword scraped brick, sending sparks flying.

He back tracked, kicking aside hound corpses. Their blood made the ground slippery, adding another obstacle to the mix.

Hackles raised, the barguest followed Braden, while its limping companion hung back.

Sweat beaded on Braden's face and freely soaked his back. Despite his growing exhaustion, the fact that only two opponents remained and one was in no shape for another scuffle bolstered his spirits. He had enough vigor left to win this fight.

Time to finish this.

Braden stepped away from the wall.

Instead of fleeing, the barguest raised its head and howled – a long, agonized call.

A cry for help?

The air in the alleyway shuddered and an astringent stink of cinder and sulfur stung Braden's nose. Then four more hounds materialized through the walls, landing on the cobbled stones with a light fresh bounce in their steps.

Cursing, Braden drew back as the deadly reinforcements faced him, growling, teeth bared, frothy drool dripping from their snouts. The triumphant barguest was at their lead. Braden's back touched the alley wall. A desperate side-glance toward the entry showed his footman walking away.

"Garth!" His desperate plea bounced off the barrier. Garth must have reinforced it to keep sounds from attracting passersby. Without his assistance, Braden couldn't pass through that magical blockade to safety. What had once been a shield to protect innocents was now a fortification that trapped him with the enemy.

The fight was indeed about to end, but not as he'd envisioned. Giving a frustrated huff, Braden sent up a silent prayer of apology for his sad failure in his duty to protect this world. He begged for whatever miracle the Good Lord could spare and raised Agamore to defend himself.

The sword vibrated in Braden's grip, surprising him. Then it lit up as if the sun itself had risen over the dark horizon while Braden stared at it in utter shock. Agamore touched a hound in mid-leap and the beast screamed. The ear-shattering cry echoed in the narrow passage, then the hound sizzled, turning into smoke and dust in the air, before fluttering to the ground.

The remaining creatures backed away from Agamore's blazing fury. No doubt as stunned as Braden by the sword's unexpected power surge, the hounds abandoned all compulsion to fight to the death and scrambled to flee. Claws scraped stones as hound after hound vaulted over each other in a rush to speed down the alley. The wounded hound ran last, skittering as it followed its fleeing companions.

Braden, recovering from his shock at his sword's surprising flare, gave chase. Shouting in triumph, he pounded down the dark alley after them.

One glanced backward, red eyes glowering with hatred, and then the barguest streaked down the length of the lane. Like mist touched by sunlight, all the hounds vanished.

Braden slowed, stopped and bent over, hands resting on knees as he caught his breath. In his grip, Agamore's light dimmed and died, leaving the night as dark as before. The magical sword became no more than ordinary steel.

"Milord, they got away," Garth shouted at him from behind his barricade.

He spared his footman a resentful, backward glare, ready to return a quip about where had he been when his master needed help. Yet, it was probably due to Garth's spell on his sword that he had been able to fight off those hounds at the end. He should have known Garth wouldn't leave him defenseless.

Despite the use of forbidden magic, Braden was inordinately grateful to his exasperating footman for saving his life. Breathing hard and wiping at his moist forehead, he returned to the scene of the initial fight. "Bring a light."

Garth pulled out a candle from his pack, lit it with a soft-spoken incantation and then hurried over. Braden couldn't bring himself to object to the blatant use of magic, not when the same power had saved his life.

Everywhere, black splatters gleamed in the candle's flickering yellow glow. He took out one of the cloths he carried, specially protected and blessed for this purpose, and used it to wipe down his sword.

"Thank you for your help." His words were heartfelt. Garth deserved a reward for this night's work and there'd be a gold coin in it for him later tonight. "You saved my life."

"What help, milord?" Garth asked.

Did magic come so easily that he didn't even notice when he performed something as spectacular as that flaring sword? He glanced at his footman, curiosity mingling with an irrepressible flash of envy.

Braden flung the filthy cloth and his soiled gloves to the ground by the dead beasts and held Agamore out to Garth. "Thank you for making this sword light up and burn that hound. That's what finally chased them away."

"I didn't do that," Garth protested, and exchanged the weapon for a velvet bag containing ingredients with which to bless this evil-sullied ground.

"Of course you did," Braden said. "Do not worry. This once I forgive you for disobeying my order to never to use magic on me. Your spell was impressively effective."

"Milord, I swear I didn't cast such a spell." Garth slipped the great broadsword into its sheath on his back.

Head pounding with worry, Braden hid his astonishment. "Then why did you leave me unguarded?"

"I'm sorry, milord, but you looked to be thrashing them devils without any need for my help, and the night watch approached. I added a silencer spell on the shield and went to warn him off. When I returned, the hounds were fleeing, though there seemed more of 'em. So, the sword flared? Odd. It wasn't any of my doing, sir. I swear."

Braden looked at the sword hilt and then into Garth's eyes, to see if he were lying. The confused look in his servant's gaze seemed genuine. That begged the question, if Garth hadn't bespelled Agamore, what had happened in this alleyway?

Prayer answered? Dare he believe he'd been granted a personal favor from God? The thought both elated and terrified. He must seek the archbishop's guidance. See if other guards had ever been gifted such an extraordinary blessing. He shook his head. How ironic that he seemed more comfortable believing in spells than miracles.

Trying to still his unruly thoughts, Braden took out handfuls of red powder from the velvet bag, and while muttering a quiet prayer, sprinkled the holy mixture that the archbishop gave all the guards to spread over demon corpses. As he prayed, consecrating the battleground, clouds of incense smoke spewed up, bubbling over the fallen beasts, soiled material and poisonous streaks of fae blood. Soon, the ground was covered in naught but ash and sand.

"Garth, could those hounds have been waiting here for me?"

"How, milord? You only decided to come two hours ago."

"Yes, after you brought me that note earlier from Dewer suggesting we meet at White's tonight."

"Didn't like that note," Garth muttered. "Almost didn't give it to you. Should've listened to me instincts."

"Garth." Braden stopped and glared over his shoulder at his footman. "I decide which notes I read or not."

"O'course, milord. Ain't that always been the way? Though sometimes notes do get misplaced. Just happens."

Braden frowned, not liking the innocent look on his footman's wizened features. How many notes had been *misplaced* since he'd hired Garth two months ago after rescuing him from a vengeful wraith? No wonder life had become positively tedious since then.

Late for his appointment, he shook away the disturbing thought. "We'll finish this conversation later."

"You've blood on your coat, milord. Best change first. I brought spares."

By the candlelight, blood spatters were indeed prominent on his white cravat, and his coat sleeves were ruined.

With an impatient hand, Braden pulled off the neck cloth and shrugged out of his jacket. He tossed both to Garth, though he held little hope that whatever his footman produced would be suitable for White's.

From his pack, Garth fished out a replacement coat and a strip of pristine white cloth.

Braden frowned at the oddly un-creased garments coming from the cramped pack. Had Garth conjured them up?

Don't ask. Best if you don't know.

He shrugged on the new coat. It fit to perfection as if crafted by Gieves and Hawkes of Savile Row. As he tied the cravat in a loosely arranged Mail Coach style, he prayed the magical cloth would not choke him in the middle of a conversation. Satisfied he looked presentable, he strode toward the street. At the alley's entrance, the air flared and pushed him backward.

"Garth!"

"Sorry, milord," the little magician muttered and slipped to the other side of the invisible barrier without any hindrance. There, he moved some small rocks aside and spit on a larger one before wiping it clean.

Braden watched with a troubled spirit. As an ordained church guard, he had been taught that magic was a tool of the dark, just as miracles were tools of light. Convincing Garth to beware the deadly lure of the dark arts, however, had proved an exercise in futility. One Braden had given up lecturing on.

For his part, Garth often said he owed Braden his life and insisted he was devoted to his master's missions.

"That's done it, then," Garth said and the barrier shimmered and fell away.

Braden headed for the club. "I shan't be long. Stay close."

Inside White's entryway, the butler recognized Braden and said the proprietor had a missive for him. He hurried off to fetch it.

The moment the note was in Braden's hands, the first thing he noticed was the Archbishop of Canterbury's secret seal. He opened the note with suppressed excitement. Finally, a new assignment.

The dove must return to the nest.

A coded message. He sent his regrets to Dewer and abruptly left the establishment.

Down the road, Garth sat up on the carriage box beside the driver. Braden gave instructions to speed them to Lambeth Palace forthwith. He'd barely claimed his seat before the carriage lurched forward.

Soon the ripe stench of fish and refuse hinted they journeyed alongside the Thames River. On arrival at Lambeth, Garth flagrantly refused to follow orders to drive into the palace. Instead, he ordered the vehicle stopped ten feet short of the gatehouse doors.

Braden disembarked, pushing back the angry words hovering on his lips. He knew better than to resume a revolving argument. No matter how often he told Garth that the archbishop's palace was the safest home in the kingdom, he insisted on waiting outside the palace walls. His excuses varied with month, week and time of day.

"Best be careful, milord," Garth said in a warning tone, from atop the carriage. He pointed to an illusory line running parallel to the open gates. "A ley line. Could get you transported to places you don't want to visit."

Braden crossed the imaginary barrier without a backward glance or comment. In the garden, he passed a stately white fig tree heavy with fruit. Harvest time. He'd often climbed its branches as a child, hungering for a taste of those sweet morsels. He now ignored the bounty and headed for the Great Hall. From there, a butler led him toward the Blue Room. Bowing, the man left him by the door.

Braden knocked.

"Enter!" The summons was as sharp as a slap.

Braden's pulse ricocheted. He huffed an impatient sigh at his nervous reaction. Why did he let Garth's fears get the better of him? He went in. Stopping before His Grace, he descended to both knees, head bowed.

"I'm pleased to see my dove returned safely." His Grace made the sign of the cross and said a quiet prayer before extending his right hand.

Braden reverently kissed the opulent medieval gold-rimmed, amethyst ring on His Grace's middle finger. The jewel was carved with the symbol of the Green Cross.

"Arise, my son," Charles Manners Sutton said. "We have grave matters to discuss." He offered a glass of brandy.

"Thank you." Braden accepted the drink and swept the orderly, spotless, book-lined room with a fond gaze. He'd learnt his church guard theology here. Entering this room felt akin to removing tight boots and settling before a warm fire with a favorite volume.

"You look worse for wear," His Grace said, with a look of curiosity.

Braden ran a hand over his hair hoping it wasn't too disheveled. "Discovered a pack of otherworldly hounds near White's. I wondered if they'd been waiting for me."

The archbishop seemed unperturbed by the suggestion.

"Do you know why they would have done so, Your Grace?"

"I suspect they were meant to stop you from being sent to Callington."

Intriguing. His assignments took him to all corners of the British Isles *except* for Cornwall or Wales. That was witch and warlock territory. They handled their own problems without church guard interference.

"Callington, *Cornwall*, Your Grace?"

Manners nodded. "There's trouble at a parish there. A demon stole a boy brought to the church for his baptism."

"From *inside* the church? How did it enter? I understood they couldn't access holy places. Also, why take a boy?"

"How is up to you to determine and to ensure it never happens again. As to why, who knows why demons do anything in our realm, or who they collude with on any given day? The rector tells me the happening is beyond his understanding. You must uncover the truth and find and return the boy to his school in Snowdon."

Braden's eyebrow shot up. *Snowdon*? "The warlock school in Wales?"

"Snowdon," the archbishop repeated, his gaze hardening, daring Braden to question him. "The headmaster, Mattock, is the boy's father and he has sworn allegiance to the Church in exchange for our assistance. I will not turn away any seeker of God, no matter what guise he appears in."

Or whatever talent he brings to the table. Braden cringed inwardly at that uncharitable thought. He must not presume to question His Grace's judgment. After all, Braden housed and harbored Garth, who, though not intrinsically evil, did practice magic.

This sudden change in Church policy toward involvement with warlocks, however, was profoundly disturbing. His intention to ask if Sutton knew what could have caused such a startling reaction from his sword choked and died in his throat. He wanted to get out of here, to find a peaceful place to sit and think. He bowed. "If that is all, Your Grace. As always, I'm honored to serve the Church."

"There's more."

His every instinct shouted that he would not care for the rest. Spine rod straight, Braden faced the archbishop.

His Grace hesitated, cleared his throat and then spat out, "Callington houses a coven."

Braden's chest clamped like a vice. Cornwall likely housed dozens of covens. What was so special about this Callington one? Why target it? Before the order came, he guessed what he'd be asked to do, and felt betrayed to his marrow by the possible reason behind it. Another warlock favor?

"Destroy that coven."

"I beg your pardon?"

"You heard correctly."

"I heard destroy a *coven*? A coven of *witches*?"

"Correct." Sutton briskly strolled around the room, appearing agitated. He should be. This order was blatantly against Church policy.

While Braden digested the dire implications of being forced to carry out such an ill-conceived command, peril shadowed the room. Just as it had tailed the church guards three centuries ago when witch hunts had been the order of the day. Until disaster struck.

They were called church knights back then, before the king summarily executed the vast majority of them for crimes against their countrymen. Only a remnant was permitted to continue serving God in the much-needed fight against evil. Renamed church guards, the king issued a directive that they were never again to involve themselves with witch-warlock matters. That strict order had never been violated. Until now.

Braden's faith in the archbishop trembled. He staggered beneath that doubt. He might as well question if the sun would rise in the east on the morrow.

Sutton had initiated him into the church guards. He was a man whom Braden trusted to safeguard his soul.

Had trusted.

Echoes of past conversations, pages turning, ideas blossoming, faded. The walls about him shrank, hardened, roughened. The room's familiar contours narrowed to fit his form; as if he'd been laid in a grave his size and waited for dirt to cascade over.

Setting his untouched drink on a nearby table – the vibrant amber liquid still as a corpse – Braden faced the archbishop who finally returned to stand before him. "Your Grace, church guards are forbidden to interfere in witch-warlock conflicts."

"Must I remind you, sir," Sutton said in a repressive tone, "that the Church is at liberty to decide on the best course for the good of Britain's spiritual welfare without prior consultation with its guards? Remember your place. You are of a higher rank in secular life, but within the Church, you are sworn before God to follow my orders, without question."

Stung by the reprimand, Braden winced, but this was the *wrong* path for the Church to take. History had proven that point. His theological teachings reinforced it. Sutton knew better. What could have brought about this policy change? Whatever the cause, Braden had to make Sutton see sense.

"Your Grace, what if the king gets word we again target more than dark creatures of the underworld? Can we afford another Bedfordshire incident?"

"I do not need a history lesson. Besides, in this instance, we are not talking about harming innocents."

"We hadn't meant to harm innocents then."

"You have your orders." Sutton finally looked straight at him, and for a moment, Braden thought a shadow of confusion skimmed the edges of His Grace's gaze. "Go with God, my son." He gestured the *Signum crucis*.

Clear dismissal. Braden was sworn to obey. He bit on the argumentative words forming in his mouth. Swallowing his unease, he bowed. "By your command."

Down the corridor, out the front doors and across the churchyard, acid clawed at his stomach. So, the Church was to re-engage in witch hunts. Worse, they took sides in the ancient war between witches and warlocks. Why else seek to help a warlock boy while planning to raze a coven? Braden's loyalty to the Church turned a shade darker as he crossed the tree-lined pathway.

At the gatehouse doors, he sent Garth an ominous look that widened his footman's eyes with obvious alarm. The talkative man prudently chose to silence his questions. Nevertheless, as Braden entered the carriage, the little man muttered, "Knew no good would come from that accursed place."

For once, Braden agreed.

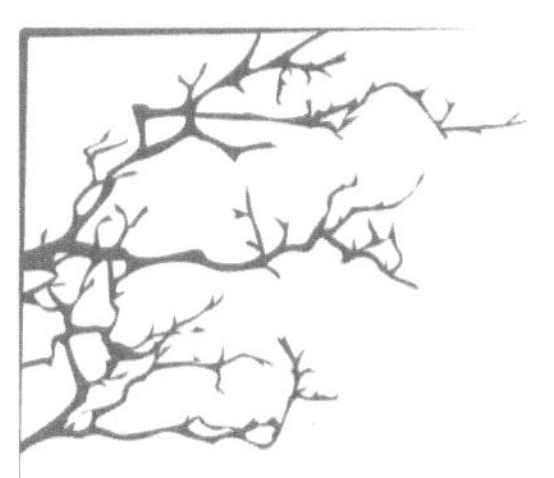

Chapter 2

Exeter, Devon

Mavis, a grey mare, shifted to allow the postilion room to maneuver straps around her broad chest. A cool brisk wind fluttered her mane. "I'm glad this carriage belongs to a lady and her maid," she said to her younger matching companion, also being harnessed. "Their conversation is bound to be more tolerable than the gentlemen's talk we're usually inundated with."

"Tired of listening to naval wood construction tips, Mavis?" Sarah asked, and neighed a mischievous laugh.

Mavis gave a rude snort, her nostrils vibrating. "If I hear one more comment about the auction price of timber, I shall bolt. Wait, I think our luck's about to improve. Look yonder at who enters the yard."

"Oohh...he's handsome!" Sarah said.

"The stallion or his riders?" Despite her scoffing tone, Mavis stood straighter and fluffed her mane.

"Definitely the stallion." Sarah's eyes widened at the black stud that strode proudly into the stable yard strewn with colorful autumn leaves. She flicked her tail in keen interest. "One of his riders is quite handsome, too. The other's gnarled, like an old oak bent by the wind. Must have been difficult for the black to carry two."

"They've ridden him hard," Mavis said. "See his sweat marks, the caked dirt on his ebony fetlocks? You'd think someone was chasing them."

"His breath gushes in steamy white puffs as if he were breathing out clouds," Sarah said in a dreamy voice. As he passed their carriage, she stomped her foot to catch the black's eye.

The stallion glanced her way and nodded his head, once, in acknowledgment.

"Oh, he's a sweet one, Mavis," she whispered, tossing her head in response. "Very well mannered. Look how his hoofs move, as if to music."

"I don't like the look of the sword the gnarly one has strapped to his back," *Mavis murmured. "Don't see folks carrying those old-fashioned weapons* *anymore."*

The taller of the riders dismounted. Ignoring his smaller companion's *ungainly struggle to get down, he turned to study their carriage.*

"Mavis, they're heading this way."

"So, I see."

"They're bringing the stallion!"

"And the sword. Let's not overlook that sword. Dear, oh dear. This could spell *trouble for us, Sarah. Makes me rethink my stand on conversations about the* *caliber of naval timber."*

MERRYN PENDRAVEN, AT eighteen years of age, walked alone along a southern Welsh road. She planned to head into Devon, and from there onto Cornwall. A long and tiring trip home. Only a few short days ago, after five long years of training, she had been thrilled to be endowed with the title, Coven Protectress of Britain, and sent on her first solo mission to Fishguard, Wales. Unfortunately, the assignment had ended up a disaster from start to finish.

First, she had been tossed out of the Fishguard coven, its sage insisting they needed no assistance there despite residing smack in the center of warlock territory. Irritated and regretting having come so far for no good reason, Merryn changed into her raven form and coasted back south, hoping to travel in the swiftest manner possible.

Then a white-tailed sea eagle, a warlock's familiar no less, had the nerve to attack her. She couldn't cast spells while transformed, so she swiftly landed and changed back to her human shape.

Though her rude attacker was now missing a few crucial tail feathers and ignominiously hopping home, she'd been unwilling to risk getting caught flying while still in Wales, which was warlock territory. Better to walk, at least down to Devon. The decision had added days to her schedule.

The only good news was that she was unharmed and there had been no witnesses to her misfortune. Well, there was the little pixie named Cri who had helped her out. Obsessed by the latest fashions, she was too busy showing off her new gown to tattle on Merryn. A gift of thanks for the light fae's invaluable assistance in pointing out the safest and quickest way out of Wales.

Close to sunset, exhausted and footsore, Merryn finally reached the Topsham Inn on the outskirts of Exeter. She opted to end this last leg of her weary journey in the comfort and warmth of an upholstered carriage. She quickly learnt the public coach was not due for another hour. Not surprising news considering her run of bad luck lately. On a positive note, this left plenty of time for a hearty meal, the first truly satisfying food she had eaten in days.

She was lingering over the last bites of a succulent braised lamb and roasted vegetables when the innkeeper delivered the disappointing news that, due to an accident, the public coach would be delayed another six hours.

Merryn's shoulders dropped in disappointment. She went outside and, chewing on her lower lip, contemplated her next move. Should she transform into her raven shape and fly home? It would certainly be less onerous than more walking or waiting endless hours for the public coach.

Happy with that plan, she looked around for a secluded area to transform. The back of the stables should serve her needs perfectly. She was on her way there when a bale of straw on the ground stirred, rustling. She hesitated, checking to see if anyone else had noticed the unnatural movement. The yard was busy with customers – a couple of grey mares were being strapped to a private carriage. She sidled closer to the bale to investigate.

"Come to the well by Laneast," the straw bale said.

"Aunt? Is that you?"

The bale seemed to settle with a sigh. "Who else, child? Meet me there before sunrise. Do not keep me waiting. Trouble brews."

"What kind of trouble?"

No response. Her aunt must have released her hold on the bale. Laneast was several miles west of Callington. Flying was now her best option.

"Miss Pendraven?" An elderly matron hurried toward her from the inn.

A neighbor. Could this day get any worse? She smiled politely. "Lady Hancock. How good to see you."

"My dear, do not tell me you travel alone?"

"Unfortunately, I'm forced to." Her aunt had taught her that the trick to lying was to make a tale sound plausible. She spoke with practiced ease. "My maid took ill. Yet Aunt Morwena requests I return post-haste. Now I hear the public coach has been delayed."

"Well, then you must come with me in my carriage, my dear. I'll not hear any arguments against the plan." The heavy-set matron pointed to the vehicle with the grey horses.

With a firm hand tucked around Merryn's forearm, the lady drew her forward. "Come along. I'm journeying to Callington as well, so am not only able to give you transportation, but chaperone you. It doesn't do for a young lady of good family to travel alone."

"Thank you, Lady Hancock," Merryn said with sincerity, for she was truly weary. The carriage would take her closer to her destination. She must simply manufacture a plausible excuse to hop out closer to Laneast.

The groom opened the carriage door and assisted Merryn inside. He then turned and helped Lady Hancock in. Instead of occupying the opposite seat, the lady sat next to Merryn, taking more than half the space. A humid scent of long days of travel and fading lilac water clogged Merryn's lungs.

She contemplated scooting across to the other seat when the lady's maid entered and took the empty spot, and placed her bag beside her. With a sigh of regret, Merryn moved her arm so it was less likely to press into her neighbor's cushy bosom.

The lady apparently took that as an invitation and leaned closer to whisper. "Have you heard of the terrible goings-on in Callington lately, my dear?"

Merryn's ears perked. "What's happened?"

"Why, young Trystan, staying with Mrs. Parnell, has been snatched. Right from the rectory. In the very midst of his baptism! Though why a boy of six would not have been baptized long before is not my place to conjecture. Can you imagine such an outrage?"

Merryn was hard-pressed to decide what outraged Lady Hancock the most – the lateness of the baptism or the stealing of the child. The latter news shook her. She knew young Trystan. He was the son of a Callington witch. The woman had intended to baptize her son? A daring move when his father was a warlock who would resent such a step. Warlocks abhorred baptisms, for the Christian ritual muted any mind controls they could place on their sons.

The stable lads heaved baggage onto the top of the carriage. The vehicle swayed under the heavy thumps. Her aunt must have been referring to this trouble. Merryn would be home soon and Aunt Morwena could inform her of all that had happened during her absence.

It galled her that when her coven was in trouble, she had been called away across half the country on a useless errand. Her eyes narrowed as frustration gave way to doubt about the legitimacy of that request from the Fishguard coven. Could she have been drawn away on purpose? Perhaps that attack by the sea eagle hadn't been to hurt her as much as to delay her. It had certainly added extra days to her journey.

Lady Hancock droned on unheard until one comment drew Merryn's attention.

"I'm sorry, Lady Hancock, I missed that. Did you say something about the fae?"

Lady Hancock's maid gasped. "Should we be talking of such things, milady?"

"Shush, Jenna," Lady Hancock said. "The little gentry are real enough, so why shouldn't we talk about them? My grandmother once told me about a mother who found her young boy switched for a fae child. Horrified, she dragged the squalling monster brat to the woods and tossed him into a raging river, for it's said that..."

"Lady Hancock," Merryn interrupted. What concerned her more were current events, not elaborate folk tales. "How are the little folk involved in this incident with Trystan?"

"That's just what I'm trying to tell you, dear. Rumor has it the child was stolen by fae."

"I see," Merryn said, tight-lipped and no longer intrigued by gossip. This type of conjecturing could lead to disaster. It would be a short leap from blaming fae to other supernatural culprits. Witch hunts were a thing of the past and Merryn's role as Coven Protectress was to ensure they never returned.

"Was a fae child substituted?" she asked, intending to scorch this rumor as she would a tick.

"No, it wasn't," Lady Hancock said. "I hadn't thought of that. You're right, of course. If it were the gentry, legend tells us they would have put one of their own in place of poor Trystan." She sounded disappointed.

"Then someone other than fae took the child." Merryn hoped they had hit on the true course of events. "Perhaps it was his father? I heard there was marriage trouble."

"I suppose," Lady Hancock said in a gush of breath, like a deflating bellow. "A havey-cavey way to go about it."

As Lady Hancock was famous for gossiping, the fae kidnapping rumor should die a quick death. Merryn nodded with satisfaction.

The father's involvement was likely. A warlock could have compelled the Fishguard coven to draw Merryn away from Callington. A warlock with a sea eagle for a familiar, perhaps?

The day Merryn visited Fishguard, those witches had acted ungrateful about her call. As if a Coven Protectress arrived there every day of every year.

What if she was young? It did not negate who she was. There hadn't been a Coven Protectress in Britain for over two decades, since the last one died in battle with a dark fae. Those creatures endowed with earth power were unmerciful. Since then, none of the witches who had tested had been found capable of handling the position or likely to survive for long in the role.

Witches had been forced to take care of their own covens for far too long. If there had been a Coven Protectress when Merryn's family came under attack five years ago, perhaps her parents and brother wouldn't now be dead. For that reason alone, Merryn took her role deeply to heart.

In fact, now she thought on it, the Fishguard coven's message of, "Be gone," was highly suspect. One of the serving witches had even whisked away Merryn's half-full plate while a forkful of eggs was headed for her mouth.

Once home, she would discover what really happened and reunite Trystan with his mother. If the Fishguard coven had played a role in this dreadful affair, woe betide them.

At a sharp knock on the carriage, Lady Hancock jumped so high that even Merryn was startled. The door swung out and a tall, young buck gazed in.

Distracted by the news about Trystan, Merryn glanced at him with mild curiosity. Her mood quickly swung to candid admiration. He had a most compelling face. All angles and arches. Like an archangel sculpture. Her heart thumped in approval and a flush warmed her cheeks.

"Good morning," he said in a polished voice that reminded Merryn of kings and knights and dances at Almack's.

She loved to dance.

"Ladies, my pardon for the interruption. May I introduce myself?"

"Of course," Lady Hancock gushed.

"Thomas Drake Saint-Clair, Earl of Braden, at your service."

Merryn doubted Lady Hancock could smile any wider. She, too, was tempted to grin like an idiot. She stifled the unruly, fully feminine, impulse.

"How do you do, my lord?" her neighbor said. "I'm Lady Hancock. My companions are Miss Merryn Pendraven and my maid, Jenna. We're on our way to Callington."

"I, too, am headed in that direction. Unfortunately, my coach broke down a way back and I hear the stage coach is likely to be several hours yet."

"Good heavens," Lady Hancock said. "Why not come with us then? Jenna, move over."

"How very kind of you, Lady Hancock. I would be delighted to join you." He turned to gesture to a short man leading a beautiful black horse. "Garth, these lovely ladies have invited us to travel with them. Pray ensure you guide the driver to miss as many holes in the road as you are able to this time. My teeth still rattle from all the craters we've visited in the past few days."

Lady Hancock adjusted her skirts to leave room for the gentleman to enter without soiling her clothing.

"Isn't this exciting," she whispered to Merryn. "He looks quite eligible, my dear, and you being unmarried must take particular note. Handsome gents – and he appears well-to-do and with a title – do not grow ten to a dozen in our Cornish moors."

Merryn's warm cheeks heated to a blaze. Had he heard that? How could he miss it?

The slight tilt of his full lips as he climbed into the carriage suggested he'd not only heard but also been amused.

She was tempted to deny she was on the lookout for a husband but prudently bit her lips. Why prolong this torture?

Once seated, he smiled and a shiver spun through Merryn like a well-cast spell. His deep blue eyes matched to perfection the azure hair ribbon woven through her braided, blond hair.

"Perhaps you ladies are acquainted with the gentleman who graciously invited me to his home in Callington," Lord Braden said. "Squire James Robin Appleton."

"Why, certainly," Lady Hancock said. The door shut and the carriage rolled forward. "The Appletons are no more than a mile from my home. On the other side of the Parnells. Oh, sir, you probably haven't heard the news."

"We shouldn't trouble his lordship with local gossip," Merryn said, hoping to waylay this beleaguered topic.

"On the contrary, Miss Pendraven," Braden said. "As I intend to stay in the area for a few weeks, I'm most interested in local happenings. What news?"

Lady Hancock leaned forward, her enthusiasm radiating about her. "A boy was kidnapped, my lord, in the most villainous manner, from Saint Agatha's church."

His blue gaze swung from Lady Hancock to Merryn, his interest obviously roused. "And I worried Callington would be a bore."

She'd never met a man with such a lively face, both animated and engaging. Despite her intention to remain tight-lipped, his captivating gaze tempted her to join in. If she weren't careful, she might blurt out that she was a witch just to see his eyes light up again.

"I had assumed the town would have no more to occupy the local constable than smuggling along the coast," he said.

"Not at all, my lord." Lady Hancock's civic pride rode her tone. "We're a thriving community with many odd happenings in the neighborhood all the time."

Merryn's panic rose and she quickly changed the subject. "What happened to your carriage, my lord?"

"The wheel snapped, Miss Pendraven."

"Was anyone injured?"

"To my groom's credit, he kept the vehicle from tipping. All has ended well, for now I've gained the delightful company of both of you."

"I hope your presence in the area will encourage Mr. Appleton to hold some parties," Lady Hancock said. "Isn't his lordship's visit quite exciting, Merryn?"

"Quite," Merryn replied and meant it. Coming from London, Lord Braden was likely a polished dancer.

He took up a great deal of space inside the carriage, but unlike Lady Hancock's horizontal expansion, his was in the vertical direction. Merryn suspected he would loom a good head over her statuesque figure. Perfect dancing height.

Even in this corner of the carriage, she gained hints of his scent. Very male. With a hint of sandalwood and soap. She liked it. She would have liked to get closer to it.

"Do you enjoy parties, Miss Pendraven?" Braden asked.

Lady Hancock responded before she could. "What young lady doesn't, my lord? You must save us both a dance."

"Why, now, I shall look doubly forward to it."

His gaze swung toward Merryn, and she underwent a disturbingly thorough study. One that would have made her squirm except, like a tightly wrapped grocery package, she was too squished into her seat to move.

"Do you enjoy dancing, Miss Pendraven?" he asked.

"What young lady doesn't, my lord?" she quipped.

The quirk of his lips said he caught her parody of Lady Hancock and was amused.

Something about this man drew her. Merryn glanced at her hands. She had learnt to her peril to distrust such instantaneous, untamed attraction. A fiendish fae-warlock had once enchanted her with his tall figure and fluid movements. He, too, had seemed polished, smooth and enticing.

She shook away the disturbing memory. Braden was nothing like that rogue. Where he had been arrogant, Braden comported himself with amicable manners. Where the warlock had been brash, Braden's words were circumspect. Where that vile villain had lied and deceived, she instinctively sensed Braden was a forthright and honest man. Still, it was prudent to be cautious.

Not that she suspected Braden of being a warlock. After her disastrous coming-out ball when she was swept off her feet by the deceptive warlock, her aunt had strenuously reinforced her lessons on how to recognize when mind power was being employed to alter her perceptions. Braden was not using such a spell. Yet, her witchly instincts insisted she keep her barriers raised and she complied.

Despite Lady Hancock's disparagement of Merryn's unmarried state, she had no illusions that would ever change. House parties and balls aside, courtship, marriage and children were for other young ladies and witches to while away their time. Long-term romantic prospects were dim for those in her line of work.

According to Aunt Morwena, a Coven Protectress's average life expectancy rarely exceeded five and twenty years - most died in battle. A fate she'd been made well aware of before she took her pledge.

In trusting any man, she would not only risk her life, but all those she was sworn to protect. When she took a lover, it could only be for a night or two, and then with someone whom she deemed worthy to risk lowering her guard.

The discussion veered back to talk of the missing boy, and Merryn returned to high alert. This time, sadly, she was unable to avert Lady Hancock's flow of words. After spilling every scrap of information about the missing child, Lady Hancock sat back, well pleased with her telling.

Into the silence, Braden spoke. "Lady Hancock, you mentioned earlier of other odd happenings at Callington. You've made me curious. What makes you define the events as out of the ordinary?"

Merryn wanted to pinch Lady Hancock and scream, *Don't speak!*

Her neighbor glanced at her before responding and Merryn groaned inwardly at the woman's conspiratorial gaze.

Whatever you're planning, Lady Hancock, pray do not act on it.

Lady Hancock could apparently neither read minds nor correctly interpret the desperate appeal on Merryn's face, for she regaled the earl with the most shocking stories. Worse, she made a point of including Merryn's role in each.

Merryn helped resolve this when such and such happened.

Merryn came to the rescue when that occurred.

When this incident blew up, only Merryn's quick thinking saved the day.

Braden looked inordinately interested. As each tale unfolded, Merryn's ears heated to volcanic status while Braden's left eyebrow rose, threatening to merge with his hairline.

The lady was obviously trying to foster the earl's appreciation of Merryn, but his many glances in her direction unnerved her. He seemed to grow more thoughtful than admiring.

She hated to imagine what he took from these stories, but prayed he wasn't intelligent enough to put all the pieces together and come up with the truth behind the accounts.

Lady Hancock's knowledge of Merryn's activities was a further shock. Was the woman uncannily perceptive about her neighbors' activities or had Merryn and her coven members become too careless and cocksure over the years?

"You seem a popular lass in Callington, Miss Pendraven," Braden said.

"She is our personal guardian angel, my lord." Lady Hancock patted Merryn's knee. "Well versed in local folklore, she has helped us out of many a scrape with the little gentry."

Right then, Merryn wished she could vanish.

"Little gentry?" Had his voice spiked? "You ladies believe in such fanciful myths?"

"Oh, they're not myths in this part of the world, my lord," Lady Hancock said in earnest. "It may seem so in London, I don't doubt. If we were in a drawing room in a townhouse at Mayfair, you can be assured I would never bring up this topic." She gave a titter of laughter. "They would think me completely mad, would they not, Merryn?"

"I don't doubt it, Lady Hancock."

"Miss Pendraven, do you, too, believe in the existence of these 'little gentry'?"

She looked him in the eye and found his return regard quite serious, as if he truly wanted to hear her view on this matter. "Not all things in heaven and earth are known to mankind," she replied, picking her words with care. "I would not presume to judge what is real or not."

"A most liberated view," he said. "Are your views a reflection of Callington's popular stance? If so, does your local rector reflect this communal spirit in his preaching?"

The question held a hint of condemnation.

Instead of snapping in defense, she decided to go on the offensive. He'd learnt much about her and her town, so it was time she probed a little into Lord Braden's character. "Are you a God-fearing man, my lord?"

"I believe in God's Truth," he said in a quiet voice. Yet, there was much weight to the lightly spoken words.

"How are we to know what is God's Truth?" she countered, then immediately regretted the question. This was a discussion for a coven gathering, not one to get into with someone she'd met inside a carriage. Especially a man.

"I would have assumed," he said, "that your Church teaching tells you all you need to know on the subject of God's Truth."

"Who teaches the Church such things?" The words were barely out of her mouth before she cringed inwardly.

Braden frowned, as if he were unused to being questioned in such a forthright manner. "Men more holy than you or I, Miss Pendraven."

Merryn nodded, and although a mantra of *Shut up, shut up, shut up* rang through her mind, she gave in to her suicidal need to continue this dangerous conversation.

"Is truth not an ever-changing commodity, my lord?" she asked, thinking, *no wonder Coven Protectresses were so short lived.* "Do not your holy men learn every day, from God, another facet of what the truth is? The advances in science alone in the last centuries have taught us that what we know today may be shown as utter falsehood tomorrow, as with our past belief that the earth was flat. What we believe tomorrow may be viewed as preposterous today. So, how is one to judge what is God's Truth when the entirety of God's Truth is as much a mystery to us today as it was yesterday?"

"You are a philosopher, Miss Pendraven." The keen light in Braden's blue eyes suggested the idea did not displease. "But philosophers must be careful, else they may be charged with heresy if the truth they pursue cannot yet be proven."

"Nothing in faith is a fact, my lord. That is why it is called faith."

"Pish posh," Lady Hancock cut in.

Merryn started, but a flush of relief suffused her cheeks at the lady's timely interruption.

"Faith in God and belief in little people has nothing to do with philosophy," Lady Hancock said. "Both are immutable facts of life." She patted Merryn's knee with a firm hand, practically pinching her. "And Merryn, dear, it does not become a lady to argue with a man about such matters. It is best left for men in universities and monasteries to thrash out such questions to the death. Do you not agree, my lord? It is more felicitous if discussions between men and women center on the best entertainments to be had."

Merryn let the matter drop, though the look on the earl's face suggested he might prefer to continue with their discussion. However, he bowed to Lady Hancock's lead and changed the subject to forms of entertainments they could stir up in the coming weeks.

Only then did her chest collapse with utter relief and she realized how tightly she'd held herself, and not just from being crushed into the side of the carriage, either.

As darkness set, they drew closer to Callington. Since witches were forbidden from using Wyhcan mind spells on humans, which past experience warned could go dangerously awry in this world, Merryn needed another way to disembark without opposition. Trickier yet, once she was out of the carriage, she needed her companions to leave the vicinity without waiting for her to return or to try to find her.

The maid had fallen asleep and Lady Hancock's head was nodding by the time a plausible plan occurred to Merryn. Her success relied heavily on her recent discovery that Lady Hancock was more aware of coven member activities, in particular Merryn's protectress duties, than any of them had thus far been aware. A risky bet, assuredly, but a necessary one with Lord Braden watching her so keenly. In fact, he seemed to sense she was up to something, for he, too, had sat up and wore a suspiciously bland expression.

A glance at the moonlit covered landscape showed they approached the turnoff for Laneast. Time to act. She shook Lady Hancock awake, and then whispered her need to deal with another bit of unusual trouble outside Callington and begged for assistance.

Lady Hancock gave her a startled look.

Merryn held her breath, wondering if she'd misjudged her. Then to her great relief, without argument or a word of censure, the lady signaled the carriage to stop and said aloud, "Miss Pendraven wishes to disembark to visit a friend who lives nearby."

Excusing herself, Merryn took her small valise tucked under her seat and stepped out the door. Once she'd descended, noting Lord Braden's upset demeanor, she gently laid a spell on the outside of the door to ensure it could not be opened until the carriage reached Callington. She couldn't risk him following her to witness her meeting with her aunt.

She moved to the front and touched each horse's forehead, bespelling the mares to keep trotting until the carriage reached town. With luck, Braden would arrive in town to have the door open as normal, and be none the wiser to her precautionary action.

She then stepped to the side of the road as the vehicle drove on, leaving Merryn behind. The groom's attention was caught with handling his willful horses. Lord Braden's servant sitting beside the driver gazed back at her with wide eyes, but he didn't say a word of protest. The carriage then turned a corner in the road and became lost to sight.

Merryn spread her arms wide. *Free at last!*

Picking up her skirts, she headed in the direction of Laneast and the meeting with her aunt. She raised her hand and cast a spell for illumination. A metal handle fit into her grip and a gentle glow from a lantern outlined her pathway ahead.

As she strode through the woods, Merryn's stiff shoulders relaxed. This was her home. These paths, the surrounding villages, Cornwall. Home to witches, as Wales was home to warlocks.

Humans were by far preferable companion to warlocks. Braden was a perfect example of that fact. She had liked the earl immensely despite their heated discussion. He had argued without making her feel dim-witted for holding opinions different from his. In fact, having only held such intellectual debates with witches, their talk had made her feel more alive and vibrant than she thought possible in a man's presence.

She hoped she'd have an opportunity to dance with him before he returned to London. She suspected she would enjoy it. She pictured herself moving about the dance floor with Braden, their hands clasped, twirling to the musical allure of a tinkling spinet.

THE FACT THAT MISS Pendraven disembarked before they'd reached Callington deeply troubled Braden. Surely it was too dangerous for a young lady to be out alone, in the dark, in the woods. Even if her friend was quite near, anything could happen between the carriage and the safety of that home.

The carriage rolled forward and on impulse he tried to open the door, to offer to act as her escort, but couldn't budge the handle. He'd knocked on the roof to stop the vehicle but it carried on without pause. He tried the door again but it remained unmovable.

The maid had awoken but her frightened, tight-lipped expression suggested he would not get far questioning her.

He turned to inform Lady Hancock that he wished to disembark, too, only to find her eyes closed and her head hanging limp off her shoulders, as if she'd nodded off. He tried shaking her awake, to no avail. Braden heaved a frustrated sigh and sat back. Soon, soft snuffling snores from Lady Hancock filled the quiet carriage.

As soon as the carriage stopped in Callington, Lady Hancock came awake with an, "Oh."

He thanked her for the ride and bid a hasty goodbye, hoping he didn't sound ungracious. This time, when he tried the door, it opened as if nothing had ever kept it shut tight.

Outside, looking worried, Garth untied the black stallion from the back of the carriage.

"Did you see where the lady who left the vehicle earlier went?" Braden whispered.

"Just stood there on the side of the road, milord, watching us drive away. Sent quivers shooting up me spine."

"There was indeed something strange in her manner. We must find her. You'll need a horse."

"Yes, sir."

As soon as they obtained Garth a mount, they trotted down the road they'd come from.

Braden didn't like it but he was forced to ask Garth to use magic to track the lady in the dark. When they finally spotted Miss Pendraven ahead, she held a lantern aloft in one hand. He breathed a heartfelt sigh of relief and his first thought was, *she's safe.*

His second – *What is she doing?*

Her arms raised, she twirled every few steps forward.

"Garth, is she performing some magical ritual on the pathway?

"No, milord," Garth said. "At least, none I can perceive. If I didn't know better, I'd say she was dancing."

Her movements did remind Braden of a closing dance often performed at balls, *La Boulanger*. After a while, he sat back on his horse and enjoyed the prospect, even going so far as to picture himself partnering her in the turns.

"Where do you supposed she's heading?" Garth asked.

"If we're lucky, she's leading us straight to her coven."

"I was afraid you'd say that," Garth muttered.

Chapter 3

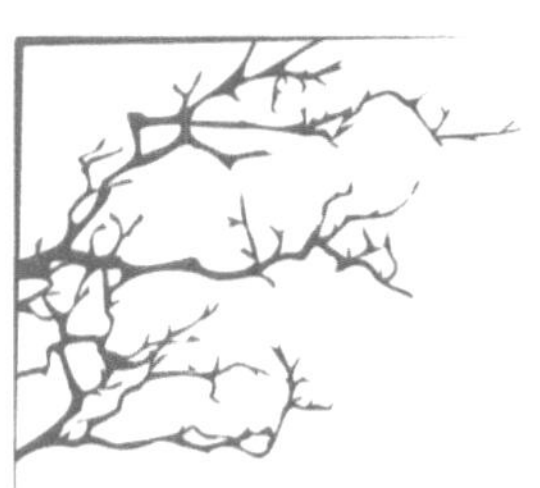

Laneast, Cornwall

"Think they'll make a request?" The wishing well posed the question to her creator.

In all the centuries that she'd listened to the prayers and hopes of those who lived nearby, her creator had never responded. Nevertheless, the well duly passed on all requests, but not once had she received an acknowledgment. There'd been no, "Thank you, I appreciate your diligent work" or "Good job." So she didn't expect a response now. She spoke anyway. It never hurt to begin a conversation, even if it went nowhere. "These ladies have been here a while but all they've done is argue. Do you think they'll come over to me?"

Silence. The well settled with a disappointed swirl of her water. After a few moments, she murmured, "Haven't had many visitors lately. Everyone's busy. When someone does come, all I hear is I need better wages, stronger shaft ladders or a fresh vein in the tin mines. I hope these two wish for something exciting."

A swell of energy enveloped her sides, warming her as if the sun had indeed risen, instead of remaining hidden below the horizon.

THEY WILL.

At this unexpected answer, the well trembled. Not only did she have visitors today, but she had been gifted with a divine response. This was indeed a special day, as she'd sensed when the sound of movement nearby awoke her.

"Do you think they'll ask about love? I like it when they ask about love."

LOVE COMES IN MANY FORMS.

Obscure. She churned her waters. Conversation was hard enough to secure with the Almighty, but must understanding be difficult to grasp, too? Not that it mattered. It was stimulating to talk with someone, especially THIS someone. The thrill of it shivered through her depths.

"I enjoy guessing what they'll ask for. I'm getting quite good. For instance, since neither of these women look like miners or widows of miners, I say the

younger one will ask about a lover. The one across from her will seek wisdom. What do you think?"

YOUR ROLE IS TO LISTEN AND HEAR PAST THE WORDS TO THEIR TRUE NEEDS.

"Oh," the well said, deflated. She wasn't good at deciphering signs and symbols and now she had to hear words that weren't spoken? She turned her attention to less troublesome matters. "What about the other two, the ones hiding in the bushes. Will they make a wish?"

THE FATE OF THIS NATION WILL REST ON THE WISH OF ONE OF THEM.

At that profound prophecy, the well splashed her stone walls in frenzied anticipation.

AN HOUR BEFORE SUNRISE, Merryn found Aunt Morwena sitting cross-legged under a large oak that shadowed the Laneast wishing well. Eyes closed, the elderly High Sage of Britain basked beneath the early morning glow that painted her fair cheeks rosy. Merryn eyed her steadfast aunt, allowing a sense of homecoming to envelop her as it always did in this lady's presence.

The dawn air was cool but carried the familiar smoky scent derived from the miners burning turf in the area. A distant shot reminded her it was partridge season. Nearby, a song thrush gave a thin, high-pitched "seep" before flying off.

Merryn approached and sat across from her aunt. The golden bed of fallen leaves crunched and rustled beneath her. Time to report in. Extending a hand, she offered the wild red cherry she'd plucked on the way, neatly pitted. One of her aunt's favorites.

Morwena Dunstan took and ate the offering, and bowed her thanks. "Blessed be, Merryn," she murmured and offered Merryn a sorrel leaf.

Merryn consumed the lemony edible, and bowed in turn. "Blessed be, Aunt."

"What did you learn in Fishguard?"

"There was no trouble there. But you have seen your share of difficulty here?"

Aunt Morwena nodded. "Young Trystan's been taken."

"By his father?"

"He says not. Mattock accuses us of hiding his son. He sent a warning to the coven threatening that if we do not return the boy within a week, there would be dire consequences. Trystan was taken three days ago."

Merryn's back stiffened with anger. How dare the warlock threaten them. What did he intend? To invade Cornwall? With few exceptions, such as the Fishguard coven in Wales, an unstated rule had prevailed for centuries that the two factions would stay out of each other's region.

The way to prevent an invasion was to find Trystan. If his father didn't have him, who did? Could Lady Hancock be right and the fae were somehow involved?

"Who else could have the boy, Aunt?"

"Who do you think?"

Merryn shivered at the light of battle in her aunt's gaze. The last time she'd seen that look had been over five years ago. The year Merryn began her training to become Coven Protectress. The day after her entire family was murdered. She said the name of her archenemy like a curse. "Dewer."

"Trystan is six, about the same age your brother was, when he and Dewer first met and became fast friends."

"Jonas and Dewer were friends?" Merryn asked, shocked. "They would have been three years apart in age."

"Yes. Dewer had few children who were permitted to befriend him. He was a lonely child. Your brother was likely awed by his new friend's half fae lineage, which linked Wyhcan heritage to earth's magic, bringing Dewer close to truly belonging on earth. During Jonas's regular visits to Wales, your father foolishly allowed the friendship between his son and Dewer to strengthen."

Merryn listened avidly. She only knew Jonas from the few months he stayed with her in Cornwall each year. She had grown to love him and was heartbroken whenever he left again for Wales. Truth be told, she was also a little envious of her brother's time with their father. During his brief visits, she often peppered Jonas with questions about their warlock father.

What happened when he stayed with their father in Wales, however, remained a mystery. Warlocks never disclosed their secrets, and Jonas was no different. After her brother's death, Aunt Morwena refused to mention Jonas's name again. The silence had been like a second death blow to a thirteen-year-old deeply grieving her parents and her beloved brother.

"What broke Dewer and Jonas's friendship?" Merryn gently prompted her aunt, hoping she would continue with this unusual sharing of family history.

"It was the fact that Dewer was never apprenticed."

"I don't understand," Merryn said, surprised. "Warlocks partner their sons with adult males for training by age ten. *Ah!* Jonas was apprenticed to a friend of father's when he turned ten."

"Exactly. I suspect that's what began the trouble between them. Dewer's warlock father was dead and his dark fae mother forbade the apprenticeship."

Wise, thought Merryn.

"I suspect Jonas secretly taught Dewer much of what he learnt," her aunt continued, "but it wouldn't be the same as being apprenticed himself."

"Still, if they were friends, why did Dewer harm my brother?"

"I doubt he meant to. Everything got out of hand when he stole him."

"Why did he do that, Aunt?"

"Without proper training, Dewer remained magically stunted. He might have hoped to apprentice with Jonas himself, and thus siphon off some of his friend's powers. Whatever his motivation, taking Jonas was a bad move. Dewer was ill prepared for the battle your parents waged to get him back. They joined forces to rescue their son. Dewer would have died if his mother had not come to his aid."

"Dewer has now had five years to recover, sulking in his black tower in Wales," Merryn warned.

"True, but despite having reached his majority, the Warlock Council repeatedly denied him access to Snowdon's crop of young warlocks to help bolster his powers."

Merryn's blood fairly thrummed with indignation. "As well they should, after what he did to my family!"

Her aunt nodded agreement. "I believe they hoped to keep him weak and thus controllable. Then along came Trystan. Another boy with a warlock for a father and a witch for a mother. Trystan has the potential to be as powerful as your brother once was. This custom of stronger warlocks tapping young apprentices for power must be stopped, Merryn. The practice breeds abuse."

"I agree but how can we affect what warlocks do? You ousted Dewer from my coming-out ball two years ago. Instead of learning from that painful lesson, he appears to have grown more daring."

"He never lacked nerve."

Merryn's clasped hands were white-knuckled. It was a Coven Protectress's duty to defend her people. She had also trained to gain the skills she would need to face Dewer and win.

"You would permit me to go after him this time?" Merryn posed the question, but wasn't requesting permission. Nothing would stop her now.

"Only to ensure Trystan's safety," Aunt Morwena said in a firm voice. "Find the boy and bring him back to Callington."

"Here? Considering the time limit, would it not be prudent to take Trystan directly to Snowdon? To his father?"

"If we prove the boy is safe in his mother's care, that may calm his father."

"The plan seems unnecessarily risky, Aunt, with warlocks on the rampage."

"Trystan would not be safe in Snowden."

"He was not safe here."

"Are you arguing with me, Merryn Pendraven?"

Her aunt's harsh-voiced question set her back. "I apologize, Aunt. I've had a trying time of late and little sleep." She smiled cajolingly to lighten the mood. "Rather than calling this an argument, would you consider I'm merely exploring the wisdom of your counsel?"

Morwena's lips twitched with the first hint of humor. "Dewer has designs on the boy, of that I am certain. Trystan is not safe anywhere. Not until he is baptized as his mother wishes. Then, he may be returned to Snowden."

This particular Christian ritual, reputedly used for the remission of original sin, had proven to have an unexpected side effect on Wyhcan children. It wove an intricate and extraordinary blessing against mind enchantments. The blessing lasted well into a Wyhcan child's early adulthood. Covens across Cornwall had been trying to replicate a spell similar to that miracle for generations, without success.

The ceremony especially hampered magical mind persuasion. Many witches heartily adopted the religious practice for their daughters. Warlocks, on the other hand, called the blessing an abomination against nature. The Warlock Council dissuaded the practice among their members.

"Has Trystan's father agreed to the ceremony?" Merryn asked.

"His father's wishes do not count."

The answer sent shock waves cascading over Merryn. The father's wishes did not count? *Not count*? When had witches begun to act like warlocks?

There was an unexpectedly militant look in her aunt's eyes. So Merryn proceeded with caution, as if she was walking barefoot along a shale-and-stone-covered Cornish beach. "Would the move not further anger the warlocks?"

"I'm willing to risk that."

"Why, when this could trigger a further confrontation?"

Her aunt's gaze skimmed half-bare trees and the dull-colored brush surrounding them before returning to spear Merryn with grim purpose. "Because of Dewer," Aunt Morwena finally replied in a seething tone. "Even if we retrieve the boy, Dewer will again try to take him - from us, from Snowden, from wherever the boy goes, unless we eliminate that which makes the boy a desirable commodity."

"But…" Merryn sat back, confused. How did what her aunt proposed, fit the witch's creed to do no harm?

"This theft of the boy should never have occurred. It's a repeat of what happened to poor Jonas."

With that admission came understanding. For the first time, Merryn saw the depth of her aunt's fury at her nephew's death. Her heart swelled with sympathy. She had thought she was alone in her pain. Her aunt, it seemed, merely hid her feelings better.

"Merryn, can you not see what this could mean for the future? If all warlock boys were baptized, none need ever again fear being used or abused by their elders."

"All?"

"We begin with one. To show how beneficial this ceremony could be. It will protect a warlock boy from being exploited by his elders but not hinder the boy's powers for his own use. When that benefit becomes clear, it is my hope baptisms will be better accepted by warlocks. There are some warlocks who would sacrifice their advancement in order to protect their child. Your father was such a man."

"My brother was never baptized," Merryn said. Or Dewer wouldn't have wanted him. *Ah!*

"Your father had agreed to the ceremony," her aunt said. "That decision might be what prompted Dewer to act."

That was news. Merryn frowned as a heavy feeling inside her shifted. For years, she had blamed her warlock father for not doing enough to keep both her mother and brother safe. If he had indeed contemplated bestowing the Christian ceremony on his son, then history *was* repeating. For the second time, Dewer had stolen a boy before he could be protected.

Her aunt continued as if she had been tending this plan for a long while. *Since Jonas's death?*

"This could give the warlock boys a chance to evolve past the emotional short-sightedness of their elders. Affect the future well-being of not only warlocks, but witches like my sister, who seem drawn to procreate with them."

The vision her aunt painted was far reaching indeed.

"You must keep a clear head in order to deal with this problem, Merryn. Do not let your thirst for revenge against Dewer cloud your judgment or you will lose sight of what we aim for."

Merryn felt as if they were about to take a step that would echo throughout history. It was a perilous move.

"Aunt, are you sure this is the wisest course? What if the boy's father acts on his threat to destroy us?"

"He has." There was worry in her aunt's eyes.

"What? How?" Merryn wanted to jump up and hit someone. If a warlock had been nearby she would have pummeled him until he screamed. Luckily, she and her aunt were alone in the forest.

"He has made a pact with the Church of England."

"Impossible," Merryn shot back, slicing her hand sideways in rejection. "The Church does not interfere with us any longer."

"They plan to now. A guard known as 'The Dove' is being sent to Callington to put an end to our coven."

The moment Aunt Morwena spoke, Merryn knew whom the Church had sent. Braden. She sat back, feeling the air thicken and congeal with dread certainty. Braden had listened to Lady Hancock's stories with such interest. She groaned aloud at all that lady had let spill during their ride.

"What is it?" Aunt Morwena asked.

"This dove has landed, Aunt. He was in the carriage with me from Exeter."

"Are you certain?"

"Yes."

Recalling how his intelligent eyes studied her so thoroughly, she shuddered. With all that talk of faith and God's Truth, what had *she* let slip? She had been as loose-tongued as Lady Hancock. Guilt and fear warred with her nerves. "What do we do now?"

"We cannot be distracted by his presence. Trystan is in danger. He is our first priority."

"But..."

"Do not worry about the church guard."

"He's an earl. Powerful both on Church grounds and by society's standards."

"I shall deal with him. You must find the boy. Begin by speaking with the rector."

All well and good for her aunt to say stay focused. Even the lure of bringing down Dewer paled next to her duty to protect those she was sworn to guard. "How can I ignore the danger to you or my coven sisters?"

"That is what I'm asking of you. Saving Trystan reaches beyond the confines of our little coven. You must keep the greater good in mind, Merryn."

She remained silent, coming to terms with what was expected of her. She must trust that her coven would be safe in her absence. Her fingers clenched and unclenched as she released her fears until a deep breath finally brought with it acceptance. "This is a dangerous game we play with the warlocks."

"It is a game we have been engaged in for centuries, ever since we disagreed on how best to deal with humans. Keep your aim high, and this time, we might win."

"WE SHOULD MOVE CLOSER," Braden said to Garth as he watched Miss Pendraven speak quietly with an older woman seated beneath an old oak.

His footman shook his head. "Wards, milord," as if that one word should explain everything.

Braden took it to mean that magical warning bells were scattered around the area. He'd witnessed Garth use such tools in their work.

While they waited, Garth adjusted his coat until he wore it inside out. "To render me safe from them nasty Cornish pixies, milord."

Braden slapped the superstitious man's hands away when he tried to do the same with Braden's morning coat.

Garth gave up with a loud disappointed sigh.

Braden turned his attention back to the two ladies. The women did nothing more than sit and talk, albeit quite animatedly. Behind him, his black Arabian stallion, Nadeem, flicked his tail with impatience.

Braden's sentiments were aligned with his steed. He'd rather be racing across the moors, eating his breakfast, or even sleeping in his comfortably warm Appleton bed than standing here staring at women who did nothing of note.

"Are you certain this is a coven meeting, milord?" Garth asked. "They look like they're just talkin' about who slept with who."

"Why would Miss Pendraven come here at sunup simply to gossip? It makes no sense."

"No more sense than thinking a witch would walk for miles instead of flyin'."

"That's merely an old wives' tale. No one can *fly*."

"Could be 'cause she didn't have her broom, I s'pose," Garth muttered in an absentminded way.

Braden might as well be having this conversation with the tree he leaned against for all the attention his servant paid him.

"Why not spell herself one, though?" Garth continued with his one-sided conversation. "As she did with the lantern?"

Braden rolled his eyes at his footman's excessive imagination. "She probably had that lantern and flint stashed away in the woods. I see no magic involvement in that."

"You believe she's a witch, else why follow her?"

"We followed to locate her coven. A coven consists of more than two witches, Garth. We must uncover who the rest are."

"Then what?" Garth asked, sounding a little nervous.

"We bring them to the Church for questioning."

"To be tortured," Garth said. "Then hanged. Or drowned. Or dismembered."

"Enough. The guards are not monsters." At least, he wasn't. Sutton's words returned to taunt that claim. *Destroy that coven.* "Garth, evil must be stopped, or it will flourish. At worst, they may be incarcerated for the rest of their lives, and be well fed and cared for. The problem here is that I have two divergent tasks. Finding out the identities of the witches and tracking down the missing boy. Trystan is my immediate concern. I want you to discover who else in this town belongs to the Callington coven."

"Me?" Garth asked, a squeak in his voice.

"Do you want to help or not?"

"Why can't I help with finding the boy?"

"He has probably been taken by demons," Braden explained, playing on Garth's fear of such beings.

"I'll keep an eye on the witches, milord. I'll do a good job."

"You'd better." Braden gave the little man a warning shove. "I'll not have you show soft heartedness with this lot."

"You can trust me, milord!"

Braden sighed, for he, too, had softened toward one of the witches. He recalled the impromptu discussion he'd had in the carriage with Miss Pendraven and his pulse leapt in remembered eagerness at that conversation. The lady's sparkling blue-green eyes had promised a passionate nature.

She stirred him both intellectually and physically. If Miss Pendraven hadn't fallen victim to the darker truths of the Devil, she would have made a stimulating companion.

The two women stood, interrupting his musing. They walked up to the well, held out their hands and, in perfect unison, dropped items down into the well.

"Oh!" Garth released a soft breath as if in awe.

"What?" Braden asked.

"Nothing."

"Garth, I know you saw something. What was it?"

"What could there be to see?" Garth asked with an innocent look, and then turned away as if he couldn't hold his master's steady regard.

Braden frowned. "Did something magical happen?"

"They're leaving."

Braden gave up on getting Garth to admit he'd seen anything supernatural and headed for his mount. "Let's go."

"I'll be right behind you, milord," Garth called out.

Braden had gone a few paces before he looked back to see Garth trotting in the other direction, toward the well. Now the witches had left, Garth probably thought it was safe to approach that area. What was he up to?

Braden followed his footman and then sat back on his horse as Garth dismounted and ran up to the well. He held out his hand and, muttering under his breath, dropped three successive prizes down into the water.

As Garth returned to his horse, Braden said, "Happy?"

"It never hurts to ask for help," Garth said, unrepentant.

"Prayer would be more useful. What did you wish for?"

"That the witches don't kill me for tracking them."

Braden hid his smile and nodded. "Appropriate."

"That the demons don't kill you for interfering in their fun."

"Thank you for thinking of me."

"And that no one gets hanged, burned, or dismembered during this journey."

"Now, Garth," Braden said in a grim tone, not liking his footman nurturing such unrealistic hopes, "you do realize your last wish is doomed to failure where evil is involved?"

Garth's shoulders slumped as he mounted and trotted off in silence.

Braden stared at the well with a frown. Among the Guards of the Green Cross, he had earned the nickname "Death's Dove" for the number of corpses that appeared wherever he was sent. His reputation did not portend a happy end for the ladies of Callington.

Still, he couldn't resist fishing out and tossing a coin into the well. As the shilling plopped, he murmured a silent prayer. He then cantered after his footman, easily passing him.

Chapter 4

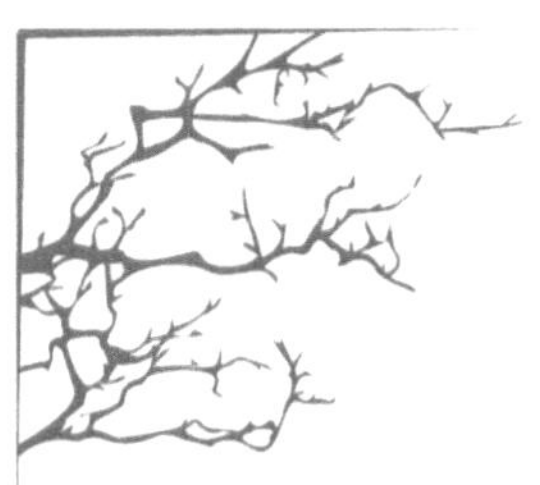

Callington, Cornwall

Saint Agatha, the solitary stone guardian of a lowly church in Callington, glanced with concern at the angel perched on her church's steeple.

The white-gowned messenger from God sat with her large wings nearly folded and her slipper-clad feet casually swinging. "The Coven Protectress is back in Callington and approaches yonder," the angel said. "She's here to investigate the missing warlock boy."

Worry slammed into Agatha like a battering north wind. Standing in her nook above the porch doors, she weighed her options and found only one was viable. "Other than granting entrance, I shall ignore the witch."

"There are others who also question what happened here the day the boy disappeared," the angel murmured. "You cannot put everyone off."

"Does...You Know Who...know what happened?"

"Do you by chance refer to the one who SEES all and KNOWS all?" The angel stared at Agatha as if she were daft. "You, my dear Agatha, are in serious trouble."

"It was not my fault!" Agatha protested. "I tried to keep them all out but my windows are broken. There's a leak in the roof. The crypt below has crumbled to such a degree, a gaping hole has opened into the underground chamber. I'm only one soul. I cannot guard everywhere. Where were you when I needed help? I did the best I could with what I had."

"Let us hope so," the angel said.

"Will you please speak to the Holy One on my behalf? Explain my side of events?"

"I have," the angel said with grave sympathy. "That is why I'm here."

"To help me protect the church?" Hope slowly rose in her wounded heart.

"I'm here to ensure all goes according to Divine plan."

Agatha sighed. She hated talking to angels because they never gave a straight answer. Her gaze drifted back toward the witch. Seeing the determination on her face, panic enveloped Agatha as solidly as her stone facade.

DESPITE HER LACK OF sleep, at ten sharp the next morning, Merryn arrived at the imposing south-facing porch of Saint Agatha's church in the center of town. She hesitated on the doorstep, checking if anyone noticed her. No one nearby.

Good.

She then glanced up at the marble statue of the church's guardian. Each of the saint's hands held one of her severed breasts. "My lady, I mean no harm to your church or its inhabitants. May I enter?"

Saint Agatha's immovable focus remained trained on the horizon. Merryn was about to lose hope of getting permission when the saint bent her stony gaze on Merryn. After a moment of contemplation, she inclined her head, once.

Merryn curtsied. "Thank you, my lady."

The saint's attention returned to the horizon in clear dismissal.

Merryn went inside. The heavy spiritual aura of the building swirled about her like the rising heat off pavement on a scorching hot day. She allowed the energies to soothe her agitated nerves. That sense of wellbeing, which a place of light always gave off, made her want to believe everything would work out after all.

No one lingered inside. Again, to her benefit. In the northwest corner of the nave, a brownie, no more than nine inches in height, diligently swept up dust balls.

She approached the little, pointy-eared cleaner. "Excuse me, sir, but do you know where I might find the rector?"

Without turning, the brownie indicated the chancel. "He's wi' a guest over there," he said with a strong Scottish brogue that rolled every "r."

Merryn gazed down the length of the pews where, at the other end of the church, from within a hidden alcove, came soft-spoken voices. While she waited for the rector to be free, she turned back to the brownie. He might have been here when Trystan was taken.

"My name is Miss Merryn Pendraven."

"I knows who ye're, Lady Protectress," the brownie said over his shoulder.

"Oh. Were you here when young Trystan came for his baptism?"

"Does I look like a clatterbags?" The brownie finally turned to face her, his pointed ears fairly twitching with visible indignation.

"The boy's in trouble." Merryn knelt on the floorboards. "I'm trying to find him and bring him home."

"Oh, that be different." Crossing one foot over the other, the brownie leaned a hand on his boom. "Shame, I thought. Waitin' until the boy was six to baptize him. What was his parents thinkin'? An' now he may never have the chance to receive holy protection."

"I'm hoping to rectify that situation. If all goes well, Trystan may yet get baptized."

"Live in dreams, do ye?"

"Do you know who took the boy?"

"Everyone kens who took him, lassie! And if ye an' yer kin' have any sense, ye'll pack up yer coven and leave Callington. I mean, that there church guard speakin' to the rector kens who ye're. I heard him ask about ye."

A shiver struck Merryn. Braden was here? Of course he was. On the same mission as herself. Who else would he seek out first but the man who saw the boy last? Exact reason she'd come.

"If you're so worried about the church guard, why are you still here?" she asked, feeling defensive. "I don't see you packing your bags to leave town."

"We're no part o' yer war." With a contemptuous look, the brownie returned to work.

"If Dewer is involved, everyone's a part of this war," Merryn said. "The church just hasn't realized it yet."

"Miss Pendraven," the rector called as he came forward from the shadows.

Merryn stood, surreptitiously blocking the brownie from the church guard's sight until the light fae vanished.

Beside the rector, the earl strode to greet her, interest sparking his eyes a breathtaking deep blue. Did he have to look quite so well turned out so early in the morning?

Next to his lordship's forest-green morning coat, cream-striped waistcoat, fluffy froth of a cravat, crisp tan breeches, and spotless shining Hessians, she and the rector could have been a hag and beggar at the marketplace seeking handouts.

Braden – hat, cane, and gloves in hand – bowed. "Miss Pendraven. A pleasure."

She curtsied. "Good morning, my lord." Though they stood a good three feet apart, every inch of her came awake as if his presence was the morning light sweeping over her.

He leaned to the side to look beyond her. "To whom were you speaking?"

"Did it seem as if I was speaking with someone?"

"The lady was probably praying, my lord," the rector said. "She was on her knees."

"Facing away from the rood?" The earl's eyebrow rose in challenge as his gaze swung from her to the cross above the rood beam that divided the nave from the chancel.

"Ah, I see where you gained the misimpression," Merryn said, trying to think past the confused clutter of her thoughts. She gestured to a dark corner. "I saw a ball of dust."

A fluffy bundle of dust suddenly filled her palm. Guessing at its origins, she sent a silent *thank you* to the brownie who put it there, and brought her right hand around to show the two men. "I bent to pick this up."

The elderly churchman chuckled and took the globe of cobwebs and dirt off her fingers. "There never seems to be an end to the collection of dust in this old building."

Braden's lips curved with a hint of skepticism. "It seems as if you are ever helpful, Miss Pendraven. From rescuing troubled souls to cleaning grubby churches. Is there anything you do not play a hand in?"

Merryn returned his direct stare without blinking, her backbone as unyielding as her devotion to Cornwall, to Callington, to her coven. "It is my duty to do what I can, my lord."

"For this place of worship?" he asked in a sharp tone, "or to elsewhere?"

"Where else would she worship but here?" the rector asked, sounding confused. "This section of Callington has but one church. We value her greatly in our little community. However, she cannot do everything. I was telling his lordship, Miss Pendraven, that the church is in desperate need of funds for renovations."

Braden took the dust ball out of the rector's restless fingers and studied the fluff of dirt. Then his gaze met Merryn's. "From the little I've seen, Miss Pendraven, it appears the church is not the only part of Callington in need of a little celestial shine."

Her throat clenched, blocking her airway. If lack of breathing weren't enough to cope with, her stomach fluttered under his direct probe. A clear symptom of her continued, illogical and ill-timed attraction to this perilous man.

Despite her body's lack of sense, she decided she no longer wished to dance with him. Not if he made a habit of destroying covens. For that made him worse than a warlock, which dug deep indeed. She forced herself to breathe, to think clearly – easier once her head stopped swimming from lack of air.

What she truly wanted was to show this upstart church guard that Callington did not require his assistance to tidy up its affairs. This town had her and that was ample.

In an act of symbolic defiance, she snatched at the dust ball Braden held in his palm. Before she could withdraw with her stolen prize, his fist clamped around her fingers.

The startlingly intimate clasp sent sparks shooting up Merryn's arm.

Was that hum an angel singing in the rafters?

No. It must be the wind blowing through a hole in the roof. Still, she could have stood there for all eternity, letting him hold her as if she were a lover from whom he didn't wish to part. His eyes proposed things far more pleasurable than retribution.

The rector's hands descended on top of both of theirs, interrupting his lordship's mesmerizing hold. Merryn breathed in relief.

"Now, now." The rector pried their clenched fingers apart to free the dust ball crushed within. "There is plenty for all to do."

Merryn withdrew her hand. Could that be disappointment in Braden's eyes? Even if so, it didn't come close to equaling the regret that swarmed her at breaking that deliciously dangerous contact.

I'm such a fool!

"We must work together," the old churchman said. "Then what is required will be accomplished faster and easier. Do you not agree, my lord? Miss Pendraven? What we truly need is funds."

"Perhaps," Braden said. "Is your chaperone waiting outside for you, Miss Pendraven?" he asked, adroitly changing the subject from church finances to Merryn's failings.

"Oh, she doesn't need a chaperone to come to Saint Agatha, my lord," the rector said. "Miss Pendraven lives not far from here and everyone hereabout knows her."

"Hmmm...so it would seem," Braden murmured. "Still, these are dangerous times. I doubt it's safe for a young lady to walk alone. Not after the unfortunate occurrence of that boy going missing."

"Snatched, my lord," the rector corrected. "Not merely missing. Sad, sad event. One moment he stood before me, the next the whole church turned into bedlam. I went to see what caused the ruckus, and when I returned, the child was gone."

"Surely his parents noticed someone taking him?" Braden asked.

"Only his mother was beside him, but she missed what happened, for it suddenly became dark, despite it being midday. As if God himself hid the sun from us."

"Sounds more like the work of the Devil," Braden said.

"Or one of his minions," Merryn mused, thinking of Dewer.

His lordship gave her a sharp look.

Did I say that out loud?

"What worries me," his lordship continued, turning back to the rector, "is how such an abomination could have taken place inside a church."

Point well taken. As a witch, even Merryn couldn't enter without the saint's permission. Perhaps the one she should question was Saint Agatha.

"I've a few errands to run," she said to the rector. "I'll come back later, shall I?"

"I hope it isn't anything urgent?" the old man asked. "Is your aunt well, Miss Pendraven?"

"Perfectly," Merryn said.

"I believe the elderly, too, must take extra precaution now winter approaches." The earl gave her another look that unnerved. "The evening air can be chilly once summer heat passes, so I warn my aged relatives to stay indoors at night. I would suggest you give your aunt the same advice, Miss Pendraven."

Merryn stared at him in bewildered silence. He returned her regard. In that instant, she guessed he had seen her by the wishing well with her aunt last night.

But how? She'd ensured he couldn't get out of Lady Hancock's carriage until it reached Callington. Yet, somehow, he had traced her to Laneast.

Her aunt underestimated this church guard if she believed she could handle him on her own.

"That is excellent advice," the rector said, breaking into the uncomfortable silence. "About the elderly not risking a cold by being out in the night air. I shall add that note to my sermon this coming Sunday."

The obsequiousness in his voice bothered her. Her attention swung from the troublesome earl to the rector. Was he that desperate for funds?

She glanced around the church with a new perspective. For the first time, boarded-up windows and tattered tapestries took prominence. A musty smell permeated the air as if rot had invaded the space, seeking a comfortable place to settle.

She must speak to Aunt Morwena about aiding this little church. Trouble was, with the depleting mining industry, times were difficult, especially if one did not resort to smuggling. Perhaps the coven could arrange a bake sale to help raise funds. Many of the witches were excellent cooks or had such talent working for them. But that must wait until later. For now, her focus was finding Trystan.

"I'll leave you two to your discussion then." Merryn bid them both goodbyes. Curtseying, she walked away, her mind turning to her next interview.

Yet, all the way to the porch doors, her shoulder blades twitched as if Braden's stare bore into them.

Once outside, noting no one else was about the churchyard, Merryn looked up at the statue. "My lady, may we speak?"

The statue of Saint Agatha did not move. Merryn's shoulders dropped with resignation.

How long might this take? Braden could walk out that door at any moment. She wasn't ready to face him again, not just yet. Whenever he drew near, she could not rid herself of an acute awareness of his presence. Even knowing who he was and what he represented made not a jot of difference. How could such attractive features and that daunting sensual energy have all been packaged into one man? It left a myriad of others sadly wanting.

Forget him, she chided herself. *You've more pressing matters to worry about.*

Another glance up showed the statue remained immobile and uncommunicative. She was about ready to give up, then shook her head. She couldn't walk away when Trystan needed her. "I wonder if a truth spell would work on a church," she murmured aloud.

The saint tilted her head downward. "What troubles you, my child? Are you fleeing from a suitor? Do you need my protection?"

Merryn hid a smile at the suddenly conversant saint. "No, my lady. I seek information."

"I see," Saint Agatha said, and Merryn received the distinct impression the saint was on the verge of losing interest.

"A boy was brought here for baptism two weeks ago," Merryn said quickly, hoping to get her question out before Agatha moved on to more pressing matters. "He was six years old. Before the baptism could take place, he was stolen. Do you know who took him or where he is now?"

"I'm the patron saint of martyrs, torture victims and eruptions," Saint Agatha replied, adjusting her arms as if to hold her severed breasts in a more comfortable position. "Does your request fall into one of those categories?"

"I thought you were the patron saint of bell ringers," Merryn said.

Saint Agatha frowned. "That is a misconception," she replied with asperity. "Are you a bell ringer?"

"No. However, I am searching for someone who may have fallen victim to imprisonment."

"A *boy*?"

That didn't sound promising. "I seek him on behalf of his grieving mother who is worried her son may be in peril."

"Very well, then. What is it you wish to know?"

"How could a man with ill intentions in his heart have gained entry into the church?"

"You have answered your own query. Why do you bother me with it?"

Merryn frowned, thinking through her words. Her eyes widened as comprehension settled. "A woman stole the boy?"

The saint shrugged her marble shoulders. "A witch, a hellhound, a warlock, they were all here that night. Any one of them could have taken him."

"And you let them into the church?"

"I'm not the boy's guardian! And the church is in need of repair. If you truly wish to do some good, you'd see to my weakening structure, not beleaguer me about a missing boy."

"He's an innocent in trouble." Merryn wove her way through the saint's illogic, and back to the crux of the matter. "While he was inside your church, were you not compelled to protect him from all harm?"

The lady's eyebrow rose with cynicism. "How innocent could he be? He had not been baptized for *six years*. Besides, his father is a warlock and his mother a witch. Such disparate unions are fraught with difficulties. You should know, also being a child of such a merger. Nevertheless, I gave them permission to enter. After all, God teaches us to be generous of spirit and open to those who seek the greater truth."

Merryn sighed. At least they were in agreement with that theological outlook.

"Best if you forget that whole unpleasant episode," the saint continued, her gaze returning to the horizon. "I have."

"I cannot forget the boy and walk away," Merryn replied. "I will not abandon him."

The saint's gaze swung back to her with such ferocious swiftness, Merryn teetered on her heels.

"The boy is a powerful warlock in his own right, though untrained," Saint Agatha said in a hard voice. "As powerful as you, Protectress, I don't doubt. What harm could possibly come to him? We all do what we can, but sometimes we must step back and let the world take a turn to see how events evolve."

The saint then shut her eyes as if she wished to blot out Merryn's existence as easily as she seemed to have Trystan's.

Merryn ground her teeth in frustration. She stared up at Saint Agatha's stony pose for a restrained count of ten and then asked in as calm a tone as she could muster, "Would you at least relay the details of what happened that night?"

The earl's voice said, "Talking to yourself, Miss Pendraven? Or are you praying again?"

Merryn lowered her gaze and found his lordship leaning against the closed porch door. How had he come out and she not heard him? Had he been listening to her for long? The one time she needed to sense his presence and he'd crept up on her like a snake in the sand.

Braden glanced up as if to study the saint before training his inquisitive glance back on her. "I gained the impression from our conversation in the carriage that you were not quite so pious."

"I believe in the Maker, my lord, so why would I not pray when troubled?"

"What troubles you this fine morning, Miss Pendraven?"

He looked as if he really wanted to know. She even suspected that, if she confided in him, he would try to help her. How odd, especially when she knew he'd been sent here to roust her and her sister witches out of Callington as if they were a virulent infection that needed to be purged by leeches.

"Thank you for your concern, my lord, but nothing troubles me that I wish to discuss at this moment. Excuse me."

"Wait."

The plea sounded urgent. She turned back, suspicious, but curious, too. "Yes?" Then realized she now stood a step below him, a most disadvantageous position to take with an enemy. Yet, since she'd paused, going back up seemed childish.

"I feel moved to find this missing boy, Miss Pendraven," Braden said and came forward until he was one step below her, so they stood eye to eye. On equal terms.

Merryn wanted to stomp her foot with frustration. This man's every action put her sadly out of curl. Why could he not act uncouth, rude, domineering, or at the least, self-serving? Then she would have enjoyed clouting him on the head and not cared a wit about straying from the witch's code. Instead, she wanted to smile and be agreeable to all his wishes.

"I suspect, Miss Pendraven," he continued, watching her with a keenly probing glance, "that you feel much as I do."

Not unless you're considering ravishing me on these church steps, my lord.

"From our talk inside the church and, earlier, I could tell that you care deeply for those who reside in this quaint town."

He looked sincere. He had truly listened to her. A most perplexing man.

"In the past, you've come to the rescue of many residents in Callington," he continued in a voice that stroked. "I feel certain you will not sit idly by during this crisis."

Merryn blushed at his accurate assessment of her character. Warmth rose up her face. As if he were unable to tear away, his gaze followed that flow of blood, heating her further without a touch.

She shut her eyes and ordered herself to be calm. If she stood here staring into his enigmatic eyes much longer, she would fall so hopelessly in love with this man, she might as well put a noose around her neck or light the bonfire herself.

"What is it you wish from me, my lord?" she asked in a quiet subdued voice, looking at him with the gravest of concern. *Pray, do not say anything nice.*

"I would like your help."

That was a shock. Was he earnest? It took her a moment to respond with the only possible answer to such an alliance. "No, my lord."

"I'm a stranger here. You know your way about Callington better than I. You could show me where best to begin my search."

"No."

"Anyone could have come upon you last night."

Her eyes widened at his direct speech. Was he openly admitting he'd followed her?

"Pray, be sensible, Miss Pendraven. It's much too dangerous to go about on your own. At least accept my services as your escort while we search for young Trystan?"

"No, no, no." Her heart hammered wildly. She was unsure if her palpitations were from fear of him or a wild attraction to him for caring enough about her to be worried. No man had ever shown her such concern. Not even her father, who had left her solely in her mother's care shortly after birth, only returning to act the parent when his son was in danger.

She took a deep breath and spoke in a harsh tone. "My lord, if I may be so bold as to say, it is you who must be sensible in this situation. I can hardly be seen going about town in your exclusive company. If it offends you to see me on my own, I shall endeavor, henceforth, to always be accompanied by a chaperone on my journeys."

She held her hand up when he would have spoken. She pointed to the gold bejeweled band around his right forefinger. "All subtlety and double talk aside, my lord, by your engraved ring, I know you are perfectly aware the two of us play for different teams. We cannot become allies, for we belong to warring camps."

He frowned, though he must know this for a fact. It was as if once spoken aloud, the concept became deeply troubling and unwelcome.

She curtsied and bid him good day before departing. On reaching the pavement, she shot a backward glance and that was to her detriment. For he still stood there, appearing so gravely distraught that her heart squeezed in sympathy.

She smiled to ease his upset a little. "I do wish you the best of luck with your quest, my lord. For I would have Trystan found safe and sound, no matter by whom."

Merryn hurried away toward the main street, shocked by her daringly blunt speech, and to a Guard of the Green Cross, no less.

Had he really meant that he wished to join forces to uncover this mystery? *No.* He must have wanted to keep her close so he could trap her into admitting she was a witch. Well, she had admitted as much just now, and he could make of it what he wanted. Her prime concern at this moment was finding Trystan, not worrying about what Lord Braden might or might not do.

Merryn hurried down Callington's main street. With purpose, she put aside thoughts of his lordship and focused on her conversation with Saint Agatha. The saint had said a witch, a hellhound and a warlock had entered the church that night. The warlock could have been Dewer, or one sent by Trystan's father, but other than those in the baptismal party, who had been the witch?

The only out-of-town witch who had been in town recently was from Fishguard. The one who came to tell of her troubles in that Welsh coven. Troubles that had sent Merryn flying to Wales, leaving Callington open to attack.

She stopped mid-step. Could that Fishguard witch, Branwyn Morgan, have come with two goals? One to get Merryn out of town, and the second to snatch Trystan for the warlocks? Such collusion with warlocks was hard to credit. Yet, against all common sense and caution, the Fishguard witches did reside in the very midst of warlock territory.

Before she could hurry home to ask her aunt if the Fishguard witch had attended the botched baptism, someone called out.

"Merryn!"

A quick glance confirmed the worst possible interruption. Her cousin Emily waved from a vegetable shop's doorway across the street. With her were her cousin's two closest friends, Miss Eliza Symons and Miss Jane Bicket.

Merryn groaned. She did not have time for chitchat and that's exactly what these three young ladies excelled at. Their sole aim in life was to find a husband who would whisk them out of the wilds of Cornwall and deliver them into the light of London's high society.

Still, as Emily considered herself an injured party from a now two-year-old event, this meeting could prove brief. With that hope in mind, Merryn crossed the street.

She came to a halt on the grocer's threshold stone, which had the word *Pol* engraved on it, the name of the shop's original proprietor. Outside the establishment, barrels were filled to overflowing with parsnips, turnips and onions caked in mud. The produce's pungent fragrance bathed the air, making her hungry. It must be close to luncheon.

"Good day, Emily. Miss Symons and Miss Bicket. I hope the day finds you all well?"

"You were speaking with Lord Braden over there," Miss Bicket said in an excited whisper. "Isn't he breathtaking?"

Merryn looked back and saw his lordship still on the church's steps, looking in their direction.

"He is indeed," she replied, unable to lie about such an obvious fact. "Pray excuse me, ladies. I've an urgent errand."

She stepped to the side but Emily matched her movement and blocked her path. "Lady Hancock said you drove into town with his lordship."

"I did," Merryn said in a cautious tone.

The girls then spoke in such a rush it was hard to tell who said what.

"Lady Hancock says he's unmarried."

"And has twenty-five thousand a year."

"The girl who marries him will become a countess!"

"And be able to attend Almack's every year."

The last comment was spoken with a heartfelt sigh.

"She would know," Merryn replied. "Now, I really must dash."

"But he's coming in this direction," Miss Bicket said in a breathless whisper.

To her discredit, Merryn feared her heart sped up with as much thrill as Miss Bicket's at the news. She squashed the unruly feelings and silently wished his lordship the best of luck with these ladies.

Perhaps they could distract him from his unsettling interest in working with her. "This should offer all of you a chance to speak to him yourselves. Good day."

She had taken no more than one step before Emily looped an arm through Merryn's elbow and swung her around. "We cannot possibly converse until we've been properly introduced. You must introduce us, Merryn. You've met him." She leaned in to whisper hotly in her ear. "*And you've a deep debt to repay me, cousin!*"

She moaned at that oft-repeated threat. Emily hadn't been the only one upset by Merryn's ruined coming-out ball. Was it her fault Dewer's unexpected appearance resulted in their family's precipitous departure from London?

Passersby jostled the group of girls standing stock still in the middle of the pavement.

Lord Braden came up to them and bowed.

All but Merryn giggled.

"Ladies," he said in his polished accent. He seemed to be hiding a smile.

As their gazes met and locked, she was tempted to return the shared humor. Instead, she made introductions.

"My mama intends to hold a ball a week hence, my lord," Miss Symons said. "I hope you will be able to attend."

"Will you be there, Miss Pendraven?"

"Of course," Emily said, before Merryn could reply. "I hope you will save us all a dance, my lord."

"It would be my pleasure," Lord Braden said.

Merryn looked longingly over her shoulder, wanting to quit this idle conversation and hurry home.

"You seem distracted, Miss Pendraven," Lord Braden said.

"She has an errand to run," Emily said, thankfully releasing her painful grip on Merryn's arm. "Let us not keep you, Merryn."

Merryn quickly accepted the opening and said her goodbyes.

"May I walk you home?" Lord Braden asked and bowed his goodbyes to a crestfallen Emily and her chagrined friends. He took Merryn's abused arm before she could protest and led her down the street.

After walking silently for a short while, the earl looked at her with knowing eyes. "Is there something you wish to share with me?"

"Whatever do you mean, my lord?"

"I saw you stop abruptly on the street earlier. You've thought of something regarding Trystan's disappearance, haven't you?" Guilt swirled through her as Braden chuckled. "You are a terrible liar."

Only with him! "Why must you keep following me?"

"If you will not help me, what choice do I have?"

The man was beginning to wear down her resistance and there had been precious little to begin with. She did want to work with him, just to spend more time in his delightful company. "I cannot help you," she said, as much to him as to herself.

"Yet, you have thought of something. Tell me and I may be of help."

"Why?" She stopped and turned toward him. "Why would you wish to help me?"

"Because we are both on the same mission, Miss Pendraven. To find young Trystan." He looked over his shoulder and frowned.

She followed his glance and saw the girls walking in their direction. "We cannot continue to stand and talk here," she warned him, "or it will be about balls and such."

Taking her meaning, he continued with her down the street, picking up their pace.

"Well?" he said. "Will you allow me to assist you?"

"No." She would have shaken off his hold and moved away but he looked crestfallen. "We cannot assist each other with this task," she said in a softer tone as they crossed the muddy street.

Before she knew what he was about, he picked her up by her waist, swung her over a puddle and set her onto dry pavement.

The three girls now across the street sighed in unison, and Merryn's cheeks burned not only from embarrassment, but also from the fact that he had yet to release her. She stepped back, breaking his warm hold.

"My lord," she said in a voice that was meant to be firm but came out as breathless as Miss Bicket's. "Any help you offer me will only lead to my demise."

"How can you say such a thing?" He reared back as if she'd struck him.

"How can you deny it, my lord?" she said in a saddened tone and bid him goodbye.

For a long while, she sensed him watching her, that appalled look, no doubt, still on his handsome face.

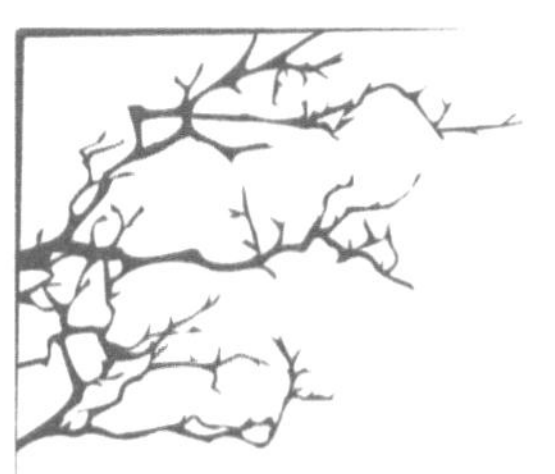

Chapter 5

"We're off to war, we're off to a glorious war!" Agamore, Braden's broadsword, sang in a booming voice, barely able to contain his delight. He loved a good fight and then the holy cleansing that followed, which connected him to all of creation in one incredible beat.

"Don't say that, Aggie," Peter, the portmanteau, moaned. "His mother told him it was time to settle down. I think we're off to find a wife." Braden's footman shoved in clothes willy-nilly and Peter just as swiftly formed shelves to accommodate the items.

He liked a tidy space, with everything neatly arranged according to size, color and need. "That witch in the carriage with us on the way here was terribly pretty," he murmured as he shook out a linen shirt and draped it over a hook to prevent creases. "I hope he chooses to wed her."

Agamore snorted as he was slipped into his sheath. "My guard doesn't want to marry, you silly twit." His words became muffled as he slid further inside his specially made and blessed leather encasement. "We're off to a holy war. There's danger afoot. Evil to vanquish. Lands to purify. This is our purpose in life. What he and I were made for. I sense great unrest in the air and I'm never wrong, while you've never been right about anything, not once."

"I'm right this time," Peter insisted. "You don't realize what his man's packing in here. If you did, you'd know we're off to find a wife, not seek a fight."

Agamore hesitated, uncertainty sliding along his steel like a soft, oil-covered cloth, but then he shook himself. "Nonsense. The footman doesn't know what my guard has in mind. We prepare for a fight. A big one. Biggest we've ever faced. We will be magnificently victorious. I can smell the battle call in my master's blood. It roils like a dragon readying to burn. We're in for a life-and-death encounter."

"Oh, there'll be an encounter, all right," Peter replied, chuckling in glee at each item the footman passed over. "The kind that will involve less of you and more of me for a change."

"I DON'T LIKE IT, MILORD," Garth muttered, strapping Agamore, encased in its leather sheath, securely across Braden's back. "She's a witch. What if she catches you following her and turns you into a vole? There're hundreds of them creatures in the Cornish moors. How will I know which one is you, so's I can try to change you back?"

"Even if such a thing were possible, and it isn't, Miss Pendraven would not change me into a vole," Braden said with studied patience. He pointed to just one pair of extra breeches for Garth to pack, for he planned to travel light.

Thinking back to the concern the lady had shown him outside the church, he added, "I think we may be mistaken about her. When I look into her eyes, I see a kind soul." Whenever they touched, a deliciously sensual feeling swept over him. The woman had the appearance of an angel but tempted him to act like the very Devil, for he'd wanted to ravish her on those church steps this morning.

"She's a witch!" Garth protested. "Underestimate her and you'll be spendin' the rest of your life in a meadow looking for nuts and carrion to feed on."

"Garth!"

"I'm just sayin', be careful, that's all. If you had any sense, you'd let me come with you."

"You need to stay here and identify the members of the coven. I expect a thorough report when I return. So, no slacking off at the pub to down ale all the while I'm gone."

"As if," Garth muttered, sounding insulted.

Braden wasn't fooled. Garth had a soft spot, and given a chance, the magician would let the whole coven escape to prevent anyone from having to face the wrath of the Church. Whether Braden agreed or not, he'd been ordered to bring down the witches of Callington, and he wasn't about to let Garth's sentimentality interfere with that duty.

"I want you to promise you'll discover which ladies in this town have been led astray in their beliefs."

"O'course, milord." Garth wore a virtuous expression that Braden distrusted. Then the man distracted him by casually shoving five shirts, three more breeches, a score of cravats, several stockings, a nightshirt and a heavy velvet nightgown into the small brown portmanteau. Next, in went two thick volumes on the fae that Braden had purchased near Exeter, and a spare pair of boots.

Garth closed the bag and buckled the three straps without any apparent effort, as if there were no more than three light items packed inside. Braden shuddered at opening that bag without Garth's magical help when the need arose. He hoped no one but him would be standing nearby.

"Is Nadeem ready?" he asked.

"Saddled and stomping to be off," Garth said. "How will you know which direction she travels in without me to guide you?"

"We know she heads north, thanks to your tracking. The rector said the only newcomer at the church during Trystan's disappearance was a Miss Branwyn Morgan, a visitor from Wales. Miss Morgan left Callington shortly after Trystan went missing."

"Ah," Garth said. "You think the boy's been whisked off to Wales."

"Precisely. Miss Pendraven is on her trail. Garth, she may be a witch, but she's not evil. Like you, she has a soft heart for her fellow man. She would have stopped any harm befalling Trystan if she'd been present when the boy was taken. I'm certain of it. I'm convinced she won't harm me."

He'd almost added, *any more than I would her*. He frowned absently at the portmanteau, feeling confused about a lot of things. He shook himself and glanced at Garth to find the little man watching him with a surprised grin.

"What's so amusing?" Braden asked with suspicion.

"Nothing, milord." Garth wiped away his smile. "I was just thinkin' you might have the right of it. Maybe I don't need to worry about you being turned into a vole, after all."

Braden nodded in approval at Garth adopting that sensible outlook. His eyes were drawn to the portmanteau packed with that impossible assortment of items. Would he ever be comfortable around magic? The Church taught that he never should. Yet, since Garth had joined him, Braden feared he'd become more acclimatized to the presence of magic than Garth had been swayed by the Church's teachings.

Swallowing that prickly thought, he said in a brusque voice, "Let's be off."

The little footman, unusually silent and thoughtful, picked up the luggage and followed Braden from the room.

Four hours later, after riding the whole way in pouring rain, Braden, feeling wet and weary, arrived at the Horse and Hound Inn, a half day's travel past Exeter. Nearing twilight, with the possibility of the sun warming the day all but gone, the air grew cold and damp.

He was not prepared to travel another mile without a sound meal in his belly and a good night's rest for both him and his steed. He ensured his tired mount was well cared for before heading out of the stables and into a bustle of people, horses and carriages. Darkness shaded the landscape in grays. The steady rain had stopped but the air was still filled with pinpricks of misty drizzle.

A post boy approached him. "Need 'elp, sir?"

Braden handed over his portmanteau and tossed the boy a coin. "Ask the innkeeper to ready a room for me and reserve a private parlor for my dinner."

The boy doffed his hat and hurried away with the bag as if it weighed nothing at all. That reminded Braden he had left Garth behind in Callington.

He had survived perfectly well in this line of work for a year without the magician's aid. This journey should show if he'd allowed himself to soften to a dangerous degree by relying too much on Garth's extraordinary abilities or if he were still in prime form.

As he headed for the inn, a flash of light behind the stables drew his attention. Curiosity triggered, he changed direction and went toward there instead. The area was bare but for a few trees. The grass-covered ground squished beneath his boots from the recent rain. All looked quiet and still. Had he imagined that spark?

Hhhissssss...

The malevolent sound sent his alarm spiking. He drew his sword and cautiously stepped forward, keeping the stables to his back.

INSIDE THE COMMON ROOM of the Horse and Hound Inn, Merryn set her teacup on the table, hardly noticing the clatter of cup meeting saucer that suggested her fingers shook ever so slightly.

The air about her shuddered, like thunder but without sound. Her skin quivered in recognition. Someone had opened a gate to the underworld - home of the dark fae.

A forbidden place for her kind, for in that realm, Wyhcan magic did not function at all. The moment a witch or warlock was foolish enough to set foot in that dark land, all connection to lines of power were severed, leaving them as vulnerable as a magic-bereft human.

She knew of only one warlock who had the ability to open a gate to the underworld at will – Dewer. His dark-fae mother's blood ran through his veins, giving him special access to both realms. She'd heard rumors his mother planned that one day he would rule her underworld kingdom. If so, Merryn wished he would get on with it and vacate this one.

Quietly, she muttered a spell of illusion over herself. Then, leaving an image of herself sitting at the table, she stood. Heart beating wildly with fear mixed with anticipation, she hurried past the people in the room, unseen. She went outdoors to check on what trouble Dewer had drawn into her world this time.

SWORD HELD AT THE READY, Braden searched the darkness behind the extensive stables. Moonlight was dimmed by feathery clouds, disguising any creatures loitering in the bushes. He listened for the hissing.

Horses neighed, men chattered and muted laughter filtered out of open doorways. Then the hiss came again, from directly overhead.

Braden sprang away from the building.

Slithering bodies wriggled down the stable's back wall. Scores of them. Snakes, but topped with hideous, distorted, human heads.

Braden slashed at the first demon that reached his feet. He scrambled away from sharp-toothed jaws that gaped open to bite. His back touched a tree trunk and something clamped onto his right shoulder, its jaws sinking through his heavy greatcoat, coat, vest and shirt as if tearing through no more than thin muslin.

Cringing in pain, he grabbed the vile thing and flung it away. He realized his mistake in backing toward the woods. Here, the creatures could reach him from above, too. Hissing surrounded him.

He twirled Agamore in a fury of slashes, trying to make a path for himself away from the cover of branches. Blood spurted. Severed heads flew.

"Now would be a good time to flare," he told his sword.

Agamore vibrated in his grip, seemed to grow lighter, but then did nothing more.

Braden swore as another creature bit through his boots. He kicked at the assailant and cut it in half. Despite having its hind end severed, the snake remained clamped onto his left shin, flapping, refusing to release its grip.

Suddenly, the horrors paused, as if something other than eating him had caught their attention. They stood in place and swayed, as if to music.

MERRYN ALMOST TURNED tail and ran. They hadn't seen her yet. The slithering, sinuous, twirling things with their infernal hissing.

Her toes scrunched inside her shoes, her body leaned away and her head refused to turn back to that horrible sight. Her skin quivered and swore to disown her if she remained hovering within reach of this constantly moving horde.

She could pretend she'd never come to investigate this disturbance. Let Braden face these monsters on his own. He was a church guard. This was his job. What he was trained to do. He could handle this task.

She couldn't leave.

By the Maker – I hate snakes!

What to do? On the far side of Braden, a darkness pulsed, the opening to the netherworld. Standing in front of that unholy opening was the silhouette of a man. Dewer? He'd seen her, for the rogue dipped his head, reminiscent of the way he'd greeted her the first time she met him at the ball in London. "Good evening, Miss Pendraven," he'd said then. "May I have this dance?"

"No, you may not!" Merryn muttered now, words she wished she'd said then, but hadn't. Remembering her outrage at his audacity at approaching her then, and her simpering self for being flattered by his intriguing attention, spurred her anger now.

She turned her burning hatred of Dewer onto the snakes assaulting Braden. She wanted to turn the lot of them into something else, but that would not get rid of them. The gate was still open behind Dewer, throbbing like a toothache. With each second that she stood indecisive, more snakes slithered through.

She needed to turn this attack into a failure for Dewer, as he'd made that ball a failure for her. One that would make him want to send his minions back where they came from and shut that infernal gate before worse terrors made their way out.

Then she knew how. A terrible spell, one that stank of warlock mind magic, but not on a human. Witch law forbade using that kind of mind magic.

Instead, she forced herself to open wide her squinting eyes, extend clenched fingers and point at those fallen under Braden's sword – the bloody dismembered cords that still writhed, refusing to die.

In the midst of her revulsion, she imagined the tastiest of meals, something deliciously aromatic and savory. Opening her clenched jaws, she quietly spoke her spell.

Sweet herbs and pungent spices scented the warm air. Basil, sage, mint. All melting in butter over freshly cooked flesh, hot and succulent on the tongue.

BRADEN WATCHED ASTONISHED as the demon snakes slowly moved away from him. Then they spun and lunged at their decapitated brethren. In an unholy rush, they fought each other to get at those who had fallen victim to his sword or appeared weaker for having been nicked.

Even the stubborn beast that had clamped onto his boot let go, dragging its bloody stump of a back end as it slithered toward the suddenly delicious dead.

Braden backed away from the ensuing frenzy. A few noticed his movement and came at him but he dispatched them with a few quick flicks of Agamore.

Standing with his back to the stables, he watched as the beasts feasted on each other. A few gave him backward glares, as if warning him away from their food, before turning back to their meal.

Watching them in horror, Braden could think of only one thing to do. He prayed. "For tho I walk amidst the shades of death: I fear no ills," Braden recited, his voice shaky. What an abomination these creatures were. His prayer, however, appeared to trigger Agamore. Light flared from the sword.

Encouraged, he continued with a grin, his voice growing stronger and more confident. "For thou art with me, lord; Thy rod and Thy staff are my comfort."

He lunged forward. The creatures wriggled away from Agamore's bright, burning light, hissing as if in protest at having to leave behind the fresh kill scattered around Braden. Some tried to drag away what they could.

With renewed vigor, Braden attacked, his sword's touch turning any within his reach to ash. The fight to vanquish evil now brought a sense of enjoyment. This was why he was a church guard. Swifter than he could mark their passage, those that could still move, disappeared from sight, leaving behind only the fallen.

"Good riddance," he called after them, raising his sword, wishing he'd had a chance to slay more.

A strange hum sounded. Braden stepped toward it, to the left, when a force flung him backwards, slamming him against the stable wall. Heat erupted all around him, and Agamore flared even brighter.

He tried to move but something held him in place, like a giant hand pressing on his chest. The humming died, as if a door had slammed shut on a noisy room. Braden was released and he stumbled before regaining balance. Agamore's light died, the steel cooled and quieted, as if it, too, realized its work was done.

He stepped forward cautiously, sword still held at the ready and caught sight of movement. He sprang at the spot. There was nothing.

He checked to see if anything hid to the side of the building. No. His pulse slowed and he breathed, allowing his tension to settle. Sweat dotted his forehead in the cool moist night air and his wet clothes were heavy on his weary frame. He was alone. Whatever had brought those unholy creatures here had left with those that remained intact.

At his feet, the carnage left behind required clean up. Reaching for a cloth, Braden began his ritual. He wiped Agamore and threw the soiled rag over the corpses. Sword returned to its sheath, he pulled out his red velvet bag and spread its contents on the soiled ground. The bodies smoked, bubbled and turned to ash.

Kneeling, he hesitated. After that fight, this ground felt vile, denigrated, damaged in a profound way. He wanted his words, his prayers to reach deep into the earth, symbolically as well as literally. He drew Agamore and with hands gripped around the hilt, he thrust the sword downward until it was half buried in the wet ground. He closed his eyes and muttered his prayers, consecrating this defiled ground and returning it to God's care.

Finished with his work, Braden sheathed Agamore and went back to the inn. A troubling question niggled at him. What had triggered these demons to come here, behind this inn, at this moment? Had Garth painted a sign on his back as a jest for leaving him behind? He stifled the urge to check.

The snakes' sudden appearance seemed as inexplicable as the hounds that attacked him in London.

He flexed his shoulder where he'd been bitten, but the pain had dulled. He stopped near a lantern at the front of the inn and checked his left Hessian. Fang holes were present but, like his right shoulder, his calf did not hurt. Still, as hungry as he was, he would need to see to his wounds before setting to his meal, to ensure no infection took root.

Inside the inn, the innkeeper greeted Braden with enthusiasm. However, the man seemed unnerved by his inquiry about Miss Pendraven. The innkeeper quickly got himself together and advised the lady had indeed arrived not an hour ago. "Having changed and refreshed herself, she is even now in the common room having her meal, milord."

That set him back. "Common room? Why not a private parlor?"

"The inn is busy tonight, milord. I've ordered our best room emptied for your use, of course, but she did not insist on this courtesy. Rest assured, the lady has visited with us once before and dined so and no one disturbed her." The innkeeper leaned conspiratorially closer. "No one would dare, milord."

Deeply troubled, Braden left the man and went upstairs. All that conversation did was confirm his worst suspicions. Merryn Pendraven was a witch and the people here knew it.

MERRYN STOOD BEHIND the inn, swathed by shadow and puzzlement as Braden headed inside. Any normal man should have succumbed long before she came to his rescue, especially since she'd dithered long enough about deciding to help him.

Instead, Braden had skewered a dozen or more by the time Merryn cast her savory spell on the fallen fae snakes. Then his sword flared, like a lightning rod. It had burned those creatures with a touch, sending ash swirling through the air like snowflakes on a blustery winter night.

The repulsive fae snakes who were still alive had fled in terror. She'd routed them straight back toward Dewer, where they swarmed him in their rush to reach safety.

She chuckled at the memory.

As if that were not amazing enough, after Dewer shut and bolted the gate to the underworld, Braden had spread a strange powder over the corpses that incinerated the remains. High magic indeed. From a *church guard*. Then he'd plunged his amazing sword into the ground where it flared brightest yet.

Dewer's opening of the underworld gate had seemed like a disturbance in the air. This new conjuring by Braden had touched everything – the ground, the buildings, *her*. She held out a hand, which still quivered and shook.

Her aunt said church guards did not work magic. It was against their laws. Braden's work certainly hadn't had the scent of magic. Rather, it reeked of something more elemental. As if, through him, and his amazing sword, the Maker reached down to destroy the evil that soiled his domain.

She shivered at the thought. With trepidation, she tiptoed toward the area where Braden had plunged his sword. Kneeling, she touched the soil with her gloved hand. The ground still vibrated, as if great power had been channeled into the land here.

She pulled off the top portion of her right glove and examined her tingling fingertips. Under the moonlight, there was an odd glow on her skin. She flexed her elbow – her arm felt healthy and strong. As if in coming in contact with this blessed soil, she, too, had been blessed in some way.

The power of that sword left her in abject awe. Then her pulse shot up, and she sprang to her feet, swinging about to glare at where Braden had disappeared into the inn.

Was this how he intended to destroy her coven? Had the Church discovered a new weapon to use against Wyhcans? Was that why they again dared raise the ghost of their old witch-hunts? What chance would witches have to survive against the power of such a sword?

Merryn's fists clenched. She needed time to think, to plan, to come up with a defense against Braden and his blasted sword. Instead of returning to the inn, she circled its perimeter on the pretext of searching for Dewer. She didn't really expect to find the fae-warlock, for the cowardly villain had been on the other side of the gate when it finally shut.

On her quiet, lonely patrol, a disquieting doubt trailed her worried steps. If the *Maker* were on Braden's side, could, nay, *should* witches oppose him?

Her sentry duty finished, Merryn slid unnoticed between those who rushed about within the inn's entryway and took the place of the image of herself she'd left behind. Braden was not in sight. No doubt he was sequestered in a private parlor.

Once seated, she waved at a waiter to refresh her now ice-cold meal. All that pacing outside had helped her come to one conclusion. While Braden could be inordinately dangerous to her coven, if swayed from killing them, he might prove to be equally helpful.

While waiting for her new meal to arrive, she seriously considered Braden's earlier offer of help. He'd insisted on following her anyway, so why not put him and his extraordinary sword to her use?

BRADEN HURRIED UPSTAIRS to see to his wounds, clean himself and change into some dry clothes. He wanted to get back downstairs before Miss Pendraven retired for the night. He had a few choice words to share with the young woman.

What was she thinking eating alone in a public parlor? Witch or not, such behavior was unseemly and downright dangerous. Society imposed rules of proper conduct for young women of good standing to protect their safety and chastity.

Braden entered his room and the brunt of his anger switched to Garth for over-packing his portmanteau. Why was it that no one ever listened to him? He'd said he would be on his own and only needed a few items. What if the thing exploded when he unbuckled it? How was he to get everything back into that little case without Garth's help?

He stared at the case without touching it and then shook his head. He had just fought off a deadly horde of demonic snakes but was fearful of opening his own baggage? How absurd.

He laid Agamore on a chair by the bed and cautiously loosened the buckles of the portmanteau. He flipped open the case and jumped back expecting all those tightly packed articles to come flying out.

When all remained still, he looked inside and found a clean shirt, breeches, waistcoat, and cravat along with some smalls right at the top, ready for his use. He'd watched Garth pack that case willy-nilly. So how could only the items he needed show up at the top?

He took out the clothing and laid it on the bed. A series of servants came in then, carrying buckets of hot water and towels for his bath.

He nonchalantly watched a servant take up the portmanteau to unpack items and place them in the wardrobe. Only four things were pulled out and then the man stuck his hand in and thumped around as if searching for more before coming up empty-handed. He shut the case and put the baggage away and Braden released the breath he'd unconsciously been holding.

He dismissed the servants and undressed himself, for he didn't want the inconvenience of having to explain all the bite marks. Standing in front of a tall looking glass, he pulled off his great coat and cravat. Off came the waistcoat and then gingerly, he pulled his shirttails out of his breeches and the entire shirt over his head. He expected the linen to cling to his bloody wound. It didn't.

For a long moment, he stared at the wound caked in blood. He flexed his muscles around it, puzzled, for he felt no pain. He took a washcloth, wet it and wiped away the blood. Beneath the mess, his flesh was unharmed. The right shoulder matched the left. No gaping holes where fangs had pierced, no torn muscles, no marks at all.

Stunned, he sat on the edge of the bed and pulled off his damaged Hessians. He undid his breeches. Threw away the sopping stockings. He cleaned the washcloth in a basin and wiped his shin. His leg was as unmarked and unharmed as his shoulder. Slowly, he turned his stunned gaze to his sword resting innocently on the chair.

Braden soaked in the warm water in a thoughtful, elated mood. His sword could not only kill but also *heal*. He didn't quite understand how it worked, but felt certain magic played no part in the process. In replaying the two occurrences when the sword had flared, Braden noticed one coincidence. Just before each event, he'd been holding Agamore in his hands and praying to God for assistance.

Relaxing in the water, he reminisced about when, as a boy of nine, he'd run rampant through an old church in search of mischief. Instead, he'd tripped over a crumbled altar, fallen and struck his head. A vision had assailed him that day, urging him to follow the way of God. It showed him a special weapon that would help him conquer dark creatures that endangered mankind.

A thrilling life for an adventurous boy to dream of, a worthwhile goal for a restless adult to claim. The day Braden found Agamore, he had been sixteen years old. It had been winter. He'd been exploring a mausoleum on his land and spotted the rusted sword lying discarded, and half buried in the snowy ground. He pulled it free, wondering, could this be the weapon his vision promised so long ago?

He'd joined the church guards soon after, seeing it as a sign that it was time to commit to a new way of life. He swore his allegiance to protect all God's creatures. His newly polished sword had proven to be a worthy tool in that endeavor. It was swifter than a bludgeon, stronger than a saber, and deadlier than a one-shot pistol. Yet, it was only since the fight in the London alleyway with those hellhounds, that the sword's incredible power manifested. It was also the first time he'd prayed while holding the sword.

Now he knew its true value, he didn't want to leave Agamore out in the open, unguarded. Carrying it to dinner would raise eyebrows, but where to hide it? His gaze was inevitably drawn to the portmanteau. He got out of the tub and quickly dried himself. Once suitably dressed, he brought the portmanteau to the bed and picked up Agamore.

He opened the case and extended the sword into it, hilt down. The luggage practically took the sheathed sword from his grip. In moments, the sword had vanished from sight.

Swallowing a nervous laugh, he held out his hand over the opening. "Agamore."

The weapon jutted back out, hilt first.

Satisfied he could retrieve the sword when needed, he put Agamore back in and replaced the portmanteau in the wardrobe.

Feeling chipper, Braden strode downstairs. He couldn't stop grinning. Before long, he was racing down the steps as if he were nine years old again.

Braden arrived at the doorway to the public room, mind in a whirl, not really seeing the crowd. The place seemed in bedlam, with voices calling for waiters, doors opening and closing everywhere, bells ringing. The hall was full of porters bringing in luggage.

The innkeeper rushed over. "Milord, your private parlor is this way."

"Has Miss Pendraven retired for the evening?"

The innkeeper looked back into the public room and pointed. "She's still there, milord."

The young lady sat by a table placed beside a large hearth, finishing the dregs of her meal. She sat in a circle of quiet amidst the mayhem of the parlor. Everyone seemed to take care to avoid her, walking a good two feet around her table and chair.

"I shall dine with the lady," Braden told the innkeeper.

The man gave him a startled look, and seemed about to protest. Braden raised his eyebrow in challenge, and the man re-thought his words and hurried away to arrange for his meal, muttering something about the "strange takes of the nobility."

The crowd of travelers, hurrying waiters, and the heat generated by three hearth fires imbued the large parlor with a sense of life and bustle. The moment he approached Miss Pendraven, an ominous silence descended on the room.

"Good evening, Miss Pendraven." Braden bowed. "We meet again. May I join you?"

She looked up, her aqua eyes not at all startled to see him. Could she have known he intended to follow her?

"My lord," she said in her quiet cultured voice. She indicated an empty chair at her table.

He stepped forward and a cold frisson of energy shivered through his body. He winced and a collective gasp rose from the watching crowd.

He looked around but found nothing that could have caused that shock – no rug or cashmere shawl he might have accidentally brushed by. A look at his audience, and everyone quickly turned back to their own business.

He combed down his hair that suddenly felt dry and flyaway instead of still damp from his bath. If he didn't know better, he'd have thought he passed through one of Garth's invisible barriers. Did witches use such barriers? They must.

Braden took his seat.

"The air in here is rather hot, is it not, my lord?" Miss Pendraven said with a bland expression. "I received a shock myself when the maid handed me my glass of wine."

So, they were to lie to each other, were they? He wasn't happy with that strategy. He liked it when she spoke directly, as she had during their impromptu theological discussion in the coach ride to Callington. That was the Merryn Pendraven he wanted to dine with.

"The young ladies in Callington will be frustrated you've left town, my lord. I'm sure word had spread that you intended to stay for a few weeks. Did you not say something about looking forward to attending dances?"

"As had you, and yet, here you are. Might I be so bold as to add, once again, sans chaperone?"

Her lips twitched. That slight movement mesmerized him. If not for the table separating them, he might have been tempted to lean over to kiss the telltale curl of her lips. To perdition with their audience!

The urge shocked him. Could Garth be right? Had Miss Pendraven bewitched him? Or did she have this sensual effect on all men?

He looked around the room. If her appeal was universal, why had none of the local lads crowding this parlor accosted her yet? Then he remembered her shield. Something more powerful than a chaperone protected this lady's virtue.

Even alone, she was safe. Then another question arose. If those here suspected a witch was among them, why did no one raise a hue and cry?

The innkeeper, with a heavily laden tray, stood respectfully back. Miss Pendraven gave permission to approach. The innkeeper, too, jumped, rattling dishes as he crossed that invisible barrier. The man laid his burden on the table and retreated, bowing profusely.

If there was to be truth spoken tonight, Braden decided he might as well begin. "Why do these people not denounce you as a witch?"

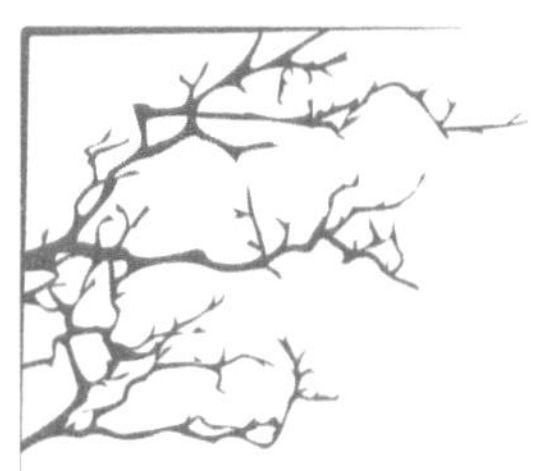

Chapter 6

"*There's a messenger coming,*" *Nuriel said, and inside the hearth his flames quivered with excitement.*

Spark, his curiosity lit, stretched his tiny candle flame as far up as he could to look over the top of the teapot and into the hearth. "Tst...tst...trouble?" He sputtered more than normal. It had been a tension-filled night.

"Very likely. Mind you, that's everywhere tonight. Never thought I'd see the day a church guard and a witch sat down for dinner together. What do they talk about?"

"This and that. Lots of under-talk, I'm not sure I'm catching everything. Who's the messenger here for?"

"The witch," Nuriel said. "Sent by her aunt. Are these two forming an alliance?"

"They seem friendly."

"How extraordinary. It's a fire sprite, by the by, the messenger that's coming."

"Ooh, tst...tst...t's serious then. Should we warn...?"

"No, best not disturb her ladyship until we know more. Appears as if this is strictly witch-guard business. I hear from the roof that the fight outside earlier was a little troublesome. Those fae snakes were swarming over the inn's rooftop, so I built up my fire in case any tried to enter by the chimney. The guard and the witch fixed that troublesome situation."

"Indeed?" Spark said.

"Yes. Can you not feel the land's response? It's fairly vibrating with strength beneath us."

"I sensed a change, but wasn't...tst...tst certain where it originated."

"It was a blessing, Spark. Haven't experienced one of those in a long while. Too long. Will be good for her."

"Think she noticed...tst...tst?"

"I had not thought of that," Nuriel said, excitement rising. "Keep your attention on the diners, Spark, in case they say anything of importance. For if this blessing awakens the lady of the inn, you can be certain we will be asked to report on it."

THERE, HE'D CALLED her a witch to her face. Braden's chest tightened as he held his breath, waiting for her response.

She looked startled but not offended. Then she nodded, as if accepting his lead toward frank conversation. "This is Cornwall, my lord. A land of magic and wonder. While Londoners remain closed to the possibility of enchanted matters, Cornishmen know how to show proper respect to this aspect of life. Little people and even practitioners of the craft receive the regard their status warrants."

By practitioners of the craft, he assumed she meant herself and people like Garth. "Who are these 'little people'? Lady Hancock mentioned 'the Gentry.' Are they the same?"

"Yes. It's said they come from the lands of faerie that intersect ours along ley lines."

About to spear a piece of meat, he snapped his head up. Garth often spoke of ley lines. Could such things truly exist?

Perhaps encouraged by his raised eyebrow, she elucidated. "Brownies, pixies, nymphs, dyads, sidhe, dwarfs. Shall I go on?"

"You believe in fairy tales, Miss Pendraven." He spoke cautiously, for he recalled the barguest he'd fought in the alleyway in London. He'd first read of such a creature in a children's folk tale. "Do you perhaps speak of hellhounds and snake demons and such? I do accept they are real."

She gave him a long silent look, as if considering her response. "My lord, there are two types of fae, those that dwell in dark places and those that reside within realms of light. Be careful you do not mistake one for the other."

An intriguing concept. In Church doctrine, there was man, made in the image of God, and there were those things spawned by the Devil that sought to corrupt man from the light of Truth. "You think there are shades within darkness?"

"There is light and dark and many shades between."

He shifted, trying to fit her answer into his worldview, and found himself cramming a square peg into a round hole. It was the same dilemma he faced every time he tried to resolve the goodness he saw in Garth with his manservant's practice of dark arts. Like that problem, he decided to shelve this one and switched to a subject he had a better hold on.

"You also mentioned practitioners of the craft. Are you admitting you are such a one?

"Will you admit you're a Guard of the Green Cross?" Merryn countered.

Before he could respond, she raised her hand.

"No," she said, "that cannot be true. Your servant is a magician. If you were truly a church guard, devoted to purging the world of those who deal with magic, why have you not condemned him to death?"

Braden's eyes narrowed with disquiet. How did she know about Garth? Would her coven attempt to harm him if his servant probed too deep into their affairs? "To my knowledge, you've never been introduced to Garth."

"Is that his name?" She wore her mysterious smile like a lady dons a fine hat.

"Garth is harmless. Hardly worthy of your notice."

"You're protective of him." She sounded pleased by that discovery. Her shoulders dropped for the first time since he sat. "My aunt told me your manservant is a magician. In her assessment, he is clever and surprisingly talented and so, possibly dangerous. Yet, despite that, rather appealing."

Her aunt had captured the very reasons why his annoying footman was fast growing into someone Braden considered more than a servant, and in fact, approaching nearer a friend. At her relative's accurate assessment of Garth, quite absurdly considering the circumstances, he felt as if he'd left Garth among trusted friends. His tension unwound.

At the drop of his guard, hunger pangs prodded his empty stomach. He returned his attention to his meal while continuing the conversation. "Your aunt is Mrs. Morwena Dunstan?"

"The very same, my lord. She says your Garth seems quite courteous to witches despite keeping company with you."

Braden looked up at that slight, but then shrugged it off as justified. In keeping with his intent to speak frankly with this captivating lady, he added, "Your aunt is the one you met by the wishing well?"

"Yes," Miss Pendraven admitted with a look that dared him to even try to harm her relative.

He took a bite of roasted goose with gravy and applesauce to gain time to consider his next words. Slowly, he savored the rich taste. Even the potatoes and peas were mouthwateringly good. The mushrooms! These Cornishmen knew how to cook well.

A glance up showed her studying him with an indulgent look, as if she enjoyed watching him take pleasure in his meal. The look stirred a deeper yearning. "You're not frightened of me, Miss Pendraven," he said, finally. "Why not? You should be."

She gave a start and then nodded. "Yes, I should be, but I find I'm not because I've come to a decision. You asked me in Callington if I would join you in finding young Trystan. I refused then but have since reconsidered. I *will* work with you on this matter, my lord."

Braden choked on the delicious goose. It took him a moment to recover and order his clamoring thoughts. He took a sip of his drink and then asked, "Why the sudden change?"

"I cannot stop you following me. We are heading in the same direction, on the same purpose."

His doubts quieted to a faint murmur. He nodded acceptance, trying to appear composed while squelching the happiness that rose at her acquiescence. He wanted to grin like a boy just given a dear present.

He hoped chewing the excellent food would keep his lips from betraying what a fool he seemed to have become since meeting this extraordinary witch.

He couldn't identify why he felt so happy. Normally, he preferred to work alone, except for Garth. He rarely joined other church guards on their missions, preferring to be the one in control. Or as his father once complained, he didn't play well with others.

Yet her assistance could potentially open whole new doors. Like Garth, she could see and do things to help ensure his mission's success faster than if he worked alone – the original reason he'd asked for her help.

Still, none of that logic explained the swell of happiness that fought to burst out. He wanted to jump up, shake his arms in the air and roar in joy. However, he refused to allow any of that irrationality to show on the surface.

Considering his strong reaction to her news, doubt crept in. Were his emotions real or, as Garth had warned, had a bewitchment been placed on him? The thought acted like a damp cloth thrown over a raging cook fire – producing a lot of confusing smoke without smothering all the flames.

"If we are to work together," he said in a grave voice that effectively hid his inner turmoil, "then I will begin by confessing that, Garth notwithstanding, I am a church guard. My primary purpose on this journey is to find the missing boy and take him to Snowdon."

"So, my aunt was correct. The Church has made a covenant with warlocks."

Made uncomfortable by her direct, accusatory glare, and his smarting conscience, Braden looked toward the flames leaping inside the hearth. "I merely carry out my orders."

"Very well," she said, though her tone cooled by several degrees. "We understand each other, and where this journey is likely to lead us to in the end."

Alas, she had heard of his second order as well. Deep sadness sank into his midriff, transforming the remnants of his scrumptious meal into desert sand. "It would seem so, Miss Pendraven."

She stared at him and he back at her. For a fleeting moment, despite their problems, he felt as if in that look, their worlds collided. Like two stars that exploded in heaven and then dropped back to earth, embers dissipating in the night air.

What could have been, would never be. Profound grief swept over him for the loss of those two stars.

"Since you have confided in me, my lord," she murmured into the silence, "I shall return the favor. My role among my people is that of Protectress of all covens in the isles of Britain."

The idea intrigued, sounding much like his calling. "Are you one of many who play this role? As we church guards protect the interests of the Church of England?"

"Only one in every generation is chosen and chooses to hold that position."

"A wide field to cover alone." He had to ask the next question, his life might one day depend on the answer. He hoped the question would not offend. She seemed too young to be given such a significant position. "Do your talents warrant the weighty responsibility, Miss Pendraven?"

She shrugged, then leaned forward to pour herself some tea. "My aunt has thus far refused to allow me to test the limits of my abilities. Still, I have dealt with warlocks, dark fae, and even a demon or two in my training. Now I can add a church guard to that list. I am sworn to protect with my life all who are under my care."

He couldn't help but be impressed, and then a little worried. "To the death?"

"To the death, my lord."

"Then Garth will indeed be let down in his wish by the well," Braden murmured, more to himself than her.

"He may at that," she answered, surprising him.

"You knew we were there?"

She shook her head, giving a self-deprecating smile. "I only guessed after our conversation inside Saint Agatha's church. I told my aunt. She found out about his concerns because he spoke them aloud."

Braden wondered how her aunt could have known what was spoken between him and Garth if they had not been nearby. Then decided, like many of Garth's magical tricks, this, too, he didn't want to delve into.

"How did you manage to follow me to Laneast?" she asked.

"Garth. He's an excellent tracker."

"I'm surprised you weren't bored, my lord. Why keep up the chase? I wasn't doing anything of interest."

He frowned at her. "You were a young lady out alone, in the dark, in the woods. What type of gentleman would leave you there unprotected?"

She blinked as if the answer surprised her.

Good! Time she took proper measure of his character. He wasn't all church guard out to destroy her world. Though why her high regard mattered, he didn't examine too closely.

"Does your Church support your connection with a magician?"

He hesitated and then shrugged, deciding truthfulness could win the night after all. He'd won her agreement to help him. "It's an experiment of sorts. The archbishop is a progressive churchman who is open to new methods of converting disbelievers toward Christian principles."

"That's assuming what Garth practices are the dark arts."

"What else could magic be?"

The lady shook her head, smiling with indulgence. "I think the whys and wherefores of magic, my lord, can wait another day. Let's instead discuss what we must face on the morrow. I am heading for…"

"Fishguard," he finished, delighted at surprising her. "Your aunt's houseguest, Miss Branwyn Morgan, was at the church when Trystan was taken. She left town the day he went missing. Another witch?"

The question remained suspended.

MERRYN TOOK A SIP OF her tea to gain time to think of a response and then cringed at the cold liquid in her teacup. She did not want to invite a servant into this intimate sphere surrounding her and Braden to refresh her pot. Gently, she slipped her hands around her cup and hoped Braden didn't notice the steam suddenly rising up.

He did. His gaze rested on her cup, roamed over to his cup, and then swung back to hers.

Hiding her smile, she returned her cup to the table. Though he apparently knew much about her, if they were to join forces, she should share some knowledge. That might also take his mind off the self-heating tea.

"When the incident with young Trystan occurred, I had been called away to Fishguard," Merryn said. "Under false pretenses, I now believe. In fact, I was attacked on the way home by a warlock's familiar, which delayed my return by several days."

Braden sat forward and took her hand. The touch sent melting warmth rolling over her like a waterfall.

His thumb gently rubbed her knuckles, sending energy shooting up her arm. "Were you hurt?"

Other than her aunt, no one had ever shown her such concern. Reluctantly, she withdrew her hand before she was tempted to return the caress. "Merely inconvenienced. The distraction required me to walk farther than I had planned and then to settle for that coach ride from Exeter."

His face relaxed and he sat back. "Then I cannot be completely unhappy, for it gave us a chance to become acquainted. But I'm confused, Miss Pendraven. I thought witches and warlocks did not consort. Yet, the Welsh witch and this warlock, who obviously set his familiar on you, sound as if they were colluding on this enterprise."

"Yes, it is unusual for a warlock and witch to work together these days," Merryn mused.

"These days?" Braden sounded intrigued. "Was there a time when witches and warlocks did not war?"

Discussing the Wyhcan lore with a human was forbidden, so Merryn prevaricated. "Witch-warlock unions are rare and thankfully so."

His hooded look and long silence said, *I understand there will continue to be secrets between us.* He gave a firm nod as if agreeing to the rules being set down. Still, his next query swam uncomfortably close to the first. "Is a warlock very different from a witch?"

Merryn settled on generalities for her answer. "Warlocks are strange and contrary. It is in their nature to make use of others, even their own children. I've never understood such unnatural ambition, to always want to be in control of everyone and everything."

"Most men lean in that direction," Braden said with a little smile.

"Do you?"

"I like control of my life. Of my destiny." He shrugged. "As such, I feel it is only fair to allow others the same liberty."

"Unless their will conflicts with the Church's teaching."

"Unless they endanger the safety of those the Church is sworn to guard."

Merryn narrowed her gaze. *Did he speak the truth?* No witch ever meant the Church harm, either to those it governed or any other innocent. His definition could allow leeway for witches to survive this upcoming conflict.

Her excitement built at the possibility. *Can I trust you, my lord?*

"What I find confounding is why Trystan's parents do not work together to find their son," Braden continued, breaking eye contact to spear a piece of apple. "If the parents are a witch and warlock, are they not more powerful together than apart? Or is there a core conflict between them that I'm unaware of?"

How to answer that? Perhaps the best response was to begin with what they both knew. "Their conflict was around the ceremony being conducted that day at the church. The boy was being baptized because his mother believed it would give Trystan the ultimate protection of the Maker."

"Yes, through forgiveness of original sin."

Merryn took a deep breath for courage and plunged past the boundaries her coven set for confiding in humans. If Braden were to be of any help, he needed to know the crux of the problem regarding Trystan. "For the offspring of a witch or a warlock, baptisms have an added benefit."

He stopped eating and stared at her. "Is it to do with the water?"

She gave a twisted smile. "It's not what you think. Water, even blessed, will not melt a witch."

"That's good to hear, for sanitary reasons." A matching smile played along his full lips.

She looked away and spoke the truth. "A baptism can impede the placing of mind magic spells on children."

"On all children?"

"All Wyhcan children."

"Wyhcan?" he said. "What is that?"

"You are an Englishman. Witches and warlocks are Wyhcans."

"So, baptisms are a protection against your powers?"

"Against mind spells, yes," Merryn corrected. "It is the reason why warlocks oppose their children receiving baptisms."

"But not witches?" He leaned forward, eyes intent. "Explain."

"Warlocks use mind-magic spells. You would call them bewitchments."

Braden's eyes widened. "That is what Church history claims happened in Bedfordshire!" Then his thoughtful gaze narrowed. "Witches cannot bewitch the same way?"

"After Bedfordshire, the High Sage of Britain forbade witches under her jurisdiction to ever use mind magic on humans."

"At what consequence?"

"Expulsion from the coven. The outcome for a witch is equal to excommunication for a Christian. As well, a permanent binding is placed on the witch preventing her from using magic again."

"Forever?"

"Until she proves herself trustworthy to the high sage. The leader of Wyhcans in Britain."

He looked stunned, and then so relieved that Merryn wondered what he was thinking.

"Getting back to baptisms, my lord, history has shown that if a warlock boy or witch girl is baptized, mind magic spells cannot penetrate that holy defense until they mature. Usually not until well after they turn fourteen or fifteen and are capable of defending themselves."

Merryn glanced at her hands. She'd clutched her fingers as thoughts of her brother intruded. She forcefully released that tensed hold and her fingers came apart trembling.

The rattling of dishes drew their attention. The innkeeper had arrived with two waiters who carried custard, ratafia cakes and a bottle of wine and clean glasses.

Receiving permission, they laid their burden on the table, cleared away the used dishes and left in record time.

Braden filled the glasses with wine and handed Merryn hers. "Sounds as if the argument between the parents was about the baptism ceremony. That makes it more likely the father is responsible for Trystan's disappearance. Yet, if so, why did he involve the Church in locating his boy? Unless the person he sent to retrieve his son did not deliver the goods. The witch from Fishguard?"

"I intend to ask her that." Merryn picked up her glass of wine and noted how the hearth's flames were perfectly steady. She checked the fire directly.

"Give your curtsies and make your goodbyes."

A fire sprite summons. From her aunt?

Merryn hoped it wasn't more bad news. She turned back to Braden, saddened at having to end their conversation. She was astounded to discover that, on reflection, tonight felt like the most enjoyable evening of her life. "It's been a long day, my lord. I hope you will forgive me if I bid you good night?"

"Will you permit me to ride with you in the carriage on the morrow? It would allow us the opportunity to discuss this problem in depth."

Though the idea delighted her, he must realize what a compromising situation that would place her in. So why make the request? Especially after posturing about her traveling without a chaperone? Then she recalled his earlier question about whether she was capable of upholding the title of Coven Protectress. Did he seek to test her talent, or her character?

A part of her was tempted to discover how she would measure up. "I shall sleep on the matter, my lord," she said, capitulating instead to caution.

She stood.

He rose. "In either case, Miss Pendraven, I would like us to depart early. If you're agreeable, we'll leave at seven in the morning."

His tone suggested the time was non-negotiable. Merryn nodded, and pulled her gloves back over her hands. She was unlikely to get a good sleep this night anyway, so why not get up early? She had wards to strengthen, protection spells to prepare, and a casting to lay that would show her the safest route to take to Fishguard.

She absently released the spell that had kept people at bay around the table. "Good night, Lord Braden." She curtsied.

He kissed her hand, lips lingering on the back of her glove.

BRADEN WATCHED HER leave – her long blond braid swinging in line with the sway of her hips. He was dearly glad to have heard that witches were forbidden to practice mind bewitchments, for that meant his feelings for this extraordinary Coven Protectress were genuine. He had taken great pleasure in her company and conversation tonight, more than with any other woman. Ever.

In fact, he had discovered more about witches and warlocks on this night than he had in all his years of Church study. Suppressing his regret at the end this intriguing interlude, he went in search of the innkeeper. He had plans to make for the morrow.

Braden had barely stepped out of the public room when the man in question rushed forward with a missive. "My lord, a message has arrived for you."

Braden took the note. He recognized the cross on the seal and the drawing of a dove beside it.

In his room, he lit a candle from the hearth and sat on the bed. He slit open the note from the Archbishop of Canterbury and read the latest news. With each dreaded word, his heart hammered with mounting worry and Garth's favorite phrase echoed in his head. *Knew no good would come from that accursed place.*

MERRYN NEEDED A CLEAR space to work in her room. She pushed the large armchair toward the wall and then moved a table aside. Tall, unlit candles arranged in a wide circle on the floorboards soon set the stage. She moved into the center and with a snap of her fingers lit each candle ablaze.

The fire sprite watched her silently from inside the hearth fire. The only sign of movement was the licks of flames that shot from the tips of its ears now and then.

"Did my aunt say what the problem was?" she asked.

"Matters be worsening, you'd best be hastening."

With a nod, she sat on the floor and sent out her call.

No response.

The little sprite watched her with the same stillness it had shown since she entered the room.

"It would help if you could give me some indication of what's upset my aunt."

"Not my place to judge, nor my role to trudge," came the fire sprite's implacable answer.

"Something's upset her enough to send you here. Should I return to Callington?"

"Called to order, it's unwise to saunter."

"Right."

The candles suddenly flickered, and Merryn breathed a sigh of relief.

"Blessed be, Aunt Morwena."

Her aunt's form appeared before her, also seated cross-legged. The high sage bowed. "Blessed be, Merryn Pendraven."

Quickly, they finished the customary ritual of exchanging gifts upon meeting.

"You have news?" Merryn said.

"The church guards are on the move from London."

"To Callington?"

"That is uncertain, but where else, considering Lord Braden's charge is to destroy us? I believe these guards were sent to support him. With warlocks possibly influencing them, anything could happen. Though they cannot truly harm us, there are many innocents here who may perish in the battle. I've put out a call for all nearby witches to gather here to protect our friends and loved ones in Callington. There will *not* be another Bedfordshire incident. Not in my lifetime. You, too, must return, Merryn. As quickly as you can. This crisis takes precedence over finding young Trystan."

"Of course," Merryn agreed, her heart hammering in fear. "But aunt, Lord Braden followed me here and tonight I made a pact with him for us to travel to Fishguard together. If I suddenly beg out of that journey, he will become suspicious."

"Why would you agree to such a foolish notion?"

Merryn explained about the human-headed snakes.

"They're called pythos," her aunt said. "Demon snakes. You obviously triumphed over them. Well done."

"Something odd happened after the fight with the pythos. Braden struck his sword into the ground and blessed the land."

"He is a man of God. Why would he not cast a blessing on land desecrated by darkness?"

"I've seen blessings laid before. This was nothing like the others. The very air quivered and a pure white light lit on the spot where his sword plunged into the ground." She paused, holding Aunt Morwena's gaze, to emphasize the next statement. "The land *healed*, Aunt!"

"What?" There was utter shock in Aunt Morwena's voice. Not surprising, for the church guards they had dealt with in the past were all perfectly normal humans with no trace of magical talent.

"Afterward, the land felt rich and healthy. Touching that soil affected me and I felt blessed as if I had knelt on holy ground. That was why I agreed to accept Braden's help. He makes a safer friend than an enemy."

Merryn came back to the present to see tears in her aunt's eyes.

"Aunt Morwena, what's the matter?"

"This changes everything."

"What do you mean?"

"If he is as powerful as you say, we cannot chance him following you back to Callington."

Merryn wrapped her arms around herself, shivering despite the warmth of the room. "He wouldn't harm us. He's a good man."

"He thinks we are evil."

"I'm trying to change his views. I don't think he will harm me. If I'm protecting you, we have a better chance of remaining safe. I'll return home."

Aunt Morwena shook her head. "You must continue with your mission."

"You need my help!"

"The best help you can give us at this point is to keep your holy guard as far away from Callington as possible, Merryn Pendraven. Pray that there are not others like him coming to this town."

"But..."

"You will need a chaperone. It cannot be anyone too powerful," her aunt warned. "We will need all the best help in Callington. In essence, you will be on your own. Be wary, Merryn. Do not place your trust where it is unwarranted."

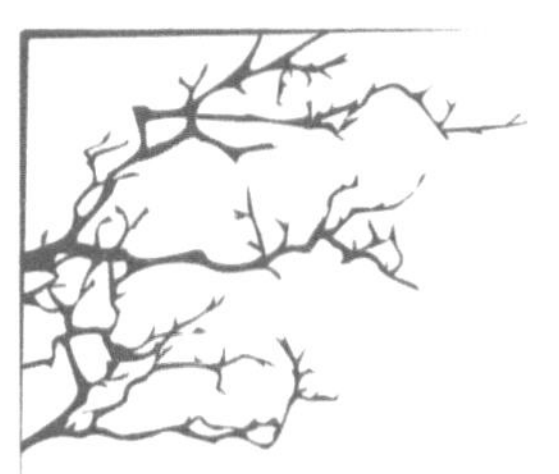

Chapter 7

Tilda, the Horse and Hound Inn, was used to her guests expressing many different emotions while staying in her rooms. Those feelings normally played like stirring harp music that lulled her while she slept. Not tonight. A disturbing burst of energy had shaken Tilda awake.

Awake!

Having retreated into her dreams from an ever-troublesome world for over two centuries, the change to her environment had acted as an unwelcome wake-up alarm. Various sections of her inn slowly integrated back, each vibrating with a sense of supreme wellness.

She didn't trust the healthy energy infusing her.

Being an elder who had witnessed centuries of evil, she wasn't ready to lower her defenses and simply accept this effervescing feeling of good at face value. Such gifts always came with a price.

The change seemed to have begun outdoors, by the stables, then swept throughout the inn and across the surrounding grounds. She would check there first. She extended her awareness to the back of the stables, and something small crashed onto the middle of her rooftop.

The slight weight transformed into something bigger, heavier and rapidly slid down the slide of her roof.

"Roof," she said, to that part of her she had yet to incorporate, "what has landed on us?"

"A wren, my lady," the roof replied in an excited voice. "And then it became a witch. She's heading toward the eaves."

Tilda huffed in impatience. Since their unexpected arrival in Britain three centuries ago, witches and warlocks had been more trouble than people. Sensing her unexpected guest's imminent and involuntary departure, Tilda enlarged and curved her roof slates until they stopped the witch from careening over the edge.

With her large bottom now cupped by the curved shelf, the elderly witch slowly turned about. "What an odd roof," she murmured. "I don't believe I was supposed to land here. Merryn won't be happy about this."

A quick inquiry to the front desk garnered the name "Merryn Pendraven," inscribed on her guest register. The young witch had been assigned to the yellow bedchamber. When Tilda asked for more information, the hearth in there said a fire sprite had recently visited.

"Ah!" Tilda murmured, listening intently to the public parlor candle impart the rest of the tale about the church guard connection to the witch.

So, a true earth healer had indeed arrived in their midst. She quivered; her defenses dropping as every part of her now uninhibitedly basked in the restorative energy that had been fed into the land beneath her foundation.

Tilda gazed out her windows at a carriage being readied under the dawn's light. A church guard and a witch working together. Times had indeed changed since she went to sleep. Perhaps it would be worth staying awake a little longer.

CLOAKED IN A FAWN-COLORED, close-fitting pelisse trimmed in white, Merryn made her careful way down the inn's wide curving stairs. Only a few lanterns lit her way. The place was eerily silent despite the recent activity of staff packing and carting away her bags.

She looked around the deserted entryway, wondering whom Aunt Morwena had sent to act as her chaperone. She hoped the lady would arrive promptly, for Lord Braden did not strike her as the patient sort.

"I shall see you at seven," he'd said last night. *Sharp,* his tone had added.

Finding no one about, she stepped outdoors and then squinted at the sudden brightness. The rain clouds had parted, offering the promise of dryness and a sunny day.

The constant overnight downpour had left the yard and roads mired in mud. In contrast to the peace inside, the yard was in an uproar. Her carriage was out and being readied. Workers' feet squelched, burped and spit mud in every direction as they ran about loading baggage and leading out horses.

She hesitated on the door stoop until eyes tender from lack of sleep spotted Braden's horse. The black stallion was tied behind her carriage. Despite not having received her permission, Braden assumed he would travel inside the carriage? The presumptuousness of the man!

The safety of her boots forgotten, she stepped into the muddy fray. One hand wielded her open umbrella downward, deflecting spray from people running about on the muddy ground. She shaded her weary eyes as she searched for the broad-shouldered brazen earl.

He came around the side of the carriage, tall and handsome in the morning light. Catching sight of her, he waved, making her heart skip. *Silly thing*. Despite her determination to remain affronted, his happy demeanor withered her anger.

"Good morning, Miss Pendraven." Braden's smile was as blinding as the sunlight flooding the yard. "I trust you've decided favorably to my accompanying you inside your carriage?" A hand at her elbow guided her expertly toward her vehicle.

"It seems you've decided for me, my lord."

"Not at all," he said. "I merely anticipated an affirmative response."

Her carriage driver climbed up to the high box, and sat, tipping his hat to her, apparently ready and eager to set off at once. Was there no one who could resist this man's wishes?

"If you deny me entry," Braden continued, "I will, of course, abide by your decision."

The answer mollified and dampened her temper. "As a matter of fact, I've decided you may ride with me." Merryn resisted his none-too-subtle urgings for her to get in. "However, we cannot leave yet."

"Why not?" A frown shadowed his cheer.

Good! Let him be discomposed for a change. She was barely awake and he had her packed and practically at the Fishguard coven's doorstep.

She lowered her voice and led him away from unintended eavesdroppers. "My aunt has agreed we may join forces, my lord. On one condition."

"How could she impose conditions when she's in Callington and we are here?" His eyebrow rose to emphasize his skepticism. "For that matter, how could you have consulted her at all?"

Merryn waited for him to rephrase his question.

His frown darkened further as it dawned on him the nature of the required communication. "I didn't realize that was possible. I don't need to know the particulars. What condition?"

"That I have a chaperone."

"Ah," he said. "A wise woman."

"Yes," Merryn agreed. "She is that and more."

"So, are we to arrange for a maid to accompany us?"

"No need. Someone from Callington is on the way."

"We cannot wait a day more, Miss Pendraven. Time is of the essence."

A movement caught her eye and she looked toward the inn. "We shan't have to, my lord." Merryn's heart warmed at who was to join her. She could not imagine a better companion on this journey. "There she is now."

Braden turned to observe an elderly woman step around the corner of the inn. One hand adjusted her deep blue bonnet covering a cascade of white curls, while the other lifted her bright yellow traveling gown to prevent it dragging in the mud.

Seeing Braden's amazement, Merryn whispered, "Even at the advanced age of five and seventy, my great aunt has a penchant for vibrant colors."

"Great aunt?" He seemed to have trouble keeping a straight face at the lady's whimsical fashion sense.

"She may have trouble coordinating every detail of matching hat color to gown," Merryn said in a stern tone, "but she possesses a merry soul and an unceasing optimism. Every encounter with her is a joyous experience."

"How did she arrive so quickly? Does she live nearby?"

Merryn hesitated and then decided there was hardly any need to hide anything at this late stage. "She would have flown, my lord."

"She what?" Braden speared her with a stunned look.

"Not on a broom!" Merryn said with a frown. "You may shed that absurd misconception about witches right this moment." She turned back to her aunt. "By the by, you should compliment her on being on time. Aunt Gwen's sense of direction's been deteriorating steadily in recent years and her prompt arrival is a marked accomplishment."

Braden looked from her to her aunt and then back, appearing thunderstruck. All sorts of uncomfortable thoughts obviously careened inside his handsome head, distressing him greatly. His frown had grown as dark as last night's thunderstorm.

Feeling uncommonly glad to have so thoroughly upset him, Merryn's mood improved. She turned to greet her elderly relative with a wide smile, extending her hand. "Good morning, Aunt."

"My goodness, child, I do not approve of such early risings. I would have you notice that I am past the stage where gallivanting around the countryside at the break of day is enjoyable."

"I'm sorry to have inconvenienced you, Aunt Gwen. Pray allow me to introduce you to the Earl of Braden. Lord Braden, this is my great aunt, Mrs. Truscott."

Her aunt curtsied

"Mrs. Truscott." Braden made a creditable bow.

"How do you do, my lord?" On rising, she gave his lordship a careful once over, squinting with inquisitive eyes. Then she leaned forward and whispered, "So, you are the young man who has sent the high sage, our coven and my great niece here into such a tizzy. I can see why. No doubt you are used to having this effect on women."

Braden blinked at the direct talk and then applied his devastating smile upon her hapless aunt. "I hope I haven't caused such an inconvenience, Mrs. Truscott. I appreciate your speedy arrival. How was your travel?" He choked at the end of that sentence as if realizing his mistake too late.

"A slight difficulty with the landing," Aunt Gwen said. Merryn got the distinct impression the old lady was avoiding her gaze. "All turned out well in the end," her great aunt finished. "I don't wish to speak of it anymore."

Braden quickly continued, as if he, too, were desperate to change the subject. "Is there anything I may do to make you more comfortable for the upcoming journey? Any food or items you would like to bring?"

Merryn, who had been rushed across the wet yard willy-nilly, marveled at how his hurry seemed to have vanished like milk spilt near a kitten.

Her great aunt seemed no more immune to his charms than any other female and melted at the gallant male attention. She gushed and pointed to the floor. "Thank you ever so much, but everything I need is in my case, my lord."

He glanced down in justified shock, for the lady hadn't been carrying anything as she crossed the yard. Yet, now a substantial wooden chest rested beside her.

"I believe we're ready to leave," Merryn said.

Braden called a stable boy over to load the lady's baggage and then helped the two women aboard.

Merryn sat beside her aunt. The elderly lady squeezed Merryn's fingers and smiled with obvious glee. Her aunt's soft delicate wrinkled skin seemed frailer than she remembered. She would have been worried at having her aunt along on this dangerous mission, except she would be safer with Merryn than with the witches set to defend Callington.

She patted her aunt's hand in comfort. Traveling here must have been a trial. Though Aunt Gwen could change herself into a wren with ease when young, as the lady grew older, her control of that talent had begun to waver. Now, the moment trouble brewed, her transformations often happened instinctively. Aunt Morwena no doubt had set a transform spell on Great Aunt Gwen before sending her on her way.

The earl entered the carriage and sat across from Merryn. He seemed to take up a large portion of the confined space and Merryn again realized what a substantial man he was. Tall, strongly built, with broad shoulders and those amazingly long legs.

A tap on the roof with his walking stick and the carriage rolled forward, jolting her against his legs until she hastily straightened. She ignored the amused quirk of his lips.

"I appreciate you ladies allowing me to ride in the comfort of your carriage," Braden said.

As his warm gaze lingered on her lips, heat suffused her cheeks.

"My niece is a special young lady," Aunt Gwen said. "Very generous and tender of heart."

Braden's gaze finally left Merryn and then swung toward her aunt. "Mrs. Truscott, are you aware of the mission your niece and I are on?"

"My lord, I am cognizant of all pertinent information. I am sure with your help young Trystan will be recovered and we will not be faced with a repeat of the tragedy that befell my great nephew."

"Your great nephew?" Braden's eyebrow rose in inquiry.

Merryn stiffened in her seat. This was a topic she rarely spoke about with anyone, not her family, and certainly not with Braden.

"Has Merryn not told you of what happened to Jonas?" Aunt Gwen asked in a surprised tone. "My dear child, do you not think he should hear of it? After all, it might involve the same players."

Merryn lowered her gaze. "That's old history, Aunt, best left buried and forgotten."

"If it relates to Trystan's case," Braden said in a quiet voice, "I would like to hear of this tale."

As the silence stretched, Merryn realized her aunt waited for her to tell the story. She heaved a resigned sigh and turned to look out the window. The cottages and shrubbery blurred as memories slowly returned. She relayed the events in short succinct sentences, not wanting to embellish any of the distasteful bits.

"When my brother was ten and I twelve, a fourteen-year-old warlock requested the Warlock Council's permission to take Jonas on as his apprentice. They and my father rightfully refused. Unwilling to accept that decision, a year later, the warlock stole my brother. My parents tried to rescue him, and were killed. My brother tried to escape and he, too, died."

She spat out the sad tale quickly, wanting the horrible words to be over, praying she would never be asked to speak them again. Still, her entire body revolted, as if she had again polluted herself with the bitterness of those past events.

On first hearing the devastating news of her parents and brother's deaths at Dewer's hands, Merryn had sworn to one day kill the fae-warlock. No, not just kill him. She had wanted to destroy everything he valued as he had done to her. She planned to torch his precious black tower that his mother built for him in south Wales. Then, she would snap and pull him apart as if she were dismantling a lobster at dinner.

Unfortunately, at thirteen, Merryn made the mistake of sharing her intention with Aunt Morwena. The elder witch had been appalled.

"First and foremost, Merryn Pendraven, witches DO NO HARM," Morwena Dunstan admonished her bloodthirsty niece. "Never assume you know the entirety of an occurrence that happened outside your sphere. It is through such impulsive angers that people do the most damage. I, too, lament my dear sister's and nephew's passing, but do you see me react with malice in my heart? That is not the witchly way. I hoped for better from you."

Drowning under waves of grief, Merryn had cringed with shame at having upset her aunt and let down the witch's code. Yet her longing for revenge never faded and had been the impetus behind her vying to become Coven Protectress. Dewer's bold invasion during her coming-out ball, where he fooled her into enjoying his company, merely added to her thirst for revenge.

She shivered, feeling cold and alone, despite the comforting arm her aunt placed around her shoulders.

"I'm sorry," Braden said, and laid a hand on hers that heated her cold fingers. "You lost your whole family. Who was this vile warlock?"

Merryn could not bring herself to say the name.

"Devlin Chase Dewer, my lord," Aunt Gwen whispered, as if saying the name might draw the warlock's ire.

"Dewer is a warlock?" Braden sounded shocked.

"You know him?" Merryn looked up. Dewer was on the fringe of high society, so it was possible Braden and he were acquaintances.

"We've met once, briefly," Braden said with a frown. "I had an appointment with him the night..." He paused to look at her thoughtfully. "Well, well, now that is interesting."

"What is?" Merryn asked. "I've been quite honest with you, my lord. Will you return the favor?"

He nodded. "While I was in London, Dewer sent me a note asking to meet him at White's. When I arrived there, a pack of hellhounds set upon me."

"Oh my!" Aunt Gwen clutched at her chest, and in that instant, she vanished. In her place, a little brown wren fluttered frantically on the seat and then flew up, banging into the sides of the carriage walls and roof.

The bird sailed past his head and he ducked.

Merryn grabbed the wren and brought it to her chest, cooing softly, soothingly. "It's all right, Aunt, you're safe."

Once the bird calmed, Merryn placed her aunt on the seat beside her and with a gentle finger stroked the soft brown feathers.

"Is that..." Braden sputtered.

"Shush."

In a flutter of feathers and finery, her aunt again sat beside her. Unlike when Merryn changed forms, her aunt returned fully clothed.

"I'm so sorry," Aunt Gwen said, a bright flush lighting her pale cheeks as she looked at Lord Braden.

Her aunt's easy use of transformation magic, even at her age, tweaked envy within Merryn for her own shortcomings. She hoped during this journey she would not be forced to change back into human form in front of Braden.

"When you mentioned those fae hounds," Aunt Gwen continued, "my heart nearly stopped."

"We understand, don't we, my lord? And Lord Braden is perfectly fine. He survived that encounter." Merryn kicked Braden until he shut his gaping mouth and sat back, blinking.

"Yes." Braden adjusted his neck cloth and jacket, though perspiration dotted his forehead.

Merryn plucked a brown feather from his hair and flicked it away, hiding her smile. "Now, where were we?"

"Devlin Chase Dewer." Braden seemed to gather his thoughts, though he didn't stop staring at Aunt Gwen.

"That fiend!" her aunt said. "I wouldn't put it past him to have sent those terrible hounds after you. But why?"

"He likely intended to stop you coming to Callington," Merryn said in a grim voice.

"As the warlocks are the ones who asked for the Church's help," Braden said, "I can't imagine why one would try to interfere."

"Dewer was expunged from the warlock community after his despicable actions," Aunt Gwen said.

"I'm still confused over how Dewer's involved," he said. "Could the witch we follow be working for him?"

"Never," both Merryn and Aunt Gwen said together.

"No witch with any sense of self-preservation would side with Dewer," Merryn said.

"Then why did this witch take Trystan?" Braden asked.

"The answer to that question is what we must find in Wales," Merryn said.

The conversation subsided as the carriage trundled along a forested pathway.

Aunt Gwen yawned wide. "That trip from Callington was tiring."

"Now is a good time to rest," Merryn said, her heart squeezing in sympathy for the stress she'd placed on her elderly aunt. "The trip is bound to prove uneventful. I will wake you when we arrive."

Aunt Gwen nodded with gratitude and rested her head on Merryn's shoulder. Merryn adjusted her arm to give the older lady a more comfortable perch. In moments, only her aunt's soft whizzes of breath disturbed the silence.

Every once in a while, the old lady vanished and a bird appeared on Merryn's shoulder, its head tucked firmly into its back, sound asleep. On the next snore, there would be her aunt, leaning against Merryn.

"I find that most disconcerting," Braden finally said, after Aunt Gwen's fourth transformation.

"Then you would find most of my family difficult to accept, my lord," Merryn replied. "For instance, I have a young cousin who, whenever she visits, casts spells to hide any personal items left unattended. We're forever searching for missing riding crops, hats, wraps, and pocket watches."

"I thought my relations were bothersome," Braden said.

His comment reminded her again how different they were. Merryn glanced outside and released a deep sigh for all that could never be. Her prospect, however, was soon interrupted by a pixie that waved at her from outside the carriage before vanishing. Merryn gasped in surprise.

"Something the matter?" Braden looked out as well.

"Not at all." She turned back to look at him wondering why the pixie had come. She had befriended this particular fae on her journey back from Wales. Could she have news about trouble at Callington or with her gown? Knowing Cri, it could as easily be either.

A thump on the carriage windowpane startled them.

Aunt Gwen sat up with a start.

Cri was back outside the carriage window.

Before Merryn could react, with a flick, Braden drew out a dagger.

Where had he kept that hidden?

The little pixie gave a frightened squeak and vanished again.

Aunt Gwen changed form and flew over to land on Braden's shoulder, chirping excitedly in his ear.

At Braden's startled expression Merryn, tried to contain her laughter and stayed his hand. "Pray, put away your weapon, my lord."

"That was a tiny demon outside, albeit a well-dressed one."

"I will grant you that evil does exist in our world. As does good. Both can manifest in different forms. Before you extinguish this tiny creature, are you not the least curious to discover which shade you may be about to encounter in this instance?"

BRADEN GLANCED AT HER hand covering his. His training shouted at him to shake off her hold, leap out of the fast-moving carriage to seek out and destroy that underworld creature. All supernatural creatures were demons sent by the Devil to test the righteous. That was a given. The wren's animated chirping, however, drowned out his sound reasoning.

Deciding to bide his time, he slipped his weapon back out of sight.

Miss Pendraven leaned close as she reached for her aunt. Her sudden nearness undid all the Church's teachings about keeping a guarded and pious distance from witches. Seemingly unaware of his inhaling her sweet scent as if it were his last breath, she plucked the wren off his shoulder and sat back.

The wren flew away just as quickly and landed on the seat beside Braden. Her aunt re-appeared. "I'm so relieved we've all settled down." She patted Braden's arm. "There's nothing to fear from that little creature, my lord."

"I shall take that under advisement, Mrs. Truscott," Braden said.

"Would you please signal the coach to stop?" Miss Pendraven asked.

He obligingly knocked on the roof with his cane.

Once the coach halted, the young lady opened the door to look outside.

"Come back," she called. "You're safe, I promise."

"Who, Miss?" the coachman asked.

"Not you," she said. "Stay on top of the coach." She sat back as if prepared to wait.

Braden glanced out the window but all appeared normal. Trees and bushes and birds. A gray squirrel scurried up a trunk with a chestnut in its mouth. Nothing out of the ordinary. No flying people in tiny blue gowns.

"What was that creature?" he asked.

"A pixie," Mrs. Truscott said.

That didn't sound dangerous. Now he thought on it, although this little creature had startled him, it hadn't exuded a sense of evil and danger. It had also looked genuinely frightened before vanishing.

He was a little disappointed if he had indeed frightened away the pixie. He always considered such creatures woven from people's imagination. "I thought only demons were real. That fairies and such were merely children's tales."

"The little people are as real as warlocks and witches and magicians and, yes, demons too," Mrs. Truscott said. "Like anyone, human or otherwise, to determine inherent goodness, one must get to know the person, their wants and desires. In most cases, it is free will that dictates the choice to do evil or good, not birthright."

Just as her aunt finished speaking, the pixie appeared on Miss Pendraven's shoulder. She sat, ankles crossed and stared intently at Braden.

Like a startled horse, his pulse shot off at a burst of speed.

The miniature creature, its wings fluttering, leaned back on tiny arms. The pixie wore a pout as she said, "Who is *he*?"

Braden got the distinct impression he was unwanted in this company. He swallowed past a rigid throat.

Miss Pendraven made the introductions.

To his utter astonishment, the pixie stood and dropped a curtsey as if they were being introduced at the arriving line at a house party. "How do you do, my lord."

Manners and instincts warred like combatants at Gentleman Jackson's. Manners won. He bowed his head, fingers itching to hold something weighty and sharp-edged.

"Do you like my new gown?" the pixie asked and twirled to show it off.

Braden raised his eyebrow in surprise.

"Miss Pendraven made it for me," the pixie said. "I wore it at the Seelie Court and all were duly impressed."

"Seelie Court?" He frowned, trying to remember his mythology.

"Our ruling order. That's why I'm here. My queen wishes Miss Pendraven to attend her at court to talk about the latest styles and fashion in London."

"How thrilling!" Mrs. Truscott exclaimed.

"I see." Miss Pendraven visibly relaxed.

What had she been expecting the pixie to tell her?

"Perhaps later," she said to the pixie. "At the moment, we're on our way to Fishguard."

"Why?" the pixie asked, and sat back down.

"We seek a witch at the coven there who may have knowledge of a missing boy."

"I shouldn't go there, if I were you," the pixie answered, arranging the folds of her skirt.

"Why not?"

"Because they're readying to burn down that coven. Besides..."

Braden's heart lurched. *Not yet! The archbishop had promised the guards would await Braden's arrival before they took such a dangerously foolish action.*

"What did you say?" Miss Pendraven asked.

Mrs. Truscott started beside Braden, her hand painfully clenching his forearm. "Did she say someone's attacking the Fishguard coven, Merryn?"

"It's all right, Aunt. Remain calm."

He absently patted the elderly lady's hand in comfort as he stared at the pixie, willing her to be silent.

"What do you mean they're readying to burn the place down?" Miss Pendraven asked. "Who are they?"

"Could the warlocks have declared war again?" A tremor shook the old lady's voice.

The fact she hadn't changed yet suggested she had taken some comfort from his touch.

"What bad timing," Mrs. Truscott continued. "Since all the witches are gathering at Callington and would not be able to come to their defense in Fishguard."

Braden turned to the older woman in shock. That was news.

"More like perfect timing," Miss Pendraven said in a hard voice that whipped at Braden's conscience.

"It's the church guards," the little fairy said, disconcerting Braden further. "They're going to set a bonfire to the coven in Fishguard. I heard the news while I was at court."

Miss Pendraven's glare had daggers aimed at him. "You knew!"

His flush of guilt damned him. The growing tenderness between them died and he shuddered at its passing. He couldn't find the words to defend himself. Anything he said would sink him further in her estimation and they both knew it.

"I thought the guards were heading for Callington," Mrs. Truscott said, in a soft frightened voice, her fingers trembling beneath his hold. "We're not prepared to defend ourselves at Fishguard," she murmured and shifted into a wren.

"How clever!" The pixie clapped her hands.

"You must let me explain," Braden finally managed to say.

"The time for explanations is over," Miss Pendraven said in a cold voice. Mouth set in a fierce line, her back ramrod straight, she refused to meet his gaze.

Mrs. Truscott returned to her human form. "Dear, oh dear. What are we to do, Merryn? Shall I fly home to tell them about the trouble in Fishguard?"

"Not enough time. I need to attend the Fishguard coven in the swiftest way possible."

"Then let's continue our journey," Braden said in a reasonable tone. "I wish to help. I'd hoped to talk the guards out of the attack."

Miss Pendraven spoke as if to herself. "Traveling by carriage will take far too long. We're still a good half a day's ride away."

"Are you going to fly again?" the pixie asked. "May I come, too?"

"Fly?" Braden asked in shock. He glanced at her aunt and then at her. "Can you, too, turn into a wren?"

Ignoring him, she brought the pixie around on her arm to speak face-to-face. "Will you ask your friends at the Seelie Court to help us?"

"I could," the pixie said, her expression falling, "but our queen's forbidden any light fae from interfering in Wyhcan conflicts again."

"Then I'm on my own. Aunt, you must stay here."

"But Merryn," Aunt Gwen began in a fretful voice.

"I'm sorry, Aunt, but I can't both protect you and work to save the Fishguard coven."

Braden worried she was about to foolishly put herself in danger to save her people. Coven Protectress or not, she was no match for a squadron of church guards. Especially if, as he now suspected, those guards were under the influence of warlocks.

"What are you planning?" he asked, knowing the answer.

"I go to Fishguard, my lord," she told him in a cold voice, finally facing him. There was such disappointment in her eyes, Braden's racing heart shriveled. "I intend to stop your guards from murdering my charges."

She leaned out the window and called up to the groom.

The man jumped down and came around the side. "Yes, Miss Pendraven?"

"Keep the carriage here until you hear from me. I might be gone several hours to a day. His lordship is not to have access to the horses, his or ours. Do you understand?"

"Yes, Miss Pendraven." The groom gave Braden a dark look that warned any attempt to escape would be met with great resistance.

"Him and what army?" Braden asked, displaying a smile meant to infuriate her henchman.

It worked.

Miss Pendraven shook her arm until the pixie flew off and hovered near the ceiling. She then raised both arms and swiped them down in a slicing gesture.

Braden frowned wondering what that meant and then remembered his trip from Exeter after she left the coach. He'd been unable to stop the carriage or disembark until they reached Callington. He rattled the door, pushing to open out. It remained unmovable as if iron barred it on the other side.

The groom grinned and called to the postillion on the lead horse, to unhook the team.

"You no longer have a say in matters, my lord," Miss Pendraven said. "Unfortunately, despite my better judgment, I've no choice but to trust that you will guard my aunt."

The words stabbed directly at Braden's abdomen. As if he would ever harm this gentle old lady. "How could you question my honor?"

His answer seemed to satisfy her, for she nodded acceptance. She gestured with her right hand and muttered under her breath.

A spell?

A more complex one than the sealing of the carriage doors. The air about them shifted and warmed, pulsing with the promise of change. She was about to leave. In an instant, she would be lost to him.

"Stay and guard Mrs. Truscott," he ordered the pixie, hoping the creature was capable of such a thing. Just as Merryn's spell ignited, he grabbed her swirling hand.

"No, you mustn't!" Mrs. Truscott cried out, panic in her voice. She muttered something and pointed at him.

The startled pixie, with her hands clasped to her chest, watched with eyes wide open. Then the world shifted and he lost sight of the inside of the carriage.

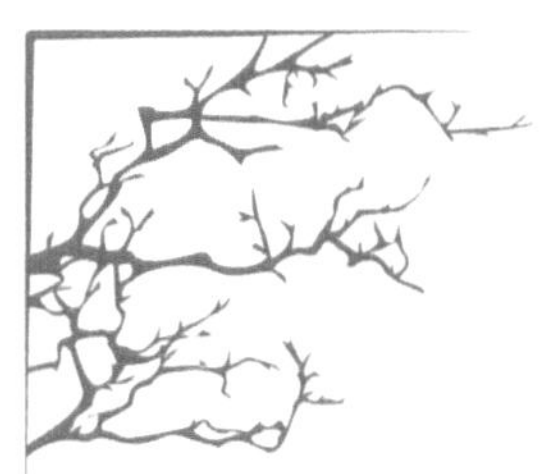

Chapter 8

"*What is this bird doing up here?*" *Anan, a cumulonimbus cloud asked his best friend, Vindr, the warm south wind.*

"It's probably a witch," Vindr said, swirling around to study all angles of the stray that had arrived so precipitately in the midst of his mushroom-shaped friend. "They go anywhere they please, with nary a 'May I.'"

"I don't think this one's a witch," Anan said, adjusting his lower layers to support his unexpected guest. "For one thing, it's male, and everyone knows witches are females. Whoops… there he goes." Gravity had taken over. He shouted in encouragement, "Flap your wings!"

Vindr whipped after the bird in high excitement. "He's going to break into a hundred little pieces when he touches ground!"

Watching the wren's accelerated descent, Anan was compelled to agree. Then an unexpected sensation shivered through every dust particle and water droplet that made up Anan, to the point where he couldn't help but release the water that had been building in him all morning.

"Vindr, you have to help him!" he shouted through the downpour, hoping his friend would hear and pay attention. Vindr could be flighty sometimes.

"Why?" Vindr asked, swirling back up.

"Orders. Just came in. It's not yet time for his lordship to return home."

"Oh," Vindr said. "Oh! That's him? He doesn't look at all the way I pictured he would. I'll get right on it." He swooped after the floundering brown wren.

BRADEN SHOUTED IN ALARM at finding himself high up in the midst of a heavy white mist. The air bathed him in icy droplets and he had one moment to catch his breath before he fell. Plunging through the vapor, he found himself midair, high above ground.

"Flap your wings!" The order hit him with astounding force, and he did as commanded. A sudden downpour railed on him, sending him plummeting again. Then a stray warm current balanced and twisted him right side up so his flapping wings could have an appreciable effect.

Wings? He had wings!

"That was a most foolish act, my lord," Miss Merryn Pendraven's voice scolded.

"What happened?" His words came out as an incomprehensible squeak.

"Let's get out of this rainfall and I'll explain."

Braden noticed with a start that he conversed with a raven. There was no time for questions.

The black bird led the way. They flew for what felt like hours but was probably only minutes. He worried he wouldn't have the strength for one more flap of water-laden wings when they cleared the rainfall. The sunshine soon warmed him but he still listed, slowing, heading downward more than straight across.

"You're a raven," he said, feeling foolish. "I thought Garth mad for suggesting you could turn me into a vole if I annoyed you." A warm wind blew beneath him and he automatically coasted on the current. "I'm a wren," he said next, mind reeling at the shocking news.

"That bird is my aunt's specialty," Miss Pendraven replied. "After you foolishly stuck out your arm, interfering with my spell, Aunt Gwen lent you a helping hand by transforming you. Then, in a panic, she accidentally transported you way up here. Realizing what she'd done, I followed as swiftly as I could. That was a dangerous action you took, my lord." The raven gave him a piercing look from a glassy black eye.

Braden accepted the scold as well deserved. "How is this possible?" He cringed. It seemed there was no end to the inanity of his conversation. "I know that you and your aunt are witches and I'm under a spell. But how is this possible?"

"You must have seen Garth do magic." Her voice softened, suggesting her temper cooled.

He was glad, for he had many questions vying for an answer. "Are you a magician, then? Is 'witch' simply another term for someone with the same ability to work magic?"

"No, my lord. Garth is as human as you, but with an innate ability to see the lines of power that thread through this land. He has simply found ways to direct and control that power."

"The ley lines he's always going on about?"

She chuckled - coming from the raven it sounded like a gurgle. He hoped it had been a chuckle and not a growl.

"Do we have much further to go?" he asked, thinking if he did not rest soon, he would fall.

"Follow me." She winged her way down.

They landed on the top bare branch of a pine that was more deadwood than leaves. The lack of foliage made finding a perch easy, though the view did nothing to ease his new terror of such impossible heights. He spread his legs to get a better grip on the slender branch, his heart drumming at an incredible pace.

"Transformations can be tiring," she said. "But we cannot stay long. Time is of the essence."

He looked at her large form, almost five times his puny size, and ferocious looking. He did not care to be on such unequal terms with this witch. Pity her aunt couldn't have changed him into a hawk or an eagle.

"Why did you not abandon me?" he asked. "I had gained the impression you despised me for withholding what I knew of the church's raid."

The raven's head turned and he slid sideways a pace, the branch bouncing alarmingly beneath his clenching claws. He was unsure what worried him more, the height or her.

"Since my aunt changed you into this bird, you are now my responsibility, my lord. I take my duties to heart."

Her words were surprising. If she spoke truly, then he had much in common with this witch – a creature the Church insisted was evil and destructive. He fluffed himself, finding that the action released some of the tension he'd built up.

All he had been taught about witches and his years of reading scholarly papers on the subject did not match what he had learnt from spending a few days in this protectress's company.

"If you are not a magician, like Garth, then what are you?" He was curious to hear her version of reality. At her continued silence, he wondered if she would answer at all.

"Are you ready for another flight?" she asked instead.

He took several breaths and nodded. Now or never. Together, they leapt into the air, wings spread out.

How amazing! He didn't plummet down as he'd half expected. He was grateful that she waited until he developed a comfortable rhythm.

"I am not like Garth," she said. "Or yourself, my lord. I am not human."

Braden's heart sank. This time it was he who could not speak, for one word reverberated in his mind. *Demon.*

She gave him a side look. At his continued silence, and perhaps at the rapid breathing that hinted at his panicked thoughts, her curious glace grew acrimonious. She gave a rude squawk. "I take leave to inform you, sir, that I may be many things, but I am not a *demon!*"

Braden's heart rate decelerated from gallop to canter. "Thank you, Lord," he murmured.

She turned her head away, refusing to look at him as they flew. He gained the impression he should apologize. *But what was she then, if not a demon?* "Who are you?"

"I suppose at this point, there is no reason to keep any more secrets." Still, she remained quiet for a long while before continuing. "My people are strangers to your world. Our land was on the brink of death until a young boy devised a clever means of transporting what remained of our people to a new world. Three hundred years ago."

Braden's mind shuddered at the news. How could this be? There was only one world where God created people. Here. Earth. He knew science had proven that earth was no longer the center of the universe, but *other inhabited worlds?* Then his mind did the time calculations. "The start of the witch trials!"

"We Wyhcans were not accustomed to the magic of this new world. Our mind magic, especially, does not function here as it did on our world. On earth, that power becomes distorted, creating false, uncontrollable illusions."

"You mentioned mind magic before. You said it was the reason for the Bedfordshire massacre."

"The witches knew church knights were coming because the warlocks had set a mind spell on them to destroy a coven in Bedfordshire. We countered to protect ourselves, to make you think there were no witches where we were. It worked. Unfortunately, the spells distorted and convinced the guards to storm a nearby village instead. The knights destroyed what they thought was a nest of witches and warlocks. What they actually did was prevent anyone from escaping and then butchered an entire village of innocent men, women and children."

"The king beheaded every one of the knights as punishment for that senseless massacre," Braden said, finishing the sad tale often told among the church guards. "He disbanded all the orders of the knights belonging to the Church of England. This is one tale to which I know the ending, for this was my reason for joining the Church instead of the army as my father wanted me to do."

"Tell me how your story ends," Merryn said. "I know the gist of it, but more from rumor than a factual retelling."

Braden nodded. "The Archbishop of Canterbury, afraid that Britain would be left spiritually unguarded, begged for leniency for his personal guards. He insisted they had never been involved in witch-hunts. That their sole purpose was to protect sovereign lands against invasion by underworld creatures that threatened the kingdom's safety."

"The Knights of the Green Cross," Merryn said. "That's why they alone were spared."

"The king changed our title to Guard of the Green Cross, stipulating that from that day forward, the Church would follow an inviolate, non-interference policy regarding witch-warlock matters."

"Until now," Merryn said.

"Yes," Braden agreed. "My personal goal in coming on this mission is to find out why."

MERRYN FELL SILENT after Braden's confession. Deep in thought, he gave his flight not one stray thought, and his little brown wings beat in perfectly harmonious rhythm.

She did not mind the hush because her throat was choked with sorrow. What happened in Bedfordshire was a tale told to all young witches in gruesome detail, so none would ever forget the consequences of using mind magic on Earth.

"Tell me more," Braden said after they had traveled a pace. There was a determined note to his tone, as if he wished, no, *needed*, to hear all she had to say. "The guards were not to interfere with witches and warlocks. Was there similar repercussion on your people's part because of what happened in Bedfordshire?"

"Witches hold themselves deeply culpable for the epidemic of hysteria that resulted in those terrible witch trials in both Europe and Britain. That is the reason why we work unceasingly to protect humans. We feel we owe your people a debt that can never be repaid."

"Warlocks do not feel the same way?"

"They were not so quick to accept blame. Just as changing shape is more a witchly practice than a warlock one, mind magic was always stronger among Wyhcan males than females. It is little wonder they refuse to live by our ban on mind magic. To this day, they cling to the hope that they can discover a means to better control their power. In doing so, they further endanger humans."

"Hence the centuries-old war between witches and warlocks," he said, sounding thoughtful. "All the pieces of this puzzle are falling into place. So, if witches do not use mind-altering power, what can they do, besides change forms?"

"We can alter the structure of the world. We see the patterns of life – of air, earth, fire and water. We can heal, alleviate suffering and encourage better weather to help crops flourish."

"Wide-ranging abilities!"

Below, the four corner towers of the Fishguard coven loomed. There was an assortment of men wearing black capes nearby but no lit torches or angry mobs waving swords. She hoped Braden had spoken truly when he said he intended to talk the guards out of attacking this coven.

"Bank to the left, my lord." She indicated a meadow far enough away to keep them undetected.

He followed. "If witches are as powerful as you say, why do you gather in Callington? Even if you suspected the church guards were headed there, you could simply leave. The same goes for the Fishguard coven. Surely we cannot truly harm you?"

"My coven and those from nearby gather to form a defense of the people of Callington, my lord, to prevent innocents from being hurt if the church guards blunder in on a blind hunt for evil, as they apparently plan to do in Fishguard. I worry that if a warlock is present and intends to assist the church guards with use of mind magic, then..."

"...what happened in Bedfordshire may be about to happen in Fishguard," Braden finished for her in a dire tone.

"All seems calm yet," Merryn said in a soothing voice. "I believe we've arrived in time. However, there is one other urgent problem I should warn you of."

"What is that?"

"I have a little difficulty with the transformation spell."

"Will I be stuck as a wren forever?"

"No, I can change you back into a human, but..."

"Yes?"

"You will change back unclothed."

There was a moment of silence. Then Braden said in a strangled voice, "Explain."

"I have yet to master transformation with clothes intact," she said, hating to admit aloud to her failing.

"For yourself, too?" This time laughter choked his words.

"This is not a laughing matter, my lord."

"Of course not," he agreed, but couldn't seem to contain his glee. "Will we need to procure some clothes for ourselves? Should we land closer to a farmhouse?"

"I can fashion clothing, but only after I'm in my natural form."

"Ah." He released another chuckle that sounded like a series of chirps.

"We must coordinate the change carefully," she said. "I, first, then you."

"As you wish."

She headed downward. He followed, tumbling into an ungainly landing. As he straightened, she moved behind a tall prickly bush and cast the spell to change back.

"Ouch," she muttered. She'd been standing too close to the holly bush.

"What's wrong?" Braden asked, his voice coming out in concerned chirps.

Merryn couldn't help smiling, thinking of the strong powerful guard reduced to a helpless little bird. Served him right for hiding the truth about the attack on Fishguard, though her anger had diminished during the flight. For a man with a twisted view of magic, he had adjusted remarkably well to being turned into a wren. At the end, he had even seemed to enjoy flying, banking and turning with grace.

Once respectably clothed, Merryn moved around the bush and found Lord Braden perched on the branch of a marsh glass-wort that bounced as he shifted.

She'd never transformed another person. Luckily, bodies tended to return to the shape they were most familiar with. The trick to the spell was to allow a transformation to happen naturally instead of forcing a change.

"It would be better if you were on the ground, my lord."

He gazed at her a moment, as if considering the request, then obligingly hopped on the grassy ground.

"Turn around please."

He obligingly swung around to show her his tail feathers.

Merryn's cheeks heated at what she must do next. She'd never seen a naked man before. Unfortunately, she could not risk looking away when she cast her spell, in case something went wrong. She must hold quite clearly in her mind what he looked like and gauge how his form should appear, taking into account the right height and weight.

She raised her hand and muttered the words of the spell. In a moment, Lord Braden stood before her completely naked.

"Well?" He gave her a mischievous glance over his shoulder at her silence. "Is the clothing spell going to take a while? Or are you merely inspecting to be certain all of me returned intact? I can assure you," he added glancing down at himself, "the front appears anatomically correct ."

Merryn swallowed hard, for she'd forgotten what she was supposed to be doing until he spoke. The clothing spell did not require her to look at him to cast it. Did he need to know that? After all, hadn't he kept secrets from her? This was quite innocent compared to his misdemeanor.

"Stand still, please," she said in a commanding tone. Her lips curved up as his fists came to rest on his lean hips.

She recited the words, pulling on one piece of clothing onto him at a time, to ensure she had chosen correctly.

White wild flowers swirled to caress his shoulders until a shirt formed that came down to his hips.

"A little lower, if you please," he said.

The shirt lengthened to drop down to mid-thigh level.

"Your change seemed to go faster." There was suspicion in his tone as leaves and branches shaped themselves into long drawers that laced up at his waist and the bottom drawstring tied at his knees. Then came tight beige breeches that hugged his thighs.

"I'm more familiar with women's fashion than men's," she explained.

He turned around, and the look in his eyes suggested devilish delight. The rogue was enjoying this experience every bit as much as she.

Now he had on his breeches and shirt, Lord Braden held his arms out to the side.

Merryn schooled her features to appear solemn. "A cravat, waistcoat and jacket next, I presume?"

"Crisp white cravat, cream waistcoat with blue stripes and cobalt jacket."

Her eyebrow shot up at the order. *Did he think he spoke to his valet?*

His eyes met hers with challenge, and something indefinably sensual.

Her knees quivered. She glanced away, afraid she'd never get him dressed if they continued with that intimate, suggestive exchange. *Coward!*

I have a coven to rescue, she silently excused herself, as the requested items draped over his well-made torso.

Stockings, Hessians and hat were last.

Fully dressed to his apparent satisfaction, he approached her.

Watching him move, Merryn decided that some men were born to wear Hessians and breeches. She forced her gaze upwards and caught such a determined look in his eyes, her heart skipped a beat in anticipation. Was she about to pay the price for her impudence in clothing him so slowly?

He stopped an arm's reach away. A proper distance, her aunt would say. Too far, her heart complained. After the recent private dressing, she found this formal void most dissatisfying.

His mischievousness was replaced by a serious, perhaps one might even say, a formal, demeanor. "Miss Merryn Pendraven," he addressed her in the tone of strangers meeting and Merryn's heart squeezed tight with disappointment. "On behalf of the King, I would like to bid you and your people a belated but heartfelt welcome to Britain. To Earth." Hat in hand, he bowed deep.

Merryn stood speechless. Her throat constricted at the unexpected words of welcome.

He straightened and donned his hat.

Could he be serious? She had to ask. "Despite the centuries of misunderstanding, pain and suffering our arrival caused your people, my lord?"

"What relationship is without its challenges?" His eyes twinkled with suppressed mirth.

Hers misted and she blinked, thinking, *Aunt will not be pleased. I'm falling in love with a church guard.*

He took one step closer, bringing him into the space she labeled *close* – the distance reserved for dear friends and family. "Now, on to more important matters," he murmured.

She was incapable of resisting his good humor, and her smile widened. "Such as?"

"You've seen me in feathers and nothing at all, Miss Pendraven. That shifts us into a new relationship."

She held her breath.

He leaned toward her. "I would like you to address me as Braden, or Thomas, whichever you prefer. I beg permission to address you as Merryn."

"Braden, it is then," she agreed, her eyes lingering on his lips, which were so close the separation seemed pointless. "I would be honored if you would call me Merryn."

She'd barely finished speaking when his kiss landed. A touch that imprinted his mark – drawing her in, arms claiming her, offering no avenue for second thoughts.

Every nerve in Merryn quivered with delight. She leaned in, enfolding him, rejecting all application to caution - in truth, she'd been waiting for this man to choose her as his lover since the first moment he stepped into Lady Hancock's carriage.

The last thing she expected him to say when he drew back from that searing, life-changing kiss was, "I smell fire."

Merryn's dazed gaze swung to the horizon. In the distance, billows of black smoke plumed into the sky.

"We're too late," she whispered, heart breaking.

Without need for words, he took her hand and they raced toward the blaze.

Merryn mouthed a spell and boulders rolled away, low hanging branches rose to let them pass beneath, and twigs, dirt and small rocks scattered to either side. A whirlwind preceded their steps, as if rolling out a safe pathway.

Breathless and spent, they neared the burning building surrounded by men carrying lit torches.

Merryn drew back into the bushes and felt his resistance. "Please, Braden, allow me to help them."

His grip loosened and she pulled free. She melded into the surrounding greenery as the first of the men turned around.

"What the blazes do you think you're doing, Dalton?" Braden demanded. "There are people inside, man."

Amidst women screaming, furniture breaking and fire crackling, Merryn could barely make out that conversation.

Leaving him to deal with the guards, she skirted around the bushes until she reached the back of the large brick structure. Though flames licked at the openings, means of escape were everywhere - broken windows, half-open doors – yet, no one ran outside.

Warlock magic at work?

Merryn cautiously approached the unguarded building's rear. Sighting no interference, she cast a spell for dirt to rise and cover the flames around one of the downstairs windows. The fire persisted. Merryn intensified her spell, urging dirt saturated in water to blanket the flames. The fire resisted, and then as if giving up the fight, with a pop and sputter, the flames around that one window died.

Picking a large rock, she flung it into the pane of glass, shattering it. The noise of breaking glass was drowned by the cacophony plaguing the air.

"Hallo!" she called into the room.

No answer. Where was everyone?

She stepped back and shook her right hand. A small bell appeared in her fist. Extending her arm inside the window of the darkened room, she rang the tiny silver bell.

A gentle tinkle sounded and then grew and flowed along all the corridors, stairs and rooms, searching out the frightened witches and human servants trapped within.

Come this way, it urged.

The chime rang with the authority of a church bell sounding the alarm, urging parishioners toward safety.

While she waited, Merryn flicked her left forefinger at leaves on the ground until they rose and formed a thick wool blanket that wrapped around her arm. She used that protected arm to clear away the sharp glass pieces so no one would be pierced as they climbed out.

The first women arrived with a shout of cheer.

They came in orderly groups – seven women at a time as per coven crisis protocol. Living in warlock-infested Wales apparently hadn't purged them of all their good sense.

Merryn helped each person climb over the windowsill and land on the ground without twisting an ankle or scraping a knee. Both the human women and witches looked terrified.

Merryn pointed toward the woods. "That way. No talking. No flying. Absolutely no magic. We're in enemy territory." Obviously, that needed emphasizing to this foolish coven. "Humans, veer toward your homes as soon as it's safe. Wyhcans keep going until you're at least a league away."

"But..." one said.

"Talk later. Go now!"

"Come, Branwyn." Another tugged at the lingering witch's sleeve, pulling her along.

Branwyn? Merryn hadn't recognized her with soot covering her face. That must be the witch that came to Callington, first to send Merryn on her goose chase to Wales and then, to steal Trystan. Could the boy be inside this burning building?

The next group of seven arrived. Still no Trystan. She helped them over the threshold, quietly urging them to run.

Merryn turned back expecting another group and found one woman, the Sage of Fishguard. She recalled speaking to this pinched-faced middle-aged witch who'd pre-emptively sent Merryn home.

What bothered her more than that slight was this woman being alone. "Is Trystan still inside?"

"The boy was never here." The sage leaned out through the window and looked about. "That fool Branwyn lost track of him inside Saint Agatha's church."

The news rocked Merryn. If Trystan never came to Fishguard, and according to Braden, the warlocks were still looking for him, then where was the boy?

As the Sage of Fishguard climbed onto the ledge of the window, Merryn blinked, swallowing bitter coldness toward a woman who had aided warlocks.

Resisting the urge to pull harder than necessary, she lent the older woman a hand in jumping to the ground.

"You can explain yourself and Branwyn's role in this disaster to the high sage," Merryn said in a cold voice, directing her to where the other witches had gone. "Join your coven as they flee for their lives."

The woman flushed at the hidden rebuke. "What about our things?"

"You should have thought of that before interfering in warlock affairs. Now is the time to thank heavens you can escape undetected."

"Not completely undetected," a man's voice said. "Where's my son?"

Merryn froze.

"You!" the sage cried out. "You promised protection but allowed those church guards to burn my coven."

The warlock, a tall gaunt looking man with fierce haunted eyes, stood with a black hound by his feet. The intelligent glint in the dog's eyes told Merryn it must be the warlock's familiar.

The man glared at the Fishguard sage. "If you wanted my help, you shouldn't have withheld my son."

Merryn swallowed a curse. A stray warlock she might have been able to handle. A vengeful father was an entirely different beast.

"We don't have him!" the sage said. "I sent word he wasn't here. We did the best we could to help you, Mr. Mattock. Why take away your protection?"

"Because warlocks are untrustworthy?" Merryn said, aghast that lesson still needed learning.

"This is none of your affair," Mattock said. "It's a personal disagreement between myself and the Fishguard witches."

"I'm their protectress." Merryn stepped forward, purposefully placing herself between him and the sage. "Their troubles are my troubles. It would serve you well to remember that, sir."

The black hound at his feet growled, baring its fangs – the attention of both warlock and hound was now effectively centered on Merryn. She gestured with her hand for the sage to back away.

"Return to Cornwall, where you belong." His hissed words twined around her mind and tempted her to accede to his order. The warlock used his magic to try to coerce her. Merryn shook her head to expel his intrusive thought.

"The boy is not here," the sage said, her voice so close Merryn guessed the silly twit hadn't used the distraction she'd provided to escape. "Branwyn failed us both."

"Liar!" Mattock's attention swung back to the coven's sage. "The boy disappeared the same time as your witch. I've confirmed the Callington coven doesn't have him, so you must."

"Dewer may have him," Merryn put in.

"Then you're a fool," he responded in a cold voice, though doubt flickered in his gaze. "I denied Dewer his request to apprentice Trystan and the Warlock Council supported my decision. He wouldn't dare steal my son."

Merryn narrowed her eyes at that. He sounded sincere.

"Trystan has to be inside," the warlock said, now sounding desperate.

She smothered her rising pity and asked in a reasonable tone, "Then why did you burn the building? Aren't you worried the flames might harm your boy as easily as it might the witches?"

"I didn't set this fire. It was burning when I arrived. The guards were under strict orders to merely watch this place, to ensure no one escaped until I arrived."

"I don't believe you," Merryn said.

"I do," the sage said. "He and his kind are our friends. We've coexisted in peace for a long while."

"Until you deceived us," Mattock said.

"We didn't."

"This discussion is pointless," Merryn said.

"Give Trystan back and I'll help put out this fire," Mattock's trail of influence slithered over her as he spoke, enticing her to believe him. Merryn was repulsed by his mind touch. Did he really think he could win her over with his paltry tricks?

She blocked Mattock's mind spell, shoving him out of her head. He staggered and looked at her in surprise. Satisfaction flared. She might be young but she was far from helpless.

"If you're not responsible for this fire, why are the flames magically enhanced to only surround doors and windows?" she asked. "These witches obviously couldn't put out those flames. Only I was able to breach it."

"What?" The sage looked back at the building.

Mattock's eyes narrowed as he, too, studied the building. "This is a trick."

"A warlock trick," Merryn said with an affirmative nod. "Same as your mind spell on the church guards that prevents them from helping those trapped inside."

"I don't know why they're not helping," Mattock said with obvious frustration. "I told them to assist before I came back here."

"Did you even consider that perhaps your new fancy mind spell might be backfiring? As all other such Wyhcan spells have done on this planet since we arrived?" Merryn asked in exasperation.

"My son's life is on the line. I had to do something."

"It's of no matter," the sage said. "My witches are no longer inside. You cannot harm us."

Merryn cringed.

Mattock's eyes narrowed and he raised his hand. Both Merryn and the sage strengthened their defense shields.

Instead of striking at them, the warlock snapped an order to his familiar and pointed to the woods. The dog raced that way.

"Quick, it's after your witches," Merryn shouted to the sage. "Help them. I'll deal with him."

For once, without hesitation, the woman raced to protect her coven members.

Heart hammering in fear, Merryn once again placed herself between warlock and sage – in time to receive a bolt of blue lightning that struck her shield. The strike shook her like a rag doll.

"The fire and the guard's reactions are not of my doing," Mattock said. "My mind spell merely enhanced what the guards desired. Our latest theory is that if Wyhcan mind magic doesn't change a human's desires, it won't be distorted."

"You never give up, do you?" Merryn said in disgust. "Even knowing how dangerous it is to practice mind magic on humans, you're trying again."

"It worked, Protectress! For the best of causes. My son is in danger. The guards wish to cleanse this land of evil. I merely provide them with a means of doing so, which is why they willingly follow me. I mean the Fishguard witches no harm, but I will not allow them to escape until they've told me what they've done with my son."

Blue light flared around her protection, the only indication that another spell had been shot at her. Merryn rocked back on her heels, her bones trembling from the force of this latest blow.

Mattock hadn't moved a muscle in warning before casting his spell. Or had he? He must have been altering her perceptions again. Unlike specific spells, a warlock's talent to work mind magic was harder to ward against. It stole past her defenses like a draft that barely fluttered leaves.

A third blast struck her, tipping her backwards onto the ground. The fourth ripped into her shield and sent her skidding painfully across the rough ground on her backside.

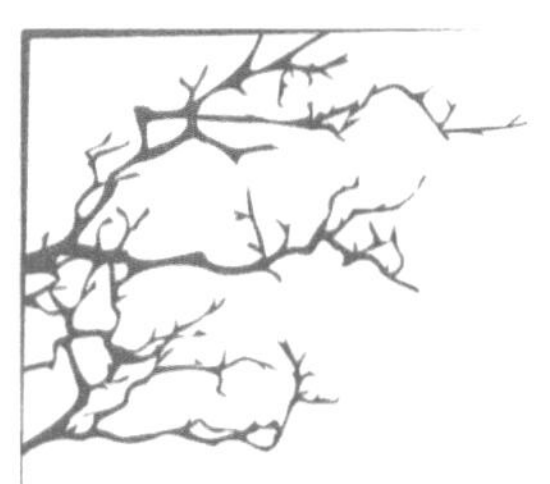

Chapter 9

"Where are you off to in such an 'urry?" Luc, an elderly fox, asked.

Mattock's familiar, Idris, paused, breathing heavy, and spared the nosy, silver-coated fox a side look. "I've been sent to find the witches that fled this way. Did you see them go by with a sharp-scented boy?"

"Nage," Luc denied in Welsh. "Just witches pelting through the woods as if the Devil himself were after 'em. You lookin' for a boy? Why?"

"Later. No time to talk." Idris returned to a chase he didn't want to be on. He wanted to be back there by the burning coven, protecting his master, but orders were orders. He'd tried to protest but the master refused to listen to advice from anyone lately.

Surprisingly, the silver fox kept pace with him. "The boy's been bad, has he?"

"No. He's a good boy." Idris said that with a sense of pride. He'd helped the master raise that boy from the time he was born, except for the rare times the boy was sent to stay with his ma. Idris wanted the boy back. He had promised Trystan he'd always watch out for him and he'd failed. "He never once pulled on my ears, not even as a baby. Always respectful. 'is pa just wants 'im back."

"Why fawr?"

"Wants the boy safe like." Idris scaled a fallen trunk and the older fox ran around the old oak and caught up. "Safe from witches?"

"Yes. No. A warlock's gone wild, and against the council's wishes, might be on the hunt for our boy. My master asked the Warlock Council for help, but they refused to stir up trouble with witches. So, he turned to the Church for help."

"The Church!"

Idris stopped, for the fox had fallen behind. In fact, panting, the fox sat down as if he didn't intend to follow Idris another step.

"You'd best find that boy quick," the fox said. "Church guards pitted against witches spells naught but trouble for everyone in their vicinity."

"It's worse than you think," Idris said. "Rumors fly the dark fae were in London Town, and closer, in Cornwall. Trouble's brewin' all 'round."

"Dark fae?" The fox scurried behind a thick bush. "I'd heard they were forbidden to enter Britain by Queen Orlagh. What's this land coming to? You go on, now. I'll stay here and call out if any evil comes your way."

Idris bounded away. He did so with a laden heart for he didn't hold much hope of finding his boy. To his nose, the only strong stench in this wood was of slightly burnt, frightened witches.

BRADEN PUSHED PAST Dalton to move closer to the burning building. The waves of heat fed by the wind buffeted him. Screams from within the inferno rang out, but a look around showed none of the guards reacting. *Had the church guards reverted to the monsters their predecessors were accused of being?*

"Who gave you authority to attack innocents, Dalton?" His rage burned in equal portion to the flames eating the building. "I will have you before the courts for this. We must save those trapped inside. Start a water line from that well."

"You misunderstand, my lord," the man replied. Instead of following orders, he tracked Braden, who paced in the front of the building looking for an opening. All the exits were covered in flames.

"When we arrived, we found the coven abandoned and the fire already lit," Dalton continued. "Someone must have warned the witches of our approach. I suspected they fled and started this fire to destroy evidence of their evil work. Surely, you cannot think I would authorize such cruelty as to burn people alive? We are well past the age of witch hunts, my lord."

Dalton's offended words clashed with the shouts for help from inside the house.

"I took a look through a window. By the number of books and paraphernalia they'd left behind," Dalton hastily drew Braden back out of harm's way as a flick of burning ash landed before them, "they did not linger to pack. There was not one person left behind. I will swear to that on a Bible," the guard finished in earnest.

"What is it about those screams for help that's beyond your understanding, sir?"

The man's startled look swung from Braden to the burning building and returned. "What screams, my lord?"

Warlock mind magic.

The answer was so obvious. Braden's rage veered toward the warlock who'd so callously used these church guards to commit this atrocity.

Feeling out of his depth, he craved Merryn's guidance. The shouts had lessened, suggesting that she at least might be making headway.

How deeply did this warlock influence extend?

"Mr. Mattock said to not put out the fire. Best if we allow the building to burn until only ashes remained."

"Who is Mattock?" Braden asked.

"The warlock liaison that accompanied us on His Grace's orders. He was here a moment ago. A tall, thin fellow with condescending eyes." Dalton leaned in to conspiratorially whisper, "I don't like working with his kind, no matter what His Grace says about them becoming converts and helping us defeat evil. Just as well, he seems to have left."

Was this Mattock responsible for altering the guards' minds so they did not assist the witches? If so, he understood now why Merryn and her witches were opposed to warlocks and their fiendishly persuasive ways. His need to speak to the archbishop shot up.

How much influence did this warlock have on Sutton? What side effect might his spells be having on His Grace? He shuddered to think what would become of these guards, the Church and England itself, if use of such influence was not instantly arrested.

Braden's right fist flexed, missing the heft of his broadsword. Agamore, however, was hidden under cloth and baggage on top of the carriage where Mrs. Truscott waited.

The burning building felt ominously quiet now, except for the crash of timber and the sputter of flames. He prayed Merryn had moved herself and her people far away. Who knew what these guards were capable of while under warlock influence?

"Has anyone reported seeing a boy nearby?" he asked, his thoughts shifting to his next problem. "One about six years old, by the name of Trystan?"

"No, my lord. I did send sentries about the place but there's no indication in which direction the witches fled or with whom. I plan to send out search parties in the morning. Too unsafe to be in these dangerous woods in the dark. We must not go behind the building. We must stay here, in the front, until daybreak."

"What?" A look up at the bright blue sky showed darkness at least a couple of hours away. Braden studied Dalton. The man's eyes were glazed, and he spoke as if he repeated a message by rote.

Dread crept up Braden's neck. If the guards were being influenced to stay here, it likely meant Mattock was at the back, with Merryn.

"Wise of you," Braden said quietly, casually inching backwards. "Best if you and the others stay on this side of the building. What are your next orders?"

The confounded fellow paced him, moving one step forward for every one Braden took back. "We're to head for Callington, my lord."

"There's been a change of plans." Braden kept his voice low and reassuring, fighting the urge to belt Dalton and run to the back. If he did, would he end up with the entire squadron of guards at his heels? "My primary duty is to find the missing boy. Dealing with the Callington coven can wait."

"What do you want us to do then?" Dalton asked.

"Go toward Cheshire. Wait there until I send word."

"But..." Dalton began.

"Those are my orders. Are they clear?"

"Yes, my lord." The man bowed, though he was obviously unhappy with the change in direction. "If you will pardon me, then, I'd best send a courier with current news to His Grace before we set off for Cheshire."

"Be quick about it." Depression settled on Braden as Dalton strode away. News that the guards were heading east instead of south would no doubt be included in that message. His orders would as quickly be countermanded.

At least this gave him a few days, a week if he were lucky, to find the boy and take him and Merryn and her aunt to safety before disaster erupted around Callington. He casually strode toward the bushes to the side of the building.

As soon as he was out of sight of any watchers, Braden raced to the back. With each pounding step, he feared a confrontation between Merryn and this Mattock would see the end to his sweet witch.

Not if I have anything to do about it. He quickly prayed to God to let him be in time. "Please keep her safe and help me help her," he muttered under his breath.

He came around the corner and skidded to a halt at the sight of Merryn lying on the ground, arms raised protectively. A tall man loomed over her in a threatening manner. *Mattock?* Braden's blood roiled in renewed rage.

"Get away from her!" He raised his right arm and energy shot from the soles of his feet, through his spine, to the tips of his raised fingers. A sweeping high-pitched hum sounded and then Agamore dropped into his grip in a flash.

He wasn't quite sure who was more startled: himself, the warlock who swung around, or Merryn who sat up with an open-mouthed gasp. He didn't have time to ponder the issue as the warlock sent a spear of light flashing toward him.

He instinctively blocked that arrow with Agamore. The instant the light struck the sword, the glow was reflected straight back to the warlock, sweeping him off his feet. He landed not two feet from where Merryn lay.

The two looked at each other in surprise and then scrambled to their feet. A black hound came barreling out of the woods barking in alarm.

Not another hellhound!

In an instant, both dog and warlock vanished. He swung around, checking where the pair would appear next.

"I don't sense either of them nearby," Merryn said, hurrying toward him.

Braden's hand still shook with the sword's vibration. He carefully lowered the still-blazing weapon. The bright flare fluttered and then died, leaving an ordinary sword in his hand.

"How did you do you that?" she asked.

Braden switched Agamore to his left hand and put a comforting arm around her shoulder. "Time for questions later," he said, mainly because he didn't have a suitable answer. "Are you all right? Is that warlock likely to return?"

"I'm well. He probably plans to return with friends." Merryn still gazed at his sword with a frown.

"Not with his church guard allies," Braden said. "I've sent them off to Cheshire. Still, the sooner we vacate these premises the better."

HAND IN HAND, MERRYN and Braden ran through the woods. She couldn't believe all the witches had fled unscathed. It had been a narrow escape. If Braden hadn't appeared like an avenging angel with his blessed sword, who knew what might have happened. Even now, their odds were slim, for that warlock was right. This was his wood. She would have to avoid using magic for that reason. It would be too easy to be tracked.

Not using magic meant no safe pathways to run through and rocks and debris were everywhere. She held her gown up to prevent tripping. Her breaths came out in puffs. All the while, Braden's reassuring grip on her hand never wavered.

They ran into a little clearing where a fox lay sprawled on the ground. At their precipitous entrance, the animal gave a frightened yip and raced into the brush. They kept going.

A glance to the side showed Braden, too, was tired. She called a brief halt by tugging at his hand.

"Rest?" He sounded out-of-breath. "Want to fly?"

The latter question sounded like a reluctant suggestion and Merryn hid her grin. "Too dangerous to use magic, and I can't use my powers while transformed."

She helped him instead to fashion a sheath from his coat so he could carry the sword at his back.

"Thank you." He slid the sword into place. Then he surprised her by pulling her close and kissing her. Slowly. Thoroughly. He stole away her last remaining breath. "That's for staying alive until I could get to you," he murmured.

They set off again, leaving Merryn's emotions spinning. Several minutes later, her lips still tingled from his touch, and her heart pounded from the thrill of that kiss.

What are you doing, Merryn? she asked in silent wonder. *He's a church guard. You're a witch. You might as well be down a mineshaft igniting a wick while covered in gunpowder.*

"This is foolish," she muttered and then realized she'd said that aloud.

"No more than Agamore appearing in my hand," Braden said. "I'm no magician, Merryn, yet suddenly, everywhere, life seems magical. That includes my feelings for you."

He has feelings for me.

"What kind of feelings?" she asked in a gasp. At least she could blame her breathlessness on the running.

He gave her a quick sideways look from deep blue eyes that dared her to suggest she did not mirror his attraction.

"Oh," she said, "those feelings."

He jumped over a high log and turned to lift her up and over it, only he didn't set her back on her feet. Instead, he rested her against him.

"Yes, those feelings." He kissed her again, long and deep, and with a promise of much more soon.

Her legs wobbled dangerously when they touched ground. He laughed and hugged her close.

"We're in danger, my lord," she said in a stern tone, but rested her face against his strong shoulder. She didn't ever want to let go. *Just one more lovely embrace,* she promised herself, wrapping her arms around his solid form.

"Yes." He sounded troubled. "More so than I ever imagined possible."

She leaned back at that. "What do you mean?"

"It occurred to me back there that if warlocks can so effectively influence the church guards and likely the archbishop, who knows what else they are capable of? All of England could be endangered."

Merryn shivered at the worry in his voice. All this time, the war had only been between witches and the warlocks. She wasn't sure she was ready to invite the rest of the kingdom into their battle. Too many people could be hurt. "Let's keep going."

They ran a while longer and then Braden called another halt. She stopped, breathing heavy, feeling the start of a stitch at her side.

"How did you keep him from influencing you?" he asked, bent over, hands on knees, breathing as heavily as she.

"I sensed his mind touch. It is not easy to discern. Your guards and your archbishop should not have been so influenced."

"What do you mean?"

"Humans react badly to Wyhcan mind magic. An ancient warlock once postulated that it had something to do with a basic human need to exercise free will. I do not understand how a warlock could have so effectively directed this event."

Braden flexed each of his legs.

Watching him, she followed suit, for every muscle ached in protest.

"Can they have discovered a way to better control their mind magic?" he asked.

"He claimed as much." She walked about the area stretching out her arms. "For centuries, warlocks have been working on a spell to make their mind magic more successful against humans." The idea that they might have succeeded terrified her.

"Can anything be done to help the church guards?"

"One of our healing witches might be able to break the spell."

He whipped her around to face him. "Merryn, that is indeed good news. Can this truly be done?"

She feared she had no easy answer. "We would need to study the problem. Even if a cure were possible, your guards may not tolerate a witch working on them. Also, there are too many who have been bespelled."

He released her with a sigh.

"We should keep going," she said. "The witches were to meet me a league from their coven. Shouldn't be much longer."

With a nod, he took her hand and off they went. The next time they stopped, he leaned against a tree trunk, pulling her to lean beside him and asked, "How about working on one person?"

Dizzy from the constant running and fear, she dropped her head onto his shoulder. It took a moment to remember what they'd been talking about. *Right. The warlock spell on the guards.* "Do you have someone in mind?"

"The Archbishop of Canterbury. He's the only one who, once he's free of warlock influence, can command all the affected guards to submit to a witch's care."

The daring idea stunned Merryn.

A cracking of a nearby branch had them both turning in alarm. Braden drew his sword and pushed Merryn behind him.

Foolish man. If a warlock were nearby, she could defend them better than Braden, even with his magic sword. Well, perhaps not better, but certainly as well.

"Who's he?" a woman's voice asked from behind a wide hawthorn bush.

"Come out and identify yourself," Braden countered.

The woman peeked around the bush, looking worriedly from Merryn to Braden. "I'm Branwyn. I'm to guide Ms. Pendraven to where the others have convened." She gave Braden a suspicious glare and added, "Alone."

Merryn stepped around Braden to face the witch. "This is Lord Braden." She indicated his sword and he obligingly lowered his weapon.

"He wears the ring of the Green Cross!" With a squeal, Branwyn returned behind the bush. "We're surely doomed."

"You were doomed the moment your coven made that foolish pact with the warlocks," Merryn replied with impatience. "Now come out and speak to us."

"The church guards are the ones that burned our building," Branwyn protested from behind cover.

Merryn gave a heavy sigh. "Though Mattock denied it, it must have been him who talked the guards into igniting the building and then he had to have magicked the fire to ensure you couldn't escape."

There was still no sign Branwyn intended to step out from behind the bush.

Braden shrugged and put away his sword.

"Who are you going to trust, Branwyn?" Merryn asked, losing what little remained of her patience. "How sound has your own or your sage's judgment proven to be in the past few days? I'm your coven protectress and I tell you it is safe to face me. Now come out this instant!"

After a moment of silence, when Merryn half expected Branwyn to have fled, the witch came out of hiding.

Her gaze was still suspiciously planted on Braden, but her timid steps brought her up to Merryn.

"Where are the other witches?" Merryn asked.

Branwyn pointed. "That way."

"Good. Now, while we go join them, tell us about Trystan." Matching words to action, Merryn set a brisk pace. Both her companions quickly followed.

"Were you sent to Callington to steal him for the warlocks?" Merryn asked. "Why didn't his father just ask the mother to return him?"

"He did! She insisted the boy must be baptized first. That riled not only Mattock, but Dewer, too, and started the trouble."

"Did Dewer steal Trystan then?" Braden asked.

"He sent his dark fae to take the boy," Branwyn said.

"How did hellhounds get inside a church?" Merryn's gaze swerved to Braden's sword as she remembered its unexpected appearance at the Fishguard coven. "A lot has been happening of late that shouldn't be possible."

"The hounds swarmed in through the bell tower entrance," Branwyn said. "I don't know how they got in there. The building is falling apart so they could have stolen in through a myriad of openings."

"As with demons, are churches normally safe from fae, too?" Braden asked, with a raised eyebrow.

"One dedicated to a saint is supposed to be protected against all supernatural beings."

"Including witches and warlocks?" he asked. "Then how were you able to enter Saint Agatha's church? As had this witch, as well as Trystan, who is a warlock. His mother, too, is a witch. Is that because the protection in that church failed?"

"Only humans can enter without the express permission of the saint," Merryn explained.

"Permission?" Braden looked thoroughly confused. Then he slowly nodded. "That's who you were talking to outside the church doors."

Merryn nodded, pleased at how quickly he grasped events. "Saint Agatha didn't say the dark fae had taken Trystan, though," she added with a frown. "Why not?"

"Probably embarrassed her building is in such sad disorder," Branwyn suggested.

"Another reason to see to that church's rebuilding," Merryn said. "Once this matter of Trystan has been resolved."

"Did you see the dark fae take the boy?" he asked.

"No, I didn't, my lord. I'd positioned myself near Trystan hoping to somehow halt the proceedings. When everything went black, I reached for him, thinking this was my chance. He wasn't there. By the time light was restored, the dark fae had left and the boy was gone. Then his mother set up one heavenly racket."

"So we don't know who took him," Braden said.

"The warlocks think I did," Branwyn cried. "I didn't!"

Merryn shook her head at her companions' utter obtuseness on this subject. Unable to contain herself, she spoke in the tone of someone responding to the question, *What color is the sky?* "Dewer took him."

Braden turned her to face him and spoke in a gentle voice. "We don't know that for certain, Merryn."

"I know," she replied, thumping her chest with a fist.

Braden stared at her in silence and asked, "Could your grief be swaying your judgment?"

The question struck her like a slap. She shook off his condescending hold and stepped away, her blood roiling hotter than when he'd kissed her. Just because he had learnt a sliver of her history, it didn't mean he knew her every rationale. He knew *nothing* when it came to Dewer.

Her words poured out like hot lava. "Who else? Who else is vile enough to attack a defenseless child? Who else controls the dark fae? Who else would have sent those hellhounds after you in London? He's probably found out by now that the warlocks asked the Church to send the Dove after him in retribution."

"The Dove! The bird of death?" Branwyn's voice spiked as her gaze swerved to Braden.

"I wasn't sent after Dewer," Braden spoke in his hatefully reasonable tone, studiously ignoring the Fishguard witch slowly backing toward Merryn. "Sutton sent me after the Coven at Callington."

"Why?" Branwyn practically shrieked the question.

"To retrieve the boy," Merryn reminded him. Why had Branwyn plastered herself to her side?

"Which I intend to," he said.

"Not if you can't see the truth when it's glaring at you."

Branwyn tugged at her sleeve.

"What's becoming glaringly obvious, Miss Pendraven," Braden continued, and she cringed at his formal use of her last name, "is that your relationship with this Dewer goes deeper than you've thus far let on."

His arms crossed and eyes narrowed, he studied her with that inscrutable look she now hated. In fact, she couldn't remember one agreeable thing about him.

"How well do you know this man?" he asked.

Branwyn tugged again.

Merryn waved her off like an annoying fly. "Warlock."

"Warlock then."

"Evil warlock."

The corner of his lips twitched with the first hint of humor, but he valiantly controlled any urge to smile. Merryn remembered one thing she did like about this domineering church guard. He had nice lips.

Branwyn's continuous tug finally broke through to her. "What is it?"

"If you're right, then we need to steal Trystan back from Dewer and return him to his father, or there will be no peace between my coven and the warlocks ever again."

"How do we do that?" Braden looked none too pleased with either of his witchly companions. "Even if Dewer has the boy, we don't know where he's hidden him."

"Black Mountain," Branwyn and Merryn replied in unison. They looked at each other and nodded in acknowledgement of that conclusion.

"Dewer's home is a tower hidden in the Black Mountain on the southern border of Wales," Branwyn explained. "It's where he took–" She stopped abruptly.

"My brother," Merryn finished through clenched teeth. "Where my parents died trying to free him."

"You're definitely not going there," Braden said in a tone of finality.

Now he sounded like Aunt Morwena. Of course, they must chase down Dewer to his lair.

"I am going, my lord," she said, reverting to his formal title. This time, neither Braden nor her aunt would stop her.

"She won't be going alone," Branwyn put in, linking fingers with Merryn's left hand in a sign of solidarity. "I will accompany her as finding Trystan is my only hope of saving my coven. I failed them once and I can't afford to do it again. The warlocks can be most unforgiving. None of us will be safe until that boy is returned to his father, unharmed."

Braden raised and lowered his arms in frustration. "If we all go traipsing up there, Dewer is sure to be alerted. We'd have a better chance if I go alone."

"No!" Merryn and Branwyn answered in unison again.

She frowned at the Fishguard witch, not liking how often they seemed in agreement. This was the witch who had conspired with warlocks not so long ago. She disengaged her hand and stepped away.

Just then, bushes rustled nearby. The Fishguard sage came out from the cover of the surrounding greenery. Behind her followed the rest of the Fishguard witches. Merryn counted eleven.

"We grew tired of waiting," the sage said, looking contemptuously at Merryn, Branwyn and Braden, as if all of her coven's misfortunes were their doing. "As for Black Mountain, we all go, or none will. I do not have faith in any of you to handle this matter with the proper delicacy that will be required to resolve the issue of young Trystan."

Merryn bit her tongue hard on her response. Of all the nerve, to accuse Merryn and Braden of indelicacy when it was this sage and her coven who had attempted to interfere with Trystan's baptism.

"I'm glad you've joined us," Merryn said instead. "We're far enough from Fishguard. Speed is now more important than remaining in human form. Time to fly."

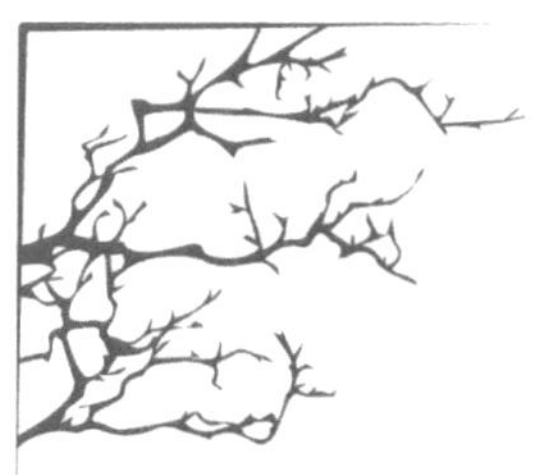

Chapter 10

"*Trouble approaches,*" *Trevor, the tallest and darkest mountain in all of southern Wales, rumbled.*

"*I've been expecting it for days,*" *Eionion, the Devil's Tablet, said in a dour tone.*

Eionion, a flat projection of rock at the mountain top, had a long history of witnessing trouble - spurting blood, terrified screams and powerful words of invocations, though the words were often muddled.

On those rare occasions when a ceremony was performed correctly, Eionion had the opportunity to touch the infinite as darkness consumed a soul or the void loomed close.

"*Hope they plan to clean up after themselves this time,*" *he muttered.*

"*The coming rain should wash you off proper,*" *Trevor replied.* "*Clouds gather overhead. They, too, sense trouble and have been grumbling about it all day.*"

"*What do you think the problem with the master is this time?*" *Eionion asked.* "*Another plea to the dark one? A battle for control? Petty theft?*"

"*Not sure. He seems of two minds about things. First, he opens the portal to the underworld, then he closes it. I hate it when he can't make up his mind.*"

"*Is he being nostalgic about that witch again?*"

"*Most likely,*" *Trevor said in his ponderous tone.* "*Wish he'd get over it. Problem is, each time he opens that blasted gate, dark fae roar out as if they've been invited to a grand feast instead of to their doom. Also, no one thinks of the mess they leave behind. A regular earthly corpse may take weeks to decompose, but a dark fae takes forever to break down and they give off a stink I never seem able to entirely shed.*"

"*You have my commiseration,*" *Eionion said with deep sympathy.* "*Been there, sniffed that.*"

WITHIN TWO HOURS, MERRYN'S group arrived at the clearing where her carriage awaited. Those who could not fly had been carried by the larger birds. Merryn stepped behind a tree to shift back to her human self and clothe herself in private.

Before Braden would allow Merryn to change him back into a wren, Merryn had to agree to give him the dignity of changing back with clothes intact, especially in front of witnesses. So, while most of the Fishguard witches chose to remain in their changed forms to conserve their magic, Branwyn alone returned to her human state. She then changed Lord Braden back with clothes intact.

The groom and post boy lounging beside the conveyance straightened and nodded to Merryn as she approached, before looking with obvious curiosity at the rabble accompanying her – cats, rabbits, deer and a flurry of birds congregating around the carriage.

Ignoring Merryn, Braden hurried to his horse's side, as if greeting an old dear friend. Now he had access to his steed, Nadeem, he planned to ride the rest of the way.

Merryn released the spell on the carriage doors.

The pixie was the first to spy her through the window. Cri cried out in excitement and flew to encircle Merryn in obvious joy. "I said they'd both be all right," she called back to Aunt Gwen. "They've brought friends!" With excited claps, the pixie flew over to say hello to the odd grouping of animals and birds.

With the groom's assistance, Aunt Gwen stepped outside. Merryn gave her a fierce hug.

The old woman held her just as tightly for a good long while. Finally releasing Merryn and cupping her cheeks with trembling fingers, she said, "I thought I'd never see you again." There were tears in her faded blue eyes. "It felt as if I were saying goodbye to your mother all over again."

"I'm sorry to have worried you." Merryn added, "Thank you for sending Lord Braden after me. He helped us all to survive."

He nodded to her, surprised pleasure in his eyes at her acknowledgement.

"Did you find that troublesome warlock boy?" Aunt Gwen asked.

"Not yet. We're headed to Black Mountain to look for him."

"Dewer's tower?" she asked in a frightened voice and changed into a wren.

Merryn picked her up and soothed her aunt's feathers, muttering soft comforting words. It took her aunt a few moments to gather herself, stop chirping in a fretful way and return to her human self.

"Merryn, dear." Her aunt's chin still quivered. "That's where your mother died. I will not have it be your grave, too."

"I have to stop him."

"Your parents couldn't." Aunt Gwen sounded uncharacteristically angry. "What makes you think you can?"

"I have help. Lord Braden and all these witches are coming with me. This time, we will be successful. I will return."

"I refuse to wait here while you go off on your own again. If you're going to Black Mountain, so am I." She snapped her fingers at the groom and ordered him to harness the horses.

Her aunt's lips were set in a determined line. The groom wrung his hands with obvious uncertainty about what to do.

Merryn exchanged a worried look with Braden.

"There's no point talking over my head with his lordship either," her aunt said. "I'll not listen to either of you, I shouldn't have listened to your parents when they insisted on going off after that rogue. I'm coming and that's final."

It was a good two days ride between here and southern Wales. Too far to fly or they'd arrive in no shape to face Dewer. Better to take the longer route, perhaps even fool any watching warlocks into thinking they were returning to Cornwall, then arrive refreshed at Black Mountain.

In the interval, perhaps, she could also talk her aunt into waiting somewhere safe instead of traipsing into the Devil's lair along with the rest of them. "Very well, Aunt. We shall all go."

She gave her nod of agreement to the hesitant groom who swung around and pulled the post boy along with him toward the horses.

"Where are you all going?" The pixie flew over. "May I come, too?"

Merryn rolled her eyes and gave up on the idea of accomplishing this without stragglers.

Even Braden's shoulders sagged as if in defeat. He came over and rubbed her back with a sympathetic hand. That felt good.

He leaned closer and whispered in her ear. "I don't like all this company. I preferred it when we worked alone."

Merryn's cheeks heated at his seductive tone. The company of her aunt, the pixie and the Fishguard witches might prove to be the best chaperonage she'd ever had. Wasn't he the one who'd once insisted she needed such protection? The irony of it made her smile.

Under Aunt Gwen's interested stare, Braden took the hint he trespassed too close. Instead of quickly withdrawing, the impudent man furtively skimmed his hand sensually down Merryn's back before he stepped away.

Aroused and then bereft, frustration descended to curdle in her belly. "I'll ride with my aunt in the carriage," she said, sounding shorter than she'd intended. She looked at the gathered milieu and softened her tone. "Anyone care to join us?"

Two of the rabbits, a few cats and a rodent took up her offer, while to the dismay of the groom, several birds landed on top of the carriage.

Braden mounted his horse. "Let's be off then."

MERRYN'S CARRIAGE MADE several stops at local inns along the way. To Braden's surprise, at each break, while the number of animals and birds present caused a stir, it did not seem to frighten anyone.

In London, at the very least, the constabulary might have been called out at such an odd event. As in Cornwall, the Welsh seemed to take unusual occurrences with a pragmatic rather than hysterical approach.

Could this acceptance be partly due to the presence in the region of witches and warlocks for the past three hundred years? They probably already believe in "the gentry." Wouldn't have been much of a leap to believe in witches and warlocks, too.

During their flight, Merryn said her people were well hidden, always present but imperceptible to humans as anything more than a neighbor, a friend, a fellow worker. With each stop, however, Braden's doubt about that assertion grew.

It was close to midnight on the second day when they arrived at a small farm situated on a plateau half way up Black Mountain. All the way there, Aunt Gwen refused to allow Merryn to go on without her. Braden approached the farmer's house to ask for shelter and food. The hope was to use this farm as their base, while they explored the mountaintop backing it.

A sheep farmer lived here with his wife and two sons. The sleepy fellow greeted Braden with a raised eyebrow and a loaded blunderbuss. Braden, despite having difficulty understanding the man's accent, managed to impress the farmer with his correct gentlemanly manner and sufficient coin. He soon put him at ease enough that the farmer offered a room in his home and use of the barn.

Braden accepted the room on behalf of Mrs. Truscott and the Fishguard sage, who had agreed to share a bed if one were available. He, Merryn, Branwyn, the groom, post boy and all the animals and birds then headed for the barn.

The farmer, apparently delighted with the coins Braden paid him, agreed to bring out bread and cheese to tide his guests until breakfast.

They'd posted the groom outside to await the farmer with the promised food, so the poor man wouldn't receive the shock of his life at seeing a dozen transformed witches encamped in his barn. Even Braden had a difficult time with that fact, not to mention the floating ball of light near the ceiling illuminating the building as if the moon itself had been enticed inside to light the place.

The groom returned with their meal. Merryn stood in line to take her portion without looking at Braden once. She'd made a place for herself in a stall he couldn't get to without passing all the other witches. There wasn't a hope of him being alone with her tonight.

With a dissatisfied grunt, he took his meal and, along with the groom and post boy, climbed to the loft. He found a quiet place away from the two who leaned over to gape and argue about the attributes of the various witches. While eating their fare, they discussed their chances between winning favors from a witch and being turned into a toad.

Braden rested his sword beside him, within easy reach in case of trouble. This close to the rogue warlock they tracked, he didn't feel at ease no matter how many wards Merryn said the witches had placed around the farm. To his mind, Agamore trumped any number of spells.

So much could go wrong. While everyone slept, Dewer could discover his mountain had been invaded. The nervous farmer could at this moment be racing to fetch the local authorities. Though Braden trusted Merryn with his life, what did he really know about these Fishguard witches? Most troubling of all, the lingering disagreement between Merryn and himself was like a sharp stone in his boot.

Despite his deep exhaustion, Braden munched on the bread and cheese. Once everyone else settled, would Merryn come to see him? With his back to a straw bale, he pondered various ways of separating Merryn from her witches. Footsteps sounded on the ladder. The other two men scrambled away from the ledge but Braden edged over to see who came.

Merryn, balancing three tin cups on a platter, climbed up to the loft.

Yes! His heart sang out. A warm glow filled him at her thoughtful gesture of bringing them drinks. Lit by a divine glow, she moved with unassuming grace up the ladder.

He then frowned, wondering how she avoided spilling a drop or tipping her tray. A look at her feet showed the rim of her skirts rising before each step. The tray, too, floated, with her hand merely skimming its underside.

Since discovering the truth about Merryn and her people, Braden had reassessed his beliefs about magic. He no longer thought of the source of magic as evil. Agamore alone testified that power could come from good, too. If indeed lines of magic were all around them, then learning to tap that bountiful source had its advantages.

The convenience factor alone made magic a useful talent. No doubt the witches sleeping below were lying on comfortable beds, ones that didn't poke one in the back or itch at the neck like his bed of straw.

Still, on closer inspection, Merryn looked tired – all the power she'd expended recently must have exhausted her.

Once she reached the top, she nodded to him but went over to the other side of the loft. The two rapscallions who'd been ogling the witches sat up and graciously accepted the offered beverages.

Finally, she came his way. "Braden."

She knelt and extended the last cup to him before setting down her empty tray.

Milk never tasted so good. The thoughtful woman had added a drop of brandy.

He imagined drinking a cup every night in bed; the delicious taste shared between kisses. Merryn smiling at him, as she did now. A sultry smile.

He swallowed convulsively and blinked to keep her face in focus. The cup in his hand was half drained. "That's good brandy."

"I thought it might help you forget your worries and assist you to sleep," she whispered. "You've had a harrowing day."

"We've all had a harrowing day." He leaned forward to steal a kiss. This was the tastiest milk he'd ever consumed. But the drink was slowing his thoughts. He drew back, swaying. "Merryn, how much liquor did you put in this?"

At her guilty look, he tossed away the rest of the milk, but too late, for he'd downed most of it.

"What else... besides brandy?"

She backed away saying, "Are all earls so suspicious?"

"Church guards are." He swore as his head tipped backward, heavy as a boulder. He straightened with difficulty and made a grab for her but she easily evaded his reach. He fell forward. Barely able to hold himself up. Past her, the groom and post boy were flat on the ground, snoring.

"Can't go...night...alone." The words come out in an incoherent slur.

"I won't be alone," she said. "You must not accompany me." Her hand brushed against his hair, gentle as a lover's touch. He grabbed for it but she moved out of reach.

"Braden," she whispered, "he's the powerful son of an underworld fae queen and a warlock. As magnificent as your sword makes you, he can still twist your thoughts without you realizing he's doing it. You could hurt us thinking you're attacking Dewer. Or if he attacks you, I might become distracted from my work. I'm sorry, but you have to stay here. Stay safe."

"Have you told him yet?" The pixie popped onto Merryn's shoulder. She gave a startled squeak as his face dropped into the straw. "You've killed him!"

"I have not. I gave him a little something to sleep."

He heard the pixie and Merryn argue in low tones. Their words echoed in his head like bubbles colliding and popping.

"Dangerss," he mumbled and got a mouth full of straw for his effort, which made the words seem even more slurred. "Blsss!"

"He swore!" the pixie said in a shocked tone.

"Are you coming?" From below. One of the witches? She spoke the truth. Not going alone. He was infinitely thankful for that, but why didn't she want his help? Didn't she trust him? Had she ever?

"Shall I stay with him?" the pixie asked.

"If you wish, but he'll be fine and we could use your help."

"I don't like the dark fae," the pixie muttered, flying by Braden's head before flitting out of his line of sight. "They have no conscience. They will rip at a girl's clothes, never mind how pretty it is."

Leaving. Must stop. Can't move, can't talk, can't help.

Chatter from below and above, like bees from a hive. Then a sharp order, like a whip cracking.

"Silence!"

Merryn. She would die. Like her mother. He would have to console Aunt Gwen. Console himself. *No!*

The barn door closed. How long would this drug incapacitate him? Minutes? Hours? Days?

His gaze flicked around the loft and fell on Agamore, resting beside the bale he'd leaned against. Only a short distance away. It might as well have been a league.

Even if it was within reach, he couldn't lift his hand, let alone the sword. It was blessed, God's special gift to him. It could perform miracles. It had come magically once before when he needed it. He opened his right fist and called with his mind, *Agamore.*

The sword remained still, an inanimate object.

Useless.

Why won't you work? Then he remembered. Prayer. Each time before it flared, he'd been praying.

Please Lord, allow me to help her, he pleaded. *I can't bear to lose her. I love her.*

The sword blazed like the North Star, lighting the loft brighter than the witches' magic ball of light. His mind cleared like clouds in a night sky dispersed by a fierce wind to allow starlight to shine through.

Slowly, he sat up, testing his strength and mobility, shocked by the sword's power, yet accepting of it. Agamore floated over to rest its hilt in his grip.

You don't think I'm capable of defending myself, eh, Merryn? Of protecting you? Standing, he whipped the sword sideways. The bale beside him fell apart, sliced in two perfect halves.

You think Dewer can cloud my judgment?

Agamore proved it could conquer her drugs, so why not warlock mind magic as well? He grinned with supreme smugness. *Let us see who needs saving tonight.*

He sheathed the sword at his back. The action dimmed the glow from the sword but still gave him enough light to see by. Feeling fully capable of defeating any warlock or witch who barred his way, he straddled the ladder and slid straight to the ground. He whistled for Nadeem.

The black stallion whinnied in acknowledgement from down the darkened corridor. A sharp kick and a stall door crashed open and then the stallion cantered along the corridor to meet his master.

Once he'd saddled his horse, they rode out of the farm on the lookout for a pathway. Everywhere appeared the same in the dark. He considered his options for a moment and then touched his hand to the sword's hilt. *Which way?*

The hilt shifted. *Left.*

He nudged Nadeem in that direction. "We must be quick, my friend. For the lady is in need of our aid, whether she will admit it or not."

Before this night ended, he intended to prove he was not a liability. *You will never mistrust me again, Merryn Pendraven.*

The light from the sword was akin to carrying a lantern at his back. Despite that illumination, and Nadeem's sure-footedness, the path was still treacherous. He wondered how Merryn and her witches made it up here on foot and then remembered her climbing that ladder with her platter of doctored milk.

Now he'd regained his strength by his own wits and God's grace, the memory of her careful climb with the intention of keeping him safe while she walked into danger no longer irked. In fact, the memory made him chuckle. Merryn Pendraven was an enchantress in every sense of the word. She was a conundrum. A powerful witch who could lift her skirts without touching them and change herself into a raven at will, yet she was unable to change herself back to human form with her clothes intact.

His humor dimmed when he pondered their future. She was a *witch*. How would he introduce her to his family? His hand tightened on the reins and Nadeem stopped short.

Braden gave a gentle kick to his steed's rump. "One worry at a time, my friend. First save the girl. Then introduce her to mother."

When the path became too steep to ride, he dismounted and led Nadeem. A heavy mist made it feel as if he were climbing blind. He prayed all the way that he wouldn't topple off the edge. The only thing guiding him onward was the touch of his sword, which never wavered when he asked for direction.

He didn't question Agamore's guidance. The answers felt as natural as the urgings of his instinct, and had the sense of feeling *right*. As if a divine hand guided him.

After an hour's strenuous climb, he topped a rise and came across a dark slab of rock. As right as his sword felt, this rock had the sense of being wrong. He halted so abruptly Nadeem bumped into his back. Every inch of Braden's soul repelled him from going closer to that black tablet. He gave the slab a wide berth.

Nadeem, too, hugged Braden's other side, keeping away from that rock.

"I don't like it either, Nadeem," Braden murmured soothingly. "Come along, boy, let's quit this area as quickly as we can."

The next curve in the bend went upward again and the mist drifted away, giving a clear view of the summit.

At the mountain's pinnacle, a lone black tower rose into the sky where it ended in closely spaced crenelations, as if a raised arm reached up to heaven with a clenched fist.

Witches surrounded the building.

"Wait here," he said to Nadeem, and raced up to the landing to find the Fishguard witches holding vigil around the tower. Each extended a broom, until they linked one to the other, forming a complete circle. Their chant created a shield that enclosed the tower.

The witches' singing made his eardrums thrum in protest. With each stanza, the light around the tower grew bright then dimmed, and grew bright again, as if the witches' power was being tested and they fought back.

Merryn, who had been standing behind the witches, calmly strode through the barrier until she stood inside the circle, facing Dewer alone. Braden's pulse shot up at the danger in which she'd placed herself.

With hands covering his ears to shut out the chanting, Braden followed Merryn beyond that magical circle. He was forcibly bounced back onto his rump. Frustrated at that failure to reach Merryn, he scrambled to his feet and hurried around the tower, searching for a weak spot in the circle.

At the very back, he stopped, surprised to see a flat checker board with giant chess pieces arranged as if in the midst of a game. He shook off the distraction and kept circling, testing the clasp of the witches.

"Let me through," he shouted, but his voice was drowned out by their continuous music.

He drew his sword and thrust it between the witches. Agamore pierced the barrier without hindrance, but when he followed its passage, he was shot him backwards so hard, he slid a few feet.

"Merryn!" he called. "Let me in."

She looked back and frowned. "You shouldn't have come. Return to the barn where it's safe."

She'd barely finished speaking when the tower door opened and a horde of black hounds streamed out, snarling and howling. The barguest was at their lead.

Braden's heart shuddered in shock. "No! Let me through. This sword can stop those hounds. It's done it before."

Everyone ignored him, even the hounds.

The hellhounds paced Merryn, testing her mettle with sudden leaps. She fought back with a flick of her arm, sending each skidding backwards. Surely she couldn't withstand an all-out attack? They would kill and ravage her flesh as he stood by helpless.

The chanting grew fierce and seemed to distract the hounds, some even lowered their heads and covered their ears with their paws. The leader, the barguest, merely shook his head as if flicking off an annoying nit and continued to circle Merryn.

Braden recognized a witch he'd spoken to before. "Branwyn, listen to me," he pleaded, "I've fought these demons before. I know how to best them. Let me through."

For a moment, her uncertain gaze flickered toward him. Then she returned her attention to the fight.

A hound leapt at Merryn. She sent a flash of light that scorched his hind end. He yelped and rolled on the ground, desperate to get away from her next strike. While Merryn was thus distracted, the barguest snuck up behind her. It jumped onto her back and toppled her to the ground.

"She's going to die," he shouted to Branwyn and the witch let go of her partner's broom, covering her eyes.

With a howl of triumph, Braden charged through. His sword flared as if recognizing old foes.

The hounds took one look at him and his sword and raced for the open door. The barguest, pinning Merryn to the ground, merely bared its teeth, dripping drool.

"Touch her and, by God, you will die," Braden promised, circling the two. "That I swear."

Merryn took that moment to magically thrust the huge beast off her back and sent it tumbling across the courtyard. While it rolled trying to gain its feet, Braden helped her rise. The barguest turned to face them with a snarl.

"Enough," a voice called from above.

The barguest appeared as startled as Braden and Merryn by the interruption. It gave a howl of protest.

"Inside, you worthless cur," his master snarled.

Though he'd only met the man once and briefly, Braden recognized Dewer. He was Braden's height but with darker hair and sharper features.

A harmless young blade out to make his mark in Town had been Braden's earlier assessment. Now he wondered how much of that evaluation had been the result of warlock mind magic influence.

The barguest still hesitated, glaring at Merryn.

"Inside," Dewer ordered the beast. "And pray I don't finish you off myself for missing your mark, twice now, by my count."

The barguest gave Braden and Merryn one last menacing snarl before obeying.

The tower door slammed shut behind it.

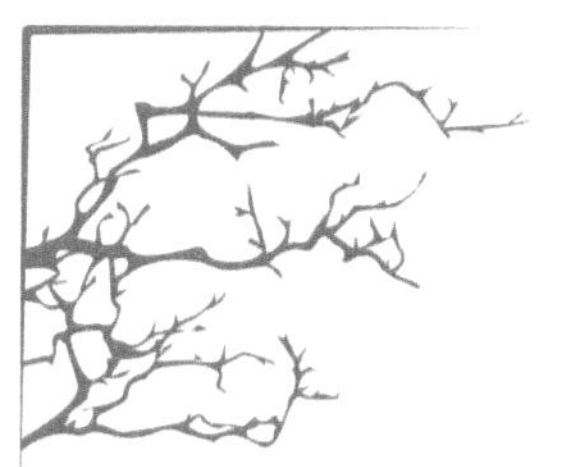

Chapter 11

Alaster, the smallest of the dark fae hounds, positioned himself as far from the others as he could inside the tower's entry room. Fights in such confined quarters were common and he didn't want to accidentally get caught up in one if he nodded off.

The stone floor was cold. Everything in this upper world was hard and uncomfortable. In the underworld, there was cushy moss, dark nooks and warm corners to hide in. Also, goblins and demons, of course. To Alaster's way of thinking, one could forgive the occasional bad turn in exchange for a few choice grassy nooks to snooze in.

As the barguest strolled into the tower entry room, Farfur, the hound closest to him, exclaimed, "You're still alive!"

Alaster snorted. The foolish hound sounded surprised. Of all of them, the barguest, the shape-changing goblin that was not a true hellhound, was the only one he'd expected to survive after the church guard arrived.

Behind the barguest, the door slammed shut of its own accord and the four hellhounds jumped in fright.

The barguest sat with a thump, his tail thwacking the ground as if intending to crack open a portal back to the underworld.

Alaster gave the barguest a worried look. "I suppose we shouldn't have run inside and left you alone with the guard. Sorry, Sax."

The barguest snarled his response.

Alaster skidded further back, wanting to plant himself at the far curve of the rough tower wall, except Bartos was there. The old hound sat awkwardly, licking around his wound. His back was still sore from where the church guard's sword had grazed him in London town. The constant pain made him bad tempered.

The master had repeatedly tried to heal Bartos, but every time he sealed the cut, by morning the wound would be open.

A glance at the festering sore and Alaster cringed. He wasn't surprised when the old hound gave a low snarl and kicked out. He obligingly retreated until they no longer touched. "The guard was carrying his cursed sword again."

"Think the master will send us home because of this?" Farfur asked from the other side of the room.

Alaster looked up in hope. No one answered and the moment passed. He sighed, resting his head on his front paws. They didn't call Farfur the "optimist" for nothing. Alaster surmised that if they ever returned home, it would be in pieces.

"It's that guard's sword that sent me running," Farfur added. "Did anyone else hear it singing? A rousing battle song, louder than the chanting witches. Made me want to sing along until I realized it sang about dismembering me."

"It's just a sword, you cowards," Sax growled. "It will break like any other mortal weapon."

"Are you daft?" Alaster asked before thinking that through.

Sax lunged for him.

He cringed, but since the old wounded hound was between him and the wall, he had no place to retreat. "You can't kill us," he pleaded, voice shaking. "We're short-handed."

Sax growled but then with a warning shake of his head that sent drool flinging, he stalked away and crouched by the door.

"I only meant none of us were safe out there with that sword," Alaster muttered.

"None of you hounds, perhaps," Sax said. "I'm not so easy to dispose of. If the usurper hadn't stopped me, the witch would be dead by now."

"You with her," Farfur said. "If you'd killed that witch, the usurper, I mean the master would have finished you off before that sword ever touched you. His order was to frighten, not kill. Also, don't call him the usurper, or I might, too, in his presence and that could be fatal."

"My orders come from higher than that half-breed fae-warlock." Sax's tone was layered with contempt. "I've been instructed to ensure the protectress doesn't survive our next encounter."

Alaster guessed from whom those orders came. The Queen of the Underworld, Dewer's mother, wasn't someone he'd want to cross.

The four hounds looked at each other with worry.

"I hate family quarrels," Alaster muttered. "They never end well. One never knows whom to trust."

"GOOD EVENING, MISS Pendraven," Dewer called down. "May I say you look particularly fetching this fine evening? Is that gown in periwinkle? Hard to see past the glow that surrounds you. What brings you to my humble abode?"

Merryn couldn't believe he was making social chitchat. He sounded as if they were both still in that ballroom in London. "Release Trystan this instant."

"Wish I could," Dewer replied with abject regret. Then he spoilt the effort by chuckling. "No, that's a lie. If I had that boy, you can be quite certain I would never let him go. He's much too difficult to catch."

"Fiend!" Merryn wished she could simply blast him into little pieces. The witch's code forbade harming another, especially without provocation. Fists clenched, she felt she could build a solid case to defend herself at a coven summit on exactly how positively provocative Dewer's innocent-sounding words really were.

"Do you think we should antagonize him like that?" Braden whispered, obviously unaware of the salt he rubbed into her open sore. He indicated the closed tower door. "Have you forgotten his hounds are behind that door?"

"I will not negotiate with a madman."

"I see you've lowered your standard for friendship. Travelling with a church guard no less. I thought better of your taste, Miss Pendraven." Dewer was all charm, and the sensual way he kept pronouncing "Miss Pendraven" rasped on her nerves. A look at Braden showed he didn't much care for the warlock's tone either.

"How well do you know Dewer?" Braden asked.

"That hardly matters," she said, but a guilty flush heated her cheeks and appeared to set off his temper.

He carefully sheathed his sword at his back, his narrowed gaze calling her a liar. Did he still hold a grudge about her drugging him? He'd overcome the potion quickly enough. Why was it she always underestimated him?

He formally bowed to the bounder. "Dewer. We meet again."

"Braden. I wonder how the archbishop would take to the news, my lord, that you're consorting with witches. Pray, forgive me. I am being remiss in my welcome. I would invite you in, but then I would be forced to kill you, and that seems such a shame, for you're all proving to be enormously entertaining."

"He obviously doesn't fear us," Braden murmured to Merryn. "Just how powerful is he?"

"I've not been serenaded before, Miss Pendraven," Dewer's insidious voice interrupted her answer. "That chanting is beautiful."

Merryn resisted the urge to fling a hefty rock at the devious warlock.

Braden indicated the surrounding witches. "Is their singing still needed? Couldn't we use their power to better use? Such as breaking through that door or restraining his hounds?"

"It's only through their music that Dewer is unable to reach us with his mind," Merryn whispered back. "If not for them, I would never have seen the door opening or the hounds coming for me."

Braden's eyes widened with comprehension.

Good! Merryn hoped he grasped the grave danger he was in. "Of all of us, you are the most vulnerable to Dewer's warlock powers. That is why I chose to leave you behind."

"Drugged me, you mean."

That didn't sound understanding or forgiving. She added, "I was concerned for your welfare."

"You're forgiven, but we will finish this discussion later."

She shivered at the ominous note in his voice. By her protective actions, had she destroyed his growing trust in her?

He nodded upwards. "The man takes the hampering of his warlock ability with good grace. I doubt I'd be as genial under the same circumstances." He then called up, "Sir, if you don't have the boy, why will you not let us in?"

"Would you let someone barge into your home uninvited, my lord?"

"I wouldn't set demons on them."

"You might set your dogs loose."

"You began this battle in London," Braden said in a hard voice. "I recognized that barguest. The very same one that almost killed Miss Pendraven just now attacked me in London, unprovoked."

Dewer smiled, unrepentant. "I accept your apology, sir."

"He's playing with us," Merryn said.

"I can see that," Braden said. "Stand aside and I'll see if I can get us inside."

"What about the hounds?"

"The sword can handle them." Braden put his shoulder to the door. He bounced back without budging the door.

"Let me try," Merryn said.

He gave her a startled look until she raised her eyebrow. "Oh, right." He bowed with a slight smile. "Have way."

Merryn raised her hand and pointed. A flare of light struck the door and it swung open. They saw the barguest sit up inside but before they could take a step, the door swung back shut.

With an angry glare up at Dewer, who merely grinned, Merryn pointed at the door again.

The moment it opened, Braden charged. Still, the door slammed shut on his face. He stepped back tenderly patting at his nose. She would have offered sympathy but it likely would have pricked his pride.

"Such persistence," Dewer called down. "We could make an incredible team, Miss Pendraven, if you would but reconsider my proposal."

"What proposal?" Braden stepped back to look up at Dewer.

"Why, marriage, of course," Dewer replied. "Did the lady not tell you we were almost betrothed?"

"We were no such thing!" Merryn replied, her cheeks burning.

Braden stepped away from her.

"Don't listen to him," Merryn pleaded. "He's unable to use his mind magic so he plays with words instead. I never agreed to marry him."

"But he proposed?" He sounded stunned.

"I did, indeed," Dewer called down. "Very nicely too, on my knee, in the balcony, under the moonlight."

"You said you'd only met him once!" Now he sounded accusing.

She could have screamed at both of them. "Dewer wasn't serious."

"I was wholeheartedly serious, my dear," the fae-warlock said, sounding affronted. "Never doubt my sincerity. I was enchanted the moment I spied a miniature portrait Jonas had of you. He often regaled me with tales of his amazing sister. For years, I searched for an opportunity to meet you in person. Your coming out ball gave me the very chance I needed. How could I resist attending? The night we met, I fell in love. You danced like an angel and kissed..."

"Silence, sir," she said, having listened to his story in utter shock. "I never kissed him," she muttered in an aside to Braden but there was deep doubt in his eyes.

She shot Dewer a killing look. "We will not listen to any more of your lies. I am deeply ashamed I ever did. You will never again convince me that you truly care for me, so don't waste your breath."

Her shame at her response to this wretched warlock at their last meeting was not something she wished to relive, especially in front of Braden. Yet, the monster had forced her to do just that. She turned to Braden, tight lipped with frustration. "This is hardly the time or place to discuss my past. We must get Trystan out of there."

He gave her a grim nod that suggested this discussion, too, was postponed, not over. He indicated the door. "Open it."

"Are you sure?" she asked with concern, thinking of his tender nose.

"Yes!"

"No need to shout," she muttered and pointed.

The door flew open. This time he saw it rebound and fiercely kicked it. The door fell off its hinges and both he and Merryn ran in. Righting itself, the door shut behind them.

They stood inside a dark chamber, completely blind. Braden drew his sword but unlike on the mountainside, Agamore did not light the way. The hounds could attack now without difficulty, for they wouldn't see them coming.

Merryn raised her arm. "Light," she said and flames lit the top of a torch in her hand.

"Excellent," Braden murmured his approval, checking the shadowy corners.

Relief washed over her as she realized they were alone. No barguest. No hounds. No fae creatures of any kind. And no Dewer. Also, no Trystan.

"Perhaps the hounds went upstairs to Dewer's room," she suggested. "He probably has Trystan imprisoned somewhere near him. He could have brought the hounds upstairs as added protection."

"There's one way to find out." Braden pointed to a set of stairs that hugged the curved wall and stretched upward. "Shall we go say hello to your friend?"

His tone was teasing but the words made Merryn's blood roil. "He's not my friend!" Why must he bait her about Dewer? She hated that villain.

"May I?" Braden indicated the torch.

At her nod, he relieved her of it and led the way up the stone staircase. "The man's home is cold and bare," Braden murmured, "something to keep in mind when considering him as suitable husband material."

If he made one more comment about Dewer and her, she determined she'd give up trying to protect Braden and just hit him.

"If he actually proposed, he must have been serious in his intentions."

He had gone up too many steps to reach him with a solid blow. Teeth gritted, she lifted her skirts as she climbed. "Dewer is a mad man. Worse, he is a warlock. Nothing they say should ever be trusted."

"He loves you."

His confident comment threw her. Was he still under the influence of the drug she'd given him in his milk? Had he not heard a word she said about the untrustworthiness of warlocks? He sounded as mad as Dewer.

She took a deep breath so her words would come out even-tempered and rational. Someone had to bring sense into this conversation. "Dewer does not know how to love," she said with feeling. "Else he would have..." She bit off the rest of that, reconsidering the direction of her thoughts.

Braden halted halfway up to look at her with mounting suspicion. "Else he would have what, Miss Pendraven?"

Oh! We are back to Miss Pendraven are we? She glared at him in silence but since he made no move to go on she gave a huff of impatience. "Else he would have known how much Jonas meant to me and realized that harming him was something I could never forgive."

Merryn turned away, unable to keep tears from falling. Braden ran down the few steps that separated them and put his free arm around her. Pulling her close, he kissed her forehead.

Why must she love the way he held her? Kissed her? Cherished her?

"I'm sorry," he whispered, sounding miserable.

She swiped at her tears. "I'm glad to remember, for it fuels my anger at the monster upstairs."

"Good girl, that's the spirit."

"I don't wish to speak about that horrid proposal ever again," she warned him as they continued their ascent.

He gave her a silent look, obviously unwilling to promise any such thing.

They came to the first landing and another closed door. This one opened easily. Finding no one inside, they continued up. It was only on the third landing that they came across a door that would not open.

Braden stood back and gestured for Merryn to use her spell on it. She pointed. "Open," she commanded and it flew inward.

The door had opened to open air and a sheer drop off the mountain. Braden swiftly grabbed Merryn and drew her back, muttering curses at the warlock.

"We're inside his tower, he controls what happens here," she said, shaking in his grip.

"I almost lost you," he whispered, holding her tight.

"His power here is strong." She took a deep breath to level her tension. "He's probably less hampered inside by the chanting spell."

"How are we to find the boy then? Trystan could be anywhere. He could have been hidden in plain sight in any of those rooms we passed on our way up. We could even have walked through that entry room below past hounds and simply not known it."

Merryn shivered at that horrendous thought. "If so, why didn't the hounds attack us?"

"It's as I said before, Dewer doesn't mean you harm."

"If all this is illusion, he could be behind that door." Merryn pushed away to look up at him. "We just can't see it."

He nodded, obviously having come to the same conclusion. "I'll go first," he said, and handed her the torch. "In case I fall, you'll be in a better position to cushion my drop than I yours."

"Of course," Merryn replied, her eyes lighting with appreciation of that plan. She stepped aside and he reached for the door. Her hand touched his and he glanced at her with surprise. "I'm glad you trust me to keep you safe."

He nodded. "I trust you with my life, Merryn," he said, and opened the door. "Though I'm unsure about my heart."

BRADEN BELIEVED THAT if he fell, Merryn would save him. Still, he drew his sword and had to muster the courage to take that first step. The crags below looked sharp. He gulped past the fear choking him. Then he stepped into the abyss.

His right foot hit a floor and he jerked back. For a moment, he was baffled for he stood in mid-air, then the room swerved into view. A cozy, carpet-covered *solid* room.

Dewer turned from the window. "I didn't think you had that in you, my lord." The warlock's gaze exposed a flash of respect, or was it worry? Whatever the emotion, it was swiftly masked behind a condescending smirk that Braden would have loved to wipe away with a swift left punch.

Merryn stepped to Braden's left and Dewer's gaze, as if drawn to a shooting star, flew toward her. For a timeless moment, neither said a word, simply staring at each other. Then Dewer gave a deep bow. "Welcome to my home, Miss Pendraven."

He sounded abjectly humble. How often had he practiced saying those words?

However much she objected to the concept, every male instinct in Braden screamed that this man desired, adored, worshiped, Merryn. Dewer acting the polished adoring madman only flung fuel onto his jealousy.

Instinctively, he drew Merryn closer, wanting to establish his claim. His free hand intimately curved around her waist. To her credit, she didn't start at the highly improper hold or withdraw from his possessive touch.

Dewer's gaze veered to him with a brooding speculation tinted in peril. A chill swept up Braden's back and plunged into his lungs, trapping his breath. His chest tightened, his fingers cramped and his body froze in place. Yet, Dewer hadn't twitched a finger.

"You won't win this battle!" Merryn's bold statement drew the warlock's attention.

Braden's breath gushed but that was the only release. He still couldn't move. He shook with the knowledge of his helplessness. Merryn must sense his vulnerability, which would be why she issued those deliberately challenging words. A tiny part of him was grateful though the largest portion screamed that it should be him protecting her.

What a joke he was. Despite his mighty blessed weapon in his grip, he wasn't able to budge his sword arm. Then he remembered. He'd forgotten to pray.

Braden sent up a silent apology to God for the neglect and humbly requested His holy assistance.

Nothing changed.

A lick of panic slid up his spine. *Please, dear Lord?* he added.

Nothing.

He shut his eyes as terror swamped him. In the midst of that torrent of worry, came what Archbishop Manners drilled into him as a lad. *For the good of all God's Children, I lay my life in your service.*

Braden repeated that phrase, releasing his anger and fear in order to mean every word.

Instantly, every nerve in his body tingled. Like a gushing stream, vibrant energy rushed to his extremities. Along with that blessing came one word, *Listen.*

Agamore, though still not glowing, came alive in his grip. The sword had more surprises than a chameleon. If the need arose now, Braden felt certain he would be more than a match for this nonchalantly powerful warlock.

He blinked and turned to Dewer with a new perspective, one born of confidence but also clarity unsullied by jealousy. That negative emotion had been swept aside like wisps of mist and replaced with an unshakable notion. *If I listen, I'll hear something of import in this darkest of towers.*

He released his tight hold on Merryn and lowered his sword arm.

Dewer and Merryn were so intent on their conversation that neither noticed the warlock's control of Braden had ended.

The warlock spoke in earnest. "I did not win the last time. Your brother's death was as much a loss to me as you."

"Don't you dare speak about Jonas!"

"We can't avoid the conversation forever. Don't you want to know what really happened to him?"

"I know what happened. He died trying to escape from you. Now give me Trystan!"

"I will not waste my breath in denials again."

"Good."

Every time these two talked, the warlock's gaze on Merryn softened. It was obvious Dewer did indeed have tender feelings for her. If the man genuinely cared, why had he harmed her brother? Her parents? Not the most cordial way to court a woman, killing off her family.

Another surprise was the state of this room. Shelves brimmed with books, scrolls and rolled maps. A table had nubs of candles as if the warlock frequented this room, perhaps reading late into the night, as Braden often did at home.

"If I had the boy," Dewer said with infinite patience, "why did I bother burning the Fishguard coven? Not that the infernal child was there either. Else he would have come screaming out along with the rest of those witches when you broke through my fire spell."

"Your spell?" Merryn sounded as shocked as Braden by the admission.

"Who else?" Dewer asked. "Trystan's father refused to act against the witches, so I had to do something to get the boy to come outside. Those witches had placed too many wards around the house for me to get in." He gave Merryn an admiring look. "Clever of you to detect the fire was not natural, Miss Pendraven."

Braden frowned as something pricked his mind. "Wait a moment. If you came to Fishguard and burned that coven in order to get the boy, then you really mustn't have Trystan."

"Exactly what I've been telling you." Dewer sounded triumphant.

It was Merryn's turn to look confused. "Then where is he?"

"Time for us to leave," Braden had no intention of discussing their next move in front of this scoundrel who'd just admitted he was indeed searching for the boy, too.

Merryn looked as if she would argue, and then her gaze fell on Dewer, who watched them with avid interest.

"Yes," she said. "We've outstayed our welcome."

"Not at all," Dewer protested. "All that effort to get in and you're not even going to stay for tea?" He snapped his fingers and a table beside him covered with open books and candles cleared, to be replaced by a plate of fresh sandwiches that made Braden's stomach growl with hunger. Beside the plate was a steaming tea service with matching cups and saucers.

"Good day," Braden said, afraid his empty stomach might unwisely accept the tempting invite. He gestured for Merryn to precede him out the door.

Before they reached it, the door slammed shut ahead of them and the bolt locked.

Braden's heart hammered in reaction and his grip tightened on his sword

"We could find the boy quicker if we worked together," Dewer said, still using that conversational tone as if the door slamming were not a terrifying threat.

"I think not," Merryn said. One gesture and the door swung back open.

Dewer came forward and took her gloved hand and kissed it. "'Till next time?"

Merryn withdrew, frowning at the warlock. "You'll allow us to leave in peace?"

All the fun vanished from Dewer's expression as he murmured in a grave tone, "On my life, Miss Pendraven, I would never harm you."

With a hand at her back, Braden urged her out of the room before the contrary warlock changed his mind. He tipped his head slightly in farewell.

Merryn went ahead. Braden looked back to check on Dewer.

The warlock shrugged, a calculating smile on his face. The look made the hairs on Braden's neck quiver, for it was obvious they were in a race with this dangerous villain to find that boy.

As the door eerily shut of its own accord, Braden sprinted after Merryn. She raced down the stairs as if she was indeed in a sprint to save Trystan's life. They both came to a crashing halt at the base of the tower.

The room that had been bare when they entered was now filled with fae hounds and the barguest. That lead beast lounged by the doorway, a wicked look in its red glowing eyes.

Braden pushed Merryn behind him and held out his sword. One of the fae hounds gave a whimper and backed away from the stairwell. The others stood to face them, growling a warning. The barguest sprang to its feet, fangs bared, hackles raised.

So, they had been here all along.

"They didn't attack last time." Cautiously, he took the last step off the stairwell.

The hounds backed up.

"Perhaps they won't bother us this time, too." Keeping his sword raised, Braden eyed the pathway to the door. "Stay behind me," he cautioned and took another step forward.

"Why is Dewer letting us see and hear them now?" Merryn whispered.

"He likes to be unpredictable," Braden replied.

They were a good seven steps from the doorway. The distance, however, wasn't the problem. Though the other hounds retreated as he and Merryn approached, the barguest refused to give ground, standing to block their path to the door.

"Any suggestions on how to deal with that one?" Braden pointed with the tip of his sword to the drooling and snarling barguest.

Merryn was silent a moment and then said, "It will let us pass."

"Any reason for your certainty?"

The silence was longer this time but finally she muttered, "If Dewer wanted to kill me, he could have tried any number of times today. He didn't."

Her reluctant admission about Dewer's intentions, both elated and deflated Braden. He gave a nod, kept the sword poised to strike and took Merryn's hand. He led them through the treacherous terrain with fae hounds on one side and the barguest on the other.

He wasn't sure if his heart pounded worse now than when he had stepped off what had looked like a precipice. Three steps and they were closer to the pack of snarling hounds.

The barguest tracked them, its hot breath brushing the back of Braden's left hand. Unlike the hounds that backed away from Agamore as if afraid its presence could end their existence, the barguest inched closer, daring Braden to strike. Either this beast had a terrible death wish or it knew something he did not.

For its part, Agamore once more glowed. It vibrated in his hand as if urging him to attack the barguest. Braden resisted. With Merryn so vulnerably close, he would not risk starting a fight. His priority was to get them both safely out of the tower.

The barguest, however, would not give an inch. It positioned itself at the door, leaning its great weight against the handle, as if daring them to reach for it.

"It hungers for a fight," he said, seeing clear hostility in the hungry gaze that followed his every movement. "I don't think it cares what its master wants."

"Then why does it not attack?" Merryn asked.

"Good question. Perhaps it's under a compulsion not to. Perhaps it needs me to instigate the clash, so it can retaliate, defend itself."

One of the hounds behind them suddenly sent out a howl and Braden jolted in alarm.

The lonely sound filled and echoed inside the confined tower. Braden's heart gave a shudder, as he remembered a similar occurrence in London.

This time, footsteps pounded down the stairs before that call died. Dewer stood at the top landing and took in their predicament. Of course, the villain would smile.

Braden clenched his teeth and said, "Your dog seems unwilling to vacate its spot by the door."

Dewer leaned his forearms on the railing and gazed at them with a grin that contradicted the pounding hurry of his steps when he first rushed in. For a moment there, he must have been worried. Had he been concerned that his precious Merryn had been hurt?

"Call him off," Merryn said, and then with reluctance added, "please."

"Of course, Miss Pendraven," Dewer said. "Your wish is my command." A flick of his wrist and the barguest went flying across the room to smash against the opposite wall. It staggered to its feet with a growl while the other hounds scurried out of its path.

Braden reeled again at the casual power the man wielded. How lucky they were to leave this tower unharmed. He bowed his own reluctant thanks, and opened the door to usher Merryn out. The faster he got her away from here, the better.

Shutting the door behind them, he sagged against the wood and breathed a silent sigh of relief. Then he muttered a heartfelt, "Bloody blazes!"

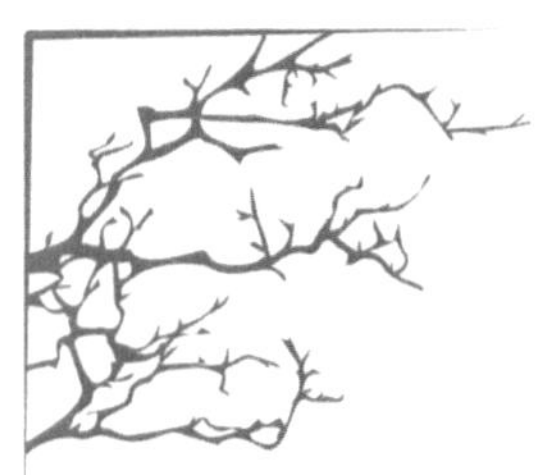

Chapter 12

As the door shut behind the guard and witch, Alaster's spiked fur settled on his twitchy spine. Outside, that infernal chanting died, to join the silence from Farfur's infernal howling that had summoned their master. The air, which had been thrumming with magic, quieted. He stretched out his hind legs, tightly clenched muscles slackening. They'd made it through another crisis.

A flash of light blinded him and then darkness descended. By the time his eyes adjusted, he found himself outside the tower, surrounded by large statues. He'd been transported onto the master's chessboard, in back of the tower. No doubt to avoid the witches out front.

The next instant, Farfur appeared beside him, knocking against one of the people-sized chess pieces.

The bishop tipped alarmingly, looking as if it would fall, then it righted itself and turned a mighty stone frown on Farfur. "GET OFF THE BOARD!"

Farfur skittered sideways and bumped into the queen. She crashed to the ground and rolled.

"OFF!" the bishop snapped again.

The queen righted herself, smoothed down her gown and slid toward Farfur with murder in her eyes.

"Blimey," Alaster said. A nearby pawn scooted across the board toward him and he sprang back.

Farfur raced between the knight and castle, heading for the edge of the board. Just as he reached the grassy verge, Alaster jumped over him to land on his other side.

"AND STAY OFF!"

As if to emphasize the bishop's order, all the chess pieces rearranged into orderly rows that faced Farfur and Alaster.

"Now what?" Farfur asked Alaster.

"We await the others?"

After several minutes, it became obvious no one else was to join them.

Farfur gave Alaster a worried look.

"Follow the witches and bring me that boy!" Dewer's voice rapped like a thunderclap inside Alaster's head.

Farfur yelped beside him.

"Shush!" Alaster warned, heart racing.

Farfur swallowed the remainder of his whine. "This night goes from bad to worse. The only good news is Sax isn't with us."

"Sax went against orders to confront the witch and guard," Alaster said. "I thought that would be the end of us all."

"He's crazy, that one," Farfur agreed. "Think the master knows Sax can't be trusted?"

Alaster gave a nervous look over his shoulder at the black tower, a dark angry projection in a star sprinkled sky. "Why else is Sax not with us?"

"Good point."

"Let's go before we lose the scent." He headed down the mountain after their prey.

"This reminds me of the last time the master stole a boy," Farfur murmured.

"Shush," Alaster snapped, looking over his shoulder as if the Queen of the Light Fae had returned to incinerate him. That powerful fae had no mercy in her soul. Out of a dozen hellhounds, only he, Bartos and Farfur had escaped and then only because they had wisely cowered behind some bushes when the magical blasting began.

Alaster recalled Bartos practically sitting on top of Farfur to keep the impulsive young hound from racing foolishly to Dewer's aid. He'd wondered at the other hound's protective gesture until he realized if Bartos hadn't done that, Farfur might have given away their location. "You should know better than to bring up that disaster."

"Why can the master not let sleeping hounds lie?" Farfur asked in a mournful voice, completely unmindful of Alaster's warning about staying off this dangerous topic.

"Can you hear what any of the witches are saying?" Alaster asked to change the subject.

"Not a word."

"I hope we find the boy soon," Alaster continued. "The master's foul mood has worsened since we lost Trystan's trail at the church."

"That was not my fault," Farfur was quick to point out.

Alaster had forgotten how sensitive his companion was on this subject. He swallowed his sigh as Farfur carried on with his usual defense.

"One minute, I had the boy's leg clamped between my jaws. The next, he'd vanished." Farfur paused to breath and then asked, "Alaster, if the Fishguard witch didn't take him, who did?"

"We'd better find out. If we fail to retrieve Trystan again, Sax will be the least of our problems."

ONCE OUTSIDE DEWER'S tower, Merryn gestured to the witches that they were leaving. The chanting died, submerging the surroundings in utter silence and darkness.

She raised her torch and said, "Light." The torch flamed and painted the witches with golden strokes.

Braden accepted her torch and held it higher. "Will you lead the way? Use your magic to find the easiest route down."

Merryn gave him a startled look. He encouraged her to use magic? A change indeed from the church guard who once insisted all magic came from the dark side. Hiding a satisfied smile, she strode forward.

Braden followed at her heels, for there was little room for two to walk side-by-side. A glance back showed, one after another, each witch raised her hand. Torches appeared in their grips and were lit. The group descended Black Mountain in a line of fire.

"They're an impressive sight," Braden murmured. "As was Dewer's exertion of power tonight."

Merryn frowned, not caring for the comparison of witch to warlock, yet they were one people, from one world. "Warlocks are a law unto themselves," she murmured, feeling a burning need to differentiate between the sexes.

"Yet some witches are drawn to them. Trystan is an example of such a union. As are you."

"What are you implying, my lord?"

"Merely that you are one people."

She shuddered at how his words mimicked her thoughts. She didn't care for the direction of this conversation. It skirted their recent argument.

As much as she would like to deny it, Braden had been right about one thing. Dewer did indeed seem genuinely taken with her. His partiality had been most obvious in his reaction to Braden.

The look shared between the two men had vibrated with mutual antagonism. They had acted male and predatory, like stags fighting over a doe. As if this doe had no choice whom she would choose as her mate. Perhaps she'd choose neither. Right now, that choice appealed.

They reached the place where Braden had left his horse and he gave her the torch while he fetched his mount.

He returned with the handsome black stallion trotting obediently behind him. Instead of taking the torch back, he took her hand. A warm clasp that left her feeling cherished and cared for. After a night of fear and anger, recriminations and terror, the tender gesture brought tears to her eyes. She glanced away, blinking to be rid of them before he noticed how vulnerable she became to his every touch.

They traveled in companionable silence down the mountainside until Braden said, "I wonder about the warlocks."

Her shoulders tensed again. "What about them?"

"Are they all truly evil?"

"They show little conscience about practicing mind magic which subverts a person's free will, both on humans and their own children. Some, like Dewer, delve into the dark arts by summoning demons and other creatures from the underworld. If they aren't evil, they are at the very least dangerous."

Reluctantly, she added, "Some witches have been known to dabble in the dark arts as well. The high sage forbids such activities. Part of my duty as Coven Protectress is to stop such users by whatever means necessary."

"Do the warlocks police their members in a similar way?"

Again, though hesitant to give warlocks any credit, she had to nod in agreement. "They purport to. Though they've done nothing to stop Dewer other than banish him from the warlock community."

He gave her a considering glance. "Is it possible witches have misjudged warlocks?"

"Even if he didn't set the fire, Mattock did nothing to interfere in the burning of the Fishguard coven," Merryn said with vehemence. "Those witches could have died if we hadn't arrived in time." She paused to allow her indignation to settle. "Warlocks may not be evil, but neither can they be trusted."

"You've told me how the events at Bedfordshire helped shape how witches behave. Is it not possible warlocks, too, learnt lessons from that shared tragedy?"

"No!" Merryn replied and then sighed, thinking of her father. "Possibly one or two, but the majority are still bad. Why pursue this line of questioning?"

He shrugged as if reluctant to bring up what was truly on his mind. "Something I heard inside the tower troubles me. You will not like hearing it."

Tight-lipped, Merryn trod on. She hadn't liked most of their conversation this night, and he had something worse? What? That Dewer might not be as evil as she knew him to be?

"You cannot possibly think to defend Dewer," she said as a statement, not a question. "He just admitted to setting a house full of witches on fire."

"Yes, he did."

"Then?"

The silence lasted for ten steps.

"Then?" she prodded, wanting to hear his insight.

"Then, if he's willing to admit to that villainy, why bother denying he harmed your brother?"

She flung his hand away. Her whole body ran cold and hot and cold again. The torch shook in her hold, fluttering the flames. "You do not know what you speak of, my lord."

"No," he admitted in a gentle voice, "but you were, what, thirteen, and not present for the crime. Are you so certain you know what happened?"

Merryn refused to speak to Braden again, marching ahead, practically running down the mountainside. Every step fed her fury as her mind replayed the horrible moment when her aunt broke the news of her parents' and her brother's deaths at Dewer's hands. Did Braden think the high sage would have lied about the event?

On and on, her mind ran in recriminations. She barged into the stables and went to the stall at the far end that she'd claimed as hers. The half door slammed behind her. She got rid of the torch and sat in a dark corner.

In time, her furious thoughts slowed and rearranged themselves. Braden was wrong. His misconceptions could easily be corrected. She simply had to get him to speak to her aunt.

For now, she wanted to do some scrying. First, she checked on the whereabouts of the church guards and Mattock and finally on Dewer. What she discovered had her heart hammering in terror.

Trystan's father led the church guards down to Callington. Dewer's whereabouts were shielded, which frightened her the most.

No more time for dithering. Since she was in southern Wales, she gauged she had a head start. If she left at first light, she and her group could arrive in Callington ahead of the guards and the warlocks.

In the meantime, her aunt must be warned.

She sat cross-legged and shook her wrist until a quill appeared and on her lap a little table with sheets of paper and a lighted candle. In order, she listed all that she wanted her aunt to do to waylay the trouble approaching beleaguered Callington.

When she was done, a good hour later, the stable was silent. The central ceiling light was reduced to just enough illumination for her dark-adjusted eyes to see by.

She stepped closer to the loft and called up, "Braden!"

Several witches sat up, murmuring sleepily. Nearby, a horse neighed.

A scuffle sounded above and Braden leaned over to shoot her an infuriating smile. "Are we on speaking terms again, Miss Pendraven?"

She took a deep breath to level her voice, so she would sound encouraging instead of murderous. She wanted him down here to hear what had happened to her brother. She'd see then if he remained so enchanted by Dewer. "I'm summoning my aunt. I beg you to attend."

"Now?"

Was that a note of alarm in his voice? *Good!* "Now."

Back inside her stall, the place shrank in size as Braden entered behind her. "Those lighted candles on the floor look dangerous," he said, nonchalantly leaning against the door.

"Their fire will never spread. This may take a while, as I have much to discuss with my aunt before we speak about Dewer."

"Such as?"

"I plan to seek her help with the archbishop's condition."

"Excellent." He pulled out a sealed missive. "This urges His Grace to go to Callington, but I'm uncertain he will receive it before trouble strikes there."

"I can help with that." She took the letter and with a flick of her hand it vanished. "Consider the letter delivered."

He shook his head in amazement. "Just as well you and your kind remain in hiding, Merryn, for the Royal Mail could not compete with such speed."

"There are many reasons why we keep our presence among humans a secret," Merryn said. "However, our current troubles have made me reconsider the wisdom of that course of action."

"I've been thinking along those lines, too," Braden said with a frown. "In London, the idea of your presence would cause widespread panic. However, in Cornwall, where your coven is established, and even in Wales, your presence might already be suspected, if not widely known."

Merryn considered that suggestion, recalling Lady Hancock's conversation in the carriage ride from Exeter to Callington. The lady had relayed much to Braden about Merryn's activities over the years. More than she'd given the woman credit for knowing. The lady also believed in the fae. The witches of Callington might have underestimated Lady Hancock, and perhaps other neighbors.

With a nod, she came to a daring decision. Stepping over the circle of candles, she sat on the straw covered floor at the center. "My aunt will be unaware you're here until I invite you into the circle, so kindly remain by the door."

At his nod, she recited the words of summoning. She'd barely finished before her aunt's face appeared before her. She blinked in surprise at the swiftness of the response.

"You're alive!" Aunt Morwena said.

"Blessed be, Aunt." Merryn held out her offering of a strand of sweet blackberries.

Her aunt heaved a sigh of relief, holding her hand to her heart and looking as if she were about to burst into tears. It was a moment before she pulled herself together and remembered to complete the ritual of exchanging gifts.

"Blessed be, indeed, child." She offered Merryn a rowan leaf. "I have followed your adventures, including your perilous confrontation of Dewer, though I couldn't see anything after you went inside his tower. Shortly after, the whole mountain became shrouded from my scrying. I feared you'd died."

"I did not. Thanks in part to the Fishguard witches' assistance and to Lord Braden's help."

"You have grown closer to this churchman."

Merryn gave a grinning Braden a dark side look. "Distance is a relative thing."

Seeing the speculation in her aunt's eyes, Merryn wondered how much her aunt's scrying had told her. Remembering Braden's kisses, a faint blush heated her cheeks.

"As grateful as I am to see you survived your encounter with Dewer, I must ask, why have you summoned me?"

"I've a number of requests to make. First, I need a healer willing to work on the Archbishop of Canterbury. We suspect that he, as well as a group of church guards, is under a warlock mind influence spell. Lord Braden says they would never have allowed the coven in Fishguard to burn with people inside. If so, they, too, will need help to be freed from warlock influence. Finally, please arrange for a protection circle around Saint Agatha's church."

"Why? Trystan isn't there. Is he?"

"I don't know where the dratted boy is. Neither does Dewer. However, the church holds the clues we need. I want to speak again with the brownie who lives there. He may know more than he admitted. Saint Agatha, too, could hold the secret to the boy's whereabouts. We must ensure no one gains access to that church before I return."

"The whole building?" Aunt Morwena sounded aghast.

"The whole building."

"How are we to do that? If the coven gathers around the church, it will raise eyebrows and we will become a standing target for the church guards. They are coming."

"I know. I have a plan." She outlined her idea and watched Aunt Morwena's eyes widen with shock.

Finally, her aunt let out a gusty laugh. "You do not ask for much, do you? What if Lady Hancock refuses to help?"

"We tell her the truth," Merryn said and Braden nodded in approval.

"Have you gone mad?" Aunt Morwena asked.

"We have lived in Cornwall for centuries," Merryn said, "believing our secret safe from discovery. I think we've misjudged our neighbors' knowledge on the matter, certainly in Callington. Tell Lady Hancock who we are, that we're trying to save Trystan. I believe she will do all in her power to help. Even to the extent of gaining the assistance of others of her acquaintance to protect us from the church guards."

"Merryn, even if the people of Callington were willing to help witches guard the church, which is a stretch by any consideration, they are human. They have no power to defend themselves against magic, and we're sworn to protect them."

"We cannot win this fight alone. We need to call on all allies, both magical and human. I intend to send a pixie to speak to her queen. She belongs to the *y tylwyth teg* group of fae. They, too, are guardians of this region and I hope they will lend us their assistance."

"Absolutely not!"

"Aunt...."

"Leave the light fae out of this, Merryn. It will only draw more trouble toward us."

"I've formed a connection to them through Cri, the pixie. I'm sure I can persuade them to help us."

"No. The *y tylwyth teg* will not help us. However, I will do as you ask regarding the rest." Her aunt spoke quickly, as if she wished to get off the topic of fae as quickly as possible. "I pray your plan works, else we put the very souls it is our duty to protect in the gravest danger."

Merryn suppressed a shudder at her aunt's words. "There's one more thing we must speak about, Aunt. I'm not alone." She gestured for Braden to step into the circle.

He did so, kneeling beside her and bowing his head in greeting to the older woman.

"Aunt, this is Thomas Drake Saint-Clair, Earl of Braden. Lord Braden, this is my aunt, Morwena Dunstan, High Sage of Britain."

Her aunt let out a hissed breath, rearing back as if she'd been betrayed.

"He's aware of who I am, who we are, our history," Merryn said. "On behalf of the king, he has offered us welcome to Britain, and to this planet."

Aunt Morwena's angry gaze went from her to Braden and returned with a deep furrow on her brow. "Why did you summon me in the presence of a church guard?"

"I need you to tell him what happened to my brother and my parents. Dewer denies killing Jonas. I need you to convince Lord Braden that Dewer is a liar. His lordship has doubts that need quelling."

"You appear to be uncannily perceptive, Lord Braden," Aunt Morwena said, wearing a frown.

"On this issue, I take no credit, my lady. I was advised that if I listened, I would hear something of import inside the Black Tower. It is merely my presumption that Dewer's denial was that information."

"By whom?" Merryn asked. "Who told you to listen?"

He shrugged, not replying.

Aunt Morwena's frown wavered and then faltered, her eyes widening. "It is as you supposed, Merryn." She sounding awed. "His God speaks to him."

"Why would the Maker lie to him?"

"Take care how you speak of the deity, young lady!"

Merryn folded her arms, doubt creeping into her heart like a pestilence. She desperately wanted this issue resolved. Now. The answer was simple. *Wasn't it?* A feverish heat swept through her body, making sweat bead on her forehead.

"Dewer murdered my brother. You said so, Aunt." The words came out more of a question than she cared for.

"I said Jonas died after he tried to escape from Dewer." Aunt Morwena sighed, more worrisome was her avoiding Merryn's direct gaze. "In doing so, the boy pulled himself out of that fiend's protection and put himself in far greater danger."

"From whom?"

Aunt Morwena twirled the twig of berries in her hand, studying the shadows between the globules as if the words she sought were hidden within that darkness.

"From whom?" Merryn's heart pounded so loud Braden and her aunt must surely hear it.

Her aunt set the berries on the ground. She'd come to a decision. "It's best if you remain ignorant for now. That is the safest course, Merryn."

"Aunt!"

"You are too close to Dewer's domain for this conversation. I will not risk losing you."

"But, Aunt…"

"When you return to Callington, where I can better protect you, I will tell you everything. Blessed be, Merryn Pendraven." With a swipe of her hand, her aunt departed.

Merryn sat in stunned silence, her protests stilling in her mouth.

Braden laid an arm around her shoulder but she found no comfort in his warm touch. The pieces of her world no longer fit together. *Who besides Dewer was her enemy?*

She stood and with a flick of her hand the candles were replaced by a lone lantern.

"Merryn." Braden stood, too.

"I'm tired. We may speak again in the morning." She didn't want to meet his caring gaze. "I need time to think about all this."

Silence stretched into uncomfortable proportions.

She heard his feet shuffle the straw as he turned to leave but then he turned back. "No."

She gave him a discouraging look. "What do you mean, *No?*"

"I do not recall gaining the privilege of time alone when my world spun out of control after your great aunt turned me into a wren. You came instantly to my rescue. Whether you see the need for my help or not, Merryn, I'm staying to offer you my guidance. That is how friends behave."

His words made her tears bud.

Strong arms pulled her to him, offering a safe haven. Against that persuasion, her resistance collapsed and her tightly held emotions broke free.

BRADEN HAD BEEN A HAIR'S breadth away from leaving. Now he held Merryn's trembling form close. The fact she let him comfort her thrilled him. It was the first sign she'd shown that she was capable of truly trusting him.

After she left him helpless and immobile in the loft, he'd been on the verge of losing hope they could ever have a future. For without trust, there could be no love.

He hugged her tight. Never again would he allow emotional distance to creep in between them. This woman belonged with him just as he did with her, body and soul.

Like the drip from a leaf after a heavy rainfall, realization sank in that Merryn was his other half. The queen to his king. His countess-to-be. The woman whom he would promise before God to love and honor, to protect and cherish, for the remainder of his days.

He finally appreciated what his stoic father had said about his own love match, of the day he first laid eyes on his bluestocking wife. Braden had thought the type of love his parents enjoyed was not for him.

"I don't understand this world anymore," she murmured against his neck.

He chuckled. "Really? I'm finally beginning to."

She glanced up, eyes puffy with shedding tears. "Then, pray, explain it to me."

He kissed her instead, starting with her adorable eyes, her nose and cheeks, before claiming her lips. The kiss was sweet and intense, with a promise of forever.

Drawing back for breath, he trailed his fingers over where his lips had roamed. He kissed her throat, inhaling her floral scent and savored her delicious taste.

Merryn groaned and tugged him closer.

"I wish the rest of our conversation could be more private," he murmured.

Her pupils wide with matching passion, she touched his cheek and a little smile played across her well-kissed lips. "Then allow me to close the door."

She stepped back and twirled her right arm above her head, pointing around the stall.

He followed the gesture with mild curiosity that grew to admiration as the space expanded and undertook a remarkable reconstruction. Solid wallpapered walls replaced the straw and wooden slats. On the center of one wall appeared a coal fireplace with a marble mantle above and small windows on either side giving a clear glimpse of the stars. Soon he stood on an Axminister carpet situated in a bedchamber that could have easily been the size of the entire barn.

Comfortable deep chairs reposed before a fireplace. A magnificent mahogany bed with tall corner posts took up the largest portion of the room. Above it, a domed top arched over the bed. He blinked in surprise, for the top floated, the edges not quite touching the ends of the posts.

A large unique painting hanging on one wall beside the bed drew Braden's distracted gaze. As he moved closer to study it, the lantern light from a nearby table swung of its own accord to shine on the painting. He'd never seen a landscape depicted like this. It had odd shades and shapes over a bright red sky.

"Where is this place?" he asked and then gasped as the painting shifted, taking him on a tour of the landscape.

"That's my home world," Merryn came up beside him. "Or what I imagine it must have looked like from writings by the original Wyhcans who arrived on earth. We call them The Travelers. Our home world became unlivable near the end."

"Did you paint this? With magic?"

"I painted it, by hand," she said with a proud little smile. "Magic merely allows you to see all of the painting without the need for a larger frame."

"I think I could get used to your magic." Taking her hand, he drew her toward the bed. High above it was a sheath attached to the wall that was the perfect size to house Agamore. He drew his sword and tossed the weapon high. Without hesitation, Agamore floated directly toward its new resting place and slid in with supreme confidence. That was all his power. He faced her. "Merryn…"

"Yes, Braden?"

"Aside from your magical and artistic talents, I would like to say that I admire who you are. You've a gentleness and strength about you that shines inside and out."

She smiled as if she enjoyed the compliment. "I'm glad you approve of my character."

His fingers tangled in her braid until the strands flowed loose about his hand. "Your hair, too, has been on my mind since the moment we met. It's as silky as I imagined."

He leaned in and rubbed his face against her cheeks, hoping she wouldn't mind his day-old stubble. "I adore your scent, you smell like lilacs."

"Thank you…oooh," she cried as he swooped her up in his arms and laid her on the high bed. Shedding his boots and stockings, he climbed up beside her.

The bed was strong and yet gave way as he bounced. Getting up onto his bare feet, he tested the incredible resilience of the mattress. "How is this bed made?"

She raised herself on her elbows and followed his exploratory leaps to all corners of the bed. "Are you asking about the technical details of its construction, my lord?"

About to say a thrilled, *Yes*, he took note of her tone and reconsidered. "Perhaps later." Kneeling, head tilted, he studied her. "I wonder…"

She watched him with an indulgent smile. "About the nature of the walls. Do you want to know if I made it of stone or brick?"

"You tease." He reclined beside her, resting his head on his fist. "All this casual use of magic is new to me." His fingers trailed the line of her gown at her bosom. "When Garth practices his craft, knowing of my disapproval, he keeps his secrets close to his chest."

She stretched with sensual grace. "What were you wondering about then?" Her voice caught as his exploring fingers slipped beneath the material.

He rested his forehead against hers, gazing intently into her eyes. "I was wondering if you could see your way clear to undressing us as easily as you dressed this room."

She licked her upper lip, her eyes pouring into his, as if seriously considering his suggestion. Then she shut her eyes and groaned as his fingers added their own brand of persuasion.

The next thing he knew, a cold breeze brushed across his bare backside. In the space of one breath, his coat, waistcoat, shirt and breeches were gone, and her hands boldly explored his chest muscles. The woman was incredible, and playful, for not one stitch of her clothing had yet been removed.

He leaned back on one folded arm and indicated her completely clothed state. "This seems a trifle unfair."

"Forming my clothing was never my strong suit," she said by way of explanation, wearing an innocent expression. "It would be easier for me later on, if you would be so kind as to oblige with their removal now."

Was she being genuine? The glint of mischief in her eyes delighted him. *The saucy minx!*

He proceeded with the requested disrobing, taking his time the way she'd done while dressing him in the woods. He unraveled each knot and tie as if it were the most painstakingly complex task until she gasped and moaned and pleaded with him to hurry.

Her gown scraped down her body with exquisite slowness, then her stays slipped off her shoulders, each layer tugged downward inch by tortuous inch.

"Is this how our lives are to play out in the future?" he asked in a feigned conversational voice. Considering his utter lack of clothing, it was impossible to disguise his readiness to claim her. "Will you always disrobe me fast but robe me slow?"

"Faster." She sounded breathlessly aroused.

Ha! He'd not even begun his best work yet.

While he had the advantage, he decided to bring up his greatest grievance. "Also, no more going off into danger without me. Promise?"

"From this day forward, Braden, I will grant you anything you want."

He hid his satisfaction and forgot all his well-laid plans to go slow. He groaned and kissed her. She was casting a spell he could no longer withstand and Braden lost control of the point of his lesson.

MUCH LATER, MERRYN awoke with a start.

An unexpected sound had intruded into the delicious dream she was enjoying. Braden slept beside her. Last night hadn't been a dream. She sat up and hugged herself, unable to stop smiling. Before he fell asleep, he'd murmured something astonishing.

Braden had said he loved her. Had he meant it? Or had it merely been the result of their lovemaking? Whichever it was, he couldn't take it back. The words had been said. Aloud. Even as his eyes closed. *I love you.*

Again, a soft noise disturbed her. She got out of bed, instincts coming on high alert, disrupting the euphoria of her thoughts and feelings.

A flick of her fingers and her clothing, scattered haphazardly around the floor, re-draped her. She walked to the window and peeked out.

One of Dewer's hounds cringed back in surprise at seeing her face. A quick spell rooted it on the spot but another she hadn't seen took off before Merryn could stop it. The trapped hellhound looked at its fleeing companion and then at Merryn. It let out a growl that sounded more fearful than threatening.

"What did you hear tonight?" she asked, afraid the hounds had heard the plans she'd made with her aunt.

The beast whined.

"Where has your friend gone?"

The hellhound bowed its head, its dark fur looking scraggly and unkempt as it sat, dropping its head as if expecting to be blasted into little pieces.

It had a right to be concerned. She couldn't let it go. If she did, the hound would either head right back to Dewer and report all it had heard or go on to Callington in search of Trystan. Neither choice was acceptable.

"I'm sorry," she said. "I can't simply release you."

The hound covered its head with its paws and Merryn rolled her eyes at its overly dramatic response.

"From whence you came, now return," she murmured and pointed at the hound. In a flash of light, a passage opened behind the beast. It howled in surprise as a whirlwind reached out and dragged the hellhound back into the underworld.

"Don't come back!" Merryn added for good measure. Satisfied, she turned around and then yelped in surprise.

Braden stood beside the bed, stark naked, sword in his hand. "You stole my clothes."

He looked none too happy as he surveyed her completely dressed form. "What did I say last night about facing danger without me?"

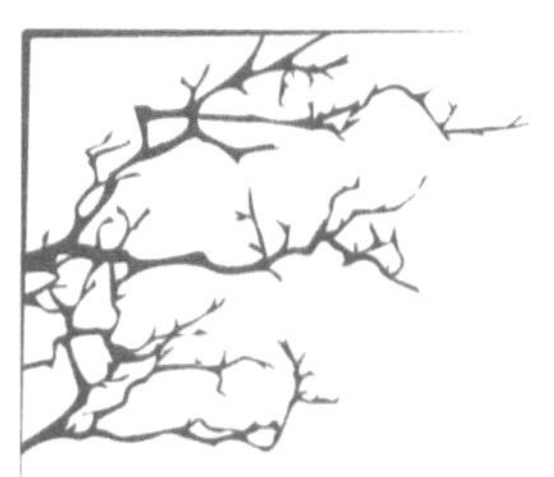

Chapter 13

Farfur ran as if death nipped at his heels. Behind him, Alaster whined and then cried out. Farfur's feet ate up the ground a smidge faster. He raced without looking back. Without hope of living past the next moment. Without knowing where to seek sanctuary.

By the time he stopped running, his lungs felt as if they had twisted inside out. The world turned fuzzy and dim. and with a soft whimper, he collapsed to the ground.

"You're sleeping on my bed," a little voice said.

Farfur opened one eye but didn't see anyone nearby.

Something poked his side. He opened the other eye and turned to find a hedgehog digging underneath where Farfur lay.

He growled and kicked the little animal away. It curled into a ball as it rolled and then unfurled and came running back at once to tunnel at Farfur's side.

"Stop that!" Farfur tried to bite the animal but the hedgehog had its back to him and he couldn't get past its spines for a really good chomp.

The hedgehog stopped long enough to order, "You must move!"

Farfur scrambled away from the large pile of leaves where he'd come to rest.

The hedgehog dug his way underneath the heap and settled.

"What're you doing?" Farfur asked.

The little animal hissed. "It's almost morning. Time for my nap."

"Oh," Farfur sank onto the ground beside the leafy pile, his legs too weary to hold him up. Napping actually sounded like a good idea.

After a few moments, a little nose poked out of the leaves and beady eyes stared at him. "Aren't you going to leave?"

Farfur thought about that question. "I can't go back to the master to report I couldn't find the missing warlock boy. That would mean certain death. It's also too dangerous to keep following the witch."

"You're not planning to stay here, are you?"

Farfur lay silently contemplating his lack of choices. "I don't know what to do."

The hedgehog stared at him for a moment. "Why don't you go find the boy as your master asked?"

Farfur huffed in impatience. "Where would I look?"

"Does this witch know where the boy is?"

"No. Though I heard her say she thinks the church where he disappeared might hold a clue."

"I bet he's hiding in there," the hedgehog said.

Farfur lifted his head and looked at the tiny bundle of leaves. "Why?"

"That's what I would've done, if I was frightened. I'd find someplace dark, like a big pile of leaves or a hollow log, to burrow into until I felt safe. Are there any dark places at the church?"

"It has underground chambers. Do you really think the boy could still be in that church? After all this time? Everyone's searched that church."

"I'm good at hiding. The boy is a warlock?"

"Yes." Farfur sat up, fatigue forgotten.

"Bet he's really good at hiding then. He could use his magic to help him."

Elated to have a goal, Farfur was instantly on his feet and racing toward Callington. "Thank you!"

"Welcome," came a sleepy response.

CONFRONTED BY BRADEN'S irate stance, Merryn retreated until her back was to the wall. She should feel contrite, but it was hard to do that when he stood before her without a stitch of clothing. To focus on his less volatile attributes, she piously raised her gaze to his hair. It was in disarray. The result of her fingers at work or a restless night in bed? In any case, he looked exceedingly delicious; she shed all guilt about not retrieving his clothes before he awoke.

He stepped past her to the narrow window. The first rays of the morning haloed his head as he peered out. "Who was out there and what was that spell you cast?"

"Two of Dewer's hounds were spying on us. One escaped but I sent the other back where he belongs."

"Just like that?" He gave her an incredulous look. "Can all witches do that?"

She frowned at the question, thinking it through. "I don't think so," she admitted. "My aunt says Wyhcan magic has even more difficulty working on fae than on humans. Possibly because the fae have their own magical powers, which are intimately tied to and derived from this world's lines of power, while Wyhcan magic has a foreign flavor that the earth seems to balk at integrating."

Braden looked vastly intrigued. Perhaps this conversation about magic was long overdue. He'd asked her once about magic and she had promised to explain but never had.

"This is the magic that Garth uses?" he asked. "The ley lines he speaks about?"

"Exactly. As for my ability to work magic, the limits have never been tested. I was chosen as Coven Protectress because my magic is stronger than most normal witches, a result of my birth. In the past, however, my aunt refused to allow me to do much, saying I wasn't ready. I believe she is still cowed by what happened to my parents and my brother and fears for my safety."

"How do you mean?"

"I, too, am the offspring of a witch and warlock. Such a union produces strong magical talents in children. That likely makes me a threat to warlocks, to underworld fae, to anyone who practices magic that harms humans, for witches are sworn to protect them with our lives."

"When we were at Dewer's tower, could you have sent those hounds back to the underworld as you did this one?"

"I tried, but his control over them was too strong."

Braden glanced back out the window. "Tonight, one got away? Do you think it heard anything of importance from our earlier discussion?"

"Possibly." Despite the tempting prospect of his rear, she twirled her fingers and clothed his lower half in fresh new smalls, breeches and boots.

He inspected his new clothes. Stepping closer to her, he lifted her chin with his left forefinger. "What about the rest?"

"I was getting to them," she said, unable to contain a happy chuckle.

The look in his eyes suggested finishing clothing him might be premature when the little pixie popped into the room and exclaimed in surprise.

Braden reluctantly released Merryn and stepped back.

She quickly finished his attire until he looked as if his valet had taken an hour to dress him. Even his sword was strapped to his back.

"Isn't she marvelous?" Cri asked.

"She is indeed." His tone spoke of more than clothes.

Merryn blushed hot.

Cri, a flutter of blue in the air, clapped her hands as she moved about the room, admiring the redecoration.

"While you speak with our guest," Braden said, "I'll pen another letter to the archbishop explaining what will happen when he arrives in Callington."

"So, it begins," Merryn said and twirled her hand at an empty spot. A little table holding a lantern appeared, then sheets of paper, ink and a pen stand. Next positioned before the table came a graceful high-back chair.

"Thank you," Braden said and sat down to write.

Cri flew over and settled on Merryn's shoulder. "I'm glad you've made up after your fight," she whispered. "I was worried."

"I, too." She brought Cri forward on her hand so they could speak face-to-face. "I have a request for your queen."

"Then you must come to court. You'd be most welcome. Her Majesty has invited you to speak on the subject of London fashion."

"I wish I could," Merryn said, "but we're in the middle of a crisis and I must return to Callington post-haste. Will you ask Her Majesty if she will assist us there?"

"Fairies are forbidden to interfere in Wyhcan affairs," the pixie said, fluttering her wings. "I wonder if I'm breaking it even speaking to you? No, the queen is aware we've spoken because I told her about the gown you gave me. So, fashion must not be part of the ban." She clapped her hands, having come to a satisfactory answer.

"Cri, please try. A boy's life hangs in the balance. Perhaps many other innocents as well."

The pixie smoothed her blue gown over her legs, arranging and rearranging the folds. "I cannot enter into Her Majesty's presence without an invite."

Merryn glanced at Braden to see if he could add his persuasion but he was at the table, deeply focused on his work.

"What must I tell her?" the pixie asked, eyes downcast.

"That Dewer is calling on the dark fae. If he's not stopped, these openings into the underworld may become uncontrollable, endangering your people as well as mine."

"That sounds like court business!" the pixie said, brightening. "Perhaps I won't get into too much trouble after all. I might even be rewarded. Do you think so?"

Merryn worried the excitement of a possible reward might make the easily diverted pixie forget the importance of the message she carried. She slipped a coiled ring from her index finger and twirled it until it shrank to a size to fit a pixie finger and offered the ring.

"If you carry my message, swiftly and accurately, this is yours to keep." She bespelled the ring to remind Cri of the message and slipped it on the pixie's forefinger.

"I'm going, I'm going," Cri said and left. Then she reappeared, flew forward to hug the side of Merryn's face, and whispered in her ear, "Thank you." She disappeared again.

Merryn released her spell on the room and it returned to its original shape.

Once she and Braden stepped out of the stall, he gave his envelope for Merryn to deliver magically. "I'll speak to the farmer about our departure. Should we eat before we leave?"

She shook her head. "We'll eat as we travel."

He gave a nod and would have left but she stopped him with a hand on his arm.

"Yes?"

She hesitated and then said, "Allow Aunt Gwen to sleep on."

He nodded, understanding her unspoken reasoning. "Not a whisper will she hear of our departure," he promised and strode out.

Branwyn joined her. "He loves you," the Fishguard witch said in a burst.

"Yes," Merryn agreed, watching his departure with as much worry for his safety as for her aunt. Did he realize what they would face when they arrived in Callington? She wasn't prepared to lose Aunt Gwen, but neither did she want to risk him.

"You love him!" Branwyn sounded more surprised by the latter concept. "A church guard."

Merryn gave her an amused smile. "He is hard to resist."

"Oh, yes," Branwyn agreed. "He's as appealing as a warlock."

That made her frown. "Warlocks are not in the least appealing. They're deadly. Don't ever forget that."

She left Branwyn to ponder that warning while she woke the rest of the sleeping Fishguard coven members, urging them to be swift but silent.

Merryn then went to see how preparations for their departure progressed at the farmhouse. The first person to come out of that building was Aunt Gwen, apparently ready for travel.

Braden, trailing her, shrugged and mouthed, "Sorry." As he passed her, he whispered, "She was dressed by the time I reached the house. I doubt she slept a wink."

The farmer and his sons followed him, each tipping his hat.

The Fishguard sage came out next. Ignoring Merryn, she went straight toward the stables where her coven members were gathered.

Merryn was left with her Great Aunt Gwen, who, though not a morning enthusiast, looked fashionably presentable in a cheerful yellow morning gown, and mismatched hat, parasol and pelisse.

"Aunt Gwen, may we speak?"

The elderly witch refused to make eye contact.

"Aunt..."

"Merryn, my mind is made up. I'm coming with you and you cannot stop me."

The farmer's wife hurried past her guests, carrying two large baskets covered in a gingham cloth. Steam rose from around the covers and Merryn inhaled the odor of fresh baked bread with gladness. She hadn't realized how hungry she was until the scent wafted by.

"I asked them to include milk, too, and cheese and cold sausages," Aunt Gwen said, watching the horses be led out of the stables by the farmer's sons.

"You don't understand how…" Merryn began.

Her Aunt Gwen turned to face her, eyes narrowed and mouth uncommonly grim. "I understand we may die today, Merryn. I understand all of our friends in Callington may perish around us. I understand we are at the brink of war with the church guards and possibly the entire underworld. What you fail to understand, my dear, is that I intend to use what little power I have at my disposal to ensure those I care for will be as protected as possible. That includes you and that dear boy who loves you. Is that clear?"

"Yes," she said, a betraying blush heating her cheeks.

Aunt Gwen held out her hands. "I do wish to speak about another matter, however."

Merryn took the elderly lady's delicate hands, warming them with hers. "Yes, Aunt?"

"I've been thinking about the Fishguard coven's agreement with the warlocks. There may be something to be understood there about warlock intent."

Merryn looked at the Fishguard witches gathering outside the stables. Distrust of them still lingered in her heart. "They did help me last night," she murmured and then looked into her aunt's troubled gaze. "You think I'm mistaken in condemning them for consorting with warlocks?"

"Unlike us, they've lived in Wales among warlocks for over a century. Is it not possible then that how they see these powerful men is closer to the truth than how we perceive them?"

"Braden said something similar." If she'd had this conversation a week ago, even a day ago, Merryn did not think she would have been as receptive. Still, she shivered. "Trusting in warlocks feels as repulsive as trusting Dewer. Yet, last night, I discovered I do not know all about that fiend either."

"Make no mistake, Merryn, Dewer's character and those of other warlocks are not the same. Dewer is a twisted man. Deserted by his warlock father and brought up by a vengeful fae mother, he can never be trusted. Your father was a warlock and your mother loved him."

"For the short time I knew him," Merryn whispered, fighting back tears, "I loved my brother."

"Exactly so."

"Last night I said to Aunt Morwena that we could not win this fight on our own."

"No truer words were ever spoken, Merryn. I think you should ask assistance from the Warlock Council. Perhaps only one or two rogue warlocks are inciting the church guards. Just think, if the Warlock Council sides with us, we would be in a stronger position to face not only Dewer's dark horde but the church guards as well."

Merryn heard the reasonableness of her aunt's counsel, yet, the thought of turning to warlocks for help sent an icy chill up her spine.

"There is reason to believe we could reach a compromise," her aunt continued. "After all, we have a common objective – the safe return of young Trystan."

"Aunt, I would worry less about taking this risky course of action if I knew you would be safe here," Merryn said. Was it asking too much for at least one member of her family to remain unharmed by this escalating fiasco?

Aunt Gwen shook her head. "When it is my time to leave this life, I shall do so with dignity and no regrets. Of that you can be quite certain." She tucked Merryn's arm around hers and patted her hand. Though she spoke with much courage, a tear rolled down her aunt's papery cheek.

Merryn wiped it away. "You are my inspiration."

"You, my child, are my heart. I could not love you more if you were my daughter. I have the utmost faith in your ability to see us safely through this troubling time. Now, do me proud."

Merryn nodded and retreated to her stall. Her hand shook as she penned a missive to the Warlock Council, requesting their help with Mattock. She informed them about his casting mind spells on the archbishop and the church guards. She then laid out her suspicions about Dewer's involvement with Trystan's disappearance. Finally, she explained about the church guards heading for Callington.

Would they accede to her request for assistance or choose to stay neutral? Time would tell.

Just as she sent off that volatile letter and stepped back outside, a horrendous rumble shook the mountainside and smoke shot up. The ground shuddered as if a giant hand shook Black Mountain.

Horses neighed in alarm and tried to run. As the rumble continued unabated, the groom, postillion and farmer had their hands full restraining them.

Braden ran out of the stables, sword drawn. Merryn followed him to the edge of the road that overlooked the side of the mountain. She coughed as dust-filled smoke billowed up, making it difficult to breathe or see.

The ground gave way before them and Braden grabbed her arm and pulled her backward. They turned and ran back. The farmer, his family and the witches shouted in terror as they fled the ground giving way all around them. In an instant, half the stable was missing.

The horses strapped to the carriage screamed and raced for higher elevation, dragging the conveyance behind them.

Merryn and Braden reached the front yard as the horrendous shaking settled. They found themselves at the edge of the farmhouse. The road behind them was gone.

The horses, what remained of them, were scrambling up the mountainside. The witches, the farmer and his family had run into the house. With terror-filled eyes, they all now peered out the windows.

Merryn was glad to see her groom and postillion inside as well but she didn't see Aunt Gwen and her heart battered in fear.

"Dewer," Braden said.

She nodded. "Did you see Aunt Gwen go inside?"

As she spoke, a little wren fluttered down to land on the ground before her. Aunt Gwen changed back to herself and wiped away some lingering feathers on her face.

Merryn hugged her aunt, breathing a heartfelt sigh and sent up a prayer of utter gratitude to the Maker. *Thank you!*

"I'm going to check around and assess the damage," Braden said.

One by one, the Fishguard witches came outside to join Merryn and her aunt. The farmer and his wife, who held their children with white-knuckled hands, soon joined them. Finally, the groom and the gangly young postillion cautiously stepped outdoors.

"Merryn, over here," Braden called.

"Go, dear." Aunt Gwen squeezed her hand in permission.

Merryn kissed her aunt's cheek and then hurried over to Braden's side.

He pointed to where his horse as well as the carriage horses had stopped, about twenty feet up the mountainside. What struck Merryn, and likely him, was the free stallions and mares that had gathered around the tied-up carriage horses. All of them nickered in distress.

"Why do you suppose they stopped there?" Braden asked.

"Because Dewer is a diabolical fiend with no mercy in his heart." Merryn picked up her skirts and climbed the slippery slope. She guessed, aside from destroying half the mountain, the warlock had built a magical fence to hold them all captive.

A few feet past where the horses had stopped, she came to an abrupt halt, bouncing back on her heels.

Braden, who had climbed after her, caught and steadied her. He had a comforting touch. "A barrier, like the ones Garth builds?"

"Yes. We can check its perimeter, but I suspect it circles the entire farm," Merryn replied. "I might be able to cross it – I'm good at crossing boundaries – but no one else could come with me."

They returned to the farmhouse to inform the others of their discovery.

"What do we do now?" her aunt said.

"We pray," Braden said, "for a miracle."

"Why did Dewer even bother?" the Fishguard sage asked Merryn. "We're capable of flying out of here."

"They're not." Merryn indicated the farmer and his family. "Besides, what makes you think the barrier doesn't go over our heads?"

"Let's find out." She nodded to one of her Fishguard witches who obligingly transformed into an eagle and took flight. She flew in an angle upwards toward a hazy layer and when she touched it, the air flared, flinging her back. She fell twirling until Merryn sent a spell to steady her and bring her in for a safe landing.

The Fishguard sage came closer to Merryn while the rest of her coven rushed over to fuss over their fallen member. "Dewer would have waited until he was off Black Mountain and onto a main road before triggering this spell. He's probably half way to Callington by now, traveling at a comfortable pace."

"Wouldn't magic of this magnitude have drained him?" Braden asked.

"The barrier spell over the farmhouse, perhaps, since that seems focused for this moment. The large one destroying half the mountain, he likely set that spell up years ago, when he had the leisure to draw on unlimited power over a length of time. He could have been working on it since my parents confronted him. No doubt as a precaution against retaliation for what happened to them and my brother."

"I hope the Callington witches are prepared for what's coming their way," the sage said. "For they'll not have help from us now."

Braden nodded to the farm family who stood apart from the rest of the group. "I'll speak to them and explain what's happened. They're probably confused."

"Tell them we'll help in any way we can," Merryn said.

"They are not our concern," the Fishguard sage said.

"We will help in any way we can," Merryn repeated in a grim voice. "We brought this ruin to this family and we are indebted to ensure they are taken care of. Or have you forgotten the witch's code, along with all our other guidelines?"

"Well said!" Braden nodded approvingly and gave the Fishguard sage a dark look before he strode off.

"Miss Pendraven," the sage began.

Merryn held up her hand for silence. "With all roads to nearby towns cut off, their sheep dead, their fields destroyed, they will starve if left alone to fend from themselves. Who knows how long it shall be before we can return, if ever. The matter is settled. We will not leave until we can find a way to help the farmer and his family."

"I strenuously disagree," the sage said in a belligerent tone. "Finding a way to break free will use up valuable magic, leaving us with little to spare on luxuries. I say we leave the humans here. They're hardy mountain folk. They'll find a way to survive."

"We leave here together or not at all," Merryn said.

"As Sage of Fishguard, I speak for all *my* witches," she said in a condescending tone that bordered on a threat.

"I'll be whacked with a broom," Aunt Gwen said, sounding thoroughly offended. "How ungrateful you sound. This family fed and gave you a bed to sleep on and you would abandon them at the first sign of trouble?"

"First sign? Have you not comprehended what Dewer did to this mountain? Think what he could do to us if we deplete our energies on unnecessary magic."

The moment they were able to, would the Fishguard witches fly off and leave Merryn and her party as stranded as the farmer and his family? At the thought, Merryn's anger exploded.

"As Coven Protectress, *I* speak for *all* witches in Britain." Merryn gave the women gathered about them a look that dared them to disagree. "You have brought this problem into our community, put untold innocent people in Callington and here in grave danger and tilted the balance of power between warlocks and witches with your flagrant disregard of our laws. You will now listen and follow my every instruction to the letter so we may extricate ourselves from this predicament. We will do so without any more harm to others. Is that understood?"

"Hear, hear," Aunt Gwen said.

The silence that followed her speech rang as sharply as the boom that had shattered the peace of Black Mountain.

Branwyn reacted first. She pushed past her sister witches and came to stand by Merryn's right side. Then another followed, and another, until all of them lined up beside Merryn.

The Fishguard sage stood alone and unsupported. Her lips quivered and tears appeared.

Merryn barely noticed for, while she had vented her anger at the Fishguard witches, a remarkable idea had spawned in her of how they could get past Dewer's barrier and travel to Callington *with* the farmer and his family.

Excitement gave an extra spring to her step as she ran to find Braden.

BRADEN. Merryn's voice brushed his ears like a lover's caress. He turned but she was nowhere in sight. "Where are you?"

To your left.

A look to that side of the house showed her gesturing at him to come over.

Hurry! came the whisper.

Would he ever become used to loving a witch? He ran the last few steps and deliberately drew her out of sight of onlookers in order to steal a kiss.

"Braden!" she exclaimed.

He silenced any objections she might pose by claiming another kiss, this time prolonging the experience, enjoying the taste of her and the heady thrill of stealing kisses.

Her fingers across his lips stopped his further plunder. "Braden, we've important matters to discuss and I cannot think rationally when you do that."

"Good. Rational thought is highly overrated."

"Not in the midst of a crisis, my lord. Pray, behave!"

He sighed and allowed her to push him back, but frowned with unconcealed frustration. A loose curl enticed him to tuck it behind her ear. "Why did you call me over if not for illicit kisses? I believe that's what the Fishguard sage assumed, considering her glare as I passed by."

"I no longer care what that she-dragon thinks. I've an idea of how we can all leave this mountain."

That had his interest. "How?"

"I believe the road may be fine and I have an idea of how to get past Dewer's barrier."

He stared at her a moment and then looked behind him to where the land fell away into a canyon. "Explain."

"Do you remember when we broke into Dewer's tower? There seemed to be no hellhounds inside. We later discovered they had been there all along but Dewer's mind magic hid them from our view."

His eyes widened at the possibility. "Now we see a cliff where the road should be. Could the road still be there?"

"Yes! Dewer is a master of illusion. The more I think on it, the more I am convinced the road out of Black Mountain still exists."

"How do we get past the barrier to test your theory?"

"How did we see the hellhounds in the tower?" Merryn asked.

"He allowed us to."

"I think he was angry with you, particularly when you put your arm around me, and that distracted him from maintaining the spell on the hounds."

Braden stared at her in silence and then nodded. "We need another distraction."

"Precisely."

"Can Dewer scry people's activities the way your aunt does?"

"I should think so. That isn't an inborn talent as much as a learnt tool for..."

He claimed her lips again, this time wrapping his feet around her legs and tipping her backwards until they landed on the grassy ground. "Follow my lead," he breathed in her ear.

"I don't understand," Merryn said in a breathless voice.

"Dewer is probably enjoying your predicament, so let's give him a good show." Merryn groaned as his mouth trailed kisses down her neck.

When one of her legs wrapped around him, Braden's pulse leapt in response.

A flash of lightning, followed by a thunderclap, slammed across the sky. Braden jumped off Merryn, sure Aunt Gwen had come to slay him for trespassing on hallowed ground.

Merryn looked up at the sky and laughed.

"What's so amusing?" he asked, thinking she laughed at his fearful reaction.

"The barrier." She pointed at the sky. "It's down. How did you know he would be watching us kiss?"

"He just trashed his mountainside. He would, of course, check to ensure the love of his life wasn't harmed during the explosion."

Merryn met his knowing gaze but then looked away. She pulled out of his hold and ran, calling to the groom. "Hurry! We must get the carriage ready before Dewer has time to rebuild his shield."

The groom and postillion raced with her to bring the carriage and horses down.

Braden observed her retreat with understanding. She wasn't ready yet to admit Dewer truly loved her because accepting that possibility unearthed too many questions about who was really responsible for her family's deaths. Leaving her to direct the groom, he strolled over to check where the road should have been. While the barrier might be down, the mountain still fell away as before.

He stepped to the edge and tested the ground with his right foot. The ground gave way and he slithered down the side of the cliff. Heart pounding, he scrambled to slow his fall and then climb up.

The farmer ran over and helped pull him up.

They sat on the edge breathing heavy. "Thank you," Braden said. He got up and walked over to Aunt Gwen who watched Merryn help the groom and postillion with the horses and carriage.

"Why does she bother?" he asked the elderly witch. "I checked. The road is definitely unusable."

"We need some way to carry the farmer and his family to safety, silly. There'll be no room inside for me anymore, however." She twirled her fingers and cast a spell that changed her into her wren form. She then flew to where the carriage was coming down the mountain.

She'd left before he could ask how they were to get the carriage and horses off the mountainside with no road.

Though still uncertain as to their plans, he ran to where Nadeem roamed. He brought the stallion down to the carriage and tied him at the back. If they were taking the vehicle, he wasn't about to leave his mount on this mountainside.

Merryn called for the farmer and his family to get inside the carriage, along with the deer and others who wouldn't be flying. Then to her groom and the postillion to take up their positions. "Quickly. Time is of the essence."

"Merryn, that road is not there. I almost fell off the edge. That is no illusion." Braden tied a nervous Nadeem to the back of the carriage, patting the horse to calm his steed as much as himself. "How do you plan to get us off the mountain?"

"My question exactly, sir," the groom called down from the rider's box.

"Help me up." She took the groom's hand, placed one foot on the steps that led up to the top seat and climbed on top of the carriage to sit beside him. "We'll have to ride up here with you so I can see where we're going."

A swish of her fingers and the wooden seat extended to either side to allow room for three.

"Oh good." Braden climbed up to sit beside her. "You have a plan."

"Of course."

"Where to, Miss Pendraven?" the groom asked from her other side.

"That way." She pointed to where the road ended in a deep drop.

"I was afraid you'd say that," the groom muttered.

"Even if I believe you could keep us safe," Braden said, "the horses will not simply leap off that edge."

"Smart beasts, unlike the rest of us," the driver muttered, clutching the reins.

"When have I ever let you down?" Merryn asked the men. "Where's your faith?"

"There's faith and then there's common sense, Merryn," Braden put in. "The horses can't be reasoned with. They believe what they see and what they see is a cliff ahead of them."

"Oh, I suppose you're right." She whirled her fingers and eye patches formed over the four horses' eyes.

"On Nadeem, too?" he asked.

"Him, too." Merryn turned to the groom. "Now you may go,"

The man groaned and looked at him for confirmation.

Braden sent a quiet but fervent prayer for their safe travel and nodded to the groom to obey Merryn's command.

The man shook his head but obligingly cracked his whip. The lead horse tentatively started forward, with the others following suit. Another snap and they moved forward again but only a step or two.

"I see they need more encouragement," Merryn said.

"They're not the only ones, miss," the groom muttered.

She twirled her fingers at the horses in front and the one at the back.

The lead horses neighed and began to step forward with confidence.

"What did you do?" Braden asked as the edge of the drop came up to them at too fast a pace.

"I have them thinking they're traveling along a flat green meadow."

The postillion shouted in alarm as they approached the cliff. The groom had shut his eyes tight.

Braden's fear made his pulse hammer like the horses' hoofs and then they were airborne.

His stomach plummeted but the carriage continued straight ahead as if, indeed, there were on solid ground.

"God preserve us," the groom said, finally opening his eyes, the reins held so tight, the bones of his knuckles showed through.

The postillion, who had been silent, gave a whoop of excitement that mirrored Braden's amazement at what they were doing.

The carriage flew through the air!

With them on it!

The little wren settled on Merryn's shoulder and cooed in her niece's ear. Behind them, one by one, other birds landed onto the carriage rooftop, while some flew past.

"They're taking turns resting," Merryn said to him, her hair whipping around her face in the wind.

"Which way do we go, miss?" the groom asked, sounding more confident.

"Head south east," Braden said. "Back to Callington."

Merryn nodded. "Yes, and hurry. We've a young boy to rescue and a coven and town to save."

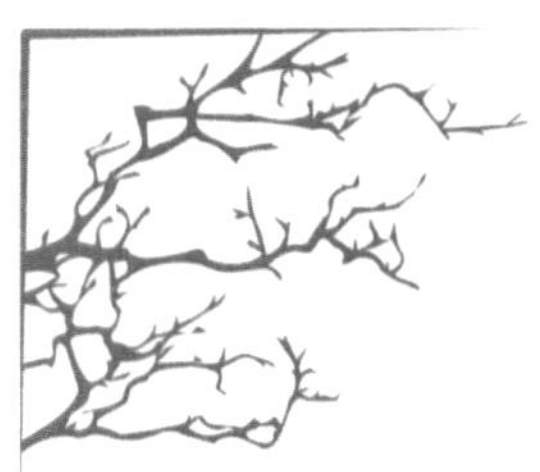

Chapter 14

Bartos looked over at Sax. The barguest's eyes glowed broodingly in the darkened tower entryway. Restless, Bartos licked around the festering wound on his left hind leg.

The tower door opened and he swung around, hopeful Farfur or Alaster was back. Instead, Eolonde, the dark fae queen, stepped in. Terror gripped him at the unexpected, unsolicited, unwanted arrival. He shrank back, shades of the past reverberating. At any moment, he expected the Queen of the Light Fae to appear and declare war, as Queen Orlagh had done the last time her sister invaded her realm and stirred Wyhcan controversy.

Sax, on the other hand, sprang up with a welcome yelp.

Traitor. The thought came unbidden. He hoped she couldn't read minds in this upper realm.

Eolonde ran her hand over Sax's back, as if he were her favorite fur rug, and bending, golden eyes glinting with dark mischief, she whispered in Sax's ear. Then the dark fae queen swept up the stairs as if she were ruler of this upper domain, too. Black Mountain shuddered with each step she took toward Dewer's study. Had her last journey to her son's tower taught her nothing? He was surprised to see her striding with such pride instead of crawling as she had after her last visit.

He'd heard Queen Orlagh of the Y Tylwyth Teg had suffered greatly, too, after that last encounter with this dark one. She had sworn to never again interfere in Wyhcan affairs. Perhaps, after recovering from her injuries, Queen Eolonde had drawn boldness from her rival's pledge. Or her current ambition outweighed caution.

The initial greeting of mother and son took place in ominous quiet. Bartos pictured each taking stock of the other's presence. Soon enough, however, familiar raised voices descended from the open door of the master's room.

Sax set to pacing the circular entryway, glancing upward whenever he passed by the stairs.

Bartos let out a deep breath of resignation and settled for a long wait. He'd begun to nod off when the queen's thunderous voice snapped open his eyes and positioned his ears on high alert.

"ENOUGH!

Was she leaving? The wish died with her next words.

"I will help you capture this boy."

Sax growled low in his throat.

"The child will increase your power in this upper world, and how can I disapprove of such a worthy goal?"

It was hard to hear past Sax's rumbles but Bartos did catch that last bit and didn't believe a word of it. No one in the underworld, least of all Her Dark Majesty, supported anyone else gaining power. He returned to licking around his wound with a worrying tongue.

"Well, then?" the master asked.

"I offer a bargain. I need a new slave. You may keep my hellhounds and I shall send you with more, if you gift me the protectress."

Bartos stopped licking, his heart pounding in fear. Not again! The last time the master and his mother fought had been over the protectress's brother. That hadn't ended well.

Even Sax looked as if he held his breath waiting for the master's answer.

"Never!"

The queen's laughter shook the tower. "You're naught but a lovesick fool. If you cannot separate your emotions from your actions, then you will never be capable of governing my kingdom."

In his corner, quivering in terror, Bartos contemplated his wound that didn't seem to be healing at all. Then the front door burst open and a magpie flew in. It headed upstairs.

"News," Sax said, leaning his front paws on the steps.

"Farfur," they heard the magpie chirp. "Near Saint Agatha's church." Message delivered, the bird flew back down and out. The front door slammed shut.

"That means the warlock boy must be there," Sax said in a low menacing voice. "The cowardly hound hopes to capture him to win the usurper's favor."

Bartos guessed Sax was more upset by the possibility of Farfur succeeding, and thus ruining Sax's plans to hand the boy over to the dark queen so he could win her favor.

In a rumble of thunder, the queen departed through a portal upstairs.

On her heels, the master's order came, "We're leaving!"

Alaster used to say this family quarrel would be the end of them all. Bartos, limping along behind Sax, agreed with him.

OUTSIDE SAINT AGATHA'S church, Lady Hancock stepped to the side of the table that housed all the baking her staff had prepared overnight. She looked to her left and right, surveying the others on the churchyard's front steps. There were manned tables topped with colorful and decorative items for sale. A most impressive gathering.

She had coerced everyone she knew into assisting with a most noble and holy cause – to protect the ailing Archbishop of Canterbury and raise funds to preserve Saint Agatha. All had arrived early this cool autumn morning. No lay-a-beds today. Heart swelling with pride, she waved to Joanna and Bessie, her closest friends, positioned two tables over.

"Kindly step aside, madam, and allow me to pass."

At the curt order, she swung around to the gentleman addressing her. There could be no mistaking that face. She'd seen it in portraits at Lambeth palace. Even expecting him, his presence left her stunned. "You're...you're..."

The man beside the irate gentleman spoke in a polished Londoner voice. "Allow me to present The Most Reverend Charles Manners Sutton, Archbishop of Canterbury."

Lady Hancock gave a hasty curtsey. "I'm deeply honored to meet you, Your Grace." Upon rising, she gave him her best court smile. "I'm Lady Hancock. If I may be so bold as to ask, what brings Your Grace to our wonderful Cornish community on this brilliant September day?"

"I'm here to see the rector of Saint Agatha. Pray step aside so I may pass."

"But you haven't tried one of my cakes." Lady Hancock moved her best china plate piled high with perfectly square cut raspberry layered cake to the edge of the table.

The archbishop looked to the plate and back at her. With a long-suffering sigh, he took a piece from the top and bit in. A dollop of raspberry splashed onto His Grace's white cravat like a drop of blood.

Lady Hancock stifled a gasp. To avoid looking at the spill, she stared into the churchman's eyes. She would faint if he blamed her for that glaring red splash.

Sutton licked his lips. "Very tasty indeed. Thank you. Now, may I go by?"

"Three shillings, please, Your Grace." She gave him her widest smile.

"I beg your pardon?"

With a hand that shook she indicated the various tables around them. "The baked goods, the stichery, the books, this is a charity event, Your Grace. We're raising funds to repair our beloved Saint Agatha." She held out her right hand, palm up.

Sutton stared at her open hand and then snapped his fingers at his companion.

The man pulled out his purse and counted out change.

"Give her all of it," Sutton snapped.

His companion started and then upended the entire contents of the purse onto Lady Hancock's open palm. Coins tumbled out and overflowed, clinking onto the ground.

"Oh dear," Lady Hancock cried out and bent to pick the fallen coins.

The man apologized and knelt to help.

While she was thus engaged, Sutton stepped around both of them and strode toward the church. Lady Hancock glanced back and saw Mrs. Morwena Dunstan and one of her young nieces move to intercept the archbishop.

With a quietly muttered oath, Sutton swerved to go around this new barrier on his path.

The women, too, stepped to the side, getting in his way.

"To that side, ladies, please." He pointed a sharp forefinger to his right.

"My profound apologies, Your Grace," the younger lady said and stepped on his right foot

Lady Hancock smothered a laugh.

"Ow!" His Grace cried out, and pulled back, losing his balance in the process. He flailed to keep from landing ignominiously down the stairs. To no avail. Like a tipped chair, he inevitably sank backwards.

Several people nearby who'd been watching the by-play reached up to slow his descent, but couldn't halt his inevitable fall.

Once on the ground, as the archbishop struggled to sit up.

Mrs. Dunstan laid her hands on either side of his face.

He pushed away her touch. "I'm fine," he said, and then went absolutely still, before slumping back.

"What have you done!" the archbishop's man cried, finally looking over at his master from beside Lady Hancock. "Get away from him. Help! Guard!"

Lady Hancock gestured to her husband and a few of his friends to approach and lift and carry the archbishop inside the church.

Meanwhile, she barred Sutton's man on the steps as he attempted to follow. Bessie and Joanna ran to either side of her, locking arms in solidarity and support.

"Sorry, sir," Lady Hancock said with a pleasant smile, "but the church is out of bounds until the end of the charity event. Except for an emergency, as in the case of His Grace."

"I must attend to His Grace," the man sputtered.

"And you may," Lady Hancock said in sympathetic tones. "Tomorrow. The church reopens then. Good day, sir."

"I will not leave the archbishop unattended. He needs my protection!"

"Inside a church?" Lady Hancock asked with a raised eyebrow. "With the rector accompanying him? Also, that was a physician who helped carry him. Be assured, all of His Grace's needs are being attended to."

The man fumed and fussed but eventually he left, muttering that he would return with reinforcements. Lady Hancock waited until he retreated to his carriage before she turned to give Mrs. Dunstan the signal she was free to act.

That lady gave a gracious nod of thanks and she and her younger companion ascended the steps.

"Mrs. Dunstan really is a witch!" Bessie whispered in an excited voice. "She must have put a sleep spell on His Grace."

"Some nights my husband tosses and turns, keeping me awake. I would love to have the ability to wield such a useful spell," Joanna murmured in a wistful voice.

The idea that her neighbor was a witch did not amaze Lady Hancock at all. In fact, she had suspected as much for years. Just as she believed every tale she'd ever heard about elves and brownies and such, despite Merryn Pendraven stubbornly refusing to confirm any of her suspicions for all these years. Still, to have the staunchly proper Mrs. Dunstan come to her and admit she was a witch to her face and then to request her help had left Lady Hancock feeling extremely privileged.

She'd quickly confided all to her two closest, like-minded friends and gained their support to rescue His Grace from a coercive spell.

"I find it fascinating they're not merely witches but people from another world," she murmured aloud.

"Terrible about their entire world being destroyed," Joanna said. "I'm glad they chose to settle in Cornwall."

Lady Hancock squeezed her friends' hands before releasing them. "God does teach us, my dears, that charity begins at home. Now let us finish what we began and raise some funds for our beloved church. Saint Agatha, too, needs our aid."

WITH CALLINGTON COVEN'S best healing witch, who was another of her nieces, at her side, Morwena stopped before the church's porch doors. She looked up at the statue above the doorway. "Saint Agatha, we mean neither you nor those under your charge any harm. May we enter?"

Saint Agatha didn't respond.

"She seems upset," her niece whispered.

"Everyone's upset, Boo-Boo," Morwena said to her teenage niece. Though only sixteen years old, Morwena trusted Grace Adair, or Boo-Boo to her close family members, to be up to the task she'd been set. Boo-Boo was a healer extraordinaire. "We are in a hurry. My spell on the archbishop will not last long."

Her niece shifted restlessly. "What if Saint Agatha won't let us in? I heard she's been cantankerous and argumentative since the boy went missing. She's refused to allow any witch to enter the church since Merryn left Callington. Though why we should be interfering in warlock activities, especially if it involves the archbishop, is beyond me."

"Shush!" Morwena said. "That argument is old and I've no more time to debate it. You will do as I ask and not question your high sage on this matter."

Morwena studied the statue of the saint holding her severed breasts. "Saint Agatha, we've come to help the archbishop. To cure him of whatever malice the warlocks have imposed on him. Will you please give us permission to enter this holy place?"

The saint bent her head to look at Morwena. "That was an archbishop who was carried inside?"

"Yes." Morwena gave a silent sigh of relief. At least the saint was talking to them. That was surely a good sign. "His name is Charles Manners Sutton."

"The Archbishop of Canterbury?" Saint Agatha asked.

"The very same," Morwena said. "He's under a spell."

"Is that why he was unconscious?"

Morwena hesitated, tempted to say, "Yes," but then she remembered Merryn's advice that it was time to ask for help. That this was not their fight alone.

"I made him sleep," she said, looking straight at the saint's marble eyes. "My healer must work on the spell he's under without his objections. Will you help us?"

"Yes," the saint said. "Anything for His Grace."

"Thank you." Morwena said and ushered her niece inside.

Before the door shut, Saint Agatha said, "Will you tell him I'm a good saint?"

Morwena came back outside. "I beg your pardon?"

"Will you tell His Grace I'm a good saint?" Saint Agatha asked. "And ask him to pray for me?"

Morwena frowned at the obvious worry in the saint's voice. "Have you done something sinful?"

"I'm the guardian of this church. I allowed a child who came here for God's blessing to be endangered."

"That was not your fault," Morwena said. "The dark fae attacked the church."

"I should have withstood their attack."

"You did your best." Morwena couldn't believe she was consoling a saint. "The Maker understands that none of us are flawless. Not even saints."

"Do you really think so?"

"I'm sure of it, my dear. Be calm. You've done an excellent job of safeguarding this church since it was built."

"I'm weak," Agatha whispered. "So very weak. My resources have been stretched to their limits and now I haven't the strength to protect myself. Will you help me?"

"How? And from what?"

"The dark fae. One is here now. Underground. He tries to enter through the old ways. I do not know how much longer I can keep him out. He's not alone. Others come. With great ill intentions toward me. They are all determined to gain entry and steal my treasure."

"What treasure?"

The saint's eyes flared open and then she clamped her mouth shut and stood straight, looking across the horizon.

Realizing she would get no more from the statue, Morwena went inside. *Could Merryn be right that this church held the secret to where Trystan could be found?*

She looked around inside the entryway to see if the Scottish brownie Merryn spoke of was anywhere near. The surfeit of dust balls and cobwebs in the corners of the church suggested the little fae had departed in search of safer terrain.

Wishing she could do the same, Morwena instead checked on her niece. The girl worked diligently on the archbishop, with the rector hovering nervously beside her.

Morwena left them to it and went in search of the stairs that led into the bowels of the church. If something was indeed attempting to enter these hallowed grounds, Saint Agatha needed help holding it at bay. At least until Merryn could arrive to lend a hand.

She opened the door to the east tower and found the stairs leading down. Shoulders back, and head up, she descended the narrow stairs.

The steps ended abruptly before a brick wall. No amount of prodding or poking at the bricks would open a doorway. Using a finger, she drew a large imaginary oval, her height. "Seal me not, open for me."

The bricks fell over into a dark room on the other side. A wave of her hands scattered the fallen bricks and puffs of dark moldy smelling clouds, forming a clear path ahead. Lifting her hem, she climbed through the impromptu doorway.

The rectangular room she entered mimicked the layout of the church above, with center and side aisles, and columns supporting three elegant arches on the left and right. A half-buried crypt at the far end drew her forward. She gauged that directly above would be the church's current altar.

Morwena checked for signs of a rude entry into the chamber but all seemed still and undisturbed. The crypt was sealed. No recent disturbance in the dust.

She held out her arms and closed her eyes, turning her sight inwards and then beyond the four walls. Abominations swarmed toward the church. Heart racing, she turned and ran toward the opening she'd created.

Before she could reach it, the fallen bricks rose and slammed into their original places, the dust settling into the crevices until Morwena was trapped inside the cellar in the dark.

The church walls trembled and Morwena thought she heard Saint Agatha whimper, "Dear God, help me."

Amen to that!

"Surely you weren't thinking of leaving yet?" a woman murmured from behind Morwena. "When the entertainment is about to begin?"

Morwena turned slowly, every nerve in her body quivering in terror. Light shone from above. One corner of the ceiling was emitting a steadily increasing sickly green glow, like a gate opening.

A beautiful dark-haired woman in an ethereal emerald confection entered through the glow and lounged on the tomb. Her legs were casually crossed and she leaned back on outstretched, slender, white arms and watched Morwena with a hard, golden gaze.

Three hellhounds followed next and sat hunched by her feet. Eyes red, hackles raised, they let out low warning growls.

"So, you are Morwena Dunstan. How do you do, my dear? I've met one of your sisters. Lovely witch. I've been meaning to discuss with you what happened to her. Perhaps it would be more enlightening to allow you to experience her fate." She laughed, a malicious, venom-filled sound.

From inside the glowing gate, snakes with deformed human heads slithered out, falling to the crypt floor with slaps and thumps. Snapping at each other in impatience, they crawled and slid over anything in their path in obvious eagerness to reach their prey.

Morwena sent out a desperate mental call, *MERRYN!* Then she raised her arms and readied to do battle.

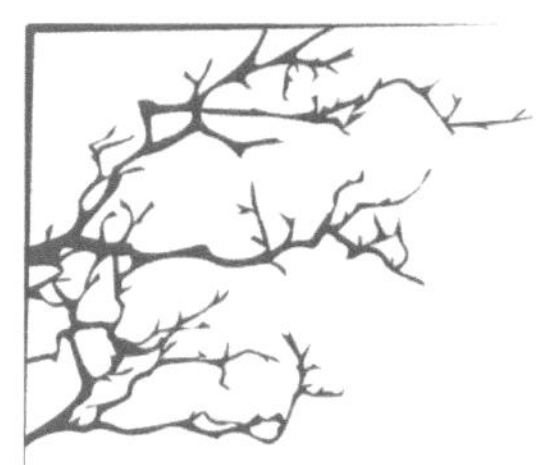

Chapter 15

Alice and her best friend, Elizabeth, resided inside the walls of Saint Agatha's church. Today, unusual chatter drew the pair of mice to a hole above the niche where the statue of Saint Agatha was set.

While Alice remained safely within the church wall, Elizabeth, the braver of the two, ventured outside to sit on Saint Agatha's right shoulder and peer at the people gathered below.

"Alice, this doesn't bode well," she called back.

No longer able to contain her curiosity, Alice poked her head out of the hole. "Looks like a tea party."

She didn't normally care for crowds. Men had a way of stomping on a mouse without particular care, while the women screamed and struck with their parasols.

"Look around." Elizabeth pointed with her front paw. "They're everywhere."

Craning her neck, Alice leaned out for a better perspective. "In the back as well?"

"The witches are. The front, sides, back."

"Why?" Alice whispered, now truly concerned. "What does it all mean?"

"Trouble, Alice. And there's more."

"What more could there be?" Alice's legs were trembling. "What else, Lizzie?"

"That." She pointed toward the sky.

Alice squinted until she spotted a dark shape looming overhead. She squealed and pulled back. "Is it an eagle?"

"Too big to be an eagle."

"A dragon?" Alice breathed out the terrifying word.

"Big enough to be one and it's coming straight for the church!"

Her friend swung around and scrambled up the saint's marble head to reach the hole where Alice hid. Her friend ran past her so quickly, Alice found herself spinning around to follow her progress.

She hurried after Elizabeth who streaked down the rood beam, skirting the base of the cross.

Her heart palpitating, Alice paused to take a much-needed breath on the far side of the Lord's bound and pierced feet.

"Come on, we have to hide," Elizabeth shouted back. "Not in the catacombs though. I heard something burrowing there earlier, trying to gain entry. It was digging. I think it was one of those hellhounds again."

Alice scampered after her friend. "Saint preserve us!"

"Better pray higher than our saint," Elizabeth said. "I showed you what happened to that poor warlock boy who came to be baptized. We don't want that happening to us."

Alice shuddered at a memory she'd valiantly tried for days to banish, and failed. She looked nervously toward the church altar where the boy had once bravely stood beside his mother. "I've not been happy since he was brought here. The church feels creepy now. I wish we could leave."

"Too late."

"Then what are we to do, Lizzie?"

"Hide. In the deepest, darkest hole we can find."

THE CARRIAGE LANDED with a clatter of hoofs, jingling harnesses and neighing horses and Braden bounced hard on his metal seat. "Next time, padded seats," he said to Merryn.

"There's going to be a next time?"

"With you, my love, I wouldn't doubt it."

"Milord." Garth ran up to them. Or more precisely, he ran around the front of the carriage. "I almost didn't believe my eyes when I looked up and saw a carriage soaring through the sky." He sounded more excited than shocked.

Braden jumped down, trying to ignore his sore rear end and his sword's suddenly agitated call from where it was strapped across his back. The other creatures from the carriage roof descended around them. He reached up to help Merryn down.

She slid trustingly into his hold. "Something's wrong."

"I know. Agamore's vibrating and I've not summoned its power. Garth!"

The little man, who had been petting the horses and shaking the postillion's hand as if to ensure he was real, hurried to his side. "Milord, you came back in a flying carriage! How does it work?"

Braden kept his arm around Merryn, for she looked decidedly shaken. "We can discuss the intricacies of flight another time. What's happening here?"

"Archbishop of Canterbury's inside Saint Agatha's church. A healing witch is working on breaking the spell cast on him. The rest of the witches mingle among the crowd. The church guards are here, too, led by a warlock. One of the archbishop's servants went to speak to them. They're in a terrible pickle about something,"

"Breathe," Braden ordered.

Garth took a gulp of air and continued. "A group of warlocks have also arrived. They've gathered to the east, by the grocer." He pointed to the opposite side of the church grounds.

"They came," Merryn said, sound astonished.

"Yes," Braden said. "The question is why."

"The plan to keep all outsiders from gaining entry into the church appears to be working," Garth continued. "No one's attempted to approach the people of Callington who effectively guard the building with their tables and chairs. Mrs. Dunstan surmised that shades of Bedfordshire keep both the warlocks and church guards back. On the fundraising front, their cakes, sugarplums and strawberry fritters are selling well. Though expensive, those tidbits are tasty."

"Enough," Braden said.

Garth took another breath.

"Where's my Aunt Morwena?" Merryn asked.

"Inside, Miss Pendraven. She lingered by that statue over the church for the longest time. I think she spoke with Saint Agatha herself."

He sounded so awed, Braden couldn't repress a smile. Garth was getting a taste of what Braden had suffered while in his remarkable footman's company. *Good!* Now he'd realize how uncomfortable it felt to be around people who could do things more extraordinary than one ever believed possible.

Thunder cracked and all of them jumped in fright. Dark clouds gathered overhead and Agamore shuddered with barely suppressed frenzy.

Braden put a hand on the hilt to settle the sword. *Be calm,* he ordered. The weapon hummed within his grip, as if trying to communicate.

The Fishguard sage turned herself from a hare into her human self beside Garth.

He squealed in fright and sidled to Braden's side.

Braden had to strain to push the man away. "Garth, kindly get a grip on yourself instead of me."

"I sense Dewer approaches," the Fishguard sage said in a dire tone.

"Then we've little time to spare." Merryn called the Fishguard witches to her. "Move among the witches here, but be inconspicuous. We do not want to alarm the warlocks before we're ready. Spread the news that momentarily a barrier must be raised around the church. Everyone, especially the people of Callington, are to be on the inside of the circle when I give the word. Go!"

She gave Braden a concerned look. "I'm worried about Aunt Morwena."

Aunt Gwen came up to Merryn's side. "Shall I search for Morwena?"

"No, please stay with me." Holding her delicate hand, Merryn gave Braden a pleading look.

"I'll check on your aunt and the archbishop."

She kissed his cheek, her hauntingly memorable scent covering him in a blanket of gratitude before she hurried away.

"Garth, stay with me," he said and headed toward the church.

Danger below! a clear and crisp voice said.

Braden stopped and looked around. "Who said that?"

"Who said what, milord?" Garth asked.

Seeing no one else nearby meant one thing. "Garth, Agamore's speaking to me."

"If you say so, milord."

The skepticism in his footman's tone irked him. "You believe a carriage can fly but not that my sword speaks to me?" He headed for the churchyard where tables laden with goods acted as a physical shield.

"You disapprove of magic, milord," Garth said from directly behind him, sprinting to catch up. "If I were the sword, I wouldn't dare speak to you."

He gave the footman a dark over-the-shoulder glare but before he could reply, someone tugged at his sleeve.

"What's happening?" An elderly gentleman stood by a table of crocheted pillow covers, his hand cupped around his right ear.

"Go toward the church steps, sir," he advised the old man.

"Has the attack on the church begun?"

Braden gave the elder a gentle nudge. "Hurry." A thunderclap accented his instruction.

He checked on Merryn but she was too busy to notice. He didn't feel right leaving her but she wouldn't be happy until her aunt was safe. The quicker he saw to that matter, the sooner he could return to lend her a helping hand.

He pushed his way past the people who crowded the steps.

"In line," Merryn called out.

Braden swung around at the order. Her tone had a magical toll to it. He guessed every witch circling the church likely heard it.

In one smooth motion, the witches stepped past the citizens of Callington. Merryn held out her free hand and a broom appeared, as it did in each witch's hand all along the circle they formed around the church. Even her Aunt Gwen held one.

The brooms were twirled until the handles pointed down. He marveled at the precision of their movement, the uniform motion. Even the British regiments, after weeks of practice, could not mimic such perfect harmony.

"Now," Merryn's call went out. In time, all the witches slammed the handles on the ground.

Spears of light sprang high up in bright lines that curved inward until they formed an arc over the church steeple.

"Come on," Braden said to Garth and hurried past the crowd musing, "I wonder why they prefer brooms? They used them by Dewer's tower, too."

"It's their staff, milord," Garth replied. "I spoke to a witch about it earlier. She said that when they first arrived on earth, their staff generated much concern and fear among humans. So, the witches took to disguising them as brooms, which was something no one questioned a woman holding. The warlocks hide their staffs in the guise of fashionable walking sticks."

"Ingenious," Braden murmured and stepped through the church doorway. Behind him Garth cried out. Turning, he found his footman sprawled on his backside.

"Garth, this is no time for tomfoolery."

"She won't let me in, milord."

"Who?"

He pointed up. "The saint."

Braden came back out and found the statue of Saint Agatha glaring at Garth. "I'm a church guard and will vouch for this man," he said, having lived through too many incredible events in the past week to question this one. "I need his help. Please let him through."

The saint nodded once.

"Come along, Garth." Braden went back inside.

Garth followed, muttering under his breath about the world going mad.

"I thought you of all people would not be shocked by what's happening here in Callington."

"Milord, I know one or two simple tricks. Since coming to Cornwall, I've seen my share of brownies and such. But talkin' statues? Flyin' carriages? This world's gone insane and no one's goin' to convince me otherwise."

Braden chuckled at the comment and then looked around. To his right, a young girl leaned over Sutton. He stepped that way but his sword pulled the other way, toward the east tower.

He changed direction and opened the tower door. "This way."

Together, they descended the circular stairs until a brick wall barred their way. "We need to go through there, Garth. Agamore suggests that's where the trouble originates. Are you able to open a door for us?"

"I can try, milord." Garth pulled out various odd objects hidden in his coat pockets and laid them on the floor.

MERRYN WAS HARDLY AWARE of Braden entering the church. Once the shield was constructed, she turned to where church guards approached with Mattock at their lead, his black mastiff familiar at his heels. Knowing how his mind spells were misfiring, the foolish warlock still continued to use them. Already the guards he'd brought were behaving oddly, for several were attacking the stone steps at the edge of her barrier, smashing at them with their sword hilts. At least by building this shield, they had safeguarded the townsfolk who came to help them. She'd only missed shielding one person.

Saint Agatha's rector strode beside Mattock.

Merryn gave a disappointed cry. Too late to bring the rector behind the shield.

On the opposite side of the churchyard, warlocks approached.

Merryn's heart fluttered with uncertainty. Was their presence here a sign that for once the warlocks intended to lend a hand instead of instigating trouble?

Before the two groups could meet, a flash of lightning struck the ground. Once the smoke cleared, Dewer stood between them, the barguest and a hellhound at his side. The hound looked wounded, one of its hind legs sagging. That surprised Merryn. She'd been sure that when Dewer came, he would bring many reinforcements from the underworld. What game did he play?

"Lower your shield, Miss Pendraven," Dewer said.

"No."

"You don't understand the danger you're in."

"With me in here, and you out there, I hardly think I'm the one in danger, sir."

Dewer glanced at the church guards to his right. Uniformly, they were attacking the church steps, mindlessly smashing at the stone steps, as if they intended to burrow their way under the shield she'd constructed. He flashed his sinister smile, convinced he had nothing to fear from that deluded quarter. He then turned to his left. The warlocks stood, arms crossed, showing no intention of interfering.

They could have been attending a race at Ascot for all the threat they showed Dewer. They were on no one's side but their own. *Warlocks!* She should have known better than to place her trust in them. Still, she, the witches and the people of Callington were safe within this barricade.

All except for the rector. If matters turned violent, he would be the only one in real danger.

Mattock's mind control on the church guards was obviously misfiring since they were ignoring all his attempts to stop their useless pounding of the steps. He finally gave up on them and came over to face Merryn.

If the guards turned their ire from the steps to those around them, the warlocks and Dewer would be well able to defend themselves, but not the rector. He wasn't even armed. His safety was her responsibility.

She could easily cross this shield, but she couldn't return behind it with the rector, not without lowering the shield first.

An it harm none, do what thou wilt.

Since Bedfordshire, her people had sworn to live by that code. She bent her head as the weight of her responsibility rose. Then Merryn, setting her shoulders back, released her hold on Aunt Gwen and purposely walked through the barrier.

"Merryn, no!" Aunt Gwen called out. She, too, tried to step through the barrier and was pushed back.

"You will not harm that boy," she told Dewer as she walked toward the rector.

"My mother's inside that church," Dewer said.

That halted Merryn's steps. "What?"

"Drop the shield and I will speak to her on your behalf."

The barguest jostled the hellhound aside and moved closer to Merryn.

"I don't believe you," she said, heart hammering.

"I assure you," Dewer said, "my mother has your high sage and will kill her without compunction. It's what she did to your parents."

"And you brought her here? You fiend!"

"I did not summon her," Dewer said in a quiet but firm tone. "Give me the boy and I will have the power to fight her."

Merryn's eyes widened. "No!"

Trystan's father echoed her reply.

She looked over at him in surprise.

He gave her an icy glare before turning to Dewer. "You will not have my son. Not for the Coven Protectress's life or to save any other witch in there."

The comment sent a wave of anger through Merryn. This warlock's wife – his son's mother – was one of the witches he'd referred to so dismissively. Did her life not matter to him either?

Merryn's chest squeezed tight with indignation. Yet, none of this must concern her at this moment. Aunt Morwena, bless her kind soul, was capable of defending herself. There was nothing she could do for her from out here.

The thought made her wonder if she'd misjudged Trystan's father. Could he, too, have come to the same reasoning about his wife? She shook off such useless speculation and focused on the rector. Him, she could still protect.

She took a step toward him and the barguest landed between Merryn and her target.

"Get back here," Dewer ordered.

The barguest ignored him and sprang at her, fangs bared.

She raised her hand to block the attack when the thing burst into flames in midair. A glance around showed every warlock present pointing at it, including Dewer.

The combined force of their attack had the barguest suspended mid-air, howling in agony. It finally dropped to the ground and lay still, a scorched shell of its former self.

The hellhound by Dewer's feet raised its head and let out a howl that sounded more triumphant than mournful.

"Silence," Dewer commanded. The noise died abruptly and the hound cowered behind his master.

Merryn wasn't certain who was more shocked, herself or everyone else, at the manner of the barguest's death. Even the church guards had stopped pounding on the steps to look over this way. She said a shaky, "Thank you." Then she rushed to the rector's side. "Are you all right, sir?"

"Oh, yes, certainly, Miss Pendraven. Mr. Mattock has been most kind. There was no need to worry."

"Good. Now, stay with me. I cannot risk being distracted again by your safety."

"Certainly, I shall be quiet as a mouse right here, behind you. We both shall." He pointed toward his feet.

Merryn spotted the little brownie. "You're still here?"

"I know me duty, missy," the Scottish brownie said. "No need ta look so surprised."

"He's been very helpful, telling me when to speak and when to keep mum," the rector whispered.

Would this day of shocks never end?

"Miss Pendraven, may we speak privately?" Dewer asked, coming up to her.

"No!" she replied succinctly. Of everyone here, she trusted him least. With so many murderous church guards and deceitful warlocks about, that was quite the honor.

"I concur." Mattock gave her his first ever nod of approval. "This involves all of us."

"Take your spell off the church guards," Merryn ordered pointing to the bewitched men.

"I did so right after they began attacking the steps," Mattock said, a guilty flush staining his cheeks. "They've stopped listening to me."

"Miss Pendraven," Dewer interrupted, "as courageous as your Lord Braden may be," his eyebrow rose in blatant skepticism, "do you truly believe him or your aunt capable of winning over the Queen of the Underworld?" His haughtiness slipped a little as he added, "I've never been able to best her, which is why I need that boy's assistance. I only want him as my apprentice. I swear I will not harm him."

Merryn was taken aback. He sounded sincere. He had just admitted to being weaker than another, something she never would have expected from this over-confident and suave warlock. Could she and her aunt have been mistaken in his character? After all, Jonas had revered him as a friend.

As if sensing her wavering toward Dewer, Mattock spoke up. "I do not believe you, sir."

Dewer's face darkened. "You dare question my integrity when you were the one who brought church guards into warlock affairs?"

That set off a tirade as Mattock brought out every grievance he held against the man, starting with Dewer's persistent attempts to steal Trystan, and going back to slights from their boyhood days.

Dewer was right on one count. A single witch, however powerful, was no match for an underworld queen. Merryn left the two sparring men and approached the warlock contingent. She needed their help if she had any hope of rescuing her aunt.

She spoke quietly, hoping to use that tried but true strategy of divide and conquer. She had something to bargain with. Trystan. After all, it had been her and her aunt's intention to eventually return the boy to the council, albeit after he was baptized. Their plan hadn't changed.

"I need to return inside the church. I promise to give the boy to the council's care, if you agree to keep Dewer here once I drop the shield."

Mattock dropped his argument with Dewer to answer her. The confounded man obviously had incredible hearing. "Will you hand my son over to me unharmed?" All signs of approval had vanished, replaced by a glare of profound mistrust.

Merryn answered truthfully. "Yes."

"That includes not baptizing him first."

Had he read her mind? At least he wasn't twisting her thoughts today. It didn't help to see Dewer break into a grin, as if he enjoyed her dilemma. In this instance, Mattock's request worked to Dewer's benefit. If the boy were baptized, he would be useless for Dewer's purposes. Of course, he sided with Mattock.

"If you do not agree," Mattock continued, "and Dewer is telling the truth about his mother invading that church..."

"I am." Hand to heart, Dewer looked altruistic.

She'd left them alone for a few moments and they'd become bosom-bows, finishing each other's sentences?

"...then your aunt and everyone else inside your barrier could die."

"I'd wager my mother's not here alone," Dewer added. "She refused to lend me more hounds because she probably intends to use them herself."

"It could end up a slaughterhouse in there," Mattock continued relentlessly, "with all of us out here watching those within the circle die a horrible death."

Merryn's bones quivered at the vile picture he painted.

Dalton, the leader of the church guards, came over to join the conversation. His hands were bloody and ravaged from his attack on the steps but his gaze was finally clear and sincere as he spoke. "You cannot mean to allow a whole-scale butchery of innocents without raising a hand to help?"

The rector, too, hurried over to her side, with the brownie riding on his shoulder.

The brownie spoke up. "The question as ah see it, lass," he looked at Merryn with grave eyes, "is whether the life of a young warlock boy whom we have no real connection with is worth risking all those we care for? Ah don't envy you having ta answer that one."

"What would you have me do, Rector?" Merryn asked, overwhelmed by her limited choices.

The old man took her hand and gave it a sympathetic squeeze. "My dear, the answer is a simple one. The boy is the responsibility of his parents, both of them. No blessing should be carried out without both of their consent." As he spoke, moisture budded in his eyes, for he must now know that with his counsel, he put the life of that child in danger.

Hot tears flooded Merryn's eyes, too, for she recognized that despite all her aunt's persuasive words about changing the course of history with this one baptism, the rector had the right of it.

This new home her people had arrived in thrived on free will, to the extent of abandoning the happiness of Heaven and opposing the will of God in order to lay claim to it. She would not be the one to thwart that worldly desire.

With her decision, came the same horror she'd felt when news arrived that her entire family had died. Her heart compressed as if pressured by a boulder.

Merryn strode up to the shield and raised her arms. When she lowered them, the shield dissipated.

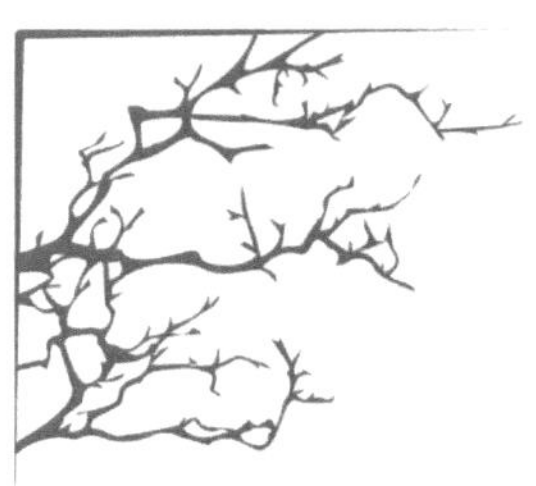

Chapter 16

Farfur hid in the shadows as a witch entered the crypt. Just his luck, the moment he placed one paw onto holy ground he was in danger of discovery. Then he heard the whispers.

The queen is coming.

The queen is coming.

The queen is coming.

Terror spiked in his heart. It was now or never.

As the witch shut her eyes and extended her arms, Farfur skirted behind her and jumped through the hole she'd bashed into the crypt wall. He raced up the stairs as if flames licked his tail. Behind him, the witch cried out and crashing bricks re-sealed the hole.

Heart pounding, feet extending the distance between him and disaster, Farfur thanked whatever luck rode his back.

At the top of the stairs, panting, he pawed open the tower door and looked in. Halfway up the nave, a young witch worked over someone lying on a pew. She looked to be healing him.

Farfur crept into the church. He double-checked to make sure no one else was nearby, large or small. Satisfied, he aimed for the chancel at the far end. That was where he'd lost the boy the last time. He wanted to see if, without other human odors to distract him, this time his nose could point him in the right direction.

He slunk past the witch working on an unconscious man. At the altar, nose to ground, he sniffed. He sought a memorable and singularly little-warlock scent.

On the morning of the baptism, Farfur had spied Trystan eating his breakfast beside his mother on the front steps of his home. Farfur had ignored the mother's spoken words and focused instead on the boy's fascinating actions.

Time and again, Trystan had dunked finger-length slices of fresh baked bread into egg before eating it. Then he'd gulped down a steaming mug of milk.

The meal had looked divinely delicious.

From his hiding place behind nearby bushes, Farfur had inhaled the smells and enviously licked his chops. Ever since, he associated the scent of fresh egg and warm milk with the boy Trystan.

A group of witches had then escorted the boy, still licking his sticky, tasty fingers, to the church.

Farfur now caught that recognizable whiff of eggy Trystan. Tail wagging in excitement, he allowed his nose to lead him straight to the boy. Then he sat down on the floor of the chancel, thoroughly perplexed. How could he possible free this child from this impossible prison? Was he even still alive?

Thunder rumbled overhead. His ears perked up at recognition of his master's drumbeat. Dewer had arrived. Good! He would surely be grateful at this piece of amazing news and perhaps be willing to forgive Farfur his past failures.

He trotted to the front door, nosed it open and came to an abrupt halt. The area reeled with people. If that weren't enough deterrent, a magical shield at the bottom of the steps separated Farfur from the master.

With a soft concerned whine, he retreated. Just in time! The church guard with that hound-slaying sword entered the church. Panicked, Farfur hid beneath a pew.

Luckily, the guard and another man went through the tower door, their footsteps clattering down the metal stairs. Thinking of what awaited them below, Farfur gave a huff of bitter humor. That should take care of that confounded sword and its interfering wielder, once and for all.

He lay still, paws crossed, and prepared to wait. Sooner or later the master would come. Farfur hoped it would be before the dark fae queen made her way upstairs. He wasn't sure he had the courage to fight Her Dark Majesty for the master's prize.

PICKING UP HER SKIRTS, Merryn raced up the church stairs.

"Go, Merryn," Aunt Gwen shouted, cheering her on.

People scrambled out of her path and then quickly reformed back into a crowd that blocked anyone following her.

The church doorway flared as she ran in and Merryn skidded to a halt, surprised to find herself already inside the church without first gaining the saint's permission. How could that have been possible, unless the saint was weaker than she'd realized. She hurriedly retreated outside and called up, "Saint Agatha, may I enter, please?"

"Hurry," the saint replied in a panicked tone. "They need you."

"Bless you." Merryn raced back in.

She heard a thump and looked over to spot Dewer sprawled on the other side of the door, swearing up at the statue. Another mystery. Saint Agatha was strong enough to stop Dewer but not Merryn? No time to ponder that now. Behind Dewer, a contingent of warlocks were pushing their way past those crowding the steps.

Merryn swung around to check the inside of the church for Braden. He was nowhere in sight. Sensing magic roiling below, she headed toward the east tower. She sped down the stairs until she spotted Garth beside an opening in the wall where bricks seemed to have been bashed in with force. A hazy barrier had been built to keep the demons from leaving the chamber and invading the rest of the church.

Merryn didn't even hesitate. She barged right in expecting no resistance, and found none. Amazing.

Garth peered in from the other side of the crude opening and said, "Oh, thank heavens you've come."

A snake dropped onto her shoulder and bit deep at her neck. She flung it off, cringing from the pain and quickly set a spell of aversion in motion. The next writhing horror that landed on her burst into flames.

Within this chamber, her aunt and Braden were fighting back a horde of underworld creatures that seemed to multiply and grow the more they were cut down. Braden's sword had flared like the North Star and she heard its battle cry.

"Welcome to hell," Braden called out. He decapitated four snakes with one swing of his sword.

"About time," Aunt Morwena gasped. Her back to the wall, she held a shield against which several hounds pounced in a vain attempt to break through. "What kept you?"

"Dewer's interference and a slight disagreement with warlocks."

"All sorted out now?" Though Aunt Morwena sounded calm, a closer look showed her face drenched in perspiration.

"Not to my satisfaction." Merryn had never seen Aunt Morwena look so frazzled. She suspected her aunt was close to her limit. She sent a bolt of energy to fortify her aunt's shield.

Aunt Morwena collapsed back and nodded her thanks.

"Well, well, if it isn't the guest of honor. Finally come to join the dance, my dear?"

Merryn looked toward the opposite end of the room where a woman rose into the air, her keen glance fixing on Merryn with avid curiosity.

"Allow me to introduce myself. I am Queen Eolonde of the *Y Tylwyth Teg*. Welcome to my domain, Miss Pendraven." She raised and lowered her arms and all the beasts in the chamber dropped to the floor and lay still.

"I believe your sister might disagree with that declaration," Aunt Morwena said. "If I recall correctly, she is the true ruler of the Welsh fae."

"This isn't Wales," Queen Eolonde snapped.

"No, this is Cornwall." Merryn said in a hard voice, "and you've entered Saint Agatha's domain. I'm her champion, come to throw you off her premises. You are not welcome in this church, Your Majesty."

"I cannot see what my boy finds so appealing about you." The Queen of the Dark Fae glided through the air toward Merryn. "You are not in the least polite. I invite you to my party and you flagrantly insult me. Is it any wonder I denied him permission to marry you?"

Merryn was stunned Dewer would have even approached his mother about that impossibility. She was about to say she would never consider such a distasteful union when caution and truth halted her words.

This was the man's mother. She probably wouldn't take kindly to Merryn calling her son a twisted maniacal fiend. Or would she consider that a compliment? In any case, for one brief moment in time, however unwisely, Merryn had been enchanted by Dewer. She cringed at the thought, but at her coming-out ball, he had literally swept her off her feet. A suave dance partner had ever been her Achilles' heel.

She couldn't help glancing at Braden. They'd yet to dance. The first time they'd met, he'd promised to partner her. Whatever his other intentions toward their future, she intended to hold him to that promise. If his lovemaking was any indication, she suspected she had nothing to fear in that quarter. The thought made her smile.

Dewer's mother seemed displeased by Merryn's distraction, and snapped her fingers in front of Merryn's face. "What? No conversation. You are a sad letdown."

"If you, like everyone else, are here for the boy, you are wasting your time," Merryn replied, forcefully bringing her mind to order. "If Trystan were here, wouldn't someone have found him by now?"

"My dearest girl, I'm not here for the boy. I'm here for you. My son promised you to me."

Looking into Queen Eolonde's eyes glittering with maliciousness, for the first time Merryn took Dewer's side on an issue. She decided his mother lied. Whatever his faults, Dewer would never betray her that way. For both his mother and Braden were right on one matter. Dewer loved her.

It was a fact she could no longer deny. The concept left a bittersweet taste in her mouth, and the rise of pity in her heart for her one-time enemy.

"I don't believe you," Merryn said.

"Believe what you will." Though Queen Eolonde sounded offhand, she looked as if Merryn's defense of Dewer had run like acid through her veins. "I need a new servant and despite your lack of wit, you will serve me satisfactorily."

"I think not." Braden positioned himself between the queen and Merryn.

Her heart warmed at his foolhardy action.

He swiped at several snakes that closed in around them. His sword cleared a path that Aunt Morwena used to approach Merryn.

"My niece is not for the taking," her aunt said to the dark fae queen.

"Afraid of losing another of your kin, dear thing?" Queen Eolonde asked in a commiserate tone. "Perhaps you'd like to bargain for her life as your sister did her son's?" She gestured with her hand and all the snakes and hounds backed away from attack. "Then let's parley."

Merryn tuned to her Aunt Morwena in shock. "What is she talking about?"

"Ancient history." Her aunt looked away, focusing on the snakes.

Trying to avoid eye contact, Aunt?

The writhing beasts watched her aunt with disdain. Waiting for the command to resume attack, they impatiently snapped at each other as if needing something on which to vent their frustration.

Merryn empathized with their mood. "Aunt!"

"Does the girl not know how her brother died?" The dark queen circled around Braden to get an unhindered view of Merryn.

"You killed him," Merryn said with rising confidence. Who else, if Dewer hadn't done the vile deed?

The dark fae laughed, head thrown back. "Priceless. I'm not a wastrel, girl. I would never harm a useful tool."

"Then how did he die?" Merryn asked.

"Your parents…"

"Shut up!" Aunt Morwena cried.

Queen Eolonde chuckled and then spoke slowly, looking Merryn directly in the eyes. "Your parents killed him."

"You lie!" Even as she said the words, this time, Merryn, devastated, sensed this fiend spoke the horrible truth.

"Do I? What would be the purpose? They struck a bargain. Give me the boy and I would not come after you."

"Me?" Merryn asked in shock. "I wasn't even there."

"They refused your bargain," Aunt Morwena spat out.

How could I not have known about this? "How did my brother die? It wasn't at my parents' hands."

"It most certainly was," Queen Eolonde said in a purring voice.

Merryn turned to Aunt Morwena in shock. Her aunt nodded once. "They couldn't risk allowing this creature to enslave him."

"So, they killed their own child?" Merryn asked in a shaky voice.

"They were aiming for her and she pushed Jonas into their line of fire. While they were in shock at that outcome, she went after them, in spite."

"They denied me what was rightfully mine," Queen Eolonde said. "No one does that and lives to tell the tale."

Merryn's heart shook in horror and deep sympathy for her parents.

"For your treachery, you were banished from entering this upper world," Aunt Morwena said. "How did you return?"

"By whom?" Merryn asked, her scattered thoughts coalescing on her aunt. "Who banished her?"

"Her sister, Queen Orlagh of *Y Tylwyth Teg,*" Aunt Morwena said.

With that answer, Merryn knew how to defeat this mad dark fae queen. "Cri!"

The little sprite in the blue gown appeared beside her. "Yes, Merryn?" She took one look at the mayhem inside the crypt and gave a frightened squeak.

Queen Eolonde spewed a string of vile epithets.

Blue light speared directly toward Cri.

Merryn spun a spell around the little pixie. "Cri, did you speak to your queen on my behalf?"

The pixie's wide eyes were transfixed on the dark fae queen who threw spell after spell at her. Each one bounced off Merryn's protection sphere, but with each strike, she came closer to breaching that barrier.

"Cri! Look at me. Did you give your queen my message?"

The pixie finally turned to make eye contact. "Yes. But she refuses to interfere in Wyhcan affairs again. She said it was a big bother last time. Besides, Callington is out of her realm. She would be willing to give you an audience to make the request again in person if you promise to make her a new ball gown. In royal blue." She then leaned closer to whisper, "Is that Queen Eolonde?"

"Yes. Now, please go tell Her Majesty about what's happening here," Merryn said. "This time she might reconsider."

In a flash the pixie vanished.

Merryn smiled grimly as Dewer's mother frantically opened a doorway back to her underworld.

Despite her earlier brave words, the dark fae queen was so frightened of her sister, she was willing to abandon this battle and her chance to gain Merryn as her slave. If that were the case, perhaps it wasn't quite time for Her Majesty to leave the dance floor. She spun a spell that formed a barrier across the gate to the underworld.

"Release me this instant!" Queen Eolonde screamed.

The crypt exploded with glittering fae light. Queen Orlagh of *Y Tylwyth Teg* had arrived in Callington inside the crypt of Saint Agatha's church.

Aunt Morwena laughed with delight. Her aunt no doubt relished this as apt punishment for what this dark fae had done to her family.

Under that blast of blinding white fae energy, every one of the hideous snakes withered and died.

Braden pulled Merryn to him as the hellhounds howled in fear and raced for the underworld gate. Merryn took pity on them and removed her obstruction across the gate, which meant Dewer's mother could also escape. The hounds leapt through to safety before their queen. Eolonde cried in agony before she, too, sputtering curses about ungrateful, disloyal and cowardly hounds, squirmed her way through the opening. Merryn slammed the door shut behind them.

In the blessedly silent chamber, Queen Orlagh hovered in the air, surrounded by a brilliance that was difficult to look into, as if the sun had come to rest inside the crypt. "Finally, we meet," she said to Merryn. "You, my dear, owe me a gown."

"It would be my pleasure to bestow such a gift for your assistance, Your Majesty," Merryn said. "Thank you for coming to our aid."

"My sister should have known better than to invade this realm again. She was always a difficult student."

"I don't understand why she came," Merryn said and asked the one question that continued to plague her. "Do you know why your sister wanted me?"

"Partially because Dewer was enamored of you and she has a jealous heart. Though I suspect it was mainly because you are a unique combination of two worlds, my dear," Queen Orlagh said in her beautiful twinkling voice. "On your birth, this world adopted you. You are both a child of Wyhca and a child of Earth."

"What do you mean?" Merryn asked. "How am I any different from Jonas or Trystan?"

"All beings that can sense the vibrations of the earth's ley lines, also sense your extraordinary connection to this world. While this land originally opposed all things Wyhcan, it has now accepted you, Merryn Pendraven, as one of its own. Have you not noticed that there are no barriers between your Wyhcan magic and our Earth magic?"

Merryn thought about that extraordinary suggestion. Then she recalled all the barriers she'd crossed recently, those formed by Wyhcan, by Fae, and even Garth's earth magic. "I can cross any magical barrier," she said.

"Much more than that, child," Queen Orlagh said. "Warlocks cannot work mind magic on our land without repercussions. Yet, you show no such obstruction."

"I have never worked mind magic on people," Merryn protested. "That is forbidden by our code."

Braden took her hand and gave her fingers an encouraging squeeze and asked, "What about the carriage horses?"

"Exactly," the fae queen said. "Did you never wonder why, at the Horse and Hound Inn, you were able to control the thoughts of those demon snakes without any repercussions? As your Lord Braden says, without backlash, you guided the horses' minds when they were flying. And just now, you shut an underworld gate. That, in itself, is extraordinary. While you may have never worked mind magic on a human, I would not put that past your ability. That makes you both powerful and prized, my dear. Be on your guard. This is neither the first nor the last time you will be tested. You are widely envied and feared, from all realms, above and below."

With those dire words of warning, the light fae queen departed.

Merryn stood stunned by the revelation.

Into that silence, Queen Orlagh's voice echoed back inside the crypt. "I shall expect you at my court once this crisis is ended, with my new gown."

Her aunt came up to her and gently touched her cheek. "I'm sorry for keeping all this from you, Merryn. I was frightened after I lost my sister. I didn't know how else to protect you."

"The boy!" Merryn pulled out of Braden's hold and raced for the opening of the crypt. She flew through the blue haze and heard Garth hurriedly dismantle his barrier so Braden and her aunt could follow.

She raced up the stairs, unable to shake the idea that without her there, Dewer might have taken Trystan. She was finally coming to accept that there was nothing she could have done for her brother, but she wasn't prepared to lose Trystan, too. Braden caught up to her and linked their fingers in silent comfort, as if he knew why she just *had* to rescue Trystan.

AT THE EAST BELL TOWER door, Braden took a deep breath before opening the door into the church.

Shouts, incrimination and fierce barks and growls greeted them. They strode past the pews lining the floor of the nave and headed toward the chancel from where all the noise emanated. It sounded as if a veritable dog fight took place by the altar.

Nearby, the rector stood by the front door's archway. Arms outstretched, he discouraged all interested on-lookers from coming inside. To Braden, that seemed like barring the door after the angry rabble had already invaded the church with their pitchforks and torches.

The old man waved them over. Braden had a hard time taking his eyes off the little man sitting on the rector's shoulder.

"What's happening over there?" Merryn asked, shouting to be heard above the din.

"They found the boy, Miss Pendraven. One of Dewer's hellhounds led them straight to him. Mattock's dog and Dewer's hellhound pace each other and are having a royal barking match."

"Does Dewer have the boy?" Merryn asked with a catch in her voice.

"Not him. The church does. Trystan's trapped in these walls. They managed to chip away enough brick and plaster to see his face but not much else."

Braden, stunned by the news, looked to Merryn for guidance. She shrugged with helpless confusion, appearing no wiser about what could be done about this disclosure.

"The saint's upset," the brownie said. "Ye'd best 'urry, lass."

Braden squeezed her trembling fingers as they walked down the nave toward the chancel.

Mattock's mastiff, Dewer's hellhound, witches, warlocks and church guards were crowded together there. The Archbishop of Canterbury seemed to be in a bitter argument with Mattock. The sight brightened Braden's heart for it meant his mentor and longtime supporter had recovered from whatever spell Mattock had placed him under.

"Let us through," Braden ordered.

Everyone moved aside, even the hounds, and the noise level dropped to a subdued rumble.

On the left wall, a portion of the boy's outline was visible. A woman, looking tearful, stood nearby. His mother?

Face in anguish, Mattock pushed his way to the woman's side and knelt by his son. He touched the tips of Trystan's fingers projecting out of the wall. "I've tried every spell at my disposal," he said, looking up at Merryn, "but I can't get him out. No one else here seems able to help, not even Dewer, unless he lies. Will you please try?"

His wife tentatively rested a hand on Mattock's shoulder, her thumb gently moving in a circle, as if she wanted to ease his pain. Braden expected the proud warlock to knock off the witch's touch. Instead, Mattock raised his free hand to cover hers, gripping her fingers as if he clung to a lifeline.

Merryn stepped up to the wall and laid her hands next to the boy's head. Seeing her deep concentration, Braden left her side to find the archbishop.

"Your Grace," he whispered, leading the churchman away for a private talk, "I'm sorry to have brought you here under false pretenses. I worried you were under the influence of a warlock spell."

"I was," Sutton replied. "Once the healer removed the spell, she explained all."

He indicated the tall, slender, brown-haired young woman Braden had seen working on the archbishop earlier. The young witch stood a little behind Dewer, her riveted gaze trained on the warlock.

"She's an articulate and well-read young lady," Sutton said, before turning his attention to Merryn. "Is that Miss Pendraven, the Coven Protectress? The healer spoke of her assistance to you."

Braden drew Sutton even further away from the crowd. "Your Grace, there's something I could not put in any missive but that you must be made aware of."

Sutton's attention turned fully in his direction, eyebrow raised in inquiry.

On the carriage flight from Black Mountain, Braden had requested permission from Merryn for this important conversation with the archbishop, and gained it. So, he felt free to begin from the beginning.

"These people, Your Grace, these warlocks and witches, known to each other as Wyhcans, are not from our world." Quickly, he recited all that he knew of the Wyhcan people's arrival on earth and subsequent violent introduction to their hosts' human culture.

Sutton listened to the tale in silence, eyes widening at moments. At the end, he gave a low whistle. "We've been so wrong, Braden," he said at the end, eyes misting up.

"The king will need to be apprised of this development, Your Grace."

"Of course," Sutton said. "This mind magic, however, is a most troublesome matter. We cannot leave ourselves vulnerable to such a threat. How do we fight it?"

"I've an idea," Braden said. "Your original concept, to accept our long-time enemy into the fold of the Church, was a sound one, Your Grace."

The archbishop's shoulders sagged as if in relief to hear his favorite student wasn't about to hold that against him.

"However," Braden continued, "it would be more useful to invite the witches into such a partnership rather than the warlocks. As a matter of fact, many of the witches, in order to blend into British society and make amends for their role in past conflicts and deaths of innocents, have already integrated themselves over the centuries into Christian culture. I believe they can be of great assistance with any mind magic threats, as that healer has proven."

Sutton nodded with enthusiasm. "I agree. Perhaps your Miss Pendraven or someone she elects can act as our liaison with the Wyhcan people. I will arrange for her to have an audience with the regent regarding this matter." The archbishop's eyes suddenly lit up and his gaze swung back toward the healer. "Do you think the healer might be able to assist with His Majesty's illness?"

"Who knows what's possible if this alliance succeeds," Braden said. "I've a request as well."

"Yes?"

"I wish to marry Miss Pendraven."

Sutton took a step back. "Are you mad? You said these people are not of earth."

"They may not be from here, but they are much like us. I intend to seek my parents' permission shortly."

Sutton shook his head. "It is the closeness of your recent association that has put this absurd idea into your head. It's your youth speaking. Danger often inflames a young man's passions. Add a beautiful woman to the mix and who could fault you for succumbing to temptation? It's nothing to be embarrassed about." He patted Braden consolingly on the back. "Give yourself a week, perhaps two, away from the lady, and I assure you, you will return to your proper senses."

"I love her, Your Grace."

Sutton frowned at him, his gaze swinging to Merryn and back to his troublesome church guard. "I cannot possibly agree to..."

"I have always thought of you as my mentor, my second father and my holy guide," Braden continued in a soft voice. "Therefore, it would please me greatly if you would perform our marriage ceremony. I am hoping you will also agree to one day be our first child's godfather."

Sutton stood there sputtering when one violently spoken word reverberated inside the church.

NO!

"Who said that?" Sutton asked.

Braden led them closer to where Merryn appeared to be having a heated conversation with the wall.

"Saint Agatha," she said in a firm voice, "please, you must release the boy."

"I cannot," a disembodied voice said.

"I understand you were protecting him. It's time to release Trystan."

"I cannot!" Loud wailing sobs vibrated through the church walls.

Aunt Morwena walked up, nodded respectfully to the archbishop, before touching Merryn's shoulder. "I spoke with the saint earlier, Merryn. She seemed much impressed by the archbishop's presence in her church. She wanted him to pray for her. To ask God to forgive her."

Merryn sent a look of appeal to Braden and then turned to Sutton. "The saint might listen to you, Your Grace. If you pray for her, perhaps she'll release the child into your custody."

"It's worth a try." Braden turned to Sutton. "This may be your one chance to not only speak to a saint, but have her respond in person."

Sutton chuckled and shook his head. "I would not have believed you if you had returned to me at Lambeth Palace with such a story. Isn't it excellent I'm here to witness this extraordinary miracle for myself? So, young lady, what must I do?"

"Lay your hand here," Merryn directed, pointing.

Sutton spanned the flat of his hands on either side of the boy's face.

"Now say your prayers, Your Grace."

He bowed his head and closed his eyes. "Heal me, O Lord and I shall be healed; save me, and I shall be saved; for thou art my praise."

As those familiar words of the Prophet Jeremiah left Sutton's lips, the church took on a bright glow.

Braden, who had closed his eyes as his mentor began his prayer, heard gasps and snapped open his eyes. There, above Sutton hovered an image of a woman in a pink square-necked gown. Her long voluminous sleeves were slashed to reveal a darker pink chemise. In each of her hands, Saint Agatha identified herself by holding up one of her severed breasts.

As Sutton wound down to the end of his prayer and made the symbol of the cross, Braden touched his shoulder. The older man looked around, startled. Braden pointed up, unable to take his eyes off the saint.

Sutton followed the direction and stumbled over the ending of his prayer. "In the name of the Father, the Son and the Holy Ghost, you are forgiven your sins and made clean in the sight of God."

"Thank you, Your Grace," Saint Agatha said with a beatific smile and faded away.

Braden felt a cool breeze behind him and turned to find the chancel no longer crowded. Only he, Merryn, Sutton, the boy's parents and the mastiff remained.

"Where did everyone go?" he asked.

Merryn looked toward the archway where the rector waved to her. He pointed to the threshold that he no longer needed to guard, because all the on-lookers were gone.

"What's happening?" Sutton asked.

"You've given Saint Agatha back her strength to defend her church," Merryn replied. "Only those she allows can now enter.

"My son is still trapped," Mattock said.

"Yes." Merryn ran her hand over the boy's chin that projected partially out of the wall. He blinked at her, but did not speak for his lips were still buried in stone. "He feels warm to the touch," she murmured. "He is still alive."

"For how long?" his mother asked.

"Saint Agatha, why will you not release the boy?" Merryn asked.

"I cannot," the saint replied, sounding more worried now than tearful. "He is no longer under my control. His body is here but not his soul. I cannot sense him anywhere in the church. Help me, Miss Pendraven. I do not wish to be responsible for this poor boy's destruction. All I ever wanted was to keep him safe. That is why I took him the day of his baptism, to save him from the hellhounds and all others who meant him harm."

"Merryn, perhaps you can release him," Braden said.

"I tried earlier and failed," she said, but obligingly walked over to the bricks that encased the boy and laid her hand on the wall by Trystan. This time, a voice inside the church whispered, *SEND MY GUARD TO ME.*

Merryn stepped back in shock, her whole body shaking in reaction. If she didn't know better, she would have sworn the Maker had just spoken to her. Then, without anyone saying a word, she sensed exactly what must happen next.

Turning to Braden, she indicated his sword. "Could you lay a blessing on the church as you did at the Horse and Hound Inn yard? Your sword had the effect of cleansing and healing the land then. Perhaps where Saint Agatha is unable to help Trystan, your blessed sword can succeed."

Braden raised his eyebrow at her surprising words; he'd been unaware she had seen him or that his prayers had indeed blessed the land to the point where she would have sensed it. Uncertain what good this would do, nevertheless, with a metallic hiss he drew Agamore. "At the inn, I struck this into soil. That's not possible here."

She wore a gentle smile. "Trust in your God, Braden."

He felt skeptical but dutifully knelt. He raised the sword and, point first, hoping he was not about to shatter the blade, aimed it into the floor and pressed downward. The sword sank into the flagstone as if piercing water, until the blade was half buried.

"Ha!" he said in shock and delight. Then with both hands on the hilt, eyes shut, he prayed. "For tho I walk amidst the shades of death, I will fear no ills, because Thou art with me; Thy rod and Thy staff have been my comfort."

The sword vibrated in his grip. In his mind's eye, it was enveloped in a bright flame. A great wave of energy churned through him, into the sword, and from there, into the heart of the church. The energy spread like a finely spun net that touched every nook and cranny of the building.

Saint Agatha cried out in joy.

His world became a land of bright lights. "Agamore," Braden whispered, "are you able to release the boy?"

A man dressed in glowing armor stepped into the light and glanced around. *I cannot see him, my lord.*

Braden strode up to the knight, not the least surprised to see his sword manifest itself in armor. To his mind, the image perfectly fit the role of the warrior blade. He would forevermore see Agamore this way. Never again would he feel alone during a fight.

Together, they searched the building.

"He has to be here," Braden said. "This is the church. There's the altar and this is the wall Trystan is buried in."

"Have you come to take me home?" a soft voice asked.

Braden swung around, as did Agamore. Then with a clatter of metal parts, Agamore dropped to his knees, head bowed.

Braden wondered at that extreme reaction and then he noticed that by the entry's archway, where the rector should have been standing, was instead a cloaked figure holding onto Trystan's hand.

Braden's legs trembled and his knees buckled. There was not a shred of doubt in his heart that he was in the presence of his Lord.

The robed figure nodded acknowledgement as Braden, too, knelt. He released the child.

With a happy laugh, Trystan ran toward them and Braden scooped the boy up in his arms.

"I heard my da and ma," Trystan said. "They weren't fighting. Idris is here, too. Barking. He's angry. That's only because he's worried. We have to tell him I'm all right."

"You must have been frightened," Braden said in sympathy.

"Yes, at first, when I found myself stuck inside a wall," the boy replied. "Then I was brought here and told you were coming to save me. I've been patiently waiting."

Braden turned his attention to the hooded figure standing motionless by the doorway.

His Lord nodded to Braden. *YOU HAVE DONE WELL, MY THOMAS*. He then turned as if to depart.

"I have a request," Braden said in a rush.

He turned back.

Tension stretched inside Braden's chest, enough to make his heart ache. At first sight of this holy figure, all his Christian teachings came racing back. He took a deep breath and fought to express a deep-seated concern that had surfaced along with those memories.

The fear, bred from years of being taught to mistrust magic because it came from evil would not fade no matter how much he'd learnt to the contrary since meeting Merryn. There still existed in his soul a quivering doubt that in accepting her and her magic, he rejected God's truth.

This was his chance to ask if his doubts were groundless. That in choosing to marry Merryn he was not alienating himself from God.

"I wish to marry Miss Merryn Pendraven. She is a witch. She practices magic. Yet, I love her."

His Lord observed him in silence, but Braden gained the surprising impression he'd amused him.

WHAT IS YOUR REQUEST?

"May I have God's blessing on our union?"

This time, the silence stretched so long Braden thought he would never breathe again.

THOMAS DRAKE SAINT-CLAIR, WHO IS MY FATHER?

The question puzzled Braden. Thinking the obvious answer was probably wrong, he said, "Merryn calls him The Maker."

As he spoke, all his doubts about magic vanished, for where would magic come from, after all, but from the Maker, the Creator. Where, but from God?

THOMAS DRAKE SAINT-CLAIR, WHO IS MY FATHER?

Braden gulped in a deep breath to feed his stunned brain that seemed to be functioning at an excessively lethargic rate. He felt as if he were a nine-year-old boy again who had fallen in an ancient church ruin one cold winter day, been gifted with a vision of Agamore and asked to save the world. "He is my God."

THOMAS DRAKE SAINT-CLAIR. WHO IS MY FATHER?

Braden floundered trying to think how to respond. He looked to Agamore. The armored knight leaned in and whispered, *"A fighter?"*

Braden shook his head, unhappy with that answer. He looked at the boy who had spent several days in the Lord's presence. "Do you know who God is?"

"A friend?" Trystan suggested in a hopeful tone.

Closer to Braden's way of thinking, but still not quite correct. Then he knew. The answer was so simple he couldn't believe he hadn't immediately gleaned the truth.

Braden said, "He is love."

AND THERE IS YOUR ANSWER.

Braden found himself back inside the church, kneeling with Agamore's hilt in his grip.

A voice in his head said, *LOVE, THOMAS, IS EVER A BLESSING UNTO ITSELF.*

THE SAINT CRIED OUT in bliss as a flow of grace embraced the building. Merryn's hurt neck abruptly stopped aching. She felt around where sharp fangs had pierced her and encountered smooth unblemished skin. She swung her elated gaze around the church, wondering if anyone else had noticed that incredible sweep of healing energy. Boo-Boo had, if that stunned look on her young cousin's face was any indication.

Sutton was staring at Braden with shocked eyes. Had the archbishop never beheld his church guard praying while he held his sword? *Obviously not.* For anyone who experienced this most magical of events could never forget it.

Beside her, the wall began to crumble and Trystan John Michael Preston fell out of his stone enclosure and landed within his father's open arms.

Merryn's heart glowed with happiness to see father and son embracing. *This is for you, Jonas*, she silently told her lost brother.

Trystan's parents hugged him, crying and kissing his forehead and cheeks. The black mastiff ran up to lick the boy's and his parents' faces with equal enthusiasm.

Mattock turned such an astonished and grateful look toward Braden; she couldn't keep a laugh from springing out.

Braden stood, sheathed his sword and put his arm around her shoulders. "That worked," he whispered, sounding pleased and not a little surprised.

This man never failed to amaze her at how unaware he seemed of his amazing abilities.

Trystan's parents conferred over the boy and then together they turned to face the archbishop.

"I've changed my mind about the boy's baptism," Mattock said.

At Merryn's gasp, he shrugged. "I had the Warlock Council and the Church at my side and still Dewer almost captured him. Principles must be put aside for once. I agree with my wife that the boy's safety takes precedence above all else."

Aunt Morwena took Merryn's hand and squeezed it tight. Her aunt's fondest wish was about to be granted.

"Your Grace," Mattock said to the archbishop, "Would you baptize our son?"

Sutton grinned and nodded, and then he asked some probing questions about both the parents' Christian religious beliefs. Looking surprised but satisfied with their answers, he said, "Seems I've several upcoming events to note in my diary. For this one, I shall need a font."

Merryn pointed to the archway, toward where the rector had hurried in preparation for the baptism. As they joined him, Merryn magically filled the tall, sculpted marble, three-sided bowl with water.

The archbishop gave her a startled look but then quickly recovered and thanked her. He blessed the water and proceeded with the ceremony. The rector and the brownie acted as official witnesses.

Once the blessing was completed, they went out to show Trystan's reappearance to those gathered outside.

Amid that loud cheer, Braden pulled Merryn back into the entryway and turned her to face him.

He had that, "I intend to claim you" look in his eyes again. One she hoped would never fade. If he meant to kiss her, she had no objections. The act was long overdue based on the agreed-upon hourly requirement.

"Yes, Braden," she said, with a fond smile.

He leaned forward to touch her lips but stopped a hairsbreadth too soon and drew back.

She frowned in concern. "Do you no longer wish to kiss me? We've found the boy. Your duty to Trystan is complete. However, I'm still a witch and you are a church guard."

"So we are." Braden tucked a stray strand of her hair behind her ear. "Which is why I am now free to ask you something I've wanted to for a while."

"Ask me what?" Merryn held her breath. She knew what she wanted him to ask but wasn't sure he was free to do so. He'd need the archbishop's permission and the holy man had foolishly left the building. She should have locked the door to bar his way. What if Braden thought his God would disapprove? Tears welled in her eyes at all the ways her heart's desire could be kept from her.

Braden knelt on one knee and Merryn caught her breath.

He took her hand and said, "Merryn Pendraven, will you marry me?"

She stared at him; her throat choked with happy tears. "Yes, yes, yes," she cried, thinking she sounded just like Cri, and not minding in the least.

She flung her arms around his neck and sealed her answer with a heartfelt kiss.

He returned her embrace with fervor. It was the sweetest kiss she'd ever experienced, for with his lips, he promised her *forever after*. For a coven protectress who hadn't expected to live past her twenty-fifth year, it was the sweetest promise ever.

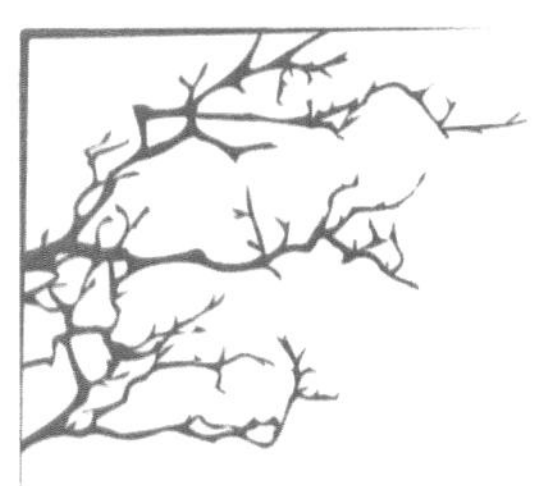

Epilogue

Ignominiously thrust outside the church by Saint Agatha, Farfur glanced around and spotted Bartos beyond the crowd.

He ran over and rubbed noses with him. He pulled back to give the other hellhound a concerned once over. "You're very warm."

"I can barely walk." Bartos lay slumped at the base of the damaged portion of the steps. "I couldn't even accompany the master up into the church." He nodded toward Dewer who was standing at the open church door, looking in. "He seems unhappy. What happened?"

"Eggy Trystan's been found and reclaimed by his parents."

Bartos laid his head down. "All is lost then."

"Not all. I heard the dark queen has fled back to the underworld. I doubt she'll return anytime soon."

"Does it matter?"

"Yes, it matters," Farfur said with indignation. "It means the master won't be tormented by her for a while."

Bartos lifted his head to nod toward Dewer. "It's not the loss of the boy or his mother's actions that upsets him. He's realized he's losing the protectress. Nothing torments him more than her. Love, Farfur, is the truest curse."

Farfur looked toward his master and gave a distressed whine, for how could he possibly help with that problem?

"What does any of it matter?" Bartos continued. "If the door to the underworld has been sealed, I cannot return to be healed. I will die here. For a moment, I sensed a healing energy in the air, but it did nothing for me."

Farfur gave a worried yip. Perhaps, there was something he could do. "Wait here." He raced to where he'd last seen the witch who'd worked on the man lying on the pew inside the nave. Could she be a healer? Might she be able to help Bartos? As he sniffed her out, people exclaimed in alarm and formed a wide berth around him. Once he reached her, he tugged at her sleeve.

She gave a started cry and raised her arm as if to strike.

He lay low, resting his head on his paws and whined his plea for mercy. When she didn't hurt him, he stood and tugged at her sleeve again, pulling her toward Bartos. She resisted and then with a sigh, let him lead her.

"What's happened to you, then?" she asked, kneeling beside Bartos. She cleared a space around the hellhound and carefully probed his wound.

Bartos growled in pain.

"I can make this better, if you let me," she said.

Farfur's ears perked in surprise. He'd never heard anyone speak so gently to a hellhound. Was this a trick?

Bartos licked her hand.

"Leave him be," Dewer snapped.

Farfur yelped in surprise and backed away. He hadn't heard the master return.

"Your hound is hurt," the witch said.

"I'll deal with him later."

"Do you know how to care for a wound this infected? How could you have allowed it to fester like this?"

"I've no time for this nonsense. There's nothing left here for me. We're leaving. Now!"

Farfur cringed, recognizing that dangerous tone.

To his surprise, instead of stepping aside, the witch stood and placed herself firmly between Bartos and the master.

"This hound needs help and I will not allow you to..."

Dewer abruptly cut her off. "We're leaving."

"Not until the hound is better," the witch protested.

"Do you mean that hellhound?" Dewer pointed to Bartos. "He's not your concern." His master set a transportation spell in motion, one that included Farfur and Bartos.

Bartos cried out, pawing at the shield and barking at the witch.

"What's the matter?" Farfur asked.

"I want to stay with her," Bartos said. "She has a gentle hand."

"Stay?" Farfur asked, confused. "With a witch?"

The witch was staring at Bartos with a startled expression, as if she sensed his wish to stay. Then she did something else entirely unwise. She reached into the spell and took hold of Bartos's neck fur.

As she pulled the hound out of his spell, Dewer looked up and released a full-throated scream of fury.

With his master's attention distracted, Farfur had one moment to decide what to do. He leapt after his friend.

The spell completed, and sent Dewer's glowering form back toward his black tower, alone. A whirlwind punctuated by a surfeit of thunder and lightning reflected the fury on his face.

The healer stared after Dewer, too, as if fascinated. She absently petted Bartos, and then she smoothed the fur on Farfur's forehead. An odd gesture that he at first ducked from, and then realized he'd enjoyed it. He tentatively wagged his tail.

"Farfur," Bartos said, "We're free."

The suggestion settled across his shoulders like an ill-fitting harness. He should be happy, he was free, he was with his friend, yet, something wasn't right. "Do you really think the master will let us go so easily?"

"He has other worries than us. At least, for a while."

Farfur played back his former master's expression before he faded away. Past Dewer's anger, there had been sorrow lines etched deep on either side of Dewer's eyes. He had lost the boy, the woman he desired, and now, his last two hellhounds. He would be utterly alone. "Bartos, what will he do without us to take care of him?"

"No longer our problem," Bartos said, but he sounded worried. He, too, was staring at the ground from where their master had vanished.

Farfur's shoulders slumped. Weighed down by an unfamiliar sense of compassion, he wanted to run after the master. Bartos was right after all. Love was, indeed, a curse.

MERRYN SAT ON THE TOP step of Saint Agatha's church and looked around at all her friends and family gathered in little groups, happily chatting. Life was beginning to slow down. Trystan was playing with his dog. His parents watched him with fond smiles a short distance away.

The most startling aspect was that the couple was holding hands. That family was likely to grow in the near future. The idea brought a happy grin to her cheeks which were already sore from smiling so much today.

Near the Mattock family stood her Great Aunt Gwen speaking to Braden's man, Garth. By the magician's hand gestures, he was asking for details about their flying carriage.

The slamming of doors swung her attention toward the roadway and a row of vehicles. The archbishop and his men were leaving Callington. Church guards had mounted horses, ready to act as their escort back to London. The guards saluted Braden as they rode by, with a few offering sly winks. With Mattock's spell removed, they were acting normal again. It was a pleasing sight.

Mattock had sworn before his council, Aunt Morwena and Braden that he would never again use mind-magic on humans no matter the incentive. He was just one warlock though. Merryn planned to keep her ears tuned for any rumors of other warlocks who might be tempted to act as foolishly, which was part and parcel of her responsibilities as Coven Protectress. The role was settling comfortably across her shoulders.

As if sensing her gaze, Braden turned away from waving off the archbishop's contingent and headed in her direction. He was swiftly accosted by Merryn's cousin Emily with her friends Miss Eliza Symons and Miss Jane Bicket, all of them flirting outrageously.

"Shameful," Lady Hancock said from behind Merryn. Before she could inform the lady that no interference was required, the matron hurried down the steps with her friends in tow to rescue him. She then ushered him toward Merryn.

He sauntered up the steps, stopping to snatch a few left-over pastries from the remnants of the bake sale. He slumped beside her and offered her one of his stolen prizes. "Where have all the witches gone?"

"Fishguard for some, with warlock escort. The rest have returned home. I'm unsure where Boo-Boo has gone."

"Who's that?"

"Sorry, my cousin, Grace. She's the one who removed the mind-spell from Archbishop Sutton."

"Ummm," Braden said, munching. "I wanted to thank her but your Aunt Morwena said she's already returned to her house. Your aunt seems worried about her. Said she left with two of Dewer's hellhounds."

"He allowed her to take them?" she asked, shocked.

He gave her a knowing side glance. "I suspect he had other matters on his mind."

Merryn looked over to the church door, remembering Braden's proposal in the entryway. Could Dewer have witnessed that precious moment? She sighed as her compassion swelled. Unrequited love was a painful emotion. Noticing Braden observing her closely, she changed the subject. Dewer was a topic she was not yet ready to discuss. "What were you and Sutton speaking about for so long?"

"With your aunt's assistance, he sent a missive to the regent to inform him about events here. His Royal Highness was apparently most intrigued. He's already sent back a message that he wants a full report, especially about Wyhcan history. How you arrived on Earth. What happened afterward."

"He'd best speak to our Lore Keeper, then," Merryn said looking off into the horizon as she remembered the elderly woman who visited occasionally to tell Wyhcan children fascinating tales of their home world. "She keeps our historical records. I haven't seen or heard from her recently. Aunt Morwena would know how to get in touch with her."

"I'll pass the contact details along," Braden said and then asked, "Are you happy, Merryn?"

She focused on him and said with sincerity, "Immensely. How could I not be when the wish I made at the Laneast well has come true."

"As did Garth's," Braden said with a tolerant smile. "What did you wish for?"

"That you would come to see my people as your friends instead of your enemy. What about you?" she asked. "Aunt Morwena said that you, too, made a wish that day."

"I wished that my God would grant me clarity about witches. Specifically, about you."

"That's why you were requested to go into the wall to retrieve Trystan," Merryn said. "It was your wish being granted."

"I suppose," Braden said. "All's well that ends well?"

"Not quite. I'm overwhelmed," Merryn said softly. "And determined, as well as a little terrified."

He sat up, brushing crumbs from his fingers. "What about, my love?"

"Overwhelmed by all Queen Orlagh revealed about the power she believes I possess. Determined to be the best Coven Protectress I can be for Britain." She paused.

"And what frightens you?" he asked, taking her hand.

"Meeting your parents."

He chuckled and kissed her knuckles.

"I want them to like me as I am, Braden, without the use of magic. Just because I can weave bewitching spells, does not mean I wish to cast one on them."

"Magic is a part of who you are, Merryn, and I accept that. I wouldn't want you any other way. You are the protectress of my heart. As for my parents, trust me, they will love you as I do. No magic required."

THE END

IF YOU WANT TO LEARN more about warlocks and the history of Wyhcans, then you've got to read **Warlock from Wales**[1], Book 2 in The Cauldron Effect series. In it, a young human woman, Mary Bryght, will set out to find the Wyhcan Lore Keeper, determined to record the history of these unexpected immigrants to her country, to her *world*, on behalf of the Prince Regent.

The secretive warlocks, well, they're unhappy about revealing who they are, where they came from, or anything else about themselves, so they send their own representative, Hugh Renfrew Price, to stop her. What will happen when these two envoys on opposing missions meet? Nothing good. Especially when love has its own mission in mind for them.

---

1. https://books2read.com/WarlockfromWales

IF YOU ENJOYED THIS story, please consider leaving a short review for this book wherever you purchased it. The review will help other readers decide if this book is worth their time.

SIGN UP TO SHEREEN'S Newsletter to learn about her new releases: http://www.subscribepage.com/c9u7e6

Thank you for reading!

Don't miss out!

Visit the website below and you can sign up to receive emails whenever Shereen Vedam publishes a new book. There's no charge and no obligation.

https://books2read.com/r/B-A-POZG-SKFV

Connecting independent readers to independent writers.

Did you love *Coven at Callington*? Then you should read *Warlock from Wales*[2] by Shereen Vedam!

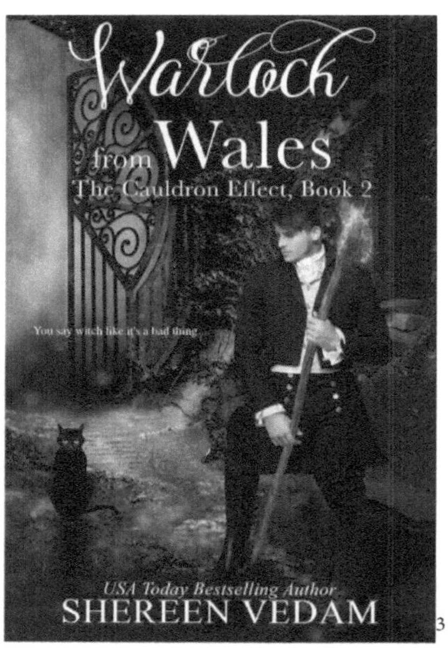

A historian in search of truth. A warlock charged to stop her.

In the year of our Lord 1816, eighteen-year-old historian MARY BRYGHT is accosted by a terrifying magical villain who threatens to destroy her brother if he doesn't reject his latest royal commission. Rushing home, she discovers that not only is she too late to stop her brother, but he's left a letter begging her to assist him by recording the details of a three-centuries-old stunning secret event.

At his father's death, HUGH RENFREW PRICE is yanked from his warlock apprenticeship by the Warlock Council and ordered to take up his father mantle as Earl of Flint. If attending boring House of Lords sessions to spy on human politicians was a bad enough chore, the Prince Regent then instructs Hugh to safeguard a human female on a mission the Warlock

---

Council insists Hugh must sabotage. However, when he meets his delightful charge, Hugh decides that life may not be so terrible after all.

Just as Hugh starts to enjoy his latest assignment, another warlock, partnered with a voracious water demon, steals Mary from under Hugh's nose. Recovering her becomes his greatest challenge, while Mary learns that not all Warlocks are created equal. Yet, how can she trust Hugh after she learns he's out to stop her mission? Finding love in this mire of intrigue will take more than magic. It might just require some unique human ingenuity.

If you enjoy stories where humans match wits against supernatural might, you'll love this magical chase across a Regency-English Countryside to preserve the integrity of history.

Scroll on up and pick up your copy.

Read more at www.shereenvedam.com.

Also by Shereen Vedam

Harrington Bay Mystery
Sage It Out
Missing You

Outside the Circle Mystery
To Capture Love
Death Takes a Detour
Death Shifts Gears
Death Smells Disaster
Death Swipes Right
Death Comes Up Short
Death is Uncovered

Tales of Ryca
Hidden
Hushed

The Cauldron Effect
Coven at Callington
Warlock from Wales
Love Spell in London

Standalone
Tales of Ryca: The Complete Series
Torn
The Cauldron Effect: The Complete Series
Believe
Innocent

Watch for more at www.shereenvedam.com.

About the Author

Once upon a time, USA Today bestselling author Shereen Vedam read fantasy and romance novels to entertain herself. Now she writes heartwarming tales braided with threads of magic and love and mystery elements woven in for good measure.

Shereen's a fan of resourceful women, intriguing men, and happily-ever-after endings. If her stories whisk you away to a different realm for a few hours, then Shereen will have achieved one of her life goals.

Please consider leaving a review wherever you purchased this book.

Read more at www.shereenvedam.com.

www.ingramcontent.com/pod-product-compliance
Lightning Source LLC
Chambersburg PA
CBHW030815210726
48290CB00002B/595